Queen of Secrets

Mafia Matriarch Series Book 1

E.J.TANDA

Tanda, E.J.
Queen of Secrets/by E.J. Tanda
ISBN: 979-8-9857497-1-7

Visit my website: www.ejtanda.com

Edited by Laura Mitchell
Proofread by Emily A. Lawrence
Book Design by Tatiana Vila
Formatted by Stacey Blake

For my Nani. All my love, your Pumpkin #1.
And to the Langone family: without all of you,
this story wouldn't exist.

Queen
of
Secrets

Prologue

HEAT SPREAD THROUGH MY BODY. A FIRE DEEP INSIDE BURNED and consumed me. Blinded by red, my mind locked somewhere between consciousness and freefall. I stood in the confines of my hallway, barely holding onto my resolve of duty to family. I'd suffered every emotion but one—rage.

The anger that lay dormant in my soul was now present. Like smoke, adrenaline crept up from the ground and slithered its way around my legs, passing my heart and settling in my brain. The toxic poison desensitized all rational thought.

This felt primal.

I wanted to be hit. Hit hard. Pain was welcomed. Pain would make me feel alive again. This time, I'd hit back. Just beyond that door was my excuse—my freedom.

My heels sank into the Persian rug fibers that lined the hallway in *our* home. I would force myself through the door and face my demons. This was *my* house. The only place I had left to go. With my dead daughter's nursery behind me, the level of violation was incomprehensible.

I unclenched my fists and threw open the bedroom door.

Rose was on top of Frank, naked, while he lay like a rag doll. The sound of the door striking the wall made her whip her head around. Her eyes were doll-like, black and lifeless. She focused on me—the woman standing in her way. Her message was clear: conquer and stake her claim, like a dog marking its territory. To Rose, this wasn't betrayal—it was a business move. A divisive power play used in my absence.

"Violetta, I told you a long time ago, you gotta make your man happy in bed." She puckered her mouth with her signature red lips and kissed the air between us while she straddled the remnants of my obligation. That was all I needed to unleash my fury.

Life would end here. Now.

Hers.

His.

Mine.

Ours.

I didn't know. I didn't care.

Part One

La Principessa

Chapter 1

The Offer

October 2002
Barbara

POOR MRS. PASSARELLI. HER PAIN WAS GONE NOW. THE OLD woman lay in her open coffin, peaceful, no more life support, safe in her eternal resting place. Frail hands held rosary beads to her chest. Cancer took her quickly.

In our short time together, I came to love her and tried not to let such things affect me. Loss was common as a senior caretaker. I prided myself on providing quality care, but sometimes God had other ideas.

"Fly with the angels," I whispered over her lifeless body. "I'll miss you, sweet girl." Once the words were out, I knew my work was done.

As I passed through the crowd of mourners to leave, Mrs. Passarelli's daughter tapped me on the shoulder. "Barbara, I wanted to thank you again for everything. My mother loved you."

"My pleasure and honor, ma'am."

"Mom wanted you to have this." She handed me a silver necklace and pendant from her pocket. "Saint Christopher. For protection. Said you'd know why she gave it to you."

Tears I'd held back rolled down my cheeks. Cheeks that stung that morning, covered in a healthy application of makeup. The shiny pendant flickered in my hands from the dreary mortuary light. Protector saint. And all this time, I thought it was understood that she was the one who needed caring.

"Thank you. It's lovely." I patted my wet cheek and wished her goodbye. "I'll be praying for you."

I didn't want to drive home and face my family. Private moments were hard to come by in a crowded house. I settled on a small bench near a weeping willow, the perfect location for me to do some weeping of my own. A few minutes had passed when a woman dressed in a business suit and holding a briefcase approached me.

"Barbara Jackson?"

"Yes?" I answered, surprised she knew my name.

"I didn't mean to startle you. May I sit?"

The woman didn't wait for an answer before she settled beside me. Diamonds on her Rolex flashed in my eyes.

"My name is Sophia Giordano. I've known the Passarelli family for years. I spent many summers here in San Jose when I was young." The woman lifted her face to the sky and inhaled deeply. "New York has nothing on California skies. So sad about Mrs. Passarelli. Such a sweet woman."

"I'll miss her dearly."

"I apologize for the timing—less than ideal, with the service and all—but I must return to New York this evening. My family needs your help. I understand you were Mrs. Passarelli's caretaker?"

"Yes."

"You came highly recommended as someone we can trust. Someone capable of discretion and confidentiality." Sofia opened her briefcase and withdrew a contract crowded with words. "The job pays twenty-five hundred a week."

My heart fluttered. Twenty-five hundred a week was more than I had made on any job. Ever. There had to be a catch.

My eyes narrowed. "You're going to have to tell me more."

"Before we continue, please sign this document." She handed me a pen, clicked open, poised to sign, and a bundle of papers with the heading *Non-Disclosure Agreement*.

"I'm not comfortable signing something I haven't read."

"Merely for insurance purposes. Standard practice in my firm."

"You're a lawyer?"

"Criminal attorney."

I didn't need more problems. But the money—*my God*—it would come in handy. What was the harm in listening? The promise of twenty-five hundred dollars a week, maybe a way out of the madness, made my knees shake. With sweaty palms, I signed on the bottom line.

"My eighty-one-year-old great-aunt has Alzheimer's. Her behavior is what you might expect, but she isn't a typical patient." Sophia lowered her voice. "How should I say this? My aunt's late husband was a member of an organized crime family. Some call it the Mafia. She might bring up her past, things that should not be repeated. She will say things that sound unusual, remarkable. Should you take this job, you will be expected to keep those *remarkable* things to yourself. Tell no one. No family. No priest. Not even the Sandman."

My throat tightened. "I am required by law to report anything she implies about harming herself or others." My voice cracked on the word *law*.

"Absolutely. Medical information may be disseminated at your professional discretion. But understand, Ms. Jackson, anything non-medical in nature must *never* be repeated. Failure to comply will result in immediate and non-negotiable termination."

I nodded. *The Mafia*. Holy shit.

"If you decide you want this responsibility, you have the job. You'd arrive at her house at ten a.m. to provide lunch and dinner, check her vitals, and spend time with her so she can get to know you. Report back to me anything alarming about her health that you feel requires further medical intervention. Then we'll go from there."

"I need time to consider."

"Certainly. It's a fair wage, given the conditions I've imposed upon you. Remember, you'd be working for me. Given your current financial status, I expect I'll hear from you before noon tomorrow."

I dug my heels firmly into the grass. "My current financial status? How do you know about that?"

Sophia looked me straight in the eyes. "I make it my business to know everything about my clients."

"You hire a private investigator or something?"

"Not exactly." The faintest smile crossed her face. "I have many resources at my disposal. If you give me your answer by noon tomorrow, I'll pay you in advance."

I nodded.

Sophia zipped her briefcase and stood to leave. "My aunt is spirited, at times, but I'm sure you'll come to love her. She's been living alone for some time, and we worry. Most of the family has moved away, and it's been hard to provide her the *right* kind of care." She handed me her business card.

"Thanks," I said, slightly dismissive, ready to end this strange conversation.

"I look forward to hearing from you, Ms. Jackson. *Ciao.*"

"What's your aunt's name?"

"Violetta Giordano. I wrote it on the back of the card along with her address."

As quickly as the mysterious woman sat beside me, she was gone—vanished like vapor into the group of mourners standing around after the service.

The job, although frightening and elusive, was almost too good to be true. The money she offered would go a long way toward my daughter's medical school bills and a car on its last legs. How could I turn down such an offer?

How hard could it be to keep an old woman's stories to myself? With the way Marcus and I were going, we'd be broke before the new year.

Something had to change.

I parked in the driveway of our tiny home. Final rays of sunset made my new pendant sparkle and reflect in the rearview mirror. Tears escaped my lids. St. Christopher, protector saint, huh? *Keep it together, Barbara.* Damn.

When I thought about what the charm represented, I knew why Mrs. Passarelli had given it to me. We never discussed it, but she must have known. I decided I'd wear it every day, hoping it would provide the protection I needed. With a deep breath, I rubbed away any leftover sadness from my face. After helping Darnell with his homework, I planned a hot soak. Long baths helped me avoid Marcus.

On my way inside, I stopped at the mailbox and fisted handfuls of bills with *late notice* stamped on the envelopes. The big red type had me gripping my stomach and made walking through the front door that much harder.

I didn't want to face Marcus. I didn't want to get into it again. Because of his gambling problem, I had to hide money or he'd spend every last penny we had. He knew today was payday, so he'd be there with his hands open, searching my purse, or on his way to the bank. Thankfully, I kept cash tucked away for emergencies. Getting and keeping a job proved to be another challenge for Marcus. His little stint in jail for falsifying checks didn't help matters much.

This was my life. I don't know how I got here, exactly. Twenty-one years into the relationship and still no wedding ring and no marriage certificate. We talked about marriage a few times but never said *I do*. Mom and Dad's divorce changed how I viewed marriage. On one hand, marriage was only a piece of paper; on the other, it was a bond and testament of love, something Marcus couldn't or wouldn't commit to. In a sick way, I still loved him, but I wasn't *in* love with him—there was a difference. So, we coexisted with two wonderful kids.

Being the main breadwinner was hard. It meant more responsibilities, and more responsibility meant more stress, which often spilled over into our relationship. Two things kept me here: the illusion of a nuclear family for my kids, something I never got, and the fear of being alone.

With the way things were, I was afraid now. Our current situation had sparked some huge resentments in me, resulting in heavy arguments that sometimes went too far. I didn't know how much more I could take from him, mentally or physically.

A shiver ran up my back.

I trudged toward the door, fanning out the bills in my hand. Shame washed over me. We desperately needed income. In days, our utilities would be shut off. I couldn't ask Leticia to get a job and pay us rent. No. I wanted her to focus on school. I thought about Sophia's offer and grappled it against my pride.

Ready to be an actress for my kids, I shoved the bills in my purse, slid my key in the lock, and brushed away a loose tear.

"Hey, guys. I'm home," I yelled from the doorway.

Leticia kissed me on the cheek, then grabbed her coat off the chair. "Hey, Mama. I'm off. Switched to nights again. I'll be in the ER now for the next few weeks, then back to days next term."

"Nights, huh? Log those hours, baby. I'm so proud of you. First doctor in the family."

"Not yet but getting there."

"You'll do it. I know you will." I patted her back. "I'll leave leftovers in the fridge."

I approached the kitchen where Darnell was doing his homework at the table.

"Mom, did you pay for my graduation pictures?" Darnell asked. "It's due by the end of the week."

My stomach clenched. "Not yet. I'll write you a check tomorrow. I can't believe my little boy is going to graduate high school this year," I said proudly.

"I have to pass chemistry first," Darnell said.

"Yes, you do. We'll work on that tonight."

I hung my purse on the chair and looked around the room. Beer bottles littered the kitchen. Marcus came in showered and dressed to go out. He stood there in his favorite black leather jacket and pants, smelling of cheap cologne. He called it his *lucky outfit*, but it wasn't lucky at all.

"Hey, baby, I need money. Me and the boys are going over to Leroy's house for poker night." Marcus kissed my cheek and rummaged through my purse for my wallet.

"Marcus, don't take it all. I lost my client. I was just at the service."

"That old bag held on for a long time."

My jaw tightened as I formed the words in my mouth. "She wasn't an old bag. She was a sweet lady." I shook my head at him.

"I feel lucky," Marcus said. "I won't be coming home empty-handed tonight. I promise you that."

"Only fifty, Marcus," I whispered in his ear so Darnell wouldn't hear me. "We need the rest." I grabbed my wallet from his hands.

"Don't you eva tell me how much I can have in my own damn house!" He yanked the wallet out of my hands.

A lump grew at the bottom of my throat. Marcus emptied the fold, dropped the wallet on the table, and slammed the door on his way out.

Into the quiet that remained, I injected all the cheer I could muster. "Well, Darnell, I guess it's just you and me for dinner tonight. Macaroni and cheese sound good? I've had a long day."

"Mac and cheese sounds good. Ya, you look tired. Are we still gonna do my chemistry project after dinner?"

"Sure, son. I love you."

"Love you too. One day, I hope you tell Dad off." Darnell pursed his lips.

"One day, baby."

After dinner and two hours of chemistry, I did online research about the Giordano family. Violetta Giordano had married a man named Frank Di Natale in 1940 but later changed her name back to Giordano. Frank was a member of the famous Molanano crime family. His father, Frank Di Natale Sr., worked directly for the crime boss, Joseph Molanano.

The Giordanos and Di Natales had ties to the Brooklyn mob. Frank Di Natale went to prison, then went missing years later. Authorities never found his body. Suspicion—not evidence—that Frank was killed by another member of the mob for bad business dealings left the San Jose police department with an unsolved crime.

As I dug deeper, I learned that Sofia was a high-profile attorney in New York who represented only a few clients. It was a short assumption that her clients probably had mob ties. What I'd read made my shoulders tighten, but I really had no other options. Ms. Giordano was an old woman who needed my help. I'd treat her like any other patient, regardless of her family background. I'd do my job, remain professional, and hope for the best.

I picked up the phone and dialed the number on Sofia's card.

Chapter 2
Hidden

I MADE MY WAY ONTO THE 680-FREEWAY, HEADING EAST. THE Giordano home was tucked away in the East San Jose foothills—private and isolated. Given the family's history, I knew why.

Once I passed Highway 101, rolling green foothills came into view. They were massive, majestic, unfamiliar. I didn't know who lived in those hills, but it made my first day with Ms. Giordano that much more frightening.

I took the Alum Rock exit and pulled into a gas station to study the map. From the looks of it, the street turned into a windy road. With my Honda on its last legs, I checked the glove box for my roadside assistance card in case authorities found me in a ditch somewhere. My fingers held tight around the steering wheel as my car climbed up the road.

Although elements of modern-day society were present, I felt like I was in a time warp: farms and ranches on both sides of me, cattle and horses roaming the fields, no strip malls. These folks seemed to be the kind of people who drank lemonade on the porch instead of coffee at the corner café.

I made the last turn around the bend and spotted the Giordano home. The property appeared more like a compound because there were several homes on it. From the little Sophia told me on the phone, Ms. Giordano had lived here since the late forties.

I parked my car in the long driveway. The main house wasn't fancy, but it seemed alive with history. A huge St. Anthony's statue faced the road and a tire swing hung from a giant oak in the front. Dozens of wind chimes decorated the porch. Made of glass, wood, and metal, they made beautiful sounds against the breeze. Everything was so pretty and inviting.

A feeling of warmth came over me and I knocked on the door.

A little woman—five feet tall with a head full of curlers—opened the door. She wore a scowl.

"Hello, Ms. Giordano. I'm Barbara Jackson."

"If you're selling something, I don't want any," she snipped.

"No, ma'am. I'm the nurse your niece, Sophia, hired."

"Nurse? Who the hell needs a nurse? I ain't sick." She slammed the door in my face.

My mouth fell open. "Sophia hired me to come check in on you," I yelled through the door.

Ms. Giordano snatched open the door again and eyed me cautiously. "Check in on me? I don't like strangers in my house. Besides, I'm fine."

"I'm sure you are. Can we talk for a minute?"

"So, you're a nurse, huh? You got identification?"

I handed her my hospital identification card.

She pulled up her glasses that hung on a chain around her neck, peered down, then shoved the card back at me.

"May I come in?"

"If you must," she relented and showed me inside.

I followed her down a narrow hallway to a living room lined with hundreds of pictures. It looked like a family shrine, full of history. A cuckoo clock chimed behind me. I placed my bag on the long wooden table and took out my instruments. "You have a beautiful home, Ms. Giordano. So many pictures on the wall."

"I have a big family."

"Let's get these tests out of the way so we can get to know each other. Can you lift your sleeve? I need to check your blood pressure."

"For what? I told you I'm fine."

"I'd like to see for myself. Please take a seat, Ms. Giordano."

She sat down, yanked up her sleeve, then shot me a dirty look. "How long you staying, anyway? *Judge Judy* is on soon."

"All day," I said as I watched the gauge. "Blood pressure looks good. Now I need a urine sample. Here." I handed her a specimen cup. "Do you need help to the bathroom?"

"Hell no, I don't. What am I supposed to do with this cup? You want me to piss in it? Pretty soon, you gonna check the color of my crap too? That'll be the day. I manage fine on my own," she barked, then went to the bathroom with her cup.

The toilet flushed.

"You okay in there?"

"I'm fine." She came out empty-handed.

"Did you leave the sample in the bathroom?"

"No. It spilled all over the floor, so I threw it away."

"Next time, I'll help you."

"The hell you will. You can clean the pee off the floor. You don't want me to slip in there, do ya? My niece wouldn't like it if I slipped while in *your care*," she said with a smug grin on her face.

Sophia *had* told me her aunt was spirited. Spirited wasn't the word I'd use.

I sat in my car in Ms. Giordano's driveway, looking at the front door to hell. For over a month, I'd been working with her. Even though I was early, I was in no rush to ring the bell for what was sure to be another day of torture.

Ms. G. was a combination of sweet and stubborn. Alzheimer's exaggerated her mood swings. She didn't like me in her home. Probably thought I'd steal something. The woman never came right out and said anything racist, but she called me names in Italian. I didn't know what they meant, but her tone suggested they were derogatory.

I didn't think much of her, either. She was a bitter old woman with nothing better to do than run her mouth. To remain professional, I ignored her snide comments and took the high road. When it came time to draw blood for testing, the pointy needle got her attention.

There were perks to the job.

Her disease made a routine essential. Our days began with a checkup where she'd complain that the blood pressure cuff was too tight, or the stethoscope was too cold. For lunch, I'd make her something nutritious to eat, but she'd complain about my cooking. I offered a compromise: I'd let her cook if I watched. I fibbed and said I wanted her to teach me. She took the bait. The agreement kept her fed and let her run her kitchen. A win-win.

Not surprisingly, Ms. Giordano was alone. It was a hard situation but one I'd seen many times before. I felt sorry for her until she'd say or do something to piss me off. On her worst days, she'd threaten to call her niece and lie that I'd broken something or that I hadn't fed her. She never called. I wondered if she forgot or if she secretly enjoyed my company.

Somewhere between watching *Judge Judy* and crocheting, she told me things. Secret, personal things. Things that her family would want me to keep quiet. As agreed, I kept my mouth shut. But her stories plagued my drive home. On a few nights, I missed the exit to my house because I was deep in thought about what she'd told me. I got a sense she needed to vent, but with her words like *made guys* and *sit-downs*, I was afraid of how much she had shared. I hoped it would pass, but it got worse. Much worse.

I applied a little more makeup to my eyes, grabbed my medical bag, and headed for the front door.

Knock, knock, knock. "Hello, Ms. Giordano. It's me, Barbara."

Beyond the door, feet shuffled across the floor. "I'm coming, damn it," she yelled, then fiddled with the lock.

"To the left, remember?"

"Don't you think I know my own house?" she asked through the door.

The door opened. Mud coated her hands and slippers. Dirty footprints dotted the hardwood floor. She avoided eye contact and held her hands behind her back.

"Have you been in the garden again, Ms. G.?"

"Big deal. I've got to get it ready for planting."

"It's November. It's not time to do gardening. Look at you. You're covered in mud, sweetheart. Let's take off your slippers so we don't trudge dirt through the house. Let's wash your hands," I said, then escorted her to the bathroom sink.

"If I put on my rain boots, will you take me to the backyard?" she asked with childlike eyes.

"If you promise not to throw my stethoscope across the room this time, I'll take you out there."

"All right, fine." She pulled up her sleeve.

With the earpieces inserted, I listened to her heart. Her heart sounded healthy as an ox.

"It's wet out today." I put the stethoscope back in my bag. "Are you sure you want to go out there?"

"I am, or I wouldn't have asked. I'm a grown woman, and I gotta ask permission to go outside in my own backyard? *Minchia,*" she scoffed. "Look, the patio is covered with leaves."

"You say that *minchia* word often. What does it mean?"

"It's a bad word. It means . . . well . . . male parts."

"Oh, okay." I shook my head. "Well, since you didn't break any of my equipment today, we'll go outside. But we need to put on your rain boots and jacket."

"Deal." She made her way to her room.

I grabbed my coat and followed her. "Would you like help?" I said, watching her almost fall when she put on her galoshes. "Here, let me help you."

"I can do it." She batted my hands away, then grabbed her jacket and looked up at me. "Can you help with the zipper? Sometimes it's hard to do with my arthritis."

This was a first. Asking for my help? "Sure," I said, then shot her a faint grin. Once dressed, we made our way to the yard.

"Hand me that broom," she said.

"Sure."

"What's with all the bruises?"

I whisked down my sleeves. "What bruises?"

"The ones on your arms. And your knuckles are all scabbed. You fall or somethin'?"

"Oh, yeah. I did. Over my son's bike. He left it in the driveway, and I tripped on it."

"Umm-hmm." She eyed me up and down. "Better be more careful next time."

"Since you seem to have things under control, I'll be sitting over here if you need me."

"I don't *need you* for anything."

"Whatever you say," I mumbled, then shook my head.

"You know this whole place is where it started for me."

"What started, Ms. G.?"

"Roots to this life. The life I was born into. *The Mafia*—all of it."

I pretended like I didn't hear the last part. Mafia was a subject best left alone. "You have a nice piece of property here."

"Where do you live?"

"Downtown."

"I lived in a big city years ago. Brooklyn. With my ex-husband," she said as she raked the leaves into a pile.

"Why Brooklyn? It's so pretty here. I don't think I'd ever leave."

"I didn't want to leave. I didn't even want to get married, but

I was forced. My father wanted to bridge our families. So, I did my duty and sacrificed—body, soul, heart. Oh, Gaetano, how I miss you so," she called out to the sky.

"What happened to your husband?" The words spilled out before I could stop myself. "I read somewhere that he went missing."

"Missing, huh? Yeah, Frank went *missing* a long time ago."

"Who was Gaetano?"

"The love of my life. Frank was just part of the arrangement."

"The arrangement?"

"With the Molanano family. One of the five families that ran this valley."

"I read about them somewhere."

"A long time ago, the type of business that ruled the Bay Area wasn't talked about. It was hidden. People that governed this place weren't elected officials or even the police. They were members of an organization bigger than anyone imagined. And we owned everyone and everything."

"Strange to think that was all right here in San Jose."

"Strange? No. Not in my day. Hand me that garbage bin over there to put these leaves in."

"Here you go." I bent down to help her.

"Thank you." She shot me a ghost of a smile.

Ms. G. handed me the broom and sat with me on the bench. "With the kind of family I was in, this was the best place to be— away from people, noise, cops. Total privacy up here. This land is all I have left. I gave them everything. And for what? To end up alone."

"You gave who everything?"

"One minute I start to feel bad for you, the next you act like a *stunad*. The mob, damn it," she huffed. "Haven't you been listening?"

"Maybe it's best we go inside," I said, irritated at her tone.

"I don't want to go inside. We just got out here. You probably think I'm lying. I never lie about the mob," she said firmly.

"I believe you, honey."

"So much history here. Like this house. It was originally built for my father's medical clinic. He was a masseuse. Some called him a healer. You're not the only one who knows the medical field. It's in my blood. I was his medical assistant."

"You never told me that."

"You never asked. You just poke me." She shot me a dirty look and rubbed her arm.

"Just doing my job."

"Yeah, my father helped lots of people. Back then, people didn't understand what a masseuse was. Folks were skeptical. There was even talk around town of him engaging in forms of witchcraft because of his unconventional ways. He used everything from leeches for bad circulation to whipped egg whites for a sore back. Believe it or not, it all worked."

I shivered at the thought of tiny slugs hanging onto people. "Leeches? Really?"

"Leeches aren't so bad. He was gifted with the healing power. He knew where to touch someone to cure them. People came from all over the country to visit him."

"Boy, I could use him now," I said, rubbing the bruises on my arms.

"He could heal most ailments, but not all. There's only one cure for what you got, and it requires more than just Band-Aids and makeup." She tapped the back of my hand.

I stopped rubbing my arm and changed the subject. "What's that building out there in the back?"

"Oh, that's the big house. We used it for parties. Made guys had sit-downs in the basement. But we were never allowed to go down there—ever." She shivered.

"You've mentioned sit-downs before."

"I have?"

"Why don't we go in for lunch?" I stood with my arm out so she could steady herself through the wet mud.

"Yeah, I'm starvin'. The food you make stinks. Look how much weight I lost since you been here. My pants are falling down," she said as she pulled at her elastic waistband.

"A turkey sandwich doesn't taste terrible."

"Turkey? Where's the *capocollo* or the *prosciutt'*, huh? Turkey tastes like crap. It's dry. I wouldn't give that to a dog. I only eat turkey at Thanksgiving, and that's with a plate full of pasta. *Maronn*. 'Turkey,' she says. Sheesh."

"Okay, I'll make you a salami sandwich. Will that make you happier?"

"Yeah. Hard to screw that up. It's not your fault. It's not in your blood."

"One day, Ms. G., I'm going to make you Southern food that will knock your socks off."

"I'll pass."

"You'll see. It's good," I said on the walk back to the house. Twenty-five hundred might not be enough for putting up with her and her snarky comments. She was a mean old bat, but I kept my mouth shut when I thought about Leticia's tuition and putting food on the table, while Marcus continued to piss it all away.

She stopped and grabbed for my arm to steady her. "They took everything from me," she mumbled as tears welled in her eyes. "I have no one now. I'm all alone."

I couldn't believe my eyes and ears. Ms. Tough-Ass had a soft spot and was crying? I wanted to help her, but something about her tears made me uncomfortable. Afraid she might push me away, I took a deep breath, reached out my arms, and patted her back awkwardly. "You won't be alone anymore. I'm right here, honey," I whispered. After a few minutes, she pushed away from me and pulled open the sliding glass door.

"I'm fine." She brushed away her tears and sat in her ragged old brown recliner. Deflated, she stared at the pictures on the wall.

"Are there any pictures of that man . . . Gaetano? Is he on the wall?"

"No, no pictures of him there."

"Tell me about him. I'm a sucker for a good love story," I said, trying to perk her up.

"When I met Gaetano that summer, it was like my soul awakened. From the moment I saw him, my heart was his. I felt alive and beautiful with him, at a time when I'd just grown into my body. He listened to my heart when I needed it. He exposed my vulnerabilities while protecting my honor. He was nothing less than chivalrous."

"He sounds amazing."

"He was." She smiled. "There are no coincidences in life. Our paths crossed when he and his family were forced to flee his hometown in Sardinia. The Black Hand bore down hard on his family, so they came here under the protection of the Antonelli family."

"The Black Hand?"

"The Black Hand, the Commission, Cosa Nostra. The mob. The Mafia. It's all the same, kid," she explained.

"Oh." I rubbed my hands together. "Antonelli? I've heard of that place. A farm, right? My son, Darnell, went there on a field trip some time ago. Are they the ones who sell dried fruit?"

"Yes. The Antonelli family has been around for years. Old man Antonelli and my father were great friends. As part of their commitment to the Mafia, my father and Antonelli hid people. Sometimes they'd take in wise guys on the run, and other times it was families hiding out from the mob. The Mafia treated it like a business deal. In exchange, my family was owed a favor. To them, it was good business. But if the Mafia back in Italy ever found out we harbored anyone, it would cause bad blood or an all-out war between the families."

"So, his family was in hiding when you met him?"

"Yes."

"Scary, but kind of romantic. Like forbidden love," I said with a wide grin.

"Forbidden, all right. I can tell you about him and all of it. I could spend the rest of my lifetime talking about my grape grower. If I don't tell someone soon, I might burst. I'm a caged animal in my own brain."

"It's all right, honey. You can tell me." I patted her shoulder. When the words came out of my mouth, I regretted them. I'd given her permission to tell me what I said I'd never tell a soul. I'd opened the floodgates, for God's sake.

"For so long, I'd closed the memories off in my mind because some memories are just too scary," she said and clasped her hands together tightly.

My throat tightened.

"In those days, when your family's connected, it's helpful to merge with other families for power and safety. Marriages bonded families together. Frank was a high-ranking member of the Molanano crime family. For my father, my marriage to him was nothing more than a business deal."

"That's so sad."

"Being married to one of the biggest gangsters in the US taught me many things. It provided me money, protection, respect, and power. But it also robbed me of freedom, independence, and the love of myself and others. That's the price you pay for the benefits. I didn't have a choice."

Her words about losing love of herself and others resonated with me. I realized that Ms. G. and I might have had more in common than I'd originally thought. I wanted to hear more. "Do you regret marrying Frank?"

"Yes, but I didn't have a choice. There's a difference between being in love with someone and living in fear of them. Our relationship became familiar, and I did what was expected of me. When you live in this world for as long as I have, you learn to accept your limitations. Some things just don't work when you're in love with someone else." She touched the gold St. Anthony's charm that dangled from her neck.

"Saint Anthony, huh? I have Saint Christopher." I pulled it out from under my shirt.

"Saint Christopher? You a Catholic?"

"No, ma'am. My last patient gave it to me. To protect me."

"Protect you from what, exactly?" Her eyebrows drew in together.

"From falling over bikes." I pulled my sleeves over my knuckles.

"Yeah, sure. Bikes." She shook her head at me.

"Go on." I leaned forward.

"Gaetano was everything. I've never told anyone the whole truth. The story I'm about to tell you is a long and complicated one and should be kept between us. Let's just say it would cause problems if certain people found out."

"Yes, your niece made me aware of that when I got the job. I won't tell anyone."

"They've probably forgotten about me by now, but if you were to tell the wrong person . . . I'm not sure I could protect you. But I'm no rat," she said loudly. "With everyone dying around me, I have no one who understands anymore."

"Do you mean they'd *hurt* me?"

"The Mafia won't just hurt you. They'll make sure you're never found again. And if that isn't enough, they'll go after your family next. That's how it works."

My heart went from first gear to overdrive. Fast. I stood.

"Excuse me for a minute. I need to use the restroom," I mumbled as I walked quickly to the bathroom.

I cupped my hand under the faucet and took a sip of water to quench my dry throat. What had I gotten myself into? Kill me and my family? No way would I let that happen. *Maybe I should leave? Yes. I'll grab my medical bag and leave. I'll tell her I can't do this. But do I know too much already?* Clearly, her extended family still had ties to this life. If they knew I'd left on my terms, maybe they'd think I'd go to the cops and kill me, anyway. *How did I get myself into this?* My stomach flipped upside down, and I wasn't sure I would be able to speak with a cherry-sized lump in my throat.

I took deep breaths and thought about my kids. Ms. G. said that sometimes you have to sacrifice for your family. So, without further thought, I marched back into the living room, ready for whatever she would throw at me.

"You okay, dear?"

"I'm fine. I think." I clutched the charm at my neck. I hoped it worked. "Okay, Ms. G. Tell me what happened with Gaetano."

"Ah yes, my beloved Gaetano. *My Guy*. I loved him so."

She sat back in her recliner and crocheted.

"I met Gaetano Sanna the summer of 1939, while picking prunes on Antonelli farms. My love for him is where my true sacrifice to the Mafia began. But what followed was so much more than I could've ever imagined. I don't regret one second with him—not one. He's the reason I survived it all. We were like two natural forces, always trying to get back to one another in a world where duty to family meant more than your own life. Every choice has a consequence, and I paid every one of them."

Chapter 3

The Visitors

San Jose, California
Summer 1939
Violetta

I DREW MY MOTHER'S HANDMADE CURTAINS ASIDE FROM OUR tiny bedroom window. Heat from the glass warmed my palms, and it was only 7:00 a.m. It would be another blazing hot June day, and I dreaded going back to the farm. My normal summer routine—picking prunes at Antonelli Farms—was sweaty, backbreaking work. But it meant more money for my family. Any chance we could make a little extra cash, we did—illegal or otherwise. Even with my father helping the Molanano family, tending to wise guys and such, residual effects of the Depression had everyone spooked.

"Bye, Vinny." I patted my little brother on the top of the head.

"When can I go with you guys?" Vinny asked.

"Trust me, you wouldn't like it, kid. You're lucky you're too young. See you tonight. *Ciao.*"

"*Andiamo*, Violetta," Pop yelled from the truck.

"Coooom-iiiiing," I yelled. Ugh. I fastened my shoes and hopped in the truck bed beside my sister and two other brothers.

"Jesus, Vi, move over," Carmela said, then pushed my legs to the side.

"Just because you're the oldest, Carm, doesn't mean you get to boss me around. There's no room," I fired back. "Paulie, move over!"

"Shut up, Vi," Paulie said.

"You know you're a real *stunad* sometimes, Paul," I said as my lip curled up on one side.

"*Stata chett!* Shut up," my big brother Tony yelled. "We're gonna be there in a few minutes. Quit complaining already."

We rode along the dirt road to Antonelli's. Dust clouds rose from the truck's tires, making it hard to see. Familiar sounds of water boatmen whistling in the trees got me thinking about how many summers we'd been doing this. My father met Antonelli not long after he and my mother moved from their hometown of Tricarico and bought land here.

Pop wanted to give our family a better life. He, like many other families, inquired about a newspaper ad that a local farmer had placed in search of people to help harvest prunes. Three cents for every forty-pound box. Pop was one of the first applicants to seek a contract with ole man Antonelli. Over the years, he and Antonelli had become good friends and confidants at a time when allegiances meant everything.

With so much weight in the back, the truck lugged past the giant metal gates at the farm entrance. Acres of trees reminded me how much I hated prune season. I rubbed my knuckles and fingers. My hands would ache when I got home tonight. On a Friday, there were only two things I looked forward to: the soda pop and the quarter we'd get at the end of the week. I guess my father thought money would keep us motivated. The faster the hours went by, the faster I'd have a cool drink in my hands and hear a jingle in my pocket.

Rewards or not, the day would drag. I couldn't wait to go home.

From the moment I started for the trees, the day felt different. Antonelli called my father over. The old farmer was a tall man with salt-and-pepper hair. I didn't know what they talked about, but their faces looked serious. They shook hands, and Pop came back over to us.

"*Signor* Antonelli have people he wan us to meet. Dey coma from a town call *Bosa*, in *Sardegna*. Dey stay wit Antonelli dis summer to help."

"Where's that? At the top of the boot or the bottom, Pop?" Tony asked.

"No in da boot. Itsa island."

"An island in Italy?" I asked.

"*Si*. He ask me if we canna make dem feel lika home. Tony maybe you canna talk to da oldest son. I ma sure he woulda like to make a fren."

"Sure, Pop. When can we meet 'em?" Tony asked.

"Right now. Letsa go. Antonelli get dem to introduce."

We followed my father to the front of the property. With sweat pouring down my back, I blistered in the sun, ready to hear from Antonelli. A slender man and his wife came before us with two little girls who were so shy, they wouldn't break away from their mother's skirt.

"Ello, everbadi, I wan you to meet da *famiglia* Sanna. Dis is *Signor* Efrem Sanna, hisa wife, Conchetta, and children, Gina and Christina and da oldest son, Gaetano," Antonelli announced.

A taller man stood behind them, backlit by the sun. He took a step forward into view.

"*Sono* Gaetano Sanna," he said, then waved to us. Soft, dark brown waves spilled down his forehead when he moved.

"Gaetano. *GUY* taaanno," I said under my breath. I loved the way it rolled off my tongue as the sound bounced between my ears. At first glance, he looked like one swell *guy* to me. Something about him got my attention. Maybe it was the way he shot me a half-crooked smile when he waved to us or the way his wavy hair crested gently behind his ears.

I was instantly drawn to him.

He looked like no one I'd ever seen before: tall and muscular, but not like a boxer type; thick and defined where it mattered; distinct facial features where his neck and jawline framed his face perfectly, like Michelangelo himself had worked away at him. But his eyes grabbed my attention the most. They were a mixture of chocolate and honey. His dark, silky eyelashes blinked slowly when the sun hit his face, giving him a relaxed and dreamy appearance.

My insides shook, and my pulse became erratic.

"Dis is da *famiglia* Sanna," said Mr. Antonelli. "Dey will stay wit us for a while. Please get to know each udder."

With a nudge from my father, my brothers swarmed the young man. In his thick accent, he tried hard to communicate. When he quieted, my brothers spoke Italian to make it easier.

I moved next to Carmela and studied him. His height made him look confident, but when he tipped his head down in between handshakes, he seemed shy and full of humility. His brief moments of silence made me want to know what thoughts lay behind those dreamy eyes.

Out of respect, he introduced himself to the rest of us. When he drew near to shake my hand, more sweat beads formed on my lips and brow. He stared into my eyes and grabbed my hand delicately.

"*Guy tano*," he repeated.

My insides quivered.

I should have tried to speak to *Signora* Sanna and the girls, but I was too interested in what my brothers and the young man talked about. Gaetano put his hands on his hips when he listened. When he spoke, his long eyelashes pinched together as he smiled between words. Like most Italians, he used his hands to weave a story. Veins swelled through his muscular arms as he moved them around to explain about his life in Italy and how stressful it was to migrate here.

And every now and again, he shot me a stare that made my knees weak. He had power over me, and I wanted nothing more than to get to know him.

After introductions, Pop, *Signor* Sanna, and ole man Antonelli went into the house to talk business while the rest of us went to work. I spent the rest of the day following Gaetano. Where he went, I went. Watching his every move, I'd find him tinkering with various equipment and talking to people. Then I'd find an area to pick where I could keep an eye on him, until Carmela started yelling my name.

"Vi, where are you?"

"What, Carm?" I returned with my half-empty tray.

"What the hell ya doin', huh? You haven't been working all day. Every time I look for you, I find you somewhere else with hardly no fruit in your tray. Stop screwing around and act your age. You're almost eighteen. I wanna go home just as bad as you do."

"I'm sorry. I don't feel well. Must be the heat," I lied.

"Well then, get water and get back to work," she said, picking up the leftover fruit that had fallen to the ground. Out of fear that Carmela might figure out my newfound interest, I complied and started picking again.

My new distraction made the hours feel longer than normal. I couldn't wait to finish so that I could go find the island boy.

"It's quitting time. Let's pack it up," Tony said as he handed me my soda and money.

I grabbed my box of prunes and followed my brother to the front of the farm. Pop motioned me over.

"Violetta, *vieni qui,*" he said as I came over to him. "Antonelli ask me if you canna drive da Sanna family to town tomorra? I gonna be busy writing da contract. *Signora* Sanna say she needa buy material to make da girls soma clothes."

"Sure, Pop. I'd love to," I said, hoping to get to know the dreamy-eyed man better.

"Okay. I tell him." His face hardened, and his tone became serious. "Pick dem up early and only take dem to places where we know da owner. And have dem back early."

"Yes, Pop," I said as he walked away. "Hey, I was thinking . . ."

He turned back toward me. "Tinking what?"

"I can teach them English if they want. I do pretty well in school. Please, Pop? I'd love to do it."

He eyed me cautiously. "I willa talk to *Signor* Sanna and you mama. But it canno interfere with you chores and when you go back to school."

"I had perfect marks last year. I'll be the first one to graduate high school. I can do it."

"I tink about it, Violetta. No promises. Time to go now. I meet you in da truck."

"Okay," I said optimistically. I looked forward to tomorrow when I'd see Gaetano again.

My pulse raced. I wanted to see him one last time before we made our way home. I scanned the fields, but he was nowhere to be found. I decided to check the main house.

"Hey, Carm, I gotta use the bathroom before we go."

"All right, but make it quick. I wanna get home."

"I'll only be a minute."

Once Carm was out of sight, I ran to the main house and looked inside the kitchen. Gaetano wasn't there. I went to the back of the house. No sign of him there, either. It wasn't until I exited the house that I saw him talking to his father. From the strong heat, he wore only his undershirt. He glistened in the sun from the sweat that dripped from his neck and chin. He took out his handkerchief to wipe his face. Even with all the sweat and dirt on his face, his eyes dazzled me and held me in place. Spellbound, my heart jumped when my father approached.

"*Minchia*. What da hell you doin'?" My father grabbed my arm and ushered me toward the truck. "You tell Carmela you go to da bathroom, and you just standin' here. Letsa go! I gotta get da money pickups ready."

Gaetano stared at me as my father forced me to the truck. My cheeks blazed. He didn't laugh at me. He looked concerned.

"Okay, Pop. Stop," I fired back and pulled my arm from his grip. "I'm a girl, and sometimes it takes longer to go to the bathroom." Playing the girl card nearly always gained his sympathies.

With softer eyes, he said, "I ma sorry. Letsa go."

I climbed into the truck bed and wrapped my dirt-covered arms around my knees. My stomach was in knots from the day's events, and I felt mortified by Pop's actions in front of the new man.

Overcome, my eyes welled up.

The farm shrank on the horizon as dust lifted from the motion of the tires. I put my head between my knees to conceal my face. As much as I hated picking prunes when we arrived, I didn't want to leave.

Once the rooster crowed, I fixed my hair in a French braid and threw on one of my nicer church outfits. As a finishing touch, and because it made me look grown up, I brushed Carmela's rouge on my cheeks and curled my eyelashes. I had eyelashes on the brain now because of the island boy. So Carmela wouldn't tease me, I carefully placed everything back on her nightstand.

Pop let me drive his black Ford pickup on occasion. It had a big bed in the back for moving stuff and for hauling the family around when we went places. He didn't mind me taking the truck because he had another car sitting in the driveway: a brand-new Cadillac LaSalle. He only took it out for church and special occasions.

I was the only girl in my household who knew how to drive. My mother was too scared to drive, and my sister never had time to learn. Pop taught me because there were times when he needed me to go and run errands for him. At first, I hated driving the truck. It had a long gear shift and stalled out all the time. After a while, I got the hang of it. On days like today, I was happy I'd learned because it meant I'd see the boy with the dreamy eyes.

With Gaetano's face still lingering in my brain, I zipped through the hills on my way to Antonelli's. I remembered his gorgeous eyes and the soft but strong way his voice tickled my eardrums.

A huge tree loomed in front of me.

I turned the wheel sharply left and slammed the brakes. The truck skidded on its tires. Tiny rocks from the dirt road flung through the air and made clanking noises as they bounced off the heavy metal frame. The fender stopped within inches of the fat oak.

"Oh my God," I screamed. I sat there for a moment, trying to catch my breath. "Damn it. Get it together, Vi. Keep your eyes on the road and not on him. You need to be *alive* to see him again."

I gathered myself up and pressed on the gas. With the orchards in the distance, I continued down the road toward the open gate.

Signora Sanna stood in front of the main house with her two little girls, but no *Signor* Sanna and no Gaetano. My heart sank to my stomach. Where was he? Maybe ole man Antonelli kept them back to work? Defeated, I parked and waved them to the truck. I'd committed to Pop that I'd take them, so I did what was asked.

"*Buongiorno, come stai?*" I asked while searching for the boy.

"*Buongiorno,*" *Signora* Sanna said, leading the girls to the back of the truck.

Our drive to town was quiet. *Signora* Sanna didn't talk much, even in Italian. The silence was awkward. At traffic stops, I'd smile at her. She kept her head down. To escape the uncomfortable quiet, I kept my eyes on the road into Goosetown. A left turn onto Bird Avenue brought us to an Italian market where they had prints and various cheap fabrics.

After I parked, *Signora* Sanna grabbed both girls by the hand and whispered something to them. They all lowered their heads. Were they praying? Even the way *Signora* Sanna was dressed seemed strange. Despite the summer heat, she wore a dark silk scarf around her neck and a big hat. Maybe she was sensitive to the sun, or maybe that's how they dressed in Italy? I didn't know what it was, but something was wrong with this family.

"The store's this way." I pointed to the building ahead.

"*Si. Prego*," *Signora* Sanna whispered to the ground.

We walked through the main street of Goosetown. Like most days, it was filled with Italians. Outside the stores, women held grocery sacks and men gathered together to chat. The yeasty smell of freshly baked bread filled the air. And the sound of screaming children chasing the water wagon down the road stung my ears. I stood outside the market while *Signora* Sanna went in to buy fabric and a few souvenirs.

"Would the girls like gelato?" I asked as she exited the store.

"No," she said firmly.

I took the hint, and we started back for the truck. She was almost emotionless. No smile, no eye contact—nothing. Something was off about her. She watched the girls as if they were made of glass. The only time she spoke was to tell them to walk faster or to say please and thank you. When we passed people in the streets, she pulled her scarf around her face. *Signora* Sanna never *really* looked at anyone when they spoke to her. At first, I thought she was rude. The more I watched, the more I became convinced she was scared. But scared of what or whom? She didn't know anyone here, so what was the problem? I was determined to find out.

Like most of the day, little conversation filled the truck cab on the ride home. I dropped them off at the doorstep of the Antonelli home and looked to see if Gaetano was around.

Tony provided the perfect cover.

"Is Tony still here?" I asked *Signora* Antonelli, who was busy in the kitchen of the main house.

"*Si*. Go to da back, Violetta," she assured me.

I searched the orchards for them. So many different families harvested, it was hard to tell workers apart. With Antonelli paying by the box, entire families packed the orchard.

In the general direction where my family usually set up, I spotted Tony talking to one of the Russo brothers. Close to my brother was another man on a ladder, who had his face buried in a tree.

My heart beat fast again.

It was him.

Gaetano's tall, denim-clad legs stood firm on the wooden ladder. While he plucked prunes from the vine, thick, corded muscles in his forearms worked beneath his skin. Moving quickly, he twisted the fruit free and dropped clusters in a cloth bag that hung over his shoulders. He was no stranger to hard work, and that attracted me even more.

He tugged—hard—on a stubborn branch. Leaves cascaded down and landed all over me. I dusted off my shoulders.

Gaetano stopped working and climbed down the steps. He took off his dirty gloves and shoved them in his pockets.

"I ma so sorry." He gently pulled a leaf from my hair and smiled.

"Thanks," I whispered. We both giggled, and I felt around in my hair for more leaves.

"I no speaka good *Inglese*. *Come si dice*? Um . . ." he stammered. "Ello, my name isa Gaetano Sanna."

He said his name to perfection. Italian, English, it didn't matter.

"It's okay. I speak a little Italian. My name is Violetta Giordano. Most people call me Vi. I'm Giuseppe's daughter." His grip was soft and tender.

"*Si*, Violetta."

"I took your mother and sisters to town today."

He slowly pulled his hand away. His palms and fingers had rough patches of calluses. Since I'd last seen him, the skin on his face, arms, and neck had turned a golden brown. The contrast of his deep black lashes against his golden skin made his eyes stand out even more. They stared at me, pensive, reflective, almost hypnotic, pulling my body toward him.

"Working hard, I see," I said as his eyes held me hostage. "Every summer, my father makes us come here, so I know the feeling."

"*Si*, itsa hard work, but Antonelli help my fater, so I happy to help."

"I don't know if your father told you yet, but I'd like to help you learn English. If you want. I'll help you study a few days a week if you like." I caught myself rambling words he probably didn't understand. "Umm, let's see here. *Posso insegnarti l'inglese.*"

"*Si. Grazie*," he said as he reached for his canteen to get a drink of water. He took a huge gulp. Water dripped off his chin onto the dry dirt next to his boots. "Uh, *si*, I woulda like dat."

"Next week? I will talk to my father to make sure it's okay. He'll probably want someone to supervise."

"What you mean supervize?" he asked.

"I don't know how it is back in Italy, but people here don't like it if a girl and boy are alone together if they aren't courting. Heck, I know people who are watched when they're being courted."

"Oh *si*, I no wanna disrespecta you fater."

"It'll be fine. We'll be fine," I said.

"*Si*, das good."

"I'll bring all the stuff we'll need. Don't worry about anything," I said, smiling.

Tony came from behind me and yanked my braid. "Where you been? No work today? How'd you get so lucky, huh?"

"Cut it out," I fussed, then fixed my hair. "I was looking for you. For your information, I drove the Sanna family in Pop's truck today. You want a ride home?"

"Hell yes, but I'm driving. Last time you drove we almost crashed. Remember?"

"Not true. You're lying," I said to Tony.

"I'm only teasin'. Can you believe it, Guy? Women drivers."

"One day we'll rule the world," I said. "You watch, Tony."

"That'll be the day, little sister," Tony teased and smiled at me fondly.

Gaetano's gaze pressed on my awareness. I glanced over my brother's shoulder and caught Gaetano staring at me again. He quickly looked down at the ground and began stacking the wooden trays of fruit on top of each other.

Tony and Gaetano kept talking in Italian. I didn't pay attention to what they were saying. All that mattered was the way Gaetano looked at me. I wasn't smart in all the ways of the world, but I knew how a boy looks when he's interested in a girl. Gaetano looked very interested.

We said our goodbyes, and I followed Tony to the truck. Because he didn't trust my driving, he got in the driver's seat, and we were on our way. While his mind was on the road, my mind was on the man with dreamy eyes. I thought about Gaetano's mother and sisters and how odd they behaved when we went to town. These strange, beautiful visitors had so many untold stories, it made them all that more mysterious and alluring. My gut told me why they were here. Much like others, they fled from the one thing my family couldn't escape: the Mafia.

Chapter 4

The Power of Words

I WOKE UP SUNDAY MORNING, SO ANXIOUS THAT I FELT SICK. My stomach flipped in circles every time I thought about the dreamy-eyed man. It didn't help that my father hadn't said one word about me teaching Gaetano English the entire weekend. If I bugged him, he'd say no. Instead, I did all my chores early and thoroughly. I wanted this so bad that I even did chores that weren't mine. I cleaned out the pigpens, fed the chickens, and washed out the horse stalls, all hoping Pop would notice and lean favorably to my proposition.

"Violetta, *vieni qui.*"

"Yes, Papa?" I said, wiping my dirty hands on my overalls.

"You mama and me, we talk. She say yes. You canna teach dat boy."

"All right." My mysterious stomach illness magically disappeared.

"But someone needa watch you. He too old."

"He's the same age as me."

"*Signor* Sanna and I, we agree to three days a week you teach dat boy. Whatever days you wan. You start eight a.m. sharp till lunch-time. Antonelli need bodies to help around da ranch, so he needa be out in da fields no later dan noon."

"Okay. And the girls?"

"No. He gonna put dem in school. Dey young enough to pick it up. But he happy you help da boy because he needa learn. *Signor* Sanna wan him in da fields for da money. Da family isa tankful to you, and to me, cause I letta you do it. Itsa good biziniss." He puffed out his chest and looped his hands around his suspenders as if he was the one who devised the plan.

"Sure. I'll start tomorrow. Thanks, Pop." I kissed him on the cheek.

"Somedays, you go to Antonelli house and *Signora* Antonelli, she watch, and sometimes you coma here and you work in da *cucina* and you mama watch. Dis boy canno be alone wit you. If I find out, no more *Inglese*." His eyes were stern.

I nodded as my shoulders sank into my frame. At least he'd agreed to my idea, and that gave me more time with Gaetano. I understood his demands and was grateful for his decision, but I felt like a two-year-old having to be watched. Even though I was almost eighteen and was ready to court, my father had to approve. I'd wallow in self-pity until the morning when I'd see Gaetano again.

I walked into the Antonelli kitchen at 8:00 a.m. *Signora* Antonelli stood over a big pot on the stove.

"*Buongiorno*, Violetta."

"*Buongiorno, Signora.*"

"You papa tell me you gonna teach da Sanna boy."

"Yes."

"Okay. You sit *here*, and he sit *ova der*." She pointed to opposite ends of her long dining room table.

With my lips pulled together in a tight line, I shook my head. I was sure that Pop had talked to her about the arrangement. When he meant separation, he wasn't kidding.

I pulled out paper, pencils, and a few beginning reader books that my little brother had. When I looked up, Gaetano stood in front of me, smiling and clean-shaven. His lightly-stained white T-shirt was tucked into his blue jeans and tiny tendrils of his hair pressed onto his forehead from his coppola cap.

I pointed to the chair on the opposite side of the table. "*Per favore*, sit there."

He took off his hat and sat.

I handed him paper and a pencil while he surveyed my face. It appeared he wouldn't just be studying English. His long, penetrating gaze made my heart flutter. Blood rushed to my cheeks.

"First, we'll start with the basics," I spoke loud enough so he'd hear me.

He nodded.

"Say . . . *hello*."

"Ello," he called back, loud enough to match my voice.

"Say *goodbye*." I waved goodbye to show him what it meant.

"*Goodbye . . . er Ciao*," he said, then moved his hands like mine.

"Yes. Good."

"Violetta, my ears, dey worka fine. Itsa *mi Inglese* dat no work too good."

We both laughed.

"I'm sorry. I thought you wouldn't hear me sitting way over there."

"No. I hear you jus fine," he said and smiled his crooked smile.

His joke broke the ice between us. Laughter was timely and needed. The rest of the session went smoothly. This was the beginning of something special, so long as we respected the rules. The constant threat of glaring eyes from our chaperone reinforced limitations and made it harder for me to get to know him in the way I'd longed for. Language barriers weren't the only thing in our way.

After a few sessions, everyone got more comfortable with the arrangement, probably so Mama and *Signora* Antonelli could hear themselves think without all the yelling back and forth across the table. With each session, we moved closer, sometimes so close that our hands brushed against each other when I'd hand him a paper or pencil. His skin felt warm, invigorating, and new. When our bodies touched, a *zing* ran right through me, quickening my pulse.

I looked forward to every session. We split our time between Antonelli's house and my house. *Signora* Antonelli brought us homemade snacks while we worked. Other times, we worked at my kitchen table where Mama would peer over her shoulder every now and again to check on us. She made sure to put her shotgun close to her so Gaetano got the message. I felt sorry for him. His eyes looked ready to pop out of his head the first time he saw her carry the rifle to the kitchen.

"I so stoopit. I neva gonna undastan da *Inglese*," Gaetano said with his hands in fists.

"You're not stupid. Don't say things like that. You're doing great. It takes practice." I laid my hand on his shoulder. When I touched him, the weight of frustration left his expression. His shoulders relaxed, and he shot me a reassuring grin, sending a bolt of lightning through my insides.

"Tank you, Violetta." He placed his hand on top of mine.

I took a deep breath to compose myself and continued with the next part of the lesson. Many times, he'd get frustrated and want to give up. He never did because we both knew our time together was precious.

Despite the exchange of an occasional smile and the obvious nervous giggle, the sessions became routine. I'd make a lesson plan the night before, and we reviewed it the next day. Once he was ready to move past my little brother's old books, I made sure to bring along classics like *Moby Dick*, *Wuthering Heights*, and even Shakespeare.

They challenged him, but I was alongside him to decode unfamiliar words and encourage him when things got hard.

There were moments we looked at each other without words and our energy connected. When I looked over his shoulder to make sure he wrote correctly, his body heat radiated against mine. It was intoxicating. His breath was sweet when he spoke. He smelled of citrus and mint. It was a fresh scent and one that made me want to get closer. As the days advanced, it was hard to control myself around him.

Gaetano aroused my senses. The way he looked at me with his deep and beautiful penetrating stares, the way his eyes held onto me, left me breathless and nervous at the same time. It did something new to my body. My heart pulsed in my groin. He'd awakened me.

"Gaetano," I said with my heart pounding against my blouse again. "Read a passage from one of the books I brought. Let's work on pronunciation." He turned to face me with the book in his hand and read a piece from *Romeo and Juliet*.

"*My bounty isa boundless as da sea, My love as deep; da more I give to dee, Da more I hava, for both are infinite,*" he read. His eyes moved up from the page and onto me, piercing with a deep intensity and reverence. He'd spoken each word with purpose and passion. The piece got away from both of us, and the words emerged gracefully over his tongue and into my heart. His choice was obvious. It was as if he'd borrowed Shakespeare's words to replace his own. We studied one another, trembling with excitement about our newfound discoveries.

"That was amazing. You pronounced every word almost perfectly." I clapped then, forgetting my surroundings. I gave him a hug. It was my first reaction to commend his efforts, but when we held on to each other, it was much more. Because our bodies met each other for the first time, the embrace made us tremble.

"Violetta, what you doin'?" Mama cracked the ravioli roller against the counter. "You canno do dat. If you papa find out, *maronn*. He gonna be mad."

Gaetano put his head down and moved away quickly.

"I'm sorry, Mama. I wasn't thinking. He did such a good job at reading. I'm proud of him." I smiled at Gaetano.

"*Si*, but you know you fater." She continued pressing the dough.

Gaetano and I didn't say much after that. We didn't have to. Words were there. Truth was there, in the air around us. I stared at the knots in the wood of our kitchen table and realized that loving someone goes beyond physical attraction. Although I gravitated to him because of his striking features and captivating eyes, it was his heart and soul I'd become acquainted with in our days together. I saw him in a different way, an intimate way in which a person exposes their mind and their true self to another, that words don't do it justice.

Although we still hadn't touched one another more than a quick handshake, a reassuring tap on the shoulder, and an accidental hug, I hoped that our desire would eventually make itself known. Nothing would keep me from seeing him alone. Not even my mother's hawk-like eyes.

Or her gun.

Because of our growing infatuation, I wanted more time with Gaetano than my three sessions a week. I waited to get Pop alone to ask him if he would consider inviting the Sanna family over for Sunday dinner. When our parents would get to talking, I hoped Gaetano and I could speak more freely. I had things I wanted to say and questions I wanted answered. Pop always reviewed his patients' charts first thing in the morning, so I knew I'd find him alone in his office.

"Hey, Pop."

"*Buongiorno*," he said as he sipped on his morning coffee. "You up early. You okay?"

"I'm fine. I was wondering . . ."

"What?"

"Well, maybe we should invite the Sanna family over for dinner. They've been here a while now, and it would be nice to get everyone together. Maybe invite the Antonellis to join?"

"Hmmm . . . Okay. I tell you mama."

"Great," I yelped, then put my head down to quiet my obvious excitement.

I skipped and whistled all the way back to the house.

With such a large family, we were used to having lots of guests for Sunday dinner. People always stopped by for one thing or another. And because Pop made our home available to various wise guys, I never knew who'd be joining us at the dinner table. Many times, different men and their families would stay with us from all over—New York, Philadelphia, New Jersey. We'd all eat together, and then, like clockwork, the men gathered in the basement of the big house, smoking stogies and talking business.

I was pretty sure that Mama wouldn't be opposed to the Sanna family coming over. She'd simply tell us to make more food. And like any given Sunday morning after church, I made raviolis with my sister and mother for dinner. This time, I'd be sitting at the table across from Gaetano. I wanted everything to be perfect.

My sister and I made over eight trays of raviolis while my mother made the gravy. The house smelled amazing. Garlic and basil filled the air. I wanted him to feel at home here, at home with me.

I put out our nicest dinner plates and silverware. I even ironed the napkins. For the finishing touch, I handpicked wildflowers and put them in a blue vase in the middle of the table. It looked so inviting, like a real restaurant.

"You ironed the napkins? Who the hell do you think is coming over here, President Roosevelt?" Carmela asked, trying to embarrass me.

"I want it to look nice, that's all." I quickly exited the room to get ready.

I pin-curled my hair in waves on the sides of my head and put on a new, fresh-pressed pink blouse and black skirt. My chest had filled out, and I could no longer button the blouse to the top. I made sure to wear an undershirt so Pop wouldn't disapprove. Then I snuck into Mama's dresser and sprayed on a little perfume. As I slipped on my shoes, a knock sounded at the front door.

I ran down the hallway, almost knocking down my little brother, eyes wide-open, ready to see Gaetano's face again.

The entire Sanna family stood in the doorway, along with Mr. and Mrs. Antonelli.

"*Avanti*," Pop said.

"*Grazie*," *Signor* Sanna said as he entered.

Signora Sanna followed along with the girls. Behind them was Gaetano. *My guy.* His eyes searched for me, and we found each other. We shared a smile. My heart leapt in my chest, and a blush heated my cheeks. I'd never had a relationship with a man, but I was pretty sure this was the closest thing I'd experienced to flirting.

The afternoon was filled with conversation about the old country and family lineage. While we passed plates of ravioli around the table, the men told stories of how Antonelli met *Signor* Sanna in the war. Gaetano and I shared a few quick glances between sips of our drinks, then buried our heads in our plates.

Once we finished eating, as expected, the women pulled the plates while the men talked.

"Hey, kids, go outside and play now," Pop said.

Pop shot Tony a look. Tony and Gaetano left the table and went outside. While I was busy clearing plates, I eavesdropped on their conversation. *Signor* Sanna explained that it was the Mafia that made them retreat from their hometown in Sardinia. He said there was a powerful family that terrorized them. He always made sure to give them money when they came to collect, but with his business on hard times, he could no longer afford to pay.

He explained that the men were known to rape the women and kill the men who didn't pay. His only choice was to flee to America, to get as far away as possible. He hated leaving the only place he called home, but he'd be less of a man if they'd raped his girls. After he told the Don he couldn't pay, they were confronted by two men in their house. His daughters screamed while one of the men held a knife to his wife's throat. The other man fondled her to scare *Signor* Sanna to pay.

"My son fought the other man when he saw what they did to his mother. That made the men even more mad," he said in Italian as he looked at Pop with somber eyes. "I told them I'd give them all the fish we'd caught that day, and I emptied the little money I had hidden in an old can. That wasn't enough. I offered them the last thing I had to give—the papers to our home. It'd been in my family for years. It was all I had left."

Pop nodded. *Signor* Sanna continued.

"We had to leave Bosa and go somewhere far away. That's when I reached out to Antonelli for help. It was hard to watch my country fade away in the distance after we boarded the ship. Everything I'd worked for, and all my memories of family—gone. But I couldn't stay after what they'd done." *Signor* Sanna's voice shook. "*Bastardi.*"

The plate slipped from my hands and crashed to the floor.

Everyone in the room turned to look at me.

"*Mi scusi, mi dispiace.* I'm sorry," I said as I picked up the pieces.

"Itsa okay, Violetta," Pop said. "Carmela, coma here and helpa you sister."

"Sure, Pop."

"*Maronn*, Vi," she whispered to me as she bent down. "What the hell happened?"

"It slipped. Don't get so mad. It was an accident." I nudged Carm, then emptied long ceramic bits into the kitchen trash.

Signora Sanna cried and spoke to my mother while she helped dry the dishes.

"I'm sorry for what happened," my mother whispered in

Italian. "If you need anything, someone to talk to, you can talk to me. Church has always helped. When we came over on the boat, we knew *Cosa Nostra* would be here. That's why we picked a place in the country. But they lurk and root themselves. No matter how hard you try to get away from them, you can't. So, we do what we can to protect our family. You are *paesani* now, so we won't let anything happen to you—as long as you can earn. And if you can't? Learn how to protect yourself." She pointed at her gun leaning against the washbasin.

Signora Sanna brushed away her tears. "*Grazie*, Adelina."

With her gun at her side everywhere she went, she stood her ground. I never realized how wise and brave she was for being in her position. She'd never allow anyone she loved to be harmed. A sense of security came over me. Her bold stance and love for us were evident.

"Violetta, go outside and check on da girls," my father called.

"Okay." It all made sense. Now I understood why *Signora* Sanna hid in Goosetown. She'd been terrorized and wanted nothing to do with *Cosa Nostra*. If they were spotted, something bad might happen.

That was why ole man Antonelli kept *Signor* Sanna and Gaetano back on the ranch with him the day that I took his wife and daughters to town. Men were always bigger targets than women. She might have been anyone's wife, but by *Signor* Sanna threatening not to pay a Don and then fleeing, those acts of rebellion were not tolerated. If he refused one Don, who was to say he wouldn't refuse another? The Sanna family would remain a target until they proved they could be earners for the Molanano family.

As much as the Sannas hated the Mafia, it was the Mafia that put Gaetano in my life. Would they accept me? With my family working for Don Molanano, would Gaetano ever pursue me? My heart fell into my stomach. I hoped that our attraction was enough for him to take a chance on me.

With a knot in my throat, I walked over to the two things that soothed me—Gaetano's eyes. I hoped I could coax him away from my brother and have some alone time. Once I was past the pig pens, I heard voices. When I turned around, I saw Pop, ole man Antonelli, and *Signor* Sanna smoking cigars and walking toward the one place where women and children weren't allowed—the basement in the big house. As the old men ventured off, I followed the sound of screaming voices. Tony and Gaetano were playing *Morra*.

"*Cinque*," Tony screamed at the top of his lungs. "I win. You threw a two, and I threw a three," he said, then collected money from his winnings.

"Der are places in Italy, *la polizia* willa put you in da *prigione* if you playa dis game," Gaetano explained.

"Prison?" Tony laughed as he grabbed another beer. "Well, over here in the States, we play *Morra* all the time. You'll be okay, kid. Don't you worry about nothin'. Cops don't come around here much. See, we have this kind of arrangement with those guys."

Gaetano took a sip of his beer.

"I'm gonna go get more beer," said Tony. "I'll be right back. Hey, Paulie, come help me carry some up here."

As they left, I walked over to Gaetano. Once again, his gaze held mine. His body stiffened as I got closer.

"Don't let my brothers tease you so much. They can be real *stunads*," I said as I stood a little closer to him.

"You brudders . . . dey funny." His eyes scanned me up and down. "I lika you dress. You looka verra nice."

"Thanks. It isn't a dress. It is a skirt, but thank you."

"A skkkirt?"

"Yes, a skirt," I said, helping him pronounce it correctly. "Your English improves every day. I'm glad I can help."

"*Si*, uh, yes. I learn a lot. Tank you," he said shyly as a soft grin spread across his face.

"It's my pleasure. I want to show you something. Come with me," I said, fully committed to my plan to be alone with him.

"Er . . . okay."

With the moonlight overhead, we walked to the barn. Horses stood in their stalls as I walked over to my favorite mare.

"This is Isabella. My father let me name her. She's put out some of our best racehorses. Her last foal won a national title. I don't ride as much as I used to, but I visit often." I rubbed her mane. She pulled her head toward mine. "Do you want to touch her?"

I placed my hand over Gaetano's to guide his touch.

"She isa verra beautiful," he said.

His warm breath grazed my ear as he moved closer. I turned to face him.

He stared down at my lips. Moonlight filtered through the barn.

"She isa verra beautiful but not as beautiful as you . . ." His eyes seemed to search for my soul. "I dona have da words in *Inglese*, but I never felt dis way before."

"Me neither. My heart feels like it is going to beat straight out of my chest."

Our noses touched and his lips grazed mine.

Tony's voice echoed through the barn.

"Hey, where you guys at?"

Gaetano and I jerked away from each other and put our hands down at our sides.

Tony rounded the corner of the stalls. "Gaetano, I got to win my money back. Let's go, kid. Smells like horse shit in here."

Gaetano followed Tony out but shot me an apologetic grin.

I waved and patted Isabella. "Well, girl, I was close, but not close enough."

Chapter 5

Babbling Brook

S UMMER ENDED. ANTONELLI FARMS QUIETED. FAMILIES THAT harvested early made their profits and headed home. Trees stood bare and the foothills thirsted for rain.

The change of season meant change for everyone. For me, it meant returning to school. Rumors persisted that the Sannas planned to move away to start over. I wanted more time with Guy, to get to know him in private ways. An impending departure made my heart feel heavy.

My family helped Antonelli winterize his farm. We put away equipment and stacked crates.

A familiar voice carried through the barn.

"Ello, Violetta," Gaetano said.

"Hello," I said shyly, remembering the encounter we had in our barn back at the ranch.

"My fater is happy wit my English. Some words are harder to say dan udders, but at least now I can speaka English," he explained, still trying to pronounce certain words correctly.

"You have come a long way. You just have to keep practicing," I said and smiled.

He nodded his head. "I ma grateful to you. Now dat my English isa betta, he tinks it will help wit da business."

"Business?"

"Yes, my fater, he tinks itsa time we find a place to live and work. In Italy, he make money as a fisherman, and he also work to make vino. He and Antonelli talk about San Francisco to work on big fishing boats, but mama, she no want to live in a big city. Antonelli tell him about a place calla Napa Valley. Mama like dat. She no want him gone all day at sea."

I drew in a trembling breath. His words verified the rumors and my biggest fears. "Napa? Oh, yes . . . I've heard it's a growing business out there. So, when are you planning to leave?"

"A few weeks."

My body stiffened. "Wow, a few weeks," I mumbled.

"Yes." He looked at the ground. "I no want to leave, but my family need da money. And my fater tink itsa betta dat we move away so no one find us."

"I want to do something nice for you for all your hard work this summer. I'd like to take you somewhere special. A place where we can be alone." My cheeks reddened.

"Okay," he said.

"Saturday at noon. I'll bring lunch. Don't worry. I'll take care of everything."

"I will see you Sataday."

"Tell your father it's our last English session, and I'll do the same."

"Gaetano!" *Signor* Sanna belted across the fields.

"I havta go now."

I would've given anything to turn back the clock and start summer over. Leaves fell and so did my heart—right into the pit of my stomach.

With Gaetano leaving in a few weeks, I was determined to make our last days together count. I crafted a graduation diploma to celebrate his hard work and crocheted a small blanket with the American flag on one end and the Italian flag on the other. In the corner, I stitched a tiny heart with the letters *Vi* in the middle so that no matter where Gaetano went, he wouldn't forget me. Next, I needed to find a place where we'd be alone.

Alum Rock Park seemed the best choice to escape into the mountains and not be seen, if Pop would agree. When I found him in the barn tending horses, I put my plan in motion.

"Hey, Pop."

"Ello, Violetta," he said as he shoveled fresh hay around the stall.

"Can I borrow the truck on Saturday?"

"Why?"

I grabbed the brush and pulled it through Isabella's mane. "Since Gaetano is leaving soon, it would be nice to give him a little graduation ceremony for all his hard work this summer."

"*Cos' è . . . graduation* cermoni?" He dug the pitchfork into the wheelbarrow of hay.

"You know, Pop, like when the school gives a diploma."

"Oh."

"I made him one, and I'd like to give it to him."

"Okay. Den have him over. Why you need da truck?"

"I'd like to take him to Alum Rock Park and show him around."

"No, you canno be alone wit dis boy."

"Please?"

My father's eyes narrowed. "Two conditions."

"Anything."

"Be home by dinner—no longer. And you havta take you brother Vinny and his friend wit you."

"Vinny? Seriously?"

"Yes. No Vincenzo, den no park." He stood, pitchfork in hand, as a faint smile covered his face.

"Fine."

"You no saya tank you?"

"Mmphm, thanks," I mumbled, then turned on my heels and marched back to the house.

Sitting on my bed, I daydreamed about Saturday. I longed to be alone with Gaetano. Although Alum Rock Park offered many attractions, from mineral baths and tea gardens to a small zoo and a huge indoor pool, I only wanted to show him a secret place. It was straight out of a fairy tale—a beautiful meadow, perfect for a picnic, next to Penitencia Creek. Best of all, a giant oak promised privacy. I had to make sure my little brother didn't get in the way.

I tossed and turned most of the night—so much so that Carmela hit me in the arm to stop me from moving. As soon as sunlight hit my eyes, I went straight for the closet and my new dress. I wanted Gaetano to remember me in this dress, instead of my old, grass-stained overalls. The fanciest dress I owned was the one my mother made me for my confirmation. This was different. I'd never dressed up for a boy before. Today I wanted to look like a grown woman for him, and I hoped this dress would do the trick.

I'd paid for it with my own money—no more Carmela hand-me-downs. I saw it in the window of Zavlaris's thrift shop. It was the most beautiful dress I'd ever seen. It was yellow with a white lace overlay, pearl-like buttons down the front, and a knee-length pleated skirt. What I liked most about it was the plunging neckline. I wanted Gaetano to find me attractive in all the ways that counted, so I gathered the dress in my hands and headed for the bathroom.

After I pinned my hair, I zipped the back and stared into the long mirror behind the door. I had a body like most Italian girls. No skin and bones. I was voluptuous. Pleased that the lace webbing hugged the contours of my body, my eyes followed the pearls that pointed toward my breasts. For the first time in my life, I felt beautiful.

On my way out, I grabbed the picnic basket from the cooler and the graduation present from the table.

"Thanks again, Pop." I kissed him on the cheek.

"Remember, be back before dark." He stared at me in my new dress. "*Maronn*," he said under his breath.

"I will." I shut the door behind me.

I walked to the truck where my brother and his friend waited in the back.

"Vin, once we get there, you and Giovanni can go off to the pool. I'm gonna show Gaetano the grounds of the park."

"Pop said you have to watch me. You wouldn't want me to tell him that you were alone with a boy, would you?" he asked, his mouth twisted in amusement.

"If you dare, I'll tell Mama about the naked pinups and cigars you have hidden under your bed."

His cheeks turned bright red. "You wouldn't."

"The hell I won't." I raised my fist to his face. "You better not, or it's a knuckle sangwich for you, kid. Keep those lips closed—*capeesh*?"

"Yeah, yeah, all right. I won't say nothin'."

"Here, Vin. Hold this and don't let it slide around the back." I leaned in to hand him the picnic basket and graduation gift. When I straightened up, the lace on my dress snagged a tiny piece of metal sticking off the bumper and tore. A piece of lace hung from the hem.

"*Minchia*." I cursed. Teeth ground together, I threw open the door and cranked the engine.

While my brother and his friend played rock, paper, scissors in the back of the truck, I pulled up to ole man Antonelli's farm and parked.

I tooted the horn and flicked a few stray hairs off my forehead. Out of the corner of my eye, I saw someone coming toward me.

At first, I didn't recognize Gaetano. I was used to seeing him in his blue jeans and a white T-shirt. Today, he wore a pair of brown slacks and a starched white buttoned-down shirt with a matching vest and bowtie. He looked like a movie star. His clothes must have been his dad's because he couldn't afford a new suit on his wages at Antonelli's. But, boy, he looked good all cleaned up. His hair was brushed back and held in place with hair grease.

The sweetest part was that he had dressed up for me. It reaffirmed what I'd intended for today. I wanted to be courted by him—to be more than friends and closer than teacher and student.

As he approached the truck, he held one hand behind his back. With his sweet, half-crooked smile, he presented a beautiful, hand-picked bouquet of roses through the open window.

"They're gorgeous." I put my nose to the velvety petals and inhaled while he climbed into the passenger seat. The scent was sweet and fragrant like perfume.

"*Signora* Antonelli lemme pick dis for you for all you help. Tank you for making me feel like a real American," he said as he gazed into my eyes.

The same energy I felt when I sat close to him during the lessons radiated throughout the truck and made my heart flutter.

He turned to me and smiled. "My fater, he let me wear dis. I wanted to looka nice for you."

"You look great."

"Tank you. You looka pretty in you dress." His gaze slipped low over my plunging neckline.

The dress provided the exact result I had hoped for.

"Thank you. It's new." I ran my hands over the lace. "I have a surprise for you."

"A surprise?" he said as he raised his eyebrows.

"More like a gift for all your hard work."

"Oh, you dona have to do dat. All you help is more dan a gift," he said as he glanced at the boys in the back.

"Oh yeah, them. Don't worry. They won't bother us. They're going swimming."

"Swimming?"

"Yeah, there's a pool there."

"Um, maybe I go and take off dis clothes?"

"No, we aren't gonna swim. I'm taking you somewhere else in the park. Trust me, you'll like it."

"Hey, Gaetano, I think my sister likes you," Vinny said and laughed from the back of the truck.

I turned my head and shot Vinny a bone-chilling stare. "One more word out of you, kid, and you know what I'll do."

"Okay, okay," he said and pressed his lips into one straight line.

"Hold on tight, boys." I turned the key, and the engine roared.

We arrived at the park. My brother and his friend ran for the pool. I carefully reached for the picnic basket when Gaetano gently placed his hands on mine.

"Lemme help you," he said.

He smiled and my eyes softened. "Thank you." We walked together toward the creek.

Once we were far from people, we both relaxed. Free from the worry of someone watching our every move, I caught him smiling at me for longer periods of time. We giggled down the private trail that led toward my special place.

Alone.

"Dis isa beautiful place," he said as he scanned the golden foothills.

"I told ya." I found a nice flat area of grass.

I laid the blanket on the lawn that faced the creek and opened the picnic basket. He yanked off his bowtie and rolled up his sleeves.

"Itsa hot today."

"I'm sure you're warm in those clothes. Relax and get comfortable."

He watched as I got out the food and napkins. Once I was done, I lay down on the blanket and stared at the sky. A few billowy clouds hung overhead.

He eyed my body as I spread my dress around me.

"Come lie down and look at the clouds. They're so pretty right now. They look like scoops of vanilla ice cream." I patted the space next to me.

Suddenly shy, he took a deep breath, bent his long legs down, and laid his body alongside mine.

With our eyes on the clouds, I said, "I told you it was pretty here. It's one of my favorite places in the foothills. When my father brings us, I come here when I need to be alone. Having a big family can be hard. You have to wait forever for the bathroom, you always have to use hand-me-downs, and it feels like you can never get a minute to yourself, ya know?" I rambled.

"What isa handmidon?" he asked, puzzled.

"A hand-me-down is when you wear clothes or use something that your big sister or brother already used."

"Oh," he said, still a little confused.

"I da only boy, so I no have da handmidon, but maybe dis suit isa handmidon," he said as he undid the first two buttons of his vest.

I kicked off my sandals and let my toes grab onto the grass at the bottom of the blanket. He did the same. We lay quiet, listening to the babbling brook that moved in front of us.

"After we eat, do you want to walk through the creek? It'll feel good to cool off in the water."

"*Sí.*" He smiled. His waves loosened from the pomade.

I opened the picnic basket filled with meats, cheese, and fruit. After I prepared a plate for us, I glanced up and saw him staring at me again. Waves of heat washed over me. We filled our bellies in the sun.

"Ready to go into the creek?" I asked.

"Ready," he said and rolled up his pants.

We walked into the shallow parts of the creek. Like a gentleman, he grabbed my hand and helped me over the slippery rocks. With only two more steps to reach the other side, I leaned forward and lost my footing.

He whisked me into his thick arms. Muscles in his arms contracted as he pulled me into his frame and prevented me from slipping further.

When I looked up, his breath skimmed my face again. He scanned my body. His gaze moved from side to side as his eyelashes flickered in the filtered sunlight of the canopy overhead. Afraid to let go of his tight grip, I held on.

"My foot slipped on one of the rocks," I said, winded.

His eyes burned on me, and we stood there holding on to each other. He bent his head closer to me, and our noses touched. The pulse in his neck beat as fast as mine. He maneuvered me to another rock to get better footing and helped me up the embankment.

Once we were on flat ground on the other side of the creek, we sat on some big rocks alongside the water's edge, just staring at each other.

"What was it like to live on an island?" I asked to break the tension.

"Itsa verra beautiful. The water is clear and full of fish. My fater and I, we go fishing a lot."

"I can only imagine."

"I miss my home, but I dona tink we canna go back. My hometown used to be safe, but now da Mafia bandits, dey come take children and terrorize for money. Dey try to hurt and scare us. Den dey take our home because my fater canno pay dem."

My gaze tumbled to the ground as I heard the pain in his voice.

"In Italy, itsa much like here. Everyone helping dem or hiding from dem. My fater say we canno stay wit my moter's family in Calabria because itsa worse der, so we have nowhere to go. We have no choice. We have to leave. I watch dem come into our house and touch my moter. No *rispetto,*" he said, then spat at the ground. "I want to hurt dem, but dey put a knife to her throat, so what could I do? I no feel like a man, but if I ever see dem again, I will kill dem." His voice shook. His lips moved into a straight line and the muscles on the sides of his cheeks pulsed. "I hate dem!"

"I'm sorry. It makes me so sad that happened to you and your family. I was born into this life, and I don't know the men to be that way. I've never experienced that part. My father and mother have always protected us from that. But I'm sure you know in the little time you've been here that my family is involved. I hope that doesn't make you feel differently about me."

The minute the words came out, I regretted them. I was afraid with my admission, he would turn and run.

"I see tings. I know dey are here. No, Violetta, I no tink bad of you. I tink only good."

"I don't want you to be scared. My father and Antonelli are good people. They would never allow anyone to harm you or your family. As long as you can earn for the Molanano family, you'll be protected."

"Payment or no payment, if dey ever come to my house again, I will slice der throats," he said through clenched teeth.

"Let's go back. I have something I want to give you."

He nodded and unclenched his fists. He reached for my hand to help me back across the creek.

Once we made it to the other side, our feet were wet and cold from the river. We lay on the blanket and let the sun warm our toes.

"I have more bad news. My family isa moving up to Napa. My fater, he gonna buy a *azienda vinicola* . . . umma how do you say."

"A winery?" I asked as my jaw hung down.

"A wwinerie?"

"So, it's for sure then. You're leaving?"

"Yes. We leave first week of October. My fater want to make a business here in America. So dat my family can live here, we need to make money." Pain settled in his eyes.

My heart fell into my gut. "I understand. My father's always finding ways to make money too."

Gaetano fidgeted with the pleat of his slacks. "I ma sad we no see each udder anymore."

"It doesn't have to be the last time, does it?" My cheeks flushed.

He turned his head to mine and smiled a seductive smile. "Umma, no, it doesn't . . ."

He moved closer and cupped my cheek with his palm. And in that pivotal act of desire, our mouths met for the first time.

He tugged me closer to him, and he hardened against my leg. Our mouths moved together, and my heart hammered through my chest. I couldn't breathe. I didn't want to breathe. My senses led the way, and I followed his every movement.

When his tongue went right, I chased it. If it went left, I joined him there. Our mouths moved together until he released me and gently sucked on my bottom lip. He pulled his mouth free of mine, only to plant a soft kiss on my forehead. We both took a much-needed gulp of air. He held me against his chest and stroked my lower back.

We would never go back to the way it was before. My heart and soul were his.

"I dona want to leave you, Violetta. From da beginning I come here to da America, you always help me, and you make me feel smart. I care for you a lot," he said.

"I've never felt this way before, Gaetano," I panted as pangs of desire surged through my body.

He reached for my hair and let the curls fall through his fingers.

"I need to respect you and you *famiglia*. I no want to ever make you feel uncomfortable," he said as he brushed his lips against mine.

"You'd never do that. I know who you are," I whispered, trying to reassure him.

"What will we do when we get back to *Signor* Antonelli?"

"I don't know. We'll have to find a way to see each other. I can't let you leave, Gaetano. I just can't." I choked on the words.

"I will not leave you, *amore mio*. I will come back for you. We will find our way," he said as he entangled his fingers in mine.

I laid my head against his shoulder while he held me close. Gentle breezes blew through our hair and over our bodies.

Embracing, he hummed something in my ear. The musical vibration put me in a sort of trance. I fantasized about our future. With hollow hope, I wondered how I'd feel once I dropped him off at Antonelli's. Because I wouldn't have more time with him, my heart ached in my chest. More than anything, I wanted to be intimate with him, as lovers do.

The sun approached the horizon.

"We better get going before my father comes looking for me." I stood.

"*Si*," Gaetano said with a soft smile.

As I picked up the blanket, I remembered I hadn't given him his gifts.

"Oh, I almost forgot. I have something for you." I presented the box to him.

He unwrapped the newspaper and pulled out the blanket.

"Bravo, bravo," he exclaimed, then examined my handiwork. He pulled it over his shoulders. "Dis will be good when itsa cold in da winter."

"I sewed my initial here, at the bottom, so you won't forget about me and our time together these last few months."

With his index finger, he pulled my chin up to his. "Violetta, I never forget about you, *tesoro mio*," he said. His tender lips joined mine.

When we finally broke away, I reached into the box. "Oh hey, don't forget about this," I said as I pointed to the rolled-up paper still in the box.

He undid the satin bow, and we read it together out loud.

This document certifies that
Gaetano Salvatore Sanna
has hereby graduated from the
Giordano School of English
on this day, August 25, 1939

He admired it. "*Grazie*, Violetta, I never get diploma in Italy."

"Well, you have one. You deserve it for all your hard work."

He intertwined his fingers with mine, then kissed the back of my hand. Standing in front of me, his eyes scanned my body.

"I no have anyting to give you but da flowers," he said apologetically.

I touched his lips. "You have given me more than you know. Today you gave me a wonderful gift."

"Oh, dat. I guess, well, yes. I enjoyed it much too." He blushed slightly.

"Just so you know, you were my first kiss, but I can tell you've done this before. Where did you learn how to kiss like that?"

"I know one girl in Italy," he said with crimson cheeks.

"Have you ever been in love?" I asked impulsively.

"Not until I met you," he said and flashed me a toothy grin. He grabbed my hands and held them to his chest. "Violetta, when I met you, you so nice to me, and you make me feel safe. I know in my mind that you special to me," he whispered into my ear as he kissed my cheek. "I never feel anyting like da way I feel when I ma close to you."

We kissed again. When we finally pulled away from one another, I looked over his shoulder and saw the sun slipping behind the hills.

"*Maronn!* We better go. It's late. My brother is probably wondering where we are." I slid on my sandals and picked up the empty picnic basket. We made our way back to the truck, where Vinny and his friend waited.

I drove fast so my father wouldn't question me. As we entered the main driveway of Antonelli farms, I drove up to the front gate and parked.

"I will be a thinking about you tonight, Violetta. I hope I hava dream about you." His eyes fixed on me.

My heart fluttered like the wings of a butterfly. He grabbed his gifts and shut the door behind him.

We'd never be the same. He was my first kiss and, hopefully, my first everything.

I stared at the empty passenger seat. With the day's events circling my mind, I was somewhere in the middle of blissful smiles and tears of doom. The conflict of emotions snaked through my body and up into my throat, making it hard to breathe. I remembered what he shared with me today. My dreams for our future were in question because of how connected my family was to the mob. I wasn't sure what that meant just yet, but Gaetano remained on my lips. For a while, that was all that mattered.

Chapter 6

Viva La Giga

My family helped the Sannas pack. Antonelli and my father helped with food and essentials. My mother made clothes for the girls to have in the winter months to come. It was my job to help *Signora* Sanna stuff huge travel cases with blankets, toiletries, and other essentials they'd need to begin their new life. And when there was a break in the action, Gaetano and I met behind a tree far in the back of the farm or inside the stables. With each passing day, it became more difficult to keep our hands off each other.

"Your lips, dey taste like da skin of a plum. And your hair, itsa so soft. It tickles my face," Gaetano said as we hid behind the big house. He pushed my body up against the wall and kissed me hard and deep. My pelvis throbbed and my nipples tingled.

"Stop. Oh my God, stop. I think I hear Tony." I brushed Gaetano's hands away from my pulsing hips. "We have to be careful."

"I sorry, Violetta. I feel like I ma gonna burst."

"I know. Me too," I panted. "Tuck your shirt in before someone sees," I whispered. "Go, go, go . . ." I said in his ear.

Gaetano and I moved quickly and turned the opposite corner of the building so that Tony wouldn't spot us. To avoid questions, we walked in different directions. He went to the right, toward his sisters playing on the porch, and I walked left, straight for the bathroom. I splashed water on my face and fixed my hair.

I'd fallen in love with him. My hormones took hold, and we explored each other's bodies. But there were limits. As a Catholic girl, I had to be careful. It wouldn't sit well if I lost my virginity before marriage. So as much as we wanted to, and as close as we got, I made sure to cool things off when they got out of control.

I went to my bedroom and changed my clothes. My panties were moist, and I felt sticky. I remembered the loving words Gaetano had said to me. With his emotions, he was raw and real, sweet and innocent. None of the playboy mentality of my brother's age group had rubbed off on him yet. His soul was still pure and sincere. He was the type of man I wanted to spend the rest of my life with. I just had to make sure we weren't caught.

If Pop found out, he'd make it so I never saw Gaetano again.

With the Sanna family's departure days away, my family threw a party in their honor. Pop was happy for any excuse to gather everyone together. The idea of Gaetano's going-away party made my chest tight, but I'd find a way to be alone with him.

Carmela was in charge of the decorations. My brothers stacked cases of Lucky Lager beer next to the barbecue pit. My father and uncles cranked out homemade Italian sausage into yards of casings. I helped my mom prepare food and hang streamers.

Once I was done, it was time to get ready. I wanted to look pretty for Gaetano, so I asked to borrow one of Carmela's dresses. Reluctantly, she showed me a few she'd let me wear. They weren't her nicer dresses, but she let me try on one that was royal blue with polka dots.

"Look at you. Why you want to get all fancy for, anyways? You trying to get the Sanna boy's attention, aren't you?" Carmela said. She looked me over and her jaw hung down about a half an inch. "Tony told me he thought he saw you two eyeing each other the other day. You better be careful. If Pop finds out, *maronn . . .*"

"No. I think he's a nice boy. We're friends. I spent a lot of time with him this summer, but that's it," I fired back.

"You better not get anything on that dress, you hear?"

"I won't." I rolled my eyes in her direction.

The party was wall-to-wall family and friends, not to mention all the wise guys. I was pretty sure Pop invited them so *Signor* Sanna could make safe arrangements with his new rent collectors. These were the same men I'd seen go down into the basement many times before, coming to collect the earnings for the Molanano family week after week. Like Joey Fingers. Tony told me he got his name because he was the best at picking locks. If anyone needed to break into something, he was your guy. Then there were the big guys, like Johnny Rizzuto and Rocco Lombardo, who made their mark in San Jose. They were all part of the Molanano crime family and had been in the papers for racketeering and extortion. I called them Uncle Johnny and Uncle Rocco, and they always spoiled me. On my confirmation, they slid me envelopes stuffed with cash. They felt indebted to my father for all the times he stitched them up or removed a bullet.

Even the mayor was at the party. Anytime Pop got pushback from the cops, from the beer drops during prohibition to petty crimes, he made a call and trouble disappeared.

I said a respectful hello and kissed them on the cheek. When I was little, some of them scared me when I'd see their pistols sticking out from their unbuttoned coats. I'm not sure why their guns scared me more than my mother's shotgun.

As the night went on, people came from all over. Beers and whiskey flowed. The smell of the sausage on the grill filled the night air. Coiled like snakes, the sausages made popping noises from the heat.

My brother and father ushered the guests to the big house in the back. Sounds of music met my ears and pulled me toward the festivities. Uncle Lorenzo squeezed his accordion, and Uncle Rocco joined the polka with his violin. Uncle Joe held his bright gold trumpet in his hands while his cheeks puffed like small balloons. Together, they made music that brought everyone to the floor, clapping and dancing. The music was infectious.

My uncle yelled, "*Viva la Giga*. Everbadi dance."

When the song began, we formed a circle. *Zia* Lucia reached for my uncle Pete's arm, and the two of them made their way to the center. As they danced, we clapped to the music. When the chorus came, we grabbed arms and moved around the people dancing in the middle. As much as I wanted to let the music numb my thoughts, something was missing. The one person I wanted to dance with still wasn't here.

To waste time, I scooped up a piece of my mom's focaccia bread and sat in the corner of the room. I tried not to get anything on my sister's dress. My cousins, aunts, and uncles all danced to the music that filled the room.

The song changed. In the doorway of the big room, Gaetano stood alongside his family and the Antonellis.

"*Paesani*," my father yelled, a little drunk now. He waved to *Signor* Antonelli and *Signor* Sanna and escorted them inside to meet everyone. With a twinkle in his eye and a stogie in his hand, my father said, "After we meet everbadi, I ma gonna show you all da *salsiccia*. We make all morning for you."

The men went outside to see the sixty pounds of sausage my family prepared in their honor. My mother and Mrs. Antonelli went straight to the kitchen. *Signora* Sanna sat with her two daughters and avoided conversation. She scanned the room and stared at the men who embodied the life she'd left behind. Trying to avoid eye contact, she pulled the girls close to her. I understood why she didn't trust strangers.

Gaetano did what was expected of the men and followed his father outside. He stood around the huge barbecue pit where clouds of smoke moved around him. While he and my brothers joked around by the fire, he scanned for me in the crowd. When no one was looking, he winked.

I smiled back.

His arrival flooded me with a mix of emotions. My heart raced. I wanted to wrap my arms around his waist and kiss behind his ear, as I'd done so often, but my father's rules wouldn't allow it. The fact remained that Gaetano and I couldn't be together. At least, not yet. I broke eye contact with him.

"Everyone, it's a broom dance," my cousin, Nino, yelled into the microphone. "We play music, and when we stop, change partners. If you don't find a partner when the music starts again, you have to dance with this." He held up a broom and dipped it as if it was a dance partner.

Everyone came in from outside and swarmed the dance floor. I spotted Gaetano across the room. My cousin, Francesca, grabbed his hand.

I felt as though I'd been stabbed in the heart. She was older than me and had earned a reputation with boys.

"Attaboy, Gaetano, look at you," Tony yelled.

Gaetano caught my stare and turned his face away. To play the part, he held her hand and danced.

Blood coursed through my body. I stood there with my hands on my hips, tapping my toes, waiting for the music to stop. Gaetano flashed Francesca a few fake smiles, and she whispered in his ear.

I was about to cut in when Tony's friend, Gianni, grabbed my hand and yanked me onto the dance floor. I had no interest in Gianni, but when he came around, he tried to impress me. He had a terrible bout of acne. His face looked like a pizza. He was a nice boy, but I was not at all attracted to him. There was only one boy I wanted to dance with, and he was in someone else's arms.

Every few minutes, the dancers exchanged partners. At one point, my father led me in the dance.

"*Vieni qui*, my Violetta. Why you looka so sad? Itsa party." His breath was thick with whiskey.

"I don't know, Pop. There's a lot of people here."

"Whatcha mean a lotta people? Itsa jus da family and soma friends."

Impatiently, I scanned the room for a six-foot-tall man with a full head of brown wavy hair. The music stopped. Pop laughed and pulled away to find Mama. The accordion started again, and I had no partner. I kept my head down and trudged toward the broom.

Someone grabbed my arm. I turned and it was him—Mr. Dreamy-eyes, himself.

Gaetano smiled and pulled me into his frame.

He laughed and said, "You almost havta dance wit da broom."

"Thanks for saving me."

He drew me close, our clasped hands between our chests, and whispered, "No, Violetta, *you* da one who saved me." He kissed my ear.

Afraid that someone else saw, I recoiled. He shot me a coy smile and laughed. We floated across the dance floor. With music in my ears, I shut my eyes and pressed my cheek to his. I was with the man I loved in front of my family. His arms felt natural, safe, familiar. I wanted to stay there all night.

The music stopped. Reality pushed back.

My father studied us, his eyes pressed into lines.

My arms fell to my sides. The dance was over, and I was sweaty from all the dancing.

"Why don't we find a place to sit?" I asked.

"*Si*," Gaetano said, then searched for a place for two chairs in the corner of the room.

We sat next to each other. *Zia* Tomasina approached the

microphone and began to sing her rendition of "Sweet Violette" by the Sons of the Pioneers—a song she sang at every family party. As we listened to the bawdy, rhyming lyrics, which starred nearly all the family members, everyone laughed. Gaetano had never heard the song, but he caught on to the chorus after a few times, and he laughed with the rest of us.

On the other side of the room, my father smiled at me lovingly. I waved, and he winked.

"You fater, he want you? He looking at you," Gaetano said.

"No, I'm fine. It's a father-daughter thing."

"What? Tell me."

"When I was little, he joked that this song was for me. He called me his Sweet Violette, just like the song. He hasn't called me that for years, but whenever my aunt sings it, he lets me know he's thinking of me."

"You fater, he love you, and I know how he feels, Violetta. I want so bad to kiss you right here, in fronta everyone."

"We can't. Not yet. Soon," I said, hoping one day Gaetano would court me. Thoughts of Pop saying *no* made me feel sick.

As the night went on, many of the men got drunk. My father passed around stogies. Big shots sat outside and smoked while the women and children drank coffee and socialized.

Around midnight, my father signaled some of the men to go to the forbidden room—the basement. Once I saw my father usher the last man down, I looked for Gaetano. He stood with my brother and his friends by the pond, drinking beers and laughing. When he caught my eye, I pointed to the barn. He nodded his head. It was the one place we could be alone.

On my way to the barn, I passed the liquor table. Small hairs on the nape of my neck rose and tingled in anticipation of what was to come. I needed something to calm my nerves, so I reached for the bottle of my father's limoncello. When no one looked, I poured some in a cup and took a big gulp. It was pretty strong going down, but I didn't care. I took another big gulp, then put it back on the table and raced through the field toward the barn.

At night, the stables were cold. I grabbed a few blankets my father had put aside for the horses and searched for an empty stall. I placed a blanket on the floor and kept one for myself.

Gaetano crept into the barn.

"Violetta, where are you?" he whispered.

Horses snorted in response.

"Over here." I unbuttoned my dress and propped my clothes on a rusty nail. I grabbed the other blanket and wrapped it around my body. He stopped at the stall where I stood silent. He'd been drinking. The smell of liquor coated his breath.

"What are you doing?" he asked as he looked me up and down and noticed my sister's polka-dotted dress hanging on the side of the stall.

"I wanted to see you." I let the blanket fall off my naked body onto the floor.

His legs swayed. He tried to steady himself against a wooden beam. Once he found his footing, he examined me. I wasn't sure if he'd ever seen a naked woman before or if he was just in shock that it was me. His eyes traced the contours of my body, stopping at my breasts, then glancing at my pubic area.

As the seconds ticked on, the cold night air hardened my nipples. Goose pimples covered my arms and legs. When I shivered, he pulled me close and held me against him. He kissed me, hard. I tasted the whiskey on his breath, and it was wonderful. Limoncello had worked its way through my body, numbing my inhibitions. He moved his tongue away from my mouth and let it slide around my ear and down my neck.

An electric shock soared through my pelvis and made my heart quicken. I breathed deeper and faster as he moved his tongue toward my breasts. He first made circles around my nipples, then nibbled them tenderly. He sucked on my neck and earlobes. It was all too much. My body was about to explode.

Out of pure instinct, we dropped to the floor. I unbuttoned his shirt and undid his belt. He unzipped his pants and the part of his body that was unknown to me sprang forward toward my stomach. I stroked him and became familiar with his stiffness.

As cold as it was in there, we were both sweating and panting with want. He kissed me harder, more deliberately. He moved his mouth from my lips to my pelvis. My heartbeat followed, descending from my chest to my groin.

I reached for the soft locks of hair on his head as he made his way downward, still kissing me and tasting me. His hair tickled my thighs and made me grab onto his ears to steady myself while he continued.

Something startled him, and he stopped exploring me. Half-naked, he sat up and took a deep breath.

"Violetta, my love, we canno do dis," he said as he tried to regain himself.

"Yes, we can. I want this. You're leaving soon, and I don't know if I'll ever see you again." I grabbed his face and started kissing his cheeks.

He caressed my hands and pulled them to his chest.

"I respecta you too much. We no married. Letta me marry you first," he pleaded.

Overcome with shame for coming onto him, I wrapped myself in the blanket.

A ghost of a shiver climbed up my spine. "Marriage? You want to marry me?"

"*Si*, I do. But I needa help my fater first and den when I make more money, I marry you. Once we settled, I come for you. I talk to you fater for you hand. You deserve to be treated like *una regina*. I wanna buy you nice tings and be a good husband," he said and then kissed me with loving intensity.

"You've made me so happy, Gaetano. Don't forget about me. I

wanted to know you in this way. I'm sorry if I made things uncomfortable," I said, discouraged.

"No, my beautiful girl. You no make me feel uncomfortable, you make me happy. Becausa you choose me to do dis wit, I know youa good woman. You no be embarrassed. You so beautiful. I lucky to have you." He turned and held my face in his palms and kissed me. "I no smart man. I have no money and nutting to give you. But one day, *tesoro mio*, I will give you da world. When we getta married, I surrender my body and soul to you. I never been in love before, but if it means dat I tink about you when I wake and go to sleep, den yes, Violetta, I love you, *amore mio*."

His eyes cherished me in the moonlight. The boy who had my attention from the moment I saw him loved me and wanted to marry me. I thought how close I came to losing my virginity, how amazing it felt to have him touch me in that way. "I've never felt like this, either. I want to be with you forever." I pulled his face closer to mine and gave him one last kiss.

"When itsa safe, I talk to your fater and den I come back for you," he said, with velvet words.

Tears welled in my eyes as his words wrapped me up in more warmth than the blanket ever could. We sat in silence, our bodies exposed, dissecting and analyzing the commitment we'd made. I held on to every word. He'd pledged his heart and soul to me.

"I want dis wit you. Der will be a time for us, *amore mio*."

With tears in my eyes, I smiled at him. We dressed, and I hung the blanket on the hook in the stall. As we were about to walk out of the barn, Tony called for Gaetano.

"Oh my God, it's my brother . . . *Shhh*," I whispered.

Tony crept up behind us. "Hey, Guy, where you been? I think your pop's looking for you. Your ma wants to go home now," he said with a wry smile.

"Oh, I was talking to Violetta about da horses," he answered.

"Horses again, huh? That's the second time I caught you guys in here. You ain't doing nothin' stupid, right, Vi?"

"Of course not," I fired back with flushed cheeks.

"Yeah, Pop has bred some nice ones. Wheneva I see you next time, I'll let you ride one, but in the daytime. You ain't doing nothin' with my sister, are you?" he interrogated.

"No, no, youa sista, she my teacher, my friend."

"Okay, shy boy. Let's keep it that way." He put his arm around Gaetano's shoulders.

Numb and almost lifeless, I followed them to the car. In just a few days, everything would change. A single tear fell as I watched them drive away into the darkness.

Chapter 7

Pen Pal

CRISP MORNINGS SURROUNDED THE FOOTHILLS. THE TIME HAD come for the Sanna family to make their way for a different set of hills, a land for the grape growers and the dreamers. Decaying, fermented fruit covered Antonelli farms. A musty, rancid smell permeated the air, and tiny flies swarmed the dirt around the tree trunks.

It all looked how I felt: lifeless and rotten.

Gaetano had confided in me the details of the arrangement. His father made a deal with Mr. Antonelli and some of the Molanano family. *Signor* Sanna received seed money to begin a wine venture with the understanding that they were to give a certain percentage of their profits to the bigger families. If needed, the company would be expected to fulfill any requests from the Molanano family, including money laundering, like my father's businesses had done over the years. With this new arrangement, they answered to a higher cause—one that protected them but expected allegiance.

For the Molanano family, the arrangement meant more than making wine. More land meant more money and power. My heart ached for Gaetano and his family. As hard as they'd fought to get away from the Mafia, they were under their control again. Like my family, they realized that coming to America didn't mean they were free. And like any government, where death and taxes were inevitable, the mob functioned much the same.

Our family stood in a line, like when the Sannas had arrived three months earlier. Tony handed Gaetano a metal lock box that had two pistols for their protection, and then they shook hands. My father nodded at the rest of us, our signal to wish them well.

It was my turn to say goodbye. Because I didn't want anyone to notice my feelings for Gaetano, I fought back tears. I took a deep breath to temper my emotions. By custom, he kissed me on both cheeks, then whispered in my ear, "I love you. It willa be a little time, and we willa see each udder again."

"Write me," I whispered in his ear before pulling away. With a smile, I slipped a note in his jacket pocket. He winked at me, and I moved down the line to his parents and sisters.

After final words and hugs, we stood in the long driveway and waved goodbye. Within minutes, they drove away with my world and heart inside. My only hope was time. If things went as we'd planned, we'd soon tell my parents. Guy needed time to start his life and make the business grow. If Gaetano proved to be a hard worker and helped his father turn his business into something big, maybe my father would approve of the match. But the distance would almost kill me.

A senior now, I stomped the pavement at San Jose High School, ready to finish what I set out to do and be the first of my family to graduate. In the beginning, hours passed like days. With Gaetano gone, subjects that used to interest me became boring. Pride kept me going.

Memories of my time with Guy became a distraction. Sitting at my desk, I fantasized about him and how it would feel when he finally took my body and made me a woman. My mind flooded with questions about his new life. Was he happy? What was it like in the Napa Valley? Was he keeping up with his English? Did he think about me as much as I thought about him? I was obsessed with the possibility of our future.

Day after day, I returned from school to check the mailbox— and nothing. I worried he'd already forgotten me. I didn't hear from him until right before Thanksgiving.

I opened the mailbox and there it was—a white envelope with black writing I'd seen many times before. My heart quickened in my chest as I pressed the paper to my lips. I ran for the bathroom and ripped it open.

November 1939

Dear Violetta,

I hope you doing well. I miss you. We have secured a piece of land that should produce a nice crop. It's about one hundred acres. My father hired people to help with the soil. We can't start planting until spring, but we have much to do between now and then.

The land already has many established vines which makes it easier to start. The man who used to own the land had no children of his own. Since he was old, he decided to sell.

It's hard work. Some days my back ache from the hours of digging and carrying heavy things but I know in time it will be good. We hope to have crop ready for la prossima season.

La proprietà has a big house. I have my own room now.

My bedroom window looks out over the hills. I practice to read and write English every day. The letters help so I get better.
  I love you,
  -G

Sitting on the bathroom floor, I held the letter to my chest. His letter answered all my questions. I tried to imagine how beautiful the land looked with the rolling hills and rows of vines that lined the property. I was excited to hear that he had his own room and that he was happy. However, his words exposed my fears. From what he wrote, it would be a long time until I saw him again.

Since he'd finally written me and I knew his address, I went to my father's office and took a few envelopes and stamps to continue what was our love story's only lifeline. Instead of doing my dreadful homework, I wrote to Gaetano with newfound excitement, knowing these sentiments would convey my love for him.

My reply expressed how his letter made me feel alive again. I detailed everything about my life in school and on the farm. I told him I couldn't wait to graduate so that we could be together. I explained how hard it had been to concentrate in math class when all I thought about was him and his new life. I ended the letter by saying how happy I was for him, that I missed him, and how wonderful it would be when we saw each other again.

With shaky hands, I placed a stamp on the envelope. I didn't want anyone to notice the letter. When no one was looking, I slipped it into the mailbox.

One eyebrow cocked, my father asked, "Violetta, a card coma for you from da Napa Valley. Who you know in da Napa Valley?"

"Oh, Papa, it's the Sanna boy. I told him before he left to write to keep up his English. We're pen pals." Butterflies danced inside me.

"Wassa pin pals?"

"It's like writing to a friend back and forth. We're catching up on each other's lives."

With a troubled face, he walked away. "*Minchia* . . . Pin pals," he said under his breath and huffed past me. I hoped he would accept my story and not pry. Letters were the only way to communicate with Guy. His handwriting softened the sting of his absence. Once alone, I went to the bathroom and opened the second letter.

December 1939

Dear Violetta,

Buon Natale e Felice Anno Nuovo ~

I am sorry I no write for a long time. I been a busy. I sorry that school is hard, but you a smart girl.

My father and I have been buying big equipment to make lots of bottles of vino. He asked me to a draw a picture to make a label on the bottles. So, when I am not digging for the water, irrigazione for the grapes, I draw at night. We have problems with the water filtration, but we are gonna get it fix. We also met with a distributore to sell the vino. In spring, we gonna start things. We gonna plant new vines.

For Natale, la mia famiglia, we are planning a big dinner with a few of our new friends. We invite some families of the workers. My mother, she gonna make lots of food.

I miss you Violetta. I want to show you everything when you come visit me in summer. I can't wait to hold you in my arms again.

-G

After Christmas, the letters slowed. I was busy at school. With spring around the corner, I expected he'd be getting things ready and working the land. To dull the loss in my heart, I kept busy with friends. Some days, I went to my friend Julia's house. She always tried to get me to talk to boys, but I was never interested in any of them. When she pushed too hard, I'd always find an excuse to go home. My heart was set on one boy—a boy who was many miles away. The only certainty I had was that the sun would set tomorrow, and another long day would be behind me.

Spring made its way to the foothills, and the sun warmed the ranch. I picked flowers along the fence line. As I walked past the chicken coup, I heard a familiar, gruesome sound. Covering my ears, I ran past my father and brother slaughtering a pig. Out of the corner of my eye, Tony grabbed the metal hooks, ready to hoist the pig's body up onto the big metal rack to drain the blood into the pit beneath. The splash of the liquid hitting the dirt below made my stomach clench. I ran to my bedroom to block out the noise when I came upon Carmela placing a white envelope on my pillowcase.

"Hey, Vi, this is addressed to you. Is this that Sanna boy? You still talking to him? Does Pop know?"

"Yes. It's fine. Thanks," I said, rubbing my queasy stomach.

"You better be careful, Vi." Carmela's words trailed off as she walked back to the kitchen.

I scooped up the letter and shut the bedroom door. With shaky hands and the need for a release, I ripped open the seal.

April 1940
Dear Violetta,

Life has been hard. We have problems. My father say it get better soon. I plan to go with my father to buy machine to crush the grapes and other equipment. There is a man in

Southern California that my father know. They were in the Italian army together. His name is Bustamante. He has a big wine business there for a long time. He's will sell to my father for cheap so we are gonna go for a trip. He tell my father that there are many workers from Mexico there that want work. So we gonna go and meet with him.

My family we never see the rest of California. I am excited. I will write when we return.

Ti amo,

-G

I was happy to hear he would travel to different places. Santa Cruz was the only place I'd ever visited because my father liked to fish off the pier. I waited to hear of Gaetano's adventures upon his return.

As graduation approached, I invited him to my ceremony. I'd just turned eighteen. If he showed up, I'd tell my father that I planned on leaving for Napa and that we would marry.

Maybe his letter got lost in the mail. A few days before my graduation, I received his reply.

June 1940
Dear Violetta,

I hope you are well. I'm sorry I no write in a long time. Southern California is beautiful. We see mountains and go swimming at the beach. My father make connections with people who helped him sell his wine. I won't be back until July, so I cannot make your graduation party. I so sorry.

I have much to tell you. We make friends with the Bustamante family. They know a lot about the wine business.

Their daughter, Angelina, she know how to sell the wine. She introduce me to lots of people to help distribute.

We hire many people from Mexico. Lots of paperwork, but we need the help in the fields. They are nice people. When I get back, I want to show you the winery and everything I have been doing all this time. I will be with you soon, tesoro mio.

Love,

-G

My heart stammered in my chest. He wouldn't be here at my graduation. I wrestled with feelings of selfishness and disappointment. I'd waited so long to reunite with him, and he felt more distant than ever. As much as I wanted to deny it, he had a new life with new people. New people, like a woman named Angelina, who absorbed all his time and energy. Maybe it was innocent, but how did I know? I felt cheated and lost.

Diploma in hand, I met my family in the cafeteria. My father beamed with pride. Smiling from ear to ear, he handed out cigars to the other proud fathers.

"You see my daughter, Violetta? She isa da first Giordano to graduate," he said to a few of the other men in the room. "*Congratulazioni,*" my father said as he kissed my cheek and hugged me tight. "I so prouda you, Violetta."

"Thanks," I mumbled as I pulled away and wiped the smoke-smelling spit off my cheek.

"Good job, kid." Tony yanked on my braid and smiled.

"Letsa go home," my mother said. "I make a lot of food, and you know you fater. He invite everbadi for dinna. Carmela, she busy keeping tings warm."

On the drive home, I played with my red tassel as it dangled from my cap. I secretly hoped Gaetano would surprise me today and that I'd find his dreamy eyes peering out at me with open arms so my life could begin.

My father parked the truck, and I ran into the house. Smiling faces greeted me, but there was no sign of Gaetano. Everyone clapped and grinned, all except one man who sat alone in the corner of the living room. A cigarette hung from his bottom lip as he combed his shiny black hair back over his ears. He couldn't have been older than his mid-twenties.

Out of respect, I went around the room to say hello to everyone. When I reached the mysterious man, he shook my hand. His palms were warm and greasy, and he held my hand too tight.

"Congratulations, gorgeous. I'm Frank. Frank Di Natale."

I wiped my hand on my graduation gown. "Um, thanks. You a friend of Tony's?"

A small laugh escaped his lips. "Let's just say I'm a friend from back east." His gaze scanned my body like a lion ready to pounce.

"I have to change. Excuse me," I said dismissively.

"Sure, doll. Don't want to keep you from your guests. Besides, I'm sure we'll get to know each other a lot better in the next few weeks." He shot me a wry smile. His greasy hair hung over his bushy black eyebrows.

I knew right away why Frank was here. Like many others, he came to get away from the consequences that existed in this life. When a member of the Molanano family approached Pop for a favor, we had to do what was asked.

Something about this stranger made me uneasy. Of all the guys Pop hid, this one felt wrong, like a snake in the grass. I'd watch myself around him. I wasn't sure if it was the way his eyes looked at me like I was a piece of meat or the way he sat in the room like some big shot Mafioso, but Frank Di Natale felt dangerous.

Chapter 8

Eyewitness

East San Jose Foothills, Giordano Estate
November 2002
Barbara

I TOOK A DEEP BREATH AND PUT DOWN THE ENVELOPE, YEL-
lowed with time, and filled with Gaetano's letters. I connected to
the faces in the pictures that covered the wall behind Ms. G. She
sat quietly in her tattered brown recliner. Her eyes hadn't moved up
from her crochet needle. When she placed the paper relics in my
hands, it was as if we'd pulled out a time capsule. With Gaetano's
handwriting staring back at me now, this woman and her love story
intrigued me.

She sat with a wrinkled face and a broken mind. I imagined her
wearing a yellow dress in the arms of the man she loved. Part of me
was jealous. I'd always wanted a man to love me like that. I wished
things were better between Marcus and me and that he'd sweep me
up in his arms and spend time with me instead of chasing his dreams

at the craps tables. Most of all, I wanted my kids to be proud of us. No more disappointed faces.

I gulped. "What a story. So, what happened next?"

She turned to look at me, her eyes wide, like marbles ready to fall out of her head.

"Who are you? Why are you here?" she demanded.

"It's me, Barbara. Your nurse."

"Barbara who?" she asked, with confused eyes and a taut face.

The effects of her disease were clear. I shook my head and handed the letters back to her. She held them in her hands and examined the penmanship. Her eyelids fluttered and then she smiled.

"Oh yeah, I remember you now. You're the one who always likes to poke me with your pointy needles," she said, then rubbed at her arm.

"That's me. Trying to keep you healthy," I muttered. "Okay, since we've already been outside once today for exercise, why don't we do something that will stimulate our minds?" I grabbed a deck of cards from a side table and shook them out of the box.

"My mind works just fine, thank you," she said and continued her needlework.

"It'll be fun. You're so good. You beat me last time."

"I did?" she asked, with her head cocked to one side.

"Why don't we sit at the kitchen table, so we'll have more room?"

"If it'll get you to stop talkin' so damn much," she said sharply, then set the twisted knots of yarn on the recliner.

I followed behind her as she tottered across the black-and-white tiled kitchen floor and plopped down in a chair.

"You shuffle those cards like you play a lot."

"My boyfriend, Marcus, likes to play cards. I've learned a lot from him over the years."

"Card player, huh? What happened to your nails? They're broken."

Heat washed over me, and my cheeks stung. "I fell on my son's bike, remember?" I curled my fingers inward so she couldn't see as I manipulated the cards further. "What should we play? Blackjack? Poker?" I suggested, hoping to change the subject.

"Poker. Played it all my life."

"Really?"

"Sure. You don't marry one of the biggest Mafia men in the country and not witness a few poker games. Hell, sometimes the games went on for days. One time, Frank almost shot a guy in my kitchen for welching," she said, unaffected. "Besides, me and the girls, we used to play all the time when the guys were out doing who knows what."

"Shot a guy in your kitchen?"

"Yes. Frank had a temper. We had lots of parties. When your husband's in the mob, you stay in tight circles. Better to stick close to people who live the same kind of life. At least that way, you know they aren't rats. So, we made a kind of friendship, the girls and me. I learned a lot from them."

"So Frank was a big gambler too?"

"You could say that. That was another reason he wanted to marry me. As part of the plan, Don Molanano gave the order that Frank be sent here under the protection of my father to hide out for murder. But I learned later it was more than just that. Frank was also sent here to scout out the casino business so Don Molanano could wet his beak. What better way to get his hands dirty with Tahoe only a few hours away? In those days, the Tahoe Bay Club lodge was booming. Everything was fresh and new—ripe for the taking. So, there were lots of wise guys out there like Frank, trying to make their way."

"Marcus goes to Tahoe all too often, but I didn't realize there was organized crime up there."

"See, out here, a made guy got away with more than in New York, and the families knew it. Things were quieter, with fewer people and cops, so it was much easier to conduct business. Frank came to get away from the cops but ended up laying the groundwork to buy a casino. Then he'd report back how business was run out here."

She pulled up her reading glasses that hung from her neck, shoved the cards up to her fingerprint-dusted glasses, and fanned them out in her hands.

"All right, kid, what's the wager?" she asked, her eyes blazed with excitement.

"If I win, you have to tell me more about your time with Gaetano. I'm a sucker for a good love story."

"You are, are you?"

"Yes. And if you win, I'll let you cook. Anything you want. Best out of ten?"

"You're on," she said confidently.

At the tenth poker hand, I spread out my cards.

"Read 'em and weep. Royal flush," I gushed with pride.

"Damn it, you won. I only had three of a kind." Violetta smacked the cards on the table.

"This time I won. But you've beaten me plenty of times." I gathered the cards.

"I have?" she asked, confused again.

"Yes, you have. See right here?" I slid the long-running score sheet in front of her.

"How long we been playing?" She dragged the paper up to her thick lenses. Her mouth dropped, and her eyes grew empty.

I put my hand on hers. "What's wrong? You all right?"

"I hate having this crap." Tears welled in her eyes. "My brain doesn't work right anymore. One minute, I see everything so clear. Next, everything goes dark. You show me this paper with my name on it and games we've played, and I don't remember them."

"Honey, you're not alone. I've cared for lots of patients in your condition. That's why I'm here, to take care of you and be your friend."

"I got a lot of friends already. I don't need new ones." She pushed away from the table.

"I'm sorry you feel that way, but I still need to be here to help you. We might as well be friends."

Her eyes narrowed. "I suppose. But you need to get out more with people your own age, sweetheart. I'm close to death, so don't count on me for much longer."

"You're in good health," I said to perk her up.

"No, I'm not. I can't remember things."

"You've told me so much about your life. Antonelli farms, Gaetano, and even Frank. You have a great memory."

"Then why can't I remember what happened yesterday?"

"Just like older folks get things like heart problems or arthritis, for you, it's Alzheimer's. Everyone has something broken about them—some are seen, and some aren't. There's not one of us who doesn't know how broken feels." I blinked back tears. "But you're in good hands, and you have the benefit of new medications that a lot of my other clients didn't have. I'll be here every step of the way."

"I don't know what the hell you're talking about . . . Alzheimer's. Sounds like something you read out of a quack magazine. I'm not slow. I could make fifty trays of lasagna, drive a hundred miles, even climb a mountain, for Christ's sakes," she said. "Do you know they took away my license? I've been driving these hills all my life, and I can't even get to the market."

"I can take you anywhere you want to go."

"Yeah, yeah, but there's something about driving how I want and where I want. I used to love driving. I feel trapped."

My heart ached. I'd seen other clients struggle to find some control and independence. In Ms. G.'s case, her loss of independence absorbed her pride, and old age was the villain.

"Well, I won, so you have to tell me more about Gaetano," I said, trying to cheer her up. "How could you marry someone else after you met someone as wonderful as Gaetano? I don't know if I would've had the strength to walk away from the love of my life. How'd you do it?"

"Man, you are a one *chiaccherone*. Aren't you?"

"A chicha what?"

"Someone who likes to talk a lot." She rolled her eyes.

"Well, okay. Maybe you're too *tired*," I said, challenging her feisty spirit. "I never thought you were a *welcher*."

"I'm no *welcher*! And I'm not tired either. Don't you listen? Or do we need to get you a hearing aid too? *Maronn* . . . *tired*, she says. I wanna go sit in the living room. This hard chair hurts my ass. It's damn near numb."

We both laughed. I put the cards away and followed her to the living room. She sat and jabbed her crochet needle back into the yarn.

"So, what happened to Gaetano?"

"Where'd I leave off?"

"You'd just gotten the last letter from Gaetano, and you met Frank at your graduation ceremony."

"Oh yeah . . . Frank."

"How could your father make you marry Frank?"

"I never wanted to marry him. Frank came straight to my father about his interest in me. Frank and my father positioned our marriage to *Consigliere* Rapino as a way to unify the East Coast with the West Coast. Deep down, Frank wanted to be a boss out here, but the deal also guaranteed my family's survival, which is why my father agreed to the whole thing. It wasn't that my dad didn't love me, but sometimes in this lifestyle, it's business over pleasure. From that day forward, I was a pawn." Her lips pressed together, and she stared off into space.

"What's a *consigliere*?"

"Like an advisor to the boss. See, the Mafia has a hierarchy. There's the boss, Don Molanano, the underboss, who at the time was Frank's father, Frank Di Natale Senior. Then the *caporegimes*— they're the managers—and then you have the soldiers. When I met Frank, he was a soldier, but he moved up to *capo* because of his father."

"You said Frank was hiding. Why was he hiding?"

"They don't tell the women much in this life. Everything is hush-hush. But after some time, I learned Frank was sent to stay with us because he was accused of murdering a guy by the name of Mario Cantoni, who was linked to the Sambino family. Frank came to stay with us to hide from the cops. Along with getting a place to hide, he got an added bonus—*me*. In exchange, my father got protection from the cops and connections all over the country, from lawyers to politicians—you name it. They were all under the mob's thumb and were at our disposal."

"Why was Cantoni killed?"

"The man was a poor earner, and the Sambinos had planned to whack him for a long time. He had a falling out with the Sambino family and tried to come work for the Molanano family. Molanano didn't trust him from the start, but because Cantoni was friends with one of Molanano's nephews, Don Molanano agreed to take him in. But because Cantoni switched sides, Don Molanano thought he might be a flip-floppin' rat. He never gave him any big jobs. This pissed Cantoni off, so he started doing stuff on the side and not sharing the profits. A boss doesn't care how you make your money, so long as you give them a taste. When he found out Cantoni lied, he gave Frank the order to kill Cantoni. That's the day Frank became a made guy. Cantoni's body was found in an alley with two shots through his chest."

"So, Frank never got caught?"

"Hmmph," she said as her top lip curled up. "I wish I was that lucky. That would have changed everything. On the night Frank killed Cantoni, a witness walking his dog informed the cops they saw Frank at the scene of the crime and that he could ID him in a lineup. To protect one of his soldiers from going to prison and further implicating the family, *Consigliere* Rapino called my father and Frank was sent to us until they got a handle on things. From what I'd read in the newspapers, the informant's body was later discovered, cut up in pieces behind a pizzeria owned and operated by the Sambino family," she said with a coy smile on her face.

"Cut up in pieces! Really?"

"Yep."

"What about the witness protection program, or didn't they have that?"

"Things were a little different back then, but remember there's always someone on the inside and everyone has a price."

"I can't believe it. It's just like the movies."

"Horror movie maybe, but no—this was real life for us. The mob doesn't leave loose ends. So, Molanano ordered the hit and because of the bad blood between the families, this got the cops off the Molanano family and onto the Sambinos. Because the Sambinos didn't off this guy when they had the chance, Don Molanano felt like the Sambino family should have taken out their own trash. Feds were thrown off the trail because they thought that Cantoni was still working for the Sambinos. It was the perfect diversion. The order killed two birds with one stone. It steered the feds away from any Molanano involvement, and Frank was no longer a suspect."

"I never realized just how treacherous these men were."

"Oh yeah. When they come, it's too late."

Her story reminded me of how I felt the first day I signed the NDA with her niece, which felt like ages ago. But it was stories like these that I had to keep private, or it might be *too late* for me. My pulse raced and left me lightheaded.

"Hey, you okay, kid? You don't look too good."

"I'm fine. I still can't believe it," I croaked out with a tight throat.

"See, that's what happens when you have a lot of friends. You get away with stuff like that. That's the story, but hell, I'm no rat." The flicker of a faint smile crossed her cheeks. "And that's how I met my wonderful husband, that lousy piece of shit. To think that some *stronzo* named Mario Cantoni had the power to change my life the way he did makes me sick. I never even met the guy, but he's responsible for ruining my life and putting that monster around me. Hell, I wish I'd had the satisfaction of killing the son of a bitch myself. Maybe then things would have turned out differently." She yanked the yarn with force and jabbed the crochet needle back into her work.

"Don't get so worked up, honey. We don't need your blood pressure to rise. It's in the past." I patted her on the shoulder, knowing that my own blood pressure felt high.

Her body stiffened, and she looked me straight in the eye. "When you're as old as me and have a brain like mine, everything's in the past."

"I'm sorry, Ms. G. We don't have to talk about it anymore if you don't want to."

"No. I want to talk about it. Words are my only power now." She took a deep breath. "Now, where was I?"

"You talked about why Frank came to you that summer."

"It wasn't long after that maniac arrived that I found out what it meant to be the daughter of someone connected. This was the first time I learned about my arranged marriage—a true sacrifice and call to duty for the cause. It was a life of loss and regret. They owned me, and then they owed me," she said with an edge in her voice.

"What did they owe you?" I asked, stunned.

"The mob owed me for a few lives they took."

Chapter 9

Duty

East San Jose Foothills, Giordano Estate
June 1940
Violetta

I FOCUSED ON THE BARN OUTSIDE MY BEDROOM WINDOW. Memories flooded. Nine months had passed since I'd seen my grape grower. We'd spent so much time there, yet so much had changed since summer. Time and separation felt like a thousand paper cuts to my soul, leaving scars and ambiguity. The Sanna business flourished, and Gaetano had settled in his new home and made new friends. I wanted to be happy for him, but his absence had blown out my heart's candle, leaving only smoke.

I was at the start of my adult life. I'd finished school, and everything was in place for me to take the reins, but what kind of life would it be without him? He'd said he'd visit soon to ask for my hand in marriage, but I'd heard nothing for weeks. My father's voice pulled me out of my memories.

"Violetta, coma here."

I walked to the kitchen.

"Bring *Signor* Di Natale a plate of pasta."

"Do I have to? Why can't he come and eat at the dinner table like the rest of us? Where is he, anyway? I haven't seen him all day."

My father's eyebrows pulled together. "He no coma home last night? I no like it."

"Probably out drinking again. He already drank two cases of beer since he's been here. And there's a few bottles of your limoncello all over the porch of the big house."

"That isa none of you biziniss. Be a good girl and go bring him his dinna."

"All right." I grabbed a heaping plate of pasta and meatballs. "Have any more letters come for me?"

"No more letters. Itsa time for you to concern yourself with udder tings, Violetta. Go bring dat boy da food before it get cold. And be nice to him. He a nice boy," Pop said.

"Fine. But there's something strange with him, Pop. I feel it in my bones."

His eyes widened. "What you mean, you bones?"

"He looks at me like I'm a Thanksgiving turkey."

"Hmm . . ." Pop raised one eyebrow. "Maybe he just wanna be nice. Now go." He pointed to the backyard.

I rolled my eyes and marched to the big house.

"Mr. Di Natale? Mr. Di Natale, you here? Hello? I brought you something to eat, sir." I banged on the door.

"Yeah, yeah, I'm coming," Frank mumbled through the door, his voice groggy.

The door swung open. His hair stood in heaps on top of his head. He studied me with bloodshot eyes. It looked as though he'd slept all day.

"Come in, beautiful." A lit cigarette flickered up and down on his lips, spilling ash on the floor.

"My father asked me to bring you dinner." I handed him the plate.

He took a whiff of the pasta, then shoved the plate back in my hands, ran past me, and threw up all over my mother's rose bushes.

"Yeah, my mom *does* use a lot of garlic in her gravy," I said with a private chuckle.

"No. I'll be all right," he choked out as he coughed and groaned between gagging.

While he retched up the contents of his stomach, I peered into the big room. A small mattress cluttered the ground. What had been the dance floor was covered with empty bottles and cigarette butts. The room smelled like sweat, smoke, and liquor.

He wiped the remains of his stomach on his undershirt. "Sorry about that, doll. I had a long night. Your father's limoncello packs a punch—that's for sure. You wanna come in? I'd like the company. Gets boring in here."

"I'd rather not. You haven't been in here all day. I see you coming and going all the time."

"I have friends showing me around."

"Not that it's any of my business, but are you sure that's smart? I mean, with your situation and all."

"What do you know about my *situation*?" He tilted his head to the side and examined me.

"Not much. Only that when guys come and stay with us, there's usually a good reason for them to keep a low profile." My eyes narrowed.

He smiled. The slightest laugh came through his dry lips. "Your name is Violetta, right?"

"Yes."

"Violetta, what would you say if you and I went out sometime? I bet you could show me places. Maybe secret places . . . private places. You know, somewhere we can be *alone*, and I won't get spotted. Maybe you can even show me around this ranch. Looks pretty big." He tried to smile through his sweaty, pale cheeks.

"My father wouldn't like that."

"Really? Maybe I should talk to your father. We'll see if you're right. I got a good feeling he'd be okay with anything I tell him." He picked at leftover food particles in his teeth.

"I should get back. It's getting dark. Good night, Mr. Di Natale." I turned to go.

"Hey, Violetta?"

"Yes?"

"Don't be a stranger. My door's always open for you, gorgeous." He licked his pasty lips.

The wind kicked up around the rose bushes. A stench of hard liquor mixed with vomit surrounded me and spun around like a cyclone of bad choices and desperation, leaving me queasy and disgusted.

I ran back to the house to get as far away from Mr. Di Natale as possible. I longed for the one voice that calmed me. When no one was around, I mustered up the courage to pick up the phone.

"Yes, Operator, please connect me to the Sanna Winery in Napa Valley," I whispered into the phone.

"Hold, please," the operator responded.

Seconds of waiting felt like hours. Sweat beads formed on my upper lip and forehead. A voice answered.

"Sanna Winery, 'ello?" A woman's voice greeted me.

"Um, yes. Hello, is Gaetano Sanna available? *Signora* Sanna, is that you?"

"*Si*. Who dis?"

"It's me, Violetta Giordano, Giuseppe's daughter. I hoped to speak with your son."

After a long pause, I heard Gaetano's voice in the background. My heart jumped in my chest. I was seconds away from hearing Gaetano's soothing voice. I had so much to tell him.

"Hello . . . *Signora*, you there?"

"No. He no here. Sorry," she said, then abruptly hung up.

I couldn't breathe. Gaetano was right there. I was so close. Why wouldn't she let me talk to him? What had I done? They didn't seem to mind me being around Gaetano when I taught him English.

And then it hit me: *Signora* Sanna, walking through the streets of Goosetown with her head down, avoiding eye contact, not talking to a single soul; the way she cried to my mother in our kitchen when *Signor* Sanna told my father what happened to their family. She didn't want her son mixed up with us.

My hope diluted. I tried to bat away the one question I couldn't ignore.

Was I the enemy now?

For fear of any further miscommunication on my part, I decided to wait a few weeks before I'd write again to confirm if my suspicions were true. I hoped Gaetano would still receive my letters. I feared this was the reason I hadn't heard from him. Maybe he didn't get my letters? I closed my eyes and took a deep breath. Powerless, I dragged myself to my room, where I'd endure another restless night of sleep.

After a few days of ruminating in self-pity, I committed to staying busy. I did extra chores to pass the time. I ironed all the linens and swept the porch.

A black limousine pulled up to the front of our house.

The driver opened the passenger door. A strange-looking gentleman in a black suit and a black hat emerged. He was short and walked like a penguin, but he looked Mafia.

Pop walked straight to the limousine to greet him. They shook hands, and Pop escorted him to the front door.

"Dis is my daughter, Violetta," he gushed to the stranger. "Violetta, dis isa *Consigliere*, eh . . . *Signor* Salvatore Rapino."

"Nice to meet you, sir." I stared at his thick glasses while he examined me.

"So, da rumors are true. She isa beautiful, Giuseppe."

I stared at him quizzically. What did he mean the rumors? What rumors? I never met this man before in my life. How did he know me?

"Itsa nice to meet you, Violetta," he said, then took out his handkerchief to dry the sweat under his hat.

"Letsa go in da back where we talk privately. You like limoncello? I make my own. Itsa good," my father said proudly.

"Si. Itsa been a long day of da travel. I could use a drink or two or three," he said.

They both laughed.

"Coma in, coma in." My father ushered *Signor* Rapino to the big house in back. The two men didn't return until late that evening for dinner. Surprisingly, Frank joined us. He was all cleaned up and dressed in a suit and tie.

My father, *Signor* Rapino, and Frank all sat around the table, laughing and serving themselves seconds of gnocchi. The older men reminisced about the time they met in Sicily. Frank went on and on about how great Brooklyn was and how he missed it there. I couldn't wait for *Signor* Rapino to leave. Frank seemed to be trying to impress him and Pop even brought out his best imported cigars. They smoked while Carmela and I cleared the table. I was ready for the night to end so that I could dream about Gaetano.

"It was nice meeting you, *signore*, but I have an early morning, so I'm off to bed," I said.

"Oh. I'm sure you'll be seeing plenty more of her soon, *Sally Boy*," Frank said as he smiled at me with a wicked grin. Confused about Frank's comments, I eyed him suspiciously. "Get sleep, doll. You have a big day tomorra."

"Huh?" I asked Frank directly.

"Good night," my father interrupted.

"Good night," I mumbled, still wondering about Frank's words.

I shut the door to my room, took off my clothes, and hopped into bed. I closed my eyes and made my way for dreamland, where I hoped to see *my Guy.*

I woke up the next morning and went straight for the kitchen. Warm scents of my mother's hotcakes with browned butter and the sweetness of maple syrup tickled my nose. My mouth drooled as I loaded my plate. Mama and Carmela were busy working the dough for ravioli while Pop sipped his coffee. I had just poured myself milk when Mama and Pop exchanged strange looks.

"*Cosa c'è?* What's going on? Did something happen?" I asked and sat at the table with my full plate of pancakes and syrup.

"Violetta, we needa talk to you," my father said, his tone serious.

My heart quickened in my chest. "About what?" I asked, then took a small bite.

"Violetta, your mama and I, we decide dat you gonna marry da Di Natale boy."

I choked on my hotcake. For a moment, I thought I'd misheard. "Wait, what? No. No. I don't even know him. I can't. I . . . I . . . I'm in love with someone else. The Sanna boy—Gaetano. He wants to ask you for my hand, Papa. He said he'll visit in a few weeks." My throat became so tight, I couldn't breathe.

"We talk. And dat isa who we wan for you. He a good man and willa provide you a good life."

"No, Papa, I won't. How could you?" I shouted back.

"Violetta, itsa settled. You willa marry dis man," he said firmly.

"No. I love Gaetano, and I'm going to marry him, with or without your permission," I yelled.

"You no disrespect me in dis house," he shouted back. His fists struck the table. My plate shook.

"But, Papa . . ." Floods of tears dropped from my eyes.

"I love you, but you dona understand. Itsa good biziniss for both families. It give us more protection and more connections. He can give you a betta life. You marriage canna give us all a betta life. Please no make dis more difficult dan it is. I know he make you happy. You willa live like a queen," he said, then reached for my hand.

I pushed his hand away. "Mama, please tell him. Talk to him."

"I sorry, Violetta. I canno do anyting about it," Mama said, defeated, then turned her face away from mine.

"You no give dis boy a chance," Pop demanded. "He always nice to you. He a good boy. His father help us. It willa help da family. You have to undastan. Das da way itsa gonna be, an das it." He stormed out.

"I hate this. How dare you do this to me? You don't love me," I said as more tears fell.

"Yes, we do. It wassa hard decision, but one we havta make," Mama said as she brushed away her straggling tears with her apron and continued working the dough.

"It'll be okay, Vi," Carmela encouraged. "Look at me and Louie. I didn't love him at first, but since the day Pop brought him here, Louie has been a complete angel."

"At least you like Louie. I can't stand Frank. He makes my skin crawl. And the way he looks at me? Yuck," I said with disgust. "Pop only brought Louie around because of the trucking business, and you know it," I yelled as my blood pressure surged.

"*Basta*, Vi," Carmela shrieked with nostrils flared. "Say all you want. I love Louie, and once his father makes him manager, we're getting married and getting our own place."

"Well, Carm, I hope you're happy. You'll get what you've always wanted. *A fanabla*," I fired back. "Pop's just using your marriage the same way he plans to use mine, and you know it. I know how all this crap works. I've seen it all my life."

My mother slammed the ravioli pin against the table.

The sharp noise made me jump.

"Enough," she said.

"I'll never forgive you and Papa for this—ever," I exclaimed, then ran to my room.

I slammed the door and thought about ways to escape to Napa. I started to pack my clothes when *Signora* Sanna's face burned in my mind. I remembered how she dismissed me on the phone. Panic held me in place. Maybe she wouldn't want me there? What's worse, the mob would come find me and go after Gaetano and his family. I didn't want to bring harm to the Sannas. That would prove her right about me. But I understood enough about the men in this life that when they came calling, they meant business. Mob bosses always got what they wanted. Broken and defeated, I couldn't take any more blows to the heart. I threw my suitcase aside, flung myself on my bed, and cried for the rest of the day.

The next morning, I awoke with swollen eyes and a red nose. I'd never felt this way before. It was as if someone took out my heart and stomped on it. I loved only one man, had devoted myself to him, and my hopes for the future were destroyed. I wanted to wake up from this nightmare and be in Gaetano's arms again. But in the quiet of my room, I heard the two voices I wanted to avoid, Pop's and that *stronzo* Frank's.

As hard as I tried to stay in bed and wallow in my sorrows, my stomach growled from not eating dinner the night before. Maybe it was all the crying and nerves, but my head pounded, and my legs felt like spaghetti. I didn't remember Carmela coming to bed. Realizing I'd slept in my clothes, I dragged myself out of bed and went to the kitchen to get something to eat.

Frank and Pop sat at the table, discussing business. I had to fight the urge to run to the bathroom and throw up.

Pop pulled down the newspaper from in front of his face. "*Buongiorno*, Violetta," he said, then lowered his gaze.

"Hmmph." Hot air escaped my nostrils like an angry bull in a bullfight.

Pop straightened his paper and continued reading.

"So, Violetta, your father told you the news?" Frank asked as he lit a cigarette.

My eyes burned a hole right through Pop's newspaper. "Yes. That doesn't mean I'm happy about it," I said sharply.

"Violetta, no disrespect." Pop's words came out hard and even.

I rolled my eyes, then served myself oats from the stove.

"I'd like to get to know yous betta. How's about you show me around the ranch? The most I've seen is this here kitchen and that big room in the back."

"Yeah, sure. Anything you want. With my father's supervision, of course, right, Pop?" I said, with a smirk.

Pop's eyes squinted at me.

"I don't feel good today, Mr. Di Natale."

"Please, call me Frank. You're gonna be my wife, and I don't think we need any formal supervision, do we, Giuseppe? You trust me, right?" Frank challenged as he undid the button of his jacket to expose his pistol.

My father eyed him carefully. "Maybe I get Tony to keep an eye. I have no problems wit you as long as you sleep in da big house out back, and she's in da house by sunset. But I no wan my daughter out in da city wit you. Itsa too dangerous wit what isa goin' on. I ma sure you undastan. At least dat isa what I told your fater and *Consigliere* Rapino when we spoke. He say dey willa respect da terms for my family's safety. *Capeesh, Signor* Di Natale?"

"*Si.* All my respect, Giuseppe. Don Molanano's a great man. I'd never want to do anything to jeopardize your daughter," he said, his eyes like a fox.

Pop continued to read the newspaper. "As long as we

undastan each udder," Pop said, appearing unfazed by Frank's subtle threat and baseless words.

Frank turned to me. "Well, Violetta, we have all the time in the world to get to know each other." He blew rings of smoke in Pop's direction.

Pop fanned the smoke away with his newspaper.

"I suppose we do. I'm one lucky girl," I said with heavy sarcasm in my voice. "If you'll excuse me, I'm going to lie down." I marched straight to my room with my bowl of oats and locked the door.

"If you no coma out dat room, Violetta, you gonna force me to give you da castor oil. If you sick, then I gonna give you da medicine," Pop bellowed through my bedroom door, trying to call my bluff.

The thought of castor oil made me sit up straight in bed and dress quickly. "Ughh . . . all right. I'm coming," I yelled and stared down at the unfinished letter to Gaetano on my dresser. I yanked the brush through knots in my hair. Knots. What better way to turn Frank off than to look unattractive? I'd alter my appearance by not bathing or brushing my teeth for a few days. I'd wear old baggy clothes to hide my shape, and I'd stop brushing my hair. If I smelled bad enough, maybe he'd call the whole thing off, and I'd wake from this nightmare.

With ratted hair, dirty clothes, and garlic breath, I gave Frank the grand tour of the ranch.

The next few days were uncomfortable. I tried to stay away from Frank as much as possible. He made me nervous. One day at lunch, he rambled on about himself. During one of his long-winded monologues about how good he thought he was, I chugged a cold bottle of soda and released a big burp. I thought maybe my appalling lack of manners would disgust Frank. Instead, he ignored me and kept talking about himself. It was obvious this was nothing more than a business transaction with a few perks for him and my father.

Most days, Frank acted fake. He said something nice one minute and ordered me to get him a beer or make him a plate the next. He never showed any interest in who I was. He never asked me what I liked or who I was inside. I suppose he thought he impressed me, but it made me sick.

Worse, he often said inappropriate things to me around my parents. He showed no respect, and it bothered Pop and Tony. Frank came across arrogant; and at times, he ordered my father around. Tony and I didn't like it. But what could we say? When I wasn't trying to avoid Frank, I was off in the barn, crying my eyes out for Gaetano.

Between long bouts of depression, which kept me in bed most of the day, my mother forced me to go to Zavlaris's shop to get lace and material to make my wedding dress. With every alteration, I looked at myself in the mirror and cried. This was not what I had envisioned. Since last summer, I only thought of marrying Gaetano. I dreamed we'd marry in a big church surrounded by our families, followed by a big reception. Yet, here I was, about to marry a stranger—someone I didn't love and had no interest in.

"Stop moving, Violetta, or I ma gonna poke you wit dis needle," Mama warned while shortening my dress. I peered down at her head engulfed in white material as she basted the hem. I felt like a mummy. Dead and roaming the Earth. Heartless. Piles of satin and tulle smothered me. I suffocated in every way.

Standing in my wedding dress, I realized I was in denial. It was mid-July, and I still hadn't heard from Gaetano. With my failed attempts to turn Frank away, I couldn't put off the hurt any longer. I'd have to write to my beloved and tell him everything. It was my duty to explain my situation.

⸻

I locked myself in the bathroom and penned a goodbye letter.

July 1940

Dear Gaetano,

I hope this letter finds you well. I haven't heard from you in quite some time. I tried to call a few weeks ago, but your mother said you weren't home.

This letter is to inform you of my upcoming nuptials. My father has promised me to another man. From the little I can gather; I believe this arrangement is intended to bridge our families.

I need you to know that I still love you and do not want this other man, but my father has made this decision clear. For the safety and benefit of my family, I don't have much choice in the matter.

I wish you the best that life has to offer. And no matter where life takes me, I'll never forget you.

Love you always,

Violetta

Tears dropped onto the paper and turned my black words of misery into swirls of regret. The paper was a mess. I was a mess. I sealed the envelope and put it in the mailbox—my last letter to the man of my dreams.

⸻

At dinner that night, I dragged my fork around my plate, rearranging food. No interest in conversation, I didn't make eye contact with anyone. I went to bed early, but I was still awake when I overheard my parents talking. Mama was in tears.

"Giuseppe, we canno do dis to Violetta. She no eat. She no talk. She walk around here like a ghost. Please, you do someting. We havta get her out of dis," she said, weeping.

"I know, and it hurt me too. I hate to see her like dis. I no can do anything. I love my daughter wit all my heart, and I no wan her to be a sad, but what can I do? You know I canno back out da deal now. Don Molanano will tink I breaka da trust, and I no wan a war. Our families have always worked together over da years. Der are tings I ma tryin' to do for dis family's future, and I need his power and support to do dem. I no hava choice, and you know dat. If I betray dem, dey will kill us all," he said with a shaky voice.

When I heard my father's words and my mother's pain for me, tears fell. He loved me and he'd do anything to protect us, but the Hand was bigger than any emotion he'd ever feel, and business would always be business. To Pop, our family's survival surpassed my needs.

And just how the sun dries up a puddle after the rain, the hate moved away from my body. I felt empty. For the first time, I recognized the emotional impact this decision had on everyone, not just me. In order to survive, I'd have to surrender to the Mafia. They had won.

To avoid the possibility of bugged phones, my father passed on the message to Mr. Di Natale Sr. through trusted informants that I'd agreed to marry his son. They reported back that Mr. Di Natale Sr. wouldn't be able to attend the wedding because it would bring too much attention to his son's whereabouts. The date was set: August 31.

Before the wedding, to try and make up for my sacrifice, Pop offered a job at his clinic to be his medical assistant and bookkeeper. As part of an early wedding gift, he promised that after we were married, he and Tony would convert part of the medical office into a home for me and Frank. Then they'd build another office building somewhere else on the property. I didn't protest because I wanted to stay close to my mother if I was to have children.

Because I looked at my marriage as nothing more than a business transaction, I'd do my duty to help my family, but I had no interest in the planning of it. I left Mama in charge of every detail, including the dress, the cake, and the decorations.

On the days leading up to the wedding, Frank came home drunk. He yelled and cussed at the top of his lungs. He threw chairs around and knocked over Mama's religious yard statues. Alcohol changed him. It made me afraid of how he'd act after we were married. All my life I was around men who drank, but none of them had acted so violently. The only good thing about his drinking was his hangover the next morning. A part of me liked when he drank because he left me alone the next day.

To get ready for my new life and help keep my mind off Gaetano, Tony helped me move my belongings into my new home. Decorating with what little I had proved a good distraction. I dressed windows, hung plants, and put away pots and pans that Mama gave me—her way of letting me know my place in the home. She'd always been the subservient type and did all the cooking, cleaning, and catering for all my father's *friends*. For her, it must have felt like she'd passed the baton down to me.

For me, I felt stuck.

"*Maronn*, you gotta lot of crap," Tony said as he lugged in various boxes and bags.

"Mama gave me a lot of things from the house. She's probably gonna make Pop buy her new stuff," I said as he handed me a big box. "What about you, Tone? You ever gonna marry Christina?"

"She's a nice girl, but I don't think her father likes me too much. I bet I know why." He stared at the floor.

"Yeah. I've felt that way before. They don't like us because our family's connected."

"How would you know? Frank works for Molanano, so—"

"Not Frank's family. Gaetano's family."

"I knew it." He smiled. "And all that time you two said you looked at horses. You're a damn good liar. You didn't . . ."

"No, you *stunad*—never. Stop." I pinched his arm. "I love Gaetano, but there was something off about *Signora* Sanna. I don't think she liked us because of Pop's business with the Molanano family."

"Yeah, well, she shouldn't be saying nothin'. Just who does she think helped finance her husband's new business?" He moved another box to the table.

"True. It's strange. As much as we don't like being owned by the mob, it's given us so much. But at what cost? My life, I suppose . . ." I muttered, then rubbed away a loose tear.

"Don't be upset, Vi. From the little I know, Frank seems like a decent guy when he isn't drinkin.'"

"Yeah, you noticed that too?"

"Kind of hard not to when he comes in screaming at night."

"He scares me, Tony."

"You have nothing to worry about. I'll never let anything happen to you," he said with a hug. "Look, I gotta go. Christina's waiting for me. I told her mother I'm gonna teach her daughter how to clean my guns."

"You'll scare the crap out of her."

"I can't wait to see the look on her mother's face when I bring Pop's Tommy gun in with me when I pick her up."

"You wouldn't," I exclaimed.

"Nah, I'm kidding. But wouldn't that be a sight to see? *Maronn* . . . the look on the old bat's face," he joked.

"Thanks for helping me today. And thanks for listening."

"You got it, kid. Anytime. Things will get better." He walked out the door.

I unpacked the rest of the kitchen and started in the bedroom. While putting clothes away, I came across the yellow dress I'd worn the day Gaetano and I had our first kiss in Alum Rock Park. Waves of happier times overcame me as I sat in front of my new bedroom window. Sunlight gleamed through the glass and caught the satin fibers. I pulled the lace away from the yellow material and draped it in front of my face. My eyes looked through the tiny holes and a rush of flashbacks washed over me. I gently pulled it away and brushed my hand over its soft scratchiness. It reminded me of how it felt to run my fingers through Gaetano's hair when we kissed. I allowed myself those private moments to be alone with him.

A flash of light twinkled from the bottom of the closet. It was the latch on my old briefcase from last summer. I pulled it out from the back of the closet, drew the drapes, and locked the door. Inside were all the papers with Gaetano's handwriting. They were notes of our time together as teacher and student.

My heart sank.

I grabbed the notebook and all his letters fell out onto the floor. These were the last few things I had of him now. I reread the poetry he'd written during our lessons. I put them back into the briefcase. I'd always want to keep them safe, but I needed to hide them from Frank. So, I placed the briefcase in an old, locking filing cabinet and hid the key in the barn. It was my little private space where I'd preserve my past and connect to Gaetano whenever I wanted.

Until then, he would stay safely locked away.

Chapter 10

A Runaway Rendezvous

EVERY DAY, THE SUN ROSE AND SET. TIME MOVED IN ONE DIREC-
tion—forward. My wedding was a few weeks away, an unavoidable freight train bearing down on me. I believed Guy had read
my letter and given up on me. A deep self-loathing took hold.

Frank and a few friends invited Tony to join them for a week in
Tahoe for a guys' gambling trip. Seemed like an extravagant bache-
lor party, but I didn't complain. Frank did more than gamble. With
his frequent trips to Tahoe, his affinity for the casino business was
clear. The Molanano family had interest in buying and operating
a casino out West, so Frank scouted places where Don Molanano
could line his pockets. Frank leaving with the boys gave me time to
sort through my feelings before the big day.

I was feeding the chickens when the sound of a car horn rang
through my ears. I went out to the front to see who made all the
racket. Three men with fancy pocket squares and dark, Sicilian skin
stepped from the black Cadillac Fleetwood and opened the trunk.
I'd seen them around a few times to pick up Frank. They loaded the
car with beer and bags.

Frank strutted over to me, a cigarette dangling from his mouth. Another failed attempt at being charming.

"Hey, baby, I'll only be gone for a little while. Don't you worry, cookie. Maybe I'll win us some cash. Wish me luck, will ya, sweetie?" he said with a devilish grin.

"Luck," I said.

Frank planted a wet kiss on my lips. His breath reeked of beer and cigarettes. He tipped his hat and climbed into the car.

Tony waved at me from the back seat and off they went, screaming out the open windows all the way down the gravel road. To get his dirty smell off my lips, I ran to the bathroom to wash my face.

The phone rang.

A moment passed before Carmela knocked on the bathroom door. "Vi, you in here?"

"Yes."

"Someone's on the phone for you. Says he's an old friend. I'm gonna go help Mama pick tomatoes."

"Yeah, okay. Old friend? Maybe someone late to RSVP." I walked out and grabbed the phone. "Hello?"

"Violetta, it's me, Gaetano."

My heart stopped.

And when it finally started again, the rhythm was clunky, almost missing beats. I couldn't even get words out.

"Violetta, are you der? Please, I need to speak to you," he said with angst in his voice.

I held the phone close to my chest to check if anyone was around to hear the conversation. After I confirmed I was alone, I pushed my voice past my dry tongue.

"Yes, it's me," I croaked, holding back tears.

"I'm so sorry I no write back. I had to travel with my fater to get equipment to start da business. We stay longer than we expect. When we get back, we have many problems with da *immigrazione*. I, I—"

"It's okay, I understand. So, you received my letter?"

"Yes. It was lost under a stack of mail. When we get home, we have so much letters from the banks, *immigrazione*, labor union, and da *applicazioni*. We try to hire more workers from Mexico. I just found it. I'm so sorry, Violetta," he said with a shaky voice.

"Did your mother tell you that I called?"

"No," he said dryly. He offered no excuse.

"Sounds like you're doing well. Your business is doing great, like you hoped. Things happen, I guess," I added, a tinge of displaced anger coating my words. I wasn't mad at him. Instead, I was mad at myself for not having the guts to stand up to my father.

"Please, tell me you no marry dis man," he pleaded.

"I don't have a choice." My throat tightened.

"I love you. Lemme talk to your fater. Please, put him on da phone. I tell him how much I love you," he begged.

"It wouldn't matter. He won't listen. It's an arrangement between the two families. Deep down, you know what this means. Besides, it doesn't sound like your mother thinks I'm the best choice for you, either, and I know why . . ." I said through tears.

"Das not true. I don't care what anyone says. I love you. What I tell you last summer, I mean. I no lie. I wanna marry you."

"I love you, too, but maybe love isn't enough when you're born into the kind of family I was."

"Dis all my fault. I'm too late. I so stupid. I had so many plans for us. Please, please forgive me for dis," he said as his voice trailed off.

"Don't make this harder than it is. I'm miserable enough already," I said, weeping.

"Please no cry, *amore mio*. Lemme make dis right. Lemme speak to your fater. He will understand dat I love you. I come get you right now," he implored.

I fumbled with the phone. "No, he won't," I said, trying to muzzle my scream.

"I need to see you, Violetta. Please . . ."

As much as I heard the pain in his voice, I was hurt. I'd endured months of loneliness. I didn't like the way our voices sounded on the phone; it felt wrong and unfamiliar.

I was about to hang up when I looked over my left shoulder at the huge boxes of wedding favors and decorations sitting on the kitchen table staring me in the face. If I was to spend the rest of my life with a man I didn't love, then I would be with the man of my dreams, every day, until I was forced not to. I didn't know how I'd do it, but I'd make my way to Gaetano, no matter the cost.

"What's the latest bus to Napa?"

"The last bus arrives at four p.m. in Vallejo. Why? No, Violetta," he protested. "Don't even tink of dat. Lemme come get you. It's too long a way for you. Lemme talk to your fater first."

"No. No one can see us together. Frank has his little informants everywhere. It isn't safe for you here. I'll be at the bus station tomorrow at four o'clock."

He yelled with panic in his voice. "No, I come get you. Don't—"

"Be there," I said, then hung up.

Vallejo? Where the hell was Vallejo?

After lunch, Mama attended to the final wedding details. When no one was looking, I went into the washroom closet, pushed aside the ironing board, and grabbed a stack of hidden cash. I shoved the bills into my purse, along with the Shakespeare book Gaetano and I used last summer. The book might help us connect with one another after a year apart, alter the mood, and help transport us back to a happier time. Privately, I packed a small overnight bag and called my best friend Julia.

"Julia, it's Vi."

"Hey, how you doin'? You must be so busy with all the wedding plans. I haven't heard from you in weeks."

"I know. I'm sorry, but I need a favor."

"Sure."

"I'm going to tell my parents that I'm staying with you at your beach house in Santa Cruz for a few days. Cover for me," I whispered into the phone. "Can you pick me up so they won't question anything?"

"Okay. Where you going anyway?"

"I wish I could tell you, but I can't."

"You aren't doing nothin' that will get *us* in trouble, are you?"

Prickles of panic crawled up my back. "I'll call you later tonight after I talk to my mother and tell you the details. I owe you one."

"Yeah, all right. I'll wait for your call." She hung up the phone.

I needed to play on Mama's sympathies. I'd heard her plead with Pop to get me out of the arrangement, so I was pretty sure she'd do anything for me right now. I found her in the living room sewing a piece of lace to my wedding dress.

"You like, Violetta?"

"Umm . . . yeah, sure, I guess." I rolled my eyes. "Mama, I want to go stay with Julia for a few days."

"Julia who?"

"Julia Langone. You know, the Langone family.

"*Si*, we know da *famiglia* Langone."

"Well, see, her family has a summer home in Santa Cruz, and they invited me to go. Frank is out having fun, so I thought I'd spend the last few nights of my single life with a friend. It would do me good to be by the beach. A little fresh air, a change of scenery. She can pick me up tomorrow morning," I said, knowing that this would be the only way my parents wouldn't question me. Once Pop saw Julia, I was free to go.

Her eyes narrowed as she stopped her sewing. "So, when you coma home?"

"I don't know. A few days, maybe a week. Don't worry, I'll be back for the wedding. You always tell me that you want me to be happy, and you know how hurt I am. Getting away for a few days until I'm forced to marry that *stronzo*, Frank, would be good for me."

"When you fater coma home I talk to him, but itsa fine by me."
She went back to putting the final touches on my dress.

The next morning, as planned, Julia honked her horn for me.
Pop pulled back the curtains and waved at her in the car. "Be careful, Violetta," he said, his eyes dubious.

I avoided his stare. "I will," I murmured, then grabbed my bags
and closed the door behind me.

"Hey, Vi, get in. Throw your stuff in the back."

I closed the car door.

"So where to?"

"Downtown, to the train station," I said and looked straight
ahead.

"Yeah, okay. No problem."

After a long train ride to San Francisco, I caught a bus to Vallejo. I
pressed my head against the bus window and my eyes shifted out
of focus. The view of the horizon put me into a trance and drew me
toward the safe depths of my mind—Gaetano.

I wanted true intimacy. A moment where we exposed more
than just our souls. I wouldn't allow years of duty and tradition to
stop me from having this experience. These next few days would
be for us.

I remembered Carmela's advice about sex and the timing
method. After I counted the days in my head, a huge smile spread
across my face, knowing I'd be safe. I took a deep breath and daydreamed of his body above mine. What would it feel like when he
put himself inside me? I remembered the last time we were together
in the barn and how wonderful it felt when he touched me and
kissed me on my most private parts. I wanted my body to feel wor-
shipped with every inch of his touch. Most of all, I wanted him to
wrap his arms around me tight and shield me from my dreaded fate.

Thinking about him, I became aroused. My underwear

dampened and my breasts tickled under my bra. To collect myself, I took deep breaths and stared down at my watch. My heart quickened like the wings of a hummingbird. Twenty minutes until we'd reach the station.

Part of me dared to be vulnerable to the experience and the other, more practical part told me to be true to my circumstances. I fought off the pictures of Pop's sullen face when he'd learn that I'd lied. But I couldn't worry about their disappointment in me. I had to do this to survive. I also wasn't sure if Gaetano would tell his parents I was there. Maybe it would be better to rent a room so that *Signor* Sanna wouldn't see me and call my parents. How would they treat me if they saw me? All I could do was put trust in Gaetano's words and let chance and discovery do the rest.

I stepped off the bus, looked up, and saw Gaetano.

My whole heart stood there, waiting for me, his eyes like magnets, pulling me toward him.

I ran to him and threw my bags on the ground. My arms wrapped tight around his neck while he scooped me up and kissed me hard. Our lips were like old friends, reuniting after a long time away. I leaned into his frame while he held up my body. Our mouths explored each other, making me come alive again. While travelers moved around us, we stood our ground and demanded our moment. I didn't care who watched. In his arms, I was free.

We paused to catch our breath and assess one another. A toothy smile and bright eyes shined back at me.

"You crazy girl. You have me so worry. Lemme look at you. You are so beautiful, just like I remember. Oh, Violetta, how I miss you," he gushed, then leaned in for another strong kiss.

"I've missed you too." Words weren't enough. I wanted to crawl inside him and stay there forever.

"I cannot believe you came all dis way. I could have come get you."

"No, we couldn't take the risk. With a little help from a friend and a train and bus schedule, I made it."

"What about your fater? We have to tell him dat your here. I feel wrong to have you here like dis." He bent down to grab my bag.

"No, no. We can't. I told them I'd be with my friend, Julia. Please, I just got here. Let me enjoy this. Is there a hotel close by? I don't want to impose on your family. With what happened with your mother, I don't know—"

"No. You will be with me. We have a guesthouse on da udder side of da property where we can be alone."

"What about your family? I know why they don't like me."

"I will take care of everyting, *amore mio*," he reassured me. "Now let's go. I can't wait to show you all of it. Every day I tink of dis moment. No time to waste."

As if I was in a dream, we walked through the station. With one hand at my lower back and the other holding my luggage, he escorted me to the parking area. We stopped in front of a large pickup truck. The door had a hand-painted letter S with the sun rising behind it.

"Did you design this? I remember you said you'd been drawing."

"Yes. It took me time to decide which idea I like most, but dis one I like very much," he said with admiration.

"It's bold. I love it. I'm so proud of you. Did you paint it too?"

"Oh no. I just design. We pay an artist to come and paint on all da trucks, and road signs—even da bottles." He threw my bag in the back of the truck and opened the passenger door. "*Andiamo*, Violetta, I'm so happy you are here."

"Me too," I said and climbed into the truck.

On the drive, I held on to his arm and breathed in his scent. The smell of his starched and pressed work shirt mixed with something new I couldn't yet place. It reminded me of burnt matches—strong and woodsy. His deep scent filled the cab and stirred my desire for him. With a few more breaths of him, I let my tired, anxious head nestle in the crook of his neck. His warm body electrified me. I'd gone so long without his touch that my body ached for him. I closed my eyes and slowed my mind. I was whole again.

"I've missed you so much," I said as my throat grew thick. "So many nights I prayed I would wake up and you'd be there, but you never were. For a while, I thought God didn't hear my prayers and had forgotten about me. I thought you'd forgotten about me too."

"I never forget you. The only ting dat keep me going was dat all my work would be for you someday," he said with soft eyes.

"We have to think of somewhere to go. If they find out I'm here, they'll come for me. I swear I don't know if I can go back. I can't stand Frank. He's not a good person and when he drinks, he does bad things."

"As long as I am alive, no one will ever hurt you." His body stiffened, and his gaze seethed through the windshield.

"What can we do? Let's run away . . . Let's go to Italy. I have uncles and cousins there that might help us. Or maybe somewhere in the States. Live under new names . . . something," I pleaded. "I don't want anything to happen. Your mother already hates me," I muttered, then shifted my eyes away from him.

"No. She does not hate you. We will talk to dem and make dem understand."

"Okay, I trust you." For the first time since we left the station, I focused on the landscape. "Look at these homes. They look like castles. I've never seen anything like it."

"*Si.* It is very beautiful up here. Private and natural, the way tings should be. But not as beautiful as you." His eyes shifted from the road to me.

Gaetano made one turn off the main street. Signs for the Sanna winery lined the road. My palms tingled. We were close now. A long, paved road led to a circular driveway. The main building was massive and resembled an old Mediterranean church. The structure had arched windows and dramatic roof lines that sloped down toward the edges of its beautiful rock-covered façade.

A man stood on a tall ladder, painting the letter S on a metal sign that hung from the front of the building. Gaetano stopped the truck by the entry doors and got out. My eyes followed him as he talked to another small, stout-looking man. I couldn't hear them, but they smiled and then the short man waved to me.

I waved back.

After a quick handshake, Gaetano came back to the truck.

"Who was that?"

"His name is José. He help me run da business. He a good man and a hard worker. Dis place would not be where it is witout him. He come from Mexico. I want you to meet him soon," he said as he started the truck and continued down a small gravel road past the main building.

Swimming in fields of color, the winery grounds were vast and brilliant. I was glad we wouldn't see his parents right away. I didn't want his father to call and tell my family where I was. I needed time alone with Gaetano.

While he drove, I studied him. His dark eyelashes flickered in the sun when he looked out the truck window. I'd forgotten how beautiful and black they were against his skin. I couldn't stop staring at him. Because of all the time and distance that had passed between us, I tried to make myself familiar with him again. I paid attention to the way he moved. He dragged his fingers through his hair to push it off his forehead. He licked his lips when he was in deep thought. I'd forgotten the little things about him that took my breath away.

In the silent pockets of conversation, I listened to how hard he'd worked in the past few months to improve his English. He still had trouble with some sounds, but it was obvious that in these last few months he'd become more fluent with every passing day. I wasn't sure if he was trying to impress me, but his determination and resilience made me want him that much more. With a renewed sparkle in my soul, I laid my head on his shoulder as we moved along the tiny gravel road.

"Da guesthouse is over dat hill." He pointed forward.

"Are you sure this is okay? Won't your family wonder where you are?"

"No. It will be fine. Don't worry. Sometimes I stay out here. My fater, he never says anyting. Our property is so big dat when I'm out here working, I sometimes stay in da guesthouse or worker house."

"What's the worker house?"

"I will show you."

On our way to the guesthouse, I spotted another large structure to the side of the road. It looked like a small motel with cars parked next to it.

"Dat is for da workers. It's for da people who want to stay and work for a long time. We have hired about seventy-five people so far. A lot of dem are a from Mexico. Good people and very hardworking. It has helped us get dis moving faster. Some of da workers are on contract and stay until der contract is up. Like Antonelli, you remember?"

"Yes. Wow, seventy-five people."

"*Si*, we still need many more. One day, I introduce you to dem."

"Sounds great."

We passed the building, and another man waved to us. He and a few other men and women picked grapes from the vines and put them into big baskets. Gaetano honked his horn, and they smiled and waved.

"Hola," Gaetano yelled to them with his window down. They all looked up and smiled back. "I learn a little Spanish too."

"You sure did." I grabbed his hand.

Finally, we pulled up to the guesthouse, crafted from the same rock facia as the main house. He reached in his pockets for a set of keys and grabbed our things. I walked behind him along the flat stoned walkway to the front door, which was framed with a flower-covered trellis. Following him into our temporary nest, I plucked a white flower from the vine and tucked it behind my ear.

"You ready?" he said, looking at me with telling eyes.

He had to have suspected how I felt. If I was to stay the night with him here, we both knew what that meant. Was he as excited and nervous as me? Only time would tell.

"I hope you like it. It is far enough away dat we will have our privacy."

Once the words were out, muscles in his cheeks tightened. He swallowed hard, and droplets of sweat formed on his forehead as he fumbled with the keys. Once we were in, there were no more rules.

With a final turn of his wrist, the door opened into a beautiful entryway. The space looked like something I'd seen in a magazine. It wasn't a typical living room because it had dramatic ceiling-to-floor windows that looked onto the back hills.

I took a few steps inside, and the walls welcomed me. The main living area was furnished with a few couches. I fiddled with the radio on a small table. Music blared in and out as I shifted the dial. I turned it off and explored further. Various paintings of Italy hung on the walls, and a bookcase crowded with books stood in the corner. At the small kitchen, I glided my hands over the stone-covered walls.

I looked out the windows. Lines of little grape vines stood in rows for miles, holding on to each other. Small grapes dangled like ornaments as the light of sunset coated them.

"Violetta, come here," he said from down the hallway.

I followed his velvety voice to find him standing in the middle of the biggest bedroom I'd ever seen. A bed fit for a king and queen looked out to another view of the orchards. I anticipated what our bodies might do on it, and my heart pounded again.

I took a deep breath to calm myself and continued to explore my new space. The subtlest hints of a woman's touch were sprinkled throughout. From the white, lace sheers that draped over the canopy bedframe to sprigs of lavender that filled a few glass vases on the nightstands. It was nothing short of romantic. I threw myself onto the bed.

With a day's travels behind me now, I stared at the ceiling. I was exhausted but filled with enough adrenaline to hold sleep at bay. With my body sprawled over the soft mattress, I kicked off my shoes.

Gaetano crawled onto the bed next to me.

Our bodies side by side now, we held hands. With so much to say still lingering, I realized the conversation that lay before us would dampen the mood, but it was unavoidable. I turned to look at him as our smiles grew into pressing stares of fascination.

"I can't believe you are here," he said as he swept tendrils of my hair behind my left ear.

"I had to get out of there. My mother talks about the wedding every day. She's made the dress, bought the decorations. And my father walks around like he made one of the biggest deals in Mafia history. They betrayed me. I don't want any of it because it isn't with you." My throat tightened. "I love only you."

"Everyting will be okay. I speak to your fater, and I will make him understand. And if he does not, den I will take you away from der—somewhere no one will find us. I will protect you from him and *dem*," he said with an edge to his voice. "You are here wit me now—safe." He smiled, then traced the lines of my jaw and neck with his fingertip.

Noses touching, he lifted my chin and kissed me, passionately. When he pulled away, quiet filled the room again. As I looked into his eyes, I cast my fears aside. Amidst all the chaos and everything it took to get to him, I was sure that my love for him was bigger than any of it.

No one would take this night from me.

My underwear felt moist between my legs. My body craved him. My heart pounded, and my hips ached. His breath heavy and uneven, he threaded his fingers through my hair and drew my face to his. Our tongues met again, and I pressed my body against his frame. Like drums, our hearts beat next to each other. I moved my mouth from his lips and dragged my tongue around his ear and neck.

"I want you so bad, Violetta. I know we not married, but I love you. I never disrespect you. I have waited so long to touch your skin and kiss your tender lips," he said, panting now, then rubbed his thumb along my bottom lip.

I marveled at his face and jawline. "It's been so long."

"I know I am a selfish and jealous man to want you right here in dis bed, but I do. I want you. You are so beautiful. How can I lie so close to you and not want to take you right here, right now? I fight myself. I know what I supposed to tink and say, but my desire is too strong. I am powerless. Just look at you," he said as the back of his hand grazed my cheek. "You are mine," he said, then exhaled.

I placed my finger against his soft lips. "Shhh . . . I'm here now."

"If you are not ready, I understand. Tell me to go, and I will sleep separate from you until we are married. But if you want da same, say da word, and I will stay here wit you."

"Don't ever leave me again."

"I . . . I . . . Violetta, I need you," he said as his voice grew thick.

"I'm yours."

We began where we left off in the barn, all those months ago, kissing ardently.

He unbuttoned my dress and unhooked my bra, then climbed on top of me. His heavy, muscular build weighed me down, while my fingers glided down his back. Reflexively, his back arched from my touch.

Hungry with desire, I moaned as he sucked my nipples. With my pulse in my groin, I pulled off my dress and bra and threw them on the ground. Half-naked under him, I worked at his belt and zipper to unveil my pleasure. Filtered, golden light reflected off of the canopy above the bed, giving dimension to his body. Gleaming muscles on his arms and stomach contracted as he moved along my body while I tugged at his boxer shorts.

He reached down to yank them off his legs and pulled the white sheets over us. I reached down to stroke him. He was stiff in my hand. He kissed me fervently, muffling his moans as I massaged him.

With one hand, he stripped off my panties. Small whiskers on his face tickled as he licked my navel and trailed his tongue downward. Like waves, his tongue tasted me, again and again. Tiny reverberations echoed through my body, like dropping a penny in a bucket full of water. Goose bumps rose on my arms, and my legs shook when he inserted his fingers inside me. With every movement, the most wonderful feeling rippled through my groin, making my breathing hitch.

"Are you okay, Violetta? You are shaking. Are you afraid? Do you want me to stop?"

"No. I'm not afraid," I said as my pelvis throbbed. "Something's about to happen. I can feel it deep inside. Please don't stop," I murmured, then closed my eyes.

He moved his body downward under the sheets and pressed his mouth against my flesh. As his tongue flicked like a feather against my spot, a strange sensation materialized under my belly button. Something awakened deep inside. I weaved my hands into his hair to guide him. My body began to rise, higher and higher. Muscles in my pelvis tightened, ready to break loose. An itch that begged to be scratched, his tongue found my release.

I let go.

For seconds after, I didn't breathe. My heart didn't beat, and my ears buzzed. When I finally took a breath and opened my eyes, it felt as though my insides had blossomed like a flower.

Every muscle relaxed. Every worry, forgotten.

When he emerged from under the sheets, he studied my face and smiled. "You look so beautiful right now, so peaceful here in dis bed with me. To watch you and feel your body free itself was a gift," he said with wondrous eyes, then brushed back a few strands of hair from my face.

With renewed life, I pulled his mouth to mine again. I tasted myself on his lips. He moved his tongue up my neck, flicking it back and forth, tracing from the base up to the edge of my jaw. Without warning, his tongue plunged into my ear, and it felt like an alarm had gone off in my head. Buzzed and blazing from his kisses, my toes curled under him. "Do it. Do it right now," I panted between words.

He looked down at me with his deep, vast eyes. His eyelashes flickered with concern. "Violetta, I don't want to hurt you."

My legs like jelly, I reached for him and pulled him to me.

"I will go slow," he said as his eyebrows pulled together. "I tink I make you ready, but if it gets too much, tell me and I stop. I hope I can stop . . ." he said, then dropped his head to his chest.

"You won't have to stop. I counted like Carm told me to. We'll be fine," I reassured him.

He nodded. "Okay," he said, flushed.

His broad shoulders above me, I was seconds away from becoming a woman. Every sensation I'd fantasized about was before me. I trusted him, and I loved him, and that was enough for me to be brave. He inserted himself into me. I pressed my forehead into his right shoulder as he moved himself deeper inside. His eyes closed. He took a deep breath, slowed, and searched for my face.

"Are you all right?" he asked.

"Yes." I smiled, tangled in his embrace.

"I love you," he said, then kissed me again. He pulled my hips into him and pushed himself deeper. I shut my eyes. My pelvis stretched and burned as he made his way further and further. I took deep breaths as he propelled himself in and out.

Vulnerable under his movements, I took a deep breath. "I need your mouth on mine. Kiss me."

He bent down with moist, warm lips and swept his tongue against mine. I sucked on his bottom lip. He moved faster. After a few more thrusts, he gently pinned my knees back for a better fit. My body relaxed, and our motions became rhythmic. With every thrust, he climbed deeper inside my body. Where I wanted him to remain, forever.

Instinctively, I grabbed at the muscles of his ass and pulled him further into me.

"Ohh," he grunted. His eyes rolled back in his head.

Our thighs clapped together as we moved back and forth, both of us working toward the finish. Sweat dripped off of his chest and onto my stomach. His eyes blazed with want, and his face became serious. All at once, his muscles tightened around me. Conjoined now, his body shook as he twitched inside.

After a few seconds, he took a deep breath, then fell into my arms. I held him as his heart pounded against my breasts.

"I will cherish you always," he whispered against my neck. "Everyting I have is yours, now and forever, including my heart and soul. *Ti amo, tu sei il mio sole. La luce che illumina la mia giornata e l'ancora nel mio universo,*" he muttered, then kissed me.

"You're all I'll ever want," I spoke through swollen lips and placed my hand on his heart. We held each other while we recovered from our lovemaking. Exhausted from all the rejoining and rejoicing, we crept into a blissful sleep, protected from a world that wanted nothing more than to tear us apart.

My eyes opened slowly. Moonlight enveloped the room, casting a warm glow onto my lover's skin. I rubbed my eyes to make sure I wasn't dreaming. Disoriented, I moved across the bed and put my hand on his arm. Unaffected, he slept deeply. His skin was soft and warm. We were blessed to have shared one of life's most sacred experiences together. How incredible it felt when he entered me and our bodies instinctively did the rest. It was in the moments of recovery that we expressed our love for one another—sweet sentiments felt by both. The whole act was nothing short of magical. I didn't think it was possible to love him more, but I did.

The guesthouse took on new meaning in the dark. Without sunlight, the only warmth was our body heat. The room was absent of sound but for the occasional gentle snore that escaped his lips. He looked so peaceful that I wanted to watch him forever. Lightly, I drew an invisible line along his rib cage down to the hairs around his navel. He woke to me staring at him. Wiping sleep from his eyes, he kissed me softly.

He stretched his arms above his head and yawned. Moonlight

reflected off the whites of his eyes, and he smiled my favorite crooked smile.

"Hello, *amore mio*. Sorry, I fell asleep."

"I hope I didn't wake you. I enjoyed watching you sleep. You look so peaceful."

"I am peaceful because you are here wit me."

"There's no place I'd rather be than right here with you."

"You are my sunlight. Like da grapes dat grow outside, dey need sunlight to help dem grow. Your sunlight is *vitale* for me. It help me live and grow. Da past few months, I feel so alone here. My heart is so lonely witout you."

My brain made the connection. "Is that why your emblem has a sunrise?"

"Yes. It's because of you. You are my sunlight. I love you."

I rubbed the back of my hand against the stubble on his cheek. "And I love you."

He bent his head over mine and kissed the skin above my heart.

"It's so dark out. What time is it?" he asked, then reached for his watch on the side table and sat up quickly. "*Minchia*," he blurted out. "It's already nine o'clock. How long have I been sleeping?"

"A few hours." I played with the waves of his hair on the top of his head. He put his head between my breasts as he adjusted the straps of his watch. We sat in silence as he pressed his ear to my chest and let my body speak to him.

"I hear your heart and your stomach," he said.

We both giggled. His head bobbed up and down on my chest, making us laugh harder.

"Are you hungry? I will go to the main house and bring us food."

"Yes. I haven't eaten anything since this morning."

He jumped out of bed, and his full frame came into view. I studied his manhood as he slid his pants over his backside.

He walked over toward the bed and stood in front of me. Cupping my face in his soft, smooth hands, he recited Shakespeare,

"*Da moon shines bright. In such a night as dis, When the sweet wind did gently kiss da trees, And dey did make no noise, in such a night.*"

"*Merchant of Venice.* You remembered? Well, if I'm the sun, then you, sir, are the wind." I sat up and kissed his bare-naked chest.

"How can I ever forget our days of poetry and Shakespeare?" He bent over and whispered in my ear, "Today was more incredible dan I ever imagined. You are beautiful, and I want you to know how much I cherish you, Violetta."

I sat up on my heels and kissed him intensely. He pulled away and laughed.

"I have to get da food. We need more energy for later," he said, then winked at me. He pulled the shirt over his head and made his way out the door.

The wind. My wind.

Sounds from my stomach interrupted my newfound tranquility. It must have been from the surge of emotions and physical activity. I was on the verge of lightheadedness, so I walked over to the bathroom and sipped some water from the faucet.

I flicked on lights around our love nest and put on a nightgown. I didn't see the point of putting clothes on when I wouldn't be in them for long. Rubbing my stomach, I went straight for the kitchen to find something to nibble on while Gaetano was away. The kitchen cabinets held stale soda crackers and dry spices. There were, however, basic kitchen supplies and a bottle of Sanna wine with a few wine glasses.

I found a bottle opener and popped open the bottle. I poured two glasses and smelled its fragrant and fruity bouquet. To avoid the effects of liquor on an empty stomach, I forced myself to bite one of the stale crackers. It crushed between my teeth, and I chased it with a sip of the wine.

Glass in hand, I went to the radio and fumbled with the dial to get a good signal. A Sinatra song enveloped the room. I stretched my legs out along the couch. My body melted to his velvety voice.

The song "Polka Dots and Moonbeams" transported me to our

time in the barn, where Gaetano told me he wanted to marry me. And today, I'd given myself to him completely. I stood, eyes closed, and swayed in the dim light. When I opened my eyes, I noticed a large painting hanging on the wall next to the table. I walked over and let my hand graze the artist's paint strokes. It was a rendition of Saint Peter's Basilica. I'd only seen it in magazines. It was beautiful—the colors vibrant and bold. As I studied the painting further, two strong hands pressed at my hips.

"Ello," Gaetano whispered in my ear and kissed my neck from behind.

"Hello . . ."

He turned me around.

"Is this Saint Peter's in Rome?"

"*Si.*"

"It's beautiful. Where did you get it?"

"Tank you. I painted it."

"Oh, Gaetano, it's beautiful."

"*Grazie.*" A slow smile tugged at the edges of his lips. "When we come to America, we stopped off at da Basilica. My fater wanted us to pray for a safe and healthy voyage." Gaetano's thumb glided over the faint brushstrokes. "It is a very special place for me. After what happened to my moter, my beliefs were tested, but when I stood in dat holy place, a feeling of warmth came over me, deep inside. It was someting I can't explain. Almost like magic, and I was restored."

"One day, I hope to visit Rome."

"One day, *amore mio*, I will take you," he whispered in my ear.

Ripples of heat flushed my body. I turned to face him. "That sounds wonderful. Dance with me," I urged while my groin pulsed.

He set my glass on the table. His arms around me, the lyrics carried us away to a place just for us. Cheek to cheek, our feet glided over the floor like mist in a forest, until the music stopped, and my stomach roared again.

I laughed. "Sorry. I need to eat something."

"Yes. Let's feed you, *bella*," He led me into the kitchen where he pulled the food from a brown paper sack.

"I brought a few tings from da house—bread, *formaggio*, and some *insalata*."

I held the fresh bread to my nose and inhaled. "Mmm . . . it smells delicious."

"*You* smell delicious." He breathed into my hair. His tongue glided down my neck.

"Stop," I said and batted his frisky hands away. "I need to eat, or I'll never be able to keep up with you tonight."

After a few bites of food and some soft kisses in a loving embrace, I sipped the wine. *His* wine.

"Do you like da vino?"

"Yes, it's wonderful." I took another sip.

He grabbed the bottle.

"Open your mouth," he said and stared at my lips with his smoldering eyes.

My heart fluttered in my chest. What was he going to put in my mouth? I nodded and then opened wide. With his left hand, he tilted my chin back and gently poured the wine down my throat. I tried to hold it all in my mouth, but a few drops fell out and onto my neck. I licked my lip. A few drips stained my nightgown. Gaetano set the bottle down on the counter and licked the drops of red wine off my chin and chest. Aroused again, his erection pressed against my leg.

He picked me up and carried me to the bedroom, where we shared another few hours of lovemaking. And in the time between animalistic desire and soft strokes of tenderness, we furthered our understanding of one another and surrendered our souls. He made me feel safe and provided me with a million miles of distance from the enemy. After months of loneliness, betrayal, and presumed reproach, I'd finally sleep tonight, in his arms, loved and accepted unconditionally.

Chapter 11

To Truly See a Man

I OPENED MY EYES TO A ROOM FILLED WITH SUNLIGHT. MOVING my tired legs around the bed, I quickly realized where I was, and a grin blanketed my face. When I turned to the other side of the bed, I found a note.

I went to the main house for more clothes and food. I will see you soon.

I have so much to show you today.

Love you,

-G

While I waited for the bathwater to warm, I studied myself in the mirror. My hair was disheveled and full of knots. It felt coarse from all the movement on top of the pillows. My eyes finally looked rested. Although my body looked no different than before, I was no longer a virgin. I didn't know how I felt about that, exactly.

I lowered myself in the tub and let the warm water soften my tired muscles. Was I a sinner? Had my actions disgraced my family or myself? Would I be called a *puttana*? My intentions were honorable. I'd come to be with the man I loved, and we were defenseless to our desires. As I stepped out of the tub, I stepped away from my self-judgment. I wouldn't let it ruin my time here. I threw on my robe, sat back in bed, and waited for *my Guy* to return.

The smell of coffee woke me a second time. Gaetano stood in the doorway with a coffee cup in hand.

"*Buongiorno*, my love," he whispered, then came over to hand me the cup.

I took a sip, then he pulled my chin up to meet his smiling face.

"Good morning. I must have dozed off again. I was pretty tired after yesterday." I wrapped my legs around his torso.

"Sorry I had to leave, but I had to check da workers and make sure everyting was on schedule."

"I understand. I knew you wouldn't leave me here all alone." I teased him by exposing my right breast. He giggled and kissed me again. "What did your parents say? Do they know I'm here?" I asked sheepishly, afraid of his answers.

"I try to get away, but my moter, she stopped me when she saw me grab da food. I told her not to tell my fater and dat I wanted to talk to him, man to man. So, I did."

"What did you say?"

"My fater is worried dat dis might cause problems for us, but I told him dat I love you and want to make you my wife."

"I never wanted to cause your family any problems, but I had to see you. Maybe I should go back?"

"No, I tell him I will take a full responsibility for you here."

"What about your mother? What did she say?"

"Violetta, please understand I am a grown man and make my own decisions. But she worry about me. Just like your family worry about you. She no like da Hand."

"My family only worries about themselves," I blurted.

"Das not true. We both know what *they* do. Even for my fater, he have to give dem our home. A house dat was in his family for many generations. We leave with nutting," he said with cold eyes. "Even now dey own us."

"Your mother will never accept me because of that. I should go." I looked at my bags on the floor.

"No. You are not leaving. Dey will have to accept you if dey want me in der lives. The only ting my fater say was he would not lie if your family ask. In a few days, we will speak wit dem so dey understand everyting."

"That's reasonable. Do your parents know that you slept here with me?" I asked, embarrassed.

"Dey no say anyting, and I no tell dem."

"What are we going to do today?"

"I want you to see da vineyard and meet da workers. Dey hard-working, good people. Sometimes when we work late, dey make Mexican food and barbecue late at night. Dey tell stories. Dey are my friends now. I know all of der children."

"Their whole families come here?"

"Oh yes. The moter and fater dey work and da *nonna* come to watch the kids here. Dey are all on contract. Most of da families live here to make it easier. Dey pay little for da room, and I make sure to pay dem a good wage."

"I want to meet them. They sound wonderful."

"Yes, I want every immigrant to have a chance at a good life here in America—like me. I make sure dey treat wit *rispetto*. I learn a lot from Mr. Antonelli last summer. He show me dat people work hard when dey work togeter."

There was a deep reverence in his voice for his workers. I heard the passion behind his words and the vision he had for his vineyard. I was in awe of him.

"When da time comes, you and I will go somewhere until tings calm down or until tings can be made right between da families. And when I tink it's safe, we will get married. It may not be a big ceremony, maybe at da courthouse. We can talk about it later. But today, *amore mio*, I want to show you what I have been doing here wit da wine business." He reached for my arm and kissed the back of my hand.

"I've seen my father make wine, but nothing like this."

"Let's eat breakfast and then you get dressed."

Gaetano started his tour at the workers' cabins. He introduced me to his right-hand man, José. He lent me a smock and a pair of work boots. Gaetano introduced me to all the workers as his *special friend*.

Despite the language barriers, they laughed and joked with each other and became serious when speaking about the job at hand. Gaetano listened, then tinkered with the machinery and checked the quality of the grapes. Like a natural-born leader, he asked their opinion, then made decisions. I was pleasantly surprised to see his transition from a man who worked in the fields at ole man Antonelli's to the future owner of this huge enterprise.

We drove to a big building in the center of the property where they made wine.

Men and women stood over thousands of grapes, pulling stems and leaves off the vines to get the grapes ready to be pressed. Conveyor belts moved the grapes into gigantic wooden vats. Men turned metal apparatuses to crush the grapes. Liquid poured into enormous wooden tubs. The process was in constant motion.

"So, when can we drink the juice? How long does it have to stay in there?"

"Da grapes will stay here for a few weeks. *Così il vino fermenterà. Come si dice* . . . ferment. Come here, I want to show you someting."

With pride in his smile, Gaetano grabbed my hand and escorted me down rocky steps into a sunken tunnel that led to a huge underground room. Streams of faint light crept through, exposing wall-to-wall oak barrels stacked on top of each other. The smell of wine filled the air, aromatic and fragrant.

Hand in hand, Gaetano walked me to where they siphoned wine from the barrel. He grabbed a glass and released a lever. A glorious, garnet liquid poured out.

"Let's walk toward da light so you can see."

He handed me the flute and held it to a beam of sunlight.

"Turn it like dis," he said, moving the red liquid around in the light. "See da little bits of *sedimento*. We will still do more filtering, but at least you can taste da flavor. Now smell it."

I put my nose inside the long-stemmed glass. Fruit tones mixed with oak swirled around my nose.

"*Salute*. Take a sip and hold it in your mouth like dis." He took a big gulp and swished it around his mouth a while before swallowing. "Now you try."

I took a sip, swirled it around my teeth and tongue, and swallowed.

"Do you taste da smell in your mouth and your nose?"

A sweet bouquet of fruit and musk lingered as it coated my mouth and throat. "Yes, it's wonderful."

"I am glad you like it." He pulled me into his arms to kiss me. Our lips met again, fierce with desire. We tasted each other. When we finally pulled away to catch our breath, he clutched my hips and flashed a suggestive grin.

"Da vino, it taste good, but you taste better." He scanned my body from head to toe. When he met my eyes, his strong hands gripped my ass, followed by a flirtatious wink. The small gesture promised a wonderful day and night.

After seeing the production line, we strolled the property. He took me out to the orchards where we touched grapes still ripening in the sun.

"You know da first people who come here have many struggles. Everyting from insect infestation to prohibition and the Depression.

Many of dem have to abandon der land and start over. Only recently has dis community produced again." He rolled a grape between his fingers.

"I had no idea it was so hard on these people. I know my family struggled during the Depression, even with Don Molanano's help."

His eyes narrowed, then he looked over the land toward the horizon. "We are part of a group of new families determined to make dis work. And one day, as da business get bigger, I plan to build a hotel here and maybe a restaurant too, to attract more guests. I have so many plans for dis place." He threw the grape across the field in front of us.

"A hotel? That's amazing." The slightest twinge squeezed my stomach. If they came for me, how could I ask him to run away with me when his life and his dreams were right in front of us?

"*Si*. I learn so much in da past few months, and I see da company growing.

"I can see that even your English is improving," I said with a smile.

"Yes. Some words are still hard, but I have been practicing every day. I want to be a smart man for you," he said, then smiled. "When it is time, I want us to have a life here, Violetta. I want you to live here wit me and be part of my dreams. Our children can play in da fields. Let me give you da life you deserve." He pulled my body into his frame.

"It's beautiful here. I can't deny that," I said. "I've never lived anywhere but the ranch, and for once, it's *my* choice to stay here with you." I turned away as the wind ruffled through my hair.

"It will be *our* choice, *tesoro mio*," he said with loving eyes.

When I turned back, Gaetano was on his knees.

"Violetta Giordano, I will love you for da rest of my days. I promise to cherish you and take care of you until my last breath. Will you please marry me?" he asked, then reached for my hand. "I don't have a ring yet, but I promise you, I will give you da biggest ring I can find dat will match da size of my love for you." He kissed the back of my hand and waited for my response.

"If my decision means anything in this world, then my answer is yes. Yes, I will marry you," I said and reached for him as tears streamed down my face.

With dusty knees, he stood and kissed me strong and deep.

We spent the rest of the afternoon looking over the land. He continued to talk about our future life. With the vineyards at his back, he looked like a proud king standing over his kingdom. Gaetano was no longer an immigrant boy; he was a powerful man who would someday run an empire. He was assertive and intelligent about his craft. His words exemplified the spirit of a man who was driven and bold, all the qualities I wanted in a husband. And although he may have to conform to the Mafia in the future, clean and honest work motivated him. He was everything I wanted for the rest of my life, but what I wanted and what my father wanted were two very different things.

Chapter 12
The Weight of Freewill

THE DAYS WITH GAETANO IN THE VINEYARD FELT MAGICAL. They were everything I'd hoped for. We drank great wine and ate great food. In quiet moments, we'd sneak away to make love. After, we'd talk about the life we wanted together. Our words made our hearts converge and, without further thought, we'd be intimate again.

As we lay naked in bed, Gaetano suckled my breasts, then said, "Tonight, we go to a party in your honor."

"A party. With your parents?"

"No. José and his family want to cook for us. But we can't avoid my family much longer. We will talk to dem, together." He swept the hair from my eyes.

"I'm nervous, Gaetano. I don't want to cause any harm. I'm surprised we haven't seen them in all these days." My chest tightened.

"My fater, he getting older. He trusts me to run tings and spends most of his day listening to da radio. He like da American baseball." Gaetano laughed. "And my moter and sisters, dey no come out in da fields. With a hundred acres, we have all the privacy we need—at least for a little while." He sucked on my nipple again.

"Yes, there is nothing but grape trees for miles." I twisted my fingers into his soft hair.

"Sometimes when I stay out here, I no see my parents for days."

"You're lucky. If I was gone for that long, my family would come searching for me. In fact, I know they would because they've done it."

"What do you mean?" he asked, puzzled.

"You know, it's strange. Up until this week, I've always considered the ranch to be my safe place after what happened, but I feel secure here too," I said as an old, dark memory crept up. "I was abducted when I was a kid."

His face looked startled. "What is abducted?"

"It means someone took me away from my family when I was a little girl."

"What happened?" he asked as his eyes scanned my face.

"I wasn't more than seven or eight years old. Old enough to remember. I was at Antonelli's when my mother and father picked prunes. Because I was too small to be of any use, I was in the way a lot." The memory made the words sting as they came out. "My mother told me to go and play somewhere else. So, I wandered off . . ."

"Where did you go?"

"I must have walked a good mile or two when I saw small patches of strawberries growing alongside the road. So naturally, I picked them and ate them as I walked farther and farther away. An older man stood in front of another farmhouse. He approached me. With broken English, he said that he had larger, sweeter strawberries in the back. I followed him. When I got there, he asked me if I was thirsty, and because it was hot, I said yes. He handed me a glass of water. I remember that it tasted funny, but it was so hot, I drank it. The next thing I knew, I woke up in a strange room. They'd locked me in and shut the curtains."

Latent memories choked me up.

Gaetano kissed the frown lines between my eyes. "Violetta, you don't have to tell me anymore if you don't want."

"No. I'm all right. I haven't talked about it in a long time," I mumbled with a clogged-up throat. "My father said I was there for two days before they found me. The room got cold and dark when the sun went down. There were no lights. I'd scream for my mother."

Gaetano lifted his head from my chest and peered at me with his soft, dreamy eyes.

"A strange woman took me out only once to go to the bathroom. She spoke in a language I couldn't understand. Then she fed me a piece of bread and more of the sour water. I begged her to get my mother, and she laughed at me. I don't remember clearly because my father believes that whatever they'd put in that water drugged me. I remember being so cold and missing my home and family." I shivered.

Gaetano pulled the sheets over us and laid his head on my chest to warm me.

"By the second day, I banged on the window and door so hard my hands hurt. I tried to scream so someone would hear me. When I got too loud, the woman came in and slapped me across the face to quiet me down. Then she gave me more water, and I fell back to sleep."

My palm glided over the soft white sheets that grazed the top of my thigh.

"It wasn't until sunrise on the third day, when the mayor and my father showed up with the sheriff. I ran into my father's arms. My dad told the man he'd be sorry for what he'd done to me."

"*Amore mio*, I so sorry." He grabbed my hand and wove his fingers with mine.

"When I came home, I threw up all over my mother. My father said I looked white as a sheet and that I didn't talk for a few days. My mother held me in her rocking chair that afternoon to calm me. She sang to me. The wind tickled my arms and helped me fall asleep, safe again in my home."

"Did dey put dat man in jail?"

"No. He told the authorities that I'd wandered onto his property and that he intended to turn me over the next morning but had no phone line on the property and his truck had engine trouble. It was the trail of half-eaten strawberries on the side of the road that helped my father find me. With the help of the Molanano family, my father took the law into his hands. The man and his family were never found again."

Gaetano's eyes were wide from my admission. "I cannot believe it." He pulled his hand from mine and brushed leftover tears from my cheeks.

"There was a big write-up in the newspaper about it."

"I will never let anyone hurt you," he whispered, then wrapped me up in his arms.

"I know you won't." I turned to kiss him. "I learned that it wasn't the ranch that made me safe but the people. That was the day I made friends with the wind and vowed to never eat another strawberry. It's a good thing I still like grapes," I said with a faint laugh.

"Si it is a good ting." He became silent. His gaze held onto me.

"Years later, I realized the power of the Mafia. They made people disappear. And as much as that scared me, they'd saved me. So, with my newfound appreciation, the ranch and everyone in it became my safe place. That's why I'm so hurt by my father. All this time, he's done nothing but provide for me and take care of me by any means possible. But when he approached me about Frank, he betrayed my trust in him. He didn't listen to my needs about you. He didn't care."

"He loves you."

"Love has nothing to do with it," I said with an icy tone. My father's face burned into my mind's eye. "Let's talk about something else."

"We no have to go to da dinner party if you don't want. I'm fine to stay right in here in dis bed wit you." He wrapped his arm around me. "When you tell me dis, I tink you are like my sisters when da men come to my house and how scared dey were. You were so little, so helpless. I wish I could have protected all of you." His eyes narrowed, and his voice trailed. He gently lay back on top of me. His body shielded me from the dark memory. His heart beat against my breasts as he breathed into my hair.

"I'm fine. Honest."

"Are you sure, Violetta?" he said with a pained gaze, then rolled back over onto the pillow.

"Yes, I'm sure. In your arms, all of it melts away." I cleared my throat. "Tell me about this party you're taking me to."

"I tink you will like it. I love playing with da children. Dey are so funny, and da food is very good. It's different and spicy."

"Sounds delicious," I said, blinking away the dark memory." I closed my eyes and nestled my head into the crook of his neck, where the sound of his gentle breath soothed me.

After a few hours in bed, we dressed and drove to the workers' cabins, where many people greeted us. José introduced me to his nine-member family. With smiling faces and laughter, the children grabbed me by the hand to jump rope with them. I played while Gaetano looked at us and grinned. I motioned him over to jump rope.

"You ready?" I asked.

"*Si.*"

I held one end of the rope and José's daughter, Esperanza, grabbed the other, while Gaetano jumped.

"We are gonna go faster now," I yelled and smiled at the girl. With a flick of our wrists, we twirled the rope around in circles. Gaetano kept up for a while, then stopped, out of breath.

"What's the matter? You can't be tired already," I teased.

"*Amore mio,*" he said, lightly panting and laughing, "you know why I tired." He winked. "You don't want me to waste all my energy

jumping dis rope, do you? I don't want to fall asleep on you tonight."
He planted a soft kiss on my lips.

"No. We wouldn't want that, would we?" I teased with seductive eyes.

Gaetano and I sat on chairs by the firepit. Children sat beside us. Girls played with my hair, and the boys teased Gaetano. He was so wonderful with kids. He'd be a great father someday. An overwhelming feeling of warmth came over me.

"*Señor*, es time to eat." José handed us plates.

With the smell of smoke from the firepit and the various spices in the air, the women served us authentic Mexican dishes. I thanked them all for the meal and their hospitality. The children got up to play.

"*Señorita* Violetta," José spoke up. "I so happy to be here. *Señor* Sanna, he good man. He help me and my family. We have a home here. It is"—he struggled to find the right words—"so hard in Mexico."

"I think he's pretty great too." I reached for Gaetano's palm. He smiled at me with my favorite crooked smile and kissed the back of my hand. I saw why Guy needed to help them. They *were* him, not long ago. He wanted to provide a place for these families to work and live, as Antonelli had done for his family.

José said, "Esperanza say you beautiful." He smiled at his daughter.

"Thank you. *Gracias*." I tried to roll the R sound in my mouth. "Esperanza—what a pretty name," I said to the young woman.

"In Spanish, it means hope," José said, looking proudly at his daughter.

"How beautiful," I said. The young girl appeared to be in her mid-teens. She had long, black, velvety hair that cascaded down her back. Already taller than her father, she had his almond-shaped eyes. She peered at me, then looked over my shoulder at Gaetano. Her eyes studied my face.

"Esperanza, this a *Señor* Sanna's friend, Violetta."

"Hello. Nice to meet you." I held out my hand to her.

The girl slowly shook my hand. Her grip was firm.

Gaetano kissed my cheek and wrapped his arms around me from behind.

"So, you meet Espi?" Gaetano said with his head hanging over my shoulder.

"Espi?" I asked.

"Yes, dat is what we call her around here. Right, Espi?" Gaetano asked.

Her eyes widened again, staring at Gaetano and me. She took a deep breath and walked away.

"She's beautiful, José," I said. "Pretty soon you'll have to fight men off with a stick."

We all shared a laugh.

Gaetano turned me around and hugged me tightly. "Have I told you today dat I love you?" His words tickled my ears and sent shivers down my spine.

"You've mentioned it once or twice," I said, then giggled into his neck.

Everyone smiled. I hadn't seen so many happy people in a crowd since my graduation, and it felt good.

"Let's go sit by da fire. It will be cold soon," Gaetano said.

While we sat in the light of the fire, José said, "Look at my children. They so happy here."

The children played in the fields.

"You are a good man, José. Tank you for all your help. You are a part of my family now. You will always have a place here wit us," Gaetano said, then reached out to shake José's hand.

"You ever drink tequila, *Señorita*?" José asked me.

"Tequila?"

"I go get so you taste. We always drink wine, but tonight we celebrate like Mexicanos," he said with pride, then went to get the bottle of liquor.

"I'm glad you brought me here tonight. Your friendship with

them is wonderful. José's daughter is beautiful. If I didn't know better, I'd say she has a crush on you," I teased.

"Why you say dat?"

"The way she looks at you. I should know. That's how I looked at you when I first met you that day at Antonelli's. It's the way I still look at you." I turned to cup his face in my hands.

"I only have eyes for you," he said, then kissed me softly. "José is loyal to me. He understands. When the Molanano men come here for da money, he says dey have much experience wit men like dat in Mexico because da drugs and da poppy. Dey are no strangers to it." His upper lip twisted in disgust.

"I understand your anger, but you wouldn't have all of this if it wasn't for them. Like I told Tony, no matter how much we try to do things legitimately on our own, somehow they find ways to control everything."

"Dat was my fater's decision. I hate to give dem money we work so hard for. Dey are thieves." He spat at the ground.

"Those *thieves* saved my life, Gaetano."

"Come here," he said and motioned me over to sit with him.

I sat on his lap. With the warm fire that burned bright in front of us, he wrapped his arms around me and kissed under my ear.

"I mean no disrespect," he whispered in my ear. "You and I, we have different experience wit *Cosa Nostra*. As much as I hate dem, for what dey did to my family, dey save your life."

"I love you." I stared at the starry sky. In the dark above, I prayed Gaetano would make peace with all of it and accept me for who I was. I didn't want to have to choose between my family or him. Some wounds ran deep.

To numb my worry, I drank tequila with Gaetano and José. We sang songs in Spanish around the fire. I felt like part of a new family. I had a place here. These last few days, Gaetano made me feel like I was his true partner. He'd shared his plans for the vineyard with me and because he valued my opinion, he asked where he should put the swimming pool and how big the hotel should be. We'd gone around the grounds with our hands in the shape of a camera, imagining his vision. I'd provided my input, and he'd listened. My opinion mattered to him. Here, my voice was heard. Most of all, he showed me how much he loved me and how a man looks at a woman when he surrenders his heart to her for safekeeping.

As much as I wanted to keep his heart safe, I couldn't stop thinking what Frank would do if he discovered I was here. The whole thing made my stomach hurt.

Frank.

I'd almost forgot about him, yet how could I? As terrible thoughts bounced around in my head, I shelved them all and focused on being in Guy's arms. Alcohol took care of the rest.

After a few days of following Gaetano around during the day and lying with him at night, I was in my restful bubble, miles away from reality, perfectly content. Then Gaetano mentioned it was time to speak with his parents.

"My fater says he want to talk to us. We going der for dinner. It's time, *amore mio*, to explain everyting to dem."

Once his words were out, muscles in my neck and throat constricted. "As long as you're with me, I'm ready."

We walked hand in hand, as a united front, into the grand kitchen where his mother and sisters sat at one end of the table. With a fluttering heart, I avoided eye contact with *Signora* Sanna. Gaetano ushered us to the middle of the table where we sat together. I looked down at my plate of homemade pasta and gripped Gaetano's hand under the table. As much as the food looked appealing, I'd lost my appetite. My mouth was dry. With a shaky hand, I sipped some water.

Signora Sanna sat at the table.

"Gaetano, you mussa return her at once. Her Papa calla here dis morning. I no lie. She hasa go back," *Signor* Sanna demanded.

My heart sank at his angry words. Gaetano squeezed my hand and looked at his father.

"I don't care. Violetta no leave. We are in love. I will marry her. She no love da man she is supposed to marry. She say he is a bad man, a killer. How can I bring her back to dem, Papa? I will not," he shouted and threw his cloth napkin beside his plate.

I grabbed at his arm.

His father stood. "I willna have your mama terrorize again. Itsa bad enough dat dey will get our money and soma of our land to do as dey wish. I willa no have dem coma here to hurt us. She hasa go back, and das it," he ordered.

"She will not," Gaetano protested. "We are getting married, and if she can't be here, den I will leave wit her. I will walk away from all da headaches—all of it. I will not let dem keep taking everyting I love. No more. You can do as dey bid, but not me," he fired back.

While the two men challenged each other for control, I glanced over at Gaetano's mother. Tears flooded her eyes. Her arms wrapped around her daughters, and her body shook as she held on to the girls.

She had suffered enough for one lifetime.

No harm would come to her, or any of them. I wouldn't allow it. I shot her an apologetic stare when Gaetano grabbed my hand. We stormed out of the room, leaving our untouched food and his family in tears.

Back at the guesthouse, Gaetano paced the room. He swore in Italian and swung his fists around, denouncing his father and the Mafia. To get a moment alone from all the yelling, I retreated back to the bedroom. I stepped out of my shoes and lay on the bed. The room took on new meaning.

It was no longer our private romantic space filled with love and promising sentiment. It was the last place Gaetano and I would be together.

He stormed in after me and said, "We will leave tomorrow. I have enough money to get us far away from here. We will find a place where dey never find us—a safe place dat you need."

I took a deep breath and shut my eyes. Mentally paralyzed from the pictures of his mother's face, I mustered the courage to respond.

"They'd find us," I whispered.

"Dey no find us," he said as he unbuttoned his shirt.

"Yes, they will. Look at you. You came here to America hoping to get as far away from them as possible; yet when you arrived, you came under their thumb, like the rest of us. We will never run far enough or fast enough."

"*Bastardi*," he yelled with his hands in fists.

"I've been here a week, and I've loved every moment with you. And for the first time that I can remember, I saw myself living here with you on this beautiful land, surrounded by the love I've felt over the last few days. I felt at home, until I saw your mother's face tonight. She'll never accept me." My heart sank into my stomach.

"I love my moter, but she does not run my life. I am a man and will be treated like one," he said firmly.

"My father will search for me to the ends of the earth because of what my marriage means for my family's survival. Even if he gave us his blessing, there's too much at stake. Don Molanano would take that as a sign of disloyalty. There might be a war. No one will die, including my father, because of me," I said with quivering lips. "And Frank would murder all of you without a thought."

Gaetano swallowed my words down like sour medicine.

"He's ruthless."

Gaetano's nostrils flared. "Don't be scared. I will protect you from *him*."

"Don't you understand? They'll come for me, like when I was younger. I'm the daughter of someone connected to this life. I can't let them hurt you. I love you too much," I said with a shaky voice.

"We leave. Start over. Please . . ."

"No. I can't do that to you and your family. You just started a life here. I can't pull you away from all of this. People depend on you for their survival," I said, thinking of all the families I'd met this week.

"Tomorrow we leave. I will not let dem take any more from

me," he said with an edge in his voice. "Now let's go to bed. We have an early morning."

I replayed all possible outcomes in my mind. They all led back to one thought—pain, both physical and emotional, no matter what we did.

Sometime in the middle of the night, we made love. We were both exhausted, but we needed the release to help us relax from such an emotional day. After his final thrust, he collapsed next to me and fell asleep. His heavy arm lay against my chest.

With news of my father's call and the heat of summer filling the room, I couldn't sleep. I tiptoed into the living room and opened a window. The breeze cooled my heated skin.

My mind and heart made the connections. Was it a sign, or something to bring me back to reality? Wind that touched my body had made itself known. He was my wind. My symbol of safety. How could I ever put him in any danger?

I couldn't.

I'd leave and make the ultimate sacrifice to spare him. The world needed people like him. Sneaking out before dawn was the only way. Gaetano would never let me go. I needed to be the mind of reason here. We had devoted our hearts and bodies to each other, and he would defend me ferociously. I wouldn't allow him to do anything that would get him, or his family, killed.

José was my only way out. I'd make up a lie to get him to drive me to the bus station. I'd write Guy a letter to tell him my reasons for leaving and that this would be the last time I'd ever communicate with him. I hoped he'd find it in his heart to forgive me someday. Until then, I'd protect him.

With quiet, shaking hands, I searched for a pen and paper. In the bathroom, I locked the door. On the cold tile floor, alone with my thoughts, I wrote.

Gaetano,

With a heavy heart, I want you to know how much I love you and how much this week has meant to me. These past days were magical. From the loving things you said to me in the moonlight of our bed to the way you laughed through my favorite crooked smile, you blanketed me in tenderness and love. Thank you for sharing your life with me and making me feel part of it.

As much as it pains me to write this, I must go back. I would never be able to live with myself if anything were to happen to any of you. You deserve an exceptional life. One that you can be proud of, and one that is free from pain.

I realize now that our destinies lie on different paths. As much as I've tried to ignore it, I can't escape who I am and the family I've been born into.

I'm grateful for every memory we've ever shared. I'll never forget you and will love you always. Every day that the wind dances in the sun, I will think of you.

Do not come after me, or I will deny everything to protect you. If anyone were to find out, I don't know what Frank would do. If you love me, you'll move on with your life. I'm sorry for any pain I've caused you and your family. I hope one day you'll understand why I had to leave, and that you'll forgive me.

Please know that you are the only man to possess my soul. My answer will always be YES, but it's no longer up to me, and I know that now.

I leave here without a heart-
May God bless you and protect you,
Vi

I folded the note and placed it on the kitchen table. I climbed into bed and held him in my arms one last time.

⌣

I rose before the sun. Because I didn't want to wake Gaetano, I quietly slid on my dress and grabbed my bags and shoes. I blew him one last kiss and walked out the door. I made my way toward the workers' cabins. Walking fast in the early morning light, I held back tears so my emotions wouldn't alarm José. I found him loading equipment into his truck.

"Hello, José."

"*Hola*," he said with wide eyes. "Is everything okay with *Señor* Sanna?"

"Gaetano woke up sick today. I told him to stay warm in bed and rest. I think he has a small fever. He wanted a favor. I need to be on the first bus because my father is expecting me later this afternoon. Will you please drive me to the bus station?"

"*Si*, I can take you. Are you sure he okay?" he asked with one eyebrow cocked.

"He's fine. Maybe a cold from being outside when we drank all that smooth tequila of yours."

"You like it?"

"Oh yes, it was wonderful," I said, then looked down at my watch.

"Okay, I get the keys," he said.

While José went to get his keys, the sun rose over the horizon, warming everything in its path. Rays of light gave the land the life it needed; but for my life, there'd only be darkness.

Chapter 13

Standing on the Edge of a Knife

THE RIDE HOME TO THE RANCH WAS BRUTAL. AS THE BUS DROVE along the highway, thoughts of ending my life plagued my mind. Visions of my mother's body over my casket and her grieving face stopped me. I knew how it felt to lose someone you love, and I couldn't put her through that kind of misery. If I counted on anything, I'd be back in Gaetano's arms in heaven where I'd answer only to God—not the Mafia.

There was stillness in my world where no wind would ever rustle my soul again. My only peace of mind came in knowing that I'd saved everyone from danger.

When I arrived at the train station, I called the house for someone to pick me up.

"Tony, it's Vi. Can you come get me? I'm at the train station downtown."

"Jesus, Vi, you got everyone worried sick over here. Where you been?"

"We can talk later. Just come and get me."

"All right. It's a good thing it's me who answered this phone. Pop is ready to tan your ass."

"Yeah, I know," I said, then hung up the pay phone.

I came in the door with my head held low, waiting for the interrogation. Pop grabbed his belt off his pants and hit me across the butt. I'd been smacked with the strap before, but this time there was a lot more force than usual.

"Ouch, stop. Please," I screamed back.

"What da hella were you tinking? We worry alla night for you," he exclaimed as he went in for another blow.

Trying to dodge his advances, I hid behind Mama who, like Pop, stood screaming at me too.

"You wit dat boy? You disgrace da family. If da Molanano find out they a gonna tink you *una puttana*. It willa ruin all my plans," he scolded. "You tink I a *stunad*. I no stupid. We see Julia's moter at da church dis Sunday. She say she dona know where you are. But Julia coma here and pick you up. You lie to us." Pop's eyes blazed.

I sat on the couch, hands covering my face, and sobbed.

"Papa, please, I needed to see him one last time. I didn't sleep in the same room as him. I slept in their guesthouse. *Signor* Sanna didn't even know I was there," I said to cover any potential problems for *Signor* Sanna. "He doesn't want any bad blood between our families."

"Did dat boy tell you to coma der?"

"No, it was my idea," I said defiantly.

For the rest of the afternoon, I explained everything, except for the part that I'd slept with Gaetano. I didn't want to break Pop's heart. Another part of me thought, if I'd told them I'd had sex with Gaetano, I'd be free from Frank, for good. Frank would never take me, knowing I'd been with another man. But Frank's Sicilian ego wouldn't allow Gaetano to get away with it. He'd make him pay. Not to mention that it would cause a huge rift between my family and the Molanano family. The Molananos would take it as a breach of contract and the lines of loyalty would be drawn. If that happened, my family's safety would be in jeopardy, and all of this would have been for nothing.

"You no speaka about dis, you a hear me?" Pop commanded. "We have a lie to da Molanano family. To Di Natale. Now looka what you do. Der were rumors about you. Even you brother Tony, he lie for you. You canno tell no one what happened. You hear me?"

"Yes. I understand."

"Now you listena me. You gonna get married to da Di Natale boy and das it," he said as he smacked his belt down on the coffee table one last time before putting it back on.

I grabbed my bag and went straight to my room. When I came in, Carmela was on the bed.

"Sorry, Vi. I tried to lie for you," she said with concern.

"Thanks," I said as tears made themselves known again. "It's not your fault."

I confided everything to my sister. She knew I'd have to marry someone I didn't love. It felt cruel and unfair, but with my sacrifice, I'd saved my family and the Sanna family from danger. I held on to my sister and wailed into her arms for what felt like an eternity.

Drained from a week's worth of tears, I moped around the house with a red nose and an empty heart. I had no hunger for life and no desire for meaningless conversation. The night before my wedding, and I wanted nothing more than to be alone. I needed a place to grieve without being questioned.

As I walked around my room, looking at old pictures on the walls, I realized this was my last night here. Tomorrow, I'd be married and would leave my childhood behind. There were so many memories of my time with Carm in this room—from the tiny desk that sat in the corner where we studied as schoolgirls, to our bed where we shared secrets. The room represented my youth. Living with Frank, despite being close by, felt like I'd be miles away.

Everything about tomorrow was a lie. I'd block it all out of my mind and wait for it to be over. Then would come the hard part: being the wife of a gangster. My desperate feelings drove me to an all too familiar place—the deep, dark abyss. A place where happiness doesn't exist but where sleep is welcomed to shut off the pain. So, I lay back in bed, closed my eyes, and fell into darkness.

At two in the morning, I pulled back the drapes. Frank and Tony stood around, drinking with a group of wise guys in the back. One guy had the nerve to shoot his gun in the air.

The windows rattled.

"What the hell are they doing anyway? We have a wedding tomorrow," Carmela muttered, then turned over in bed.

"Acting stupid. You know Frank. Any excuse to party," I said and rolled my eyes. I cracked the window and yelled, "*Basta*. Shut up! We gotta get up early in the morning. What the hell are you guys doing out there? You're being so loud, Pop's gonna get mad."

"Oh yeah?" Frank yelled, then threw a beer bottle against the side of the house.

Shards of glass ricocheted off the window. Spray splashed my face.

"You tell him to come outside and say somethin' to me about the noise. I'll make as much God damn noise as I want."

"That's it. I'm going out there." I slammed the window shut and marched outside.

One step off the back porch, Frank charged at me, stinking of liquor. His eyes took me in the way an animal examines prey. He grabbed me by the shoulders and shoved me up against the back door. Hinges snapped. Frank put one hand around my throat and, with the other, he pointed in my face.

"Hey, you listen to me. I heard that when we were gone, you were out whoring around town. Is it true?" he asked, slurring his words.

I tried to push his hand off my neck, but the attempt only tightened his grip. "I don't know what you're talking about. I spent time with a friend," I said, trying to get the words out from under his hold.

His eyes burned with rage. His foul-smelling saliva pelted my face. "If I find out that you let anyone touch my property, I will fuckin' kill you and them. *Capeesh*? Nobody makes a fool out of Frank Di Natale. You got that?"

He reached under my nightgown and grabbed my crotch.

"Get your hands off me." I spat at him. "We're not married yet, you pig."

With all his body weight, Frank crushed me against the door and shoved his fingers inside me. I tried to fight him, but he was strong. After a few tugs, he whispered, "Nice and ripe just like I like 'em. Wet too. You like that, huh?" He pulled out his hand and smelled his fingers. "Mmm . . ." His eyes rolled back in his head.

I fought off the urge to vomit. It was the most disgusting thing I'd ever seen.

"What the fuck you doing to my sister?" Tony shouted, then ripped Frank off of me. With Frank's shirt twisted in his hands, Tony, a good six-foot-two, towered over Frank. "Don't you *ever* touch my sister like that again, or we'll have a problem."

Frank put his hands down. Just as Tony let him go, Frank produced a knife and stuck it to Tony's throat. "Mind your fucking business, boy. You hear me?" Frank said through clenched teeth. "This ain't none of your concern. By morning, she'll be my wife, and I'll do whatever the fuck I want with her, you hear me?"

"Yeah, yeah, all right, calm down, Frank," Tony said as he fought for footing. "Jesus Christ, man, you're drunk." Tony gripped Frank's hand to prevent him from slicing his throat.

Frank laughed and pulled the knife away from Tony's throat. "I'm the new boss of this family. If it wasn't for the Molanano family and my father, you people wouldn't have a God damn thing. Remember that." Frank spat at Tony's feet. He swayed from the effects of the alcohol and slid the knife back into his pocket. "Make no mistake, with this marriage, my family owns the Giordano family. And if you love your pop like I think you do, you'd best remember who I am."

Papa stormed out with his gun. "*Che cazzo*? What da hell isa goin' on here? We sleepin', and we hear a gun. Tell dis guys itsa time to go home," my father ordered. "Whatsa matter you, Franco? Itsa you wedding tomorra."

"My apologies, Giuseppe. We're just having fun, right, Tony?" he said and laughed a phony laugh.

"Yeah, sure. A lot of fun," Tony said under his breath, then shook his head, avoiding Pop's stare.

"Everybody, go to bed." Pop went inside and slammed the door behind him.

Tony pushed his way past me and punched a hole in the side of the house. I wondered if he would tell my father what happened.

I shook my head at Frank.

He laughed and stumbled. His body swayed. "I'm sorry. Don't be mad, doll. We were kidding around."

"You disgust me." I turned on my heels and locked the back door.

As I walked to my bedroom, I heard Frank scream into the black night air, "Disgusting, huh? A pig, you say? You stupid bitch. I'm the best man you'll ever have. Even your father thought so, and that's all that matters now. Soon, I'll be runnin' things. You guys are all hicks up here. I'm living with a bunch of hillbillies and pigs. Ain't that right? Here piggy, piggy."

I crawled back in bed and listened to Carmela snore as adrenaline coursed through my frail body, leaving me limp and nauseated. Most brides are excited the night before their wedding, but I was scared out of my mind. This was the first real glimpse I'd seen of Frank's abusive behavior. I never thought I would ever let a man lay a hand on me. Would I be strong enough to protect myself from him?

Chapter 14

Mafia Queen

East San Jose Foothills, Giordano Estate
December 2002
Barbara

THE SMELL OF PINE AND TREE WAX STUNG MY NOSE THE MO-
ment I walked into the house.

Oh no. What did Ms. G. do now?

I threw my medical bag on the table and rushed to the sound of
the television. In the living room stood one of the biggest Christmas
trees I'd ever seen. The top was bent up against the ceiling.

"Nice of you to finally show up today," said Ms. G. as she stood,
admiring her tree.

I peered down at my watch. "I'm five minutes early."

"Not according to my watch," she said, then crossed her arms.

"This is the kind of tree you see in a bank, not a house. How'd
you get it in here?"

"My nephew works at a tree lot downtown. Poor kid just got

out of prison. This is the only kind of job he can get now, so I made a call and, well, here it is. Isn't it beautiful?" She stroked one of the branches.

"Well, it looks healthy. Not at all dry," I said, inspecting the needles. "But did you have to get the biggest one on the lot?"

"My father used to get the biggest tree, so I figured I'd do the same. Besides, this is the first time in a while that I've wanted to decorate a tree. Plus, I got you to help me decorate the damn thing, so let's get started."

"You know the protocol. I have to examine you first." I reached into my medical bag for my stethoscope.

"I'm fine. Can't you see I'm fine?"

"You look great, but I still have to check you out. That's my job."

I listened to her heart, a heart that had been broken so many years ago and thought about all she'd told me and how strong she'd been. Would I have the strength to walk away from someone I loved? From what Ms. G. told me about Frank, it seemed as though our stories were more similar than I'd first thought. I looked up at her and smiled.

She pulled the stethoscope up to her mouth and spoke loudly into it. "You done yet? I told ya I'm fine."

"Yes. Things sound pretty good today." I pulled the stethoscope from my ears with a smirk on my face.

Today. With Christmas approaching, I realized I'd been here every day for almost three months. I remembered how unbearable my first few days had been. Her constant nasty tone and demands made me want to quit. I wasn't sure if it was fear of her family or her stories that made me stay, but when I looked at her now, she was different. Her stories endeared me to her.

"Hey, you okay, kid? You look all *googly*-eyed. Time to do the damn tree," she said, then tried to undo the blood pressure cuff.

Nope. I was wrong. Still as feisty as ever.

"Let's get started," I said. "Dear Jesus, please help me," I added with a whisper and grabbed for the St. Christopher's medal that hung around my neck. "Do you have a ladder? There's no way I can get the angel up there without one."

"Yeah, in the garage."

I went to the garage and flipped on the light switch. I'd never been in there before. An old red Cadillac sat partly covered with a dusty sheet. Looked like it hadn't been driven in years. Likely, since her license had been taken away.

My leg bumped into an old desk and knocked papers on the floor.

Damn. Another bruise. All I needed.

I rubbed the sting from my leg and bent over to pick up the dusty pages—medical notes for a patient named Caruso, signed G.G.

My curious mind got the best of me, and I poked around the desk drawers. Not sure what I hoped to find, but from what Ms. G. told me about this house, I never knew what I might come across.

I found old business cards. After brushing off little bits of dust, I read,

Giuseppe Giordano, Masseuse, Giordano Horse Racing and Breeding

I ran my hands through the cards and found another one.

The next one read: *Violetta Di Natale, Medical Assistant & Bookkeeper*

As I continued to snoop, I came upon a leather medical bag. Inside was an old-fashioned stethoscope, a few tarnished scalpels and retractors, and various other medical tools. Mr. Giordano had done his fair share of surgeries in his time.

I put the instruments back into the bag and shut the desk drawers. I knew Ms. G. pretty well. If I didn't come up with that ladder soon, she'd start complaining, so I continued my search.

Because she kept everything, the garage was hard to maneuver around. I contorted my body between the car and the carpentry table along the far wall. An antique shotgun hung on rusty metal hooks. Too afraid to take it down, I stroked the tarnished, cold metal barrel. I wondered if this was the same shotgun her mother once carried around the property.

"What in the hell is taking you so damn long?" Ms. G. yelled from the doorway. "It's right over there, see it? Right there in front of the old washboard," she said as she pointed to a dark corner of the garage.

I slid my body around the tight space between the car and the wall and walked where she was pointing. A wooden ladder lay on its side, next to a few cans of paint and an antique washboard. I pulled out the ladder, taking care not to hit her car.

"You know the tree ain't going to decorate itself. Oh yeah, you see that big box right there—the one with the old paint sheets around it? We need that too."

"Which one?"

"See that box? It says *Xmas*. You know how to read, don't cha? Yeah, that one with all the lights and ornaments in it. *Maronn*," she scoffed, then went back into the house.

One by one, I carried the ladder and boxes inside to set up for what appeared to be a day of Christmas decorating. I stood on the ladder and she handed me ornaments, all of which had a story behind them. She handed me something that caught my attention. It was a little crocheted framed picture of her family at someone's wedding. When I eyed it carefully, I saw that the bride had the same eyes and pointy nose as Ms. G. Blank-faced, she stood like a stone statue next to a man who must have been Frank.

He stood in a tuxedo with his hair slicked back behind his ears, a drink in one hand and a cigarette in the other. They weren't even touching. The bridal party was all smiles, except for Ms. G.'s mother, who wore a straight face.

"Is this your wedding?"

She reached for her glasses attached to a chain around her neck and held the picture close to her face.

"Yeah. How in the hell did this get in here? Thought I threw all this crap out. My mother made this for my first Christmas with

Frank here on the ranch." She tossed it back in the box. "I haven't put up a tree in a long time. Guess I missed this one. But I don't want anything on this tree to take away its beauty."

"Is that your mom's gun in the garage?"

"Yes, it is. She always carried that gun with her," she said as a tiny giggle escaped her lips.

"Why?" I asked as I unknotted strands of lights.

"On account of her first husband, who was shot dead right in front of her," she said, unfazed at her admission.

"Shot right in front of her?"

"Yes, but then she married my father."

"Why was her first husband shot?"

"He lied to the wrong people."

"What do you mean 'the wrong people'?"

"The same people I keep telling you about—the Mafia," she divulged, then tried to rearrange one of the photos that was crooked on the wall. "Let me show you."

I set aside the lights and walked over to her. She showed me a black-and-white photo of a woman holding a child in one arm and a huge rifle in the other.

"This is your mom?"

"Yes, Adelina Giordano and my baby brother, Vinny." She grinned. "Vinny is Sophia's grandfather."

"She's holding a gun so close to the baby? Wasn't she afraid it would go off or that your brother might grab it?"

"No. No one touched that gun but her. Not even my father. Things were different back then. We didn't have any mace or stuff like that. You had to protect yourself out here."

"I didn't know she was married before."

"Carmela was her child from her first marriage."

"So, your father adopted her?"

"Not formally. My father took her on as his once my mother and father got married in Tricarico, back in Italy." She grinned proudly at all the pictures on the wall. "And look here." She pointed to another picture. "Here's my sister and three brothers. Here's Carmela and Tony. Then me and my two little brothers, Paulie and Vincenzo, or Vinny as we call him. They came a little later. Paulie's in prison now. He got popped for a murder. A life sentence about twenty years ago. That's why I don't have many pictures of him up here. He writes now and again, but I haven't seen or talked to him in years. That's what happens to the men in this life: they eventually die or go to prison."

After a few hours of stringing lights and adding garland, Ms. G.'s living room looked beautiful. The tree gave the space a warm glow. Twinkling lights made her smile, and I was happy to help.

"It looks gorgeous." She grinned from ear to ear.

"Yes, it does." I sat on the couch. My tired muscles eased.

"Okay, turn on *Judge Judy*," she commanded, then grabbed for her crochet needle.

While she crocheted, I emailed my weekly medical report to her niece. "I noticed you started a new blanket. The last one was blue, but this one's pink."

"This one's gonna be a baby blanket," she said proudly.

"Oh yeah? For who? Someone you know having a baby?"

"No."

"Then what are you planning to do with it?"

"What is this—twenty questions?" she said and shook her head.

"Sorry."

"I donate them to the church. They give them to the orphanages for the kids around here."

"Oh? How nice of you," I said in disbelief, struggling to acknowledge her soft spot.

"Been doing it for years. It's a hobby, I suppose."

I examined her handiwork. "Oh yeah, that's good."

"You wanna try?" she asked, staring over the top of her glasses.

"Um ... sure."

She handed me a ball of red yarn and a small crochet needle.

"Start a chain, like this," she said, then moved her hands and fingers to show me.

I copied her movements.

"There you go. Now you've got it." She nodded in approval. "So, where you from, hon?"

"Rockhill, South Carolina."

"How'd you end up way out here in California?"

"After my parents' divorce, we moved to California to live with one of my mother's friends. But I loved it there, and most of my family lives out that way."

"Why did your parents divorce?"

"They couldn't deal with the external pressure of a biracial marriage. My dad was white."

"Yeah, that could be hard. You got a big family out in South Carolina?"

"Oh yes. Lots of aunts, uncles, and cousins."

"That's nice. I have a big family. Have I ever told you about them?"

"Yes, dear, you have," I said with a smile.

"I have?"

"Yes." I reached for her hand to ease the confusion. "You know, one day I'm going to make you Southern food. You'll love it."

"No way. If it's half as bad as how you make a *sangwich*, I'll pass."

"Sandwich?"

"Where I come from, we call it a *sangwich* with a G, damn it," she fired back, then dug her needle into her work. "Keep working. When you get it as long as you want, I'll tell you what to do next."

"Okay," I said and continued crocheting.

"I did pretty good, right?" I asked.

She inspected my woven knots with approval. "Not bad, kid."

"I'd better get going. Seems like every day I stay later and later."

"Please don't go. Sometimes when you leave, things go dark again," she said with somber eyes.

"What do you mean 'dark'?"

"I'm used to your company," she said, almost too proud to admit it.

Smiling, I said, "That makes me happy to hear. I guess I can stay a little while longer."

After a few games of cards and warming her dinner, I knew I had to leave. I was already an hour late, and Marcus would expect his dinner before he went out or I'd surely suffer the consequences.

"I have to go now. It's getting late, and my kids are expecting me."

"I understand." She looked away with sad, sullen eyes. "You go take care of those babies."

"I'll see you tomorrow, okay?"

"Yeah, if I'm still breathin'," she mumbled with the ghost of a smile on her lips.

"Why don't we cook tomorrow? You can teach me how to make ravioli. Sound good?"

"Sure," she whispered with lifeless eyes.

"See you tomorrow, darlin'," I said and grabbed my things. I hated to leave her like this, but I was worried about being late for Marcus. Out of need, I made my way down the hallway, locked the door, and sped down the hill, hoping to avoid another argument.

The next morning, I held the ice pack to my swollen lip and winced. Leticia came into my bedroom.

I hid from her stare.

"Mama, how can you let him do this to you? Look at you. Don't you have any respect for yourself? The last time I had to lie to the other nurses and tell them you're just clumsy. I hate seeing you like this. Next time I'm calling the cops."

"Leticia, you don't understand."

"What's there to understand? Daddy shouldn't hurt you."

"This is your father's house. I can't ask him to leave," I said, fighting tears.

"Well then, we should leave," she said indignantly.

"Leave and go where? I'm gonna be late. I don't want to talk about this anymore today. I've got to get ready."

"Fine, but one day it'll go too far, and then it'll be too late," she said, then left my room.

Her words stung more than my face. She was right, and the look in her eyes meant she'd lost respect for me. If I had any other kind of job, I would've called in sick, nursed my wounds, and avoided the world. But I couldn't leave Ms. G. alone. She needed me. I'd have to make sure I left on time today.

Marcus had given me a small shiner and a busted lip. I decided I'd put lots of petroleum jelly on my lip to try and hide it. If she asked, I'd say it was medicine for a fever blister. And for my eye, I'd wear my prescription sunglasses. Tell her I broke my eyeglasses.

I had to cover things up because I didn't want to go back to the insults or teasing. We'd come so far yesterday with her admission of wanting me around, and I refused to go backward.

I grabbed my sunglasses and put them on my bruised face. It was painful to slide them over my nose, but I'd only have to endure it for a few hours. Then I'd be back home where I could bury my head under a pillow in shame. I grabbed my medical bag and headed for the door.

"Hello, Ms. G. How are you today?"

"Well, I didn't die, so that's a good thing." She snickered. "Hey, why do you have your sunglasses on? We're in the house."

"I broke my other glasses, and these are prescription." I placed my bag down.

"Prescription, huh?"

"Yes," I said firmly. "You ready to make ravioli?" I asked, trying to distract her from my appearance.

"You sure you're up for it?"

"Why wouldn't I be?"

"I don't know. Sometimes I don't know about you, kid," she eyed me suspiciously. "Go and wash your hands."

I soaped up and rinsed at the kitchen sink. When I turned around, she handed me an apron.

"See that big stock pot right there? Go get it. I'll start the gravy, and you can start the dough."

"Let me turn on the gas for you."

"I can do it." She batted my hands away. "Watch me if you have to. I can't do anything without being watched anymore. I feel like I'm wanted by the FBI again. *Maronn*," she ranted on.

I lit the gas. She added olive oil and ground beef to the pan. We watched as it popped and sizzled.

"You married?" she asked while peeling garlic. "I don't see no wedding ring."

"No, not married, but with the same man for almost twenty-one years now."

Whack! The thunderous sound of her hand came down on the tiny garlic, splitting off the skin. "Twenty-one years? And this guy doesn't have the balls to ask for your hand? What a piece of . . ." She stopped herself mid-sentence and continued to dice the garlic.

"I got pregnant early, but we've been together ever since."

"How old are your kids?" She stirred the garlic in with the meat.

"Leticia is twenty, and Darnell is seventeen."

"So, this Marcus, he ever get rough with you or your kids?"

Her question was divisive and planned. She baited me, and all this time I thought I'd covered my tracks. But lie, I would. "No. Well . . . he gets angry from time to time, but don't all men?"

"No. Not *good* men," she said.

Her words hit me right in the gut. It was clear now. She knew. She was a victim like me. Our connection.

"Here, pinch the basil while I cut the other herbs."

"Pinch?"

"Yeah, you never cut basil, you just pinch it, like this." She pressed her fingers together. "See, that keeps the flavor."

"I didn't know that."

Despite the Alzheimer's, she knew her way around her kitchen. It was impressive to watch her in her element. Like most people with Alzheimer's, she couldn't always remember what happened yesterday, but she had a firm hold on the memories and events that took place in her youth. It was of no surprise that she remembered how to cook meals she'd made as a child.

She tended to the ravioli filling and sauce. Then she rolled out the dough on the table. Her arms worked tirelessly.

"You wanna try?" she asked.

"Sure."

"Okay, use the rolling pin and stretch it out like this," she said as she pulled at the ends over a pile of sprinkled flour.

I followed her movements. My arms were sore from blocking Marcus's blows. Once we had the dough spread into a thin layer, she layered the meat filling onto the dough, then covered it with another layer of thin dough.

"Okay, tuck in the sides and use this over it." She handed me the ravioli roller. "Now go slow," she instructed.

I grabbed the roller from her, started at the end, and slowly rolled it over the dough.

"There you go. Good girl, you did it. Now that you know how to do this, you can do it at home. I bet your kids are starving."

"No. They aren't starving for food. They're starving for peace," I replied with an edge in my voice.

"I'm sorry. I know what you're going through. Sometimes I don't think before I speak," she said, then patted my hand.

Questions about my family prompted pictures of their sad faces in my mind. Defeated and exposed, I undid my apron and excused myself to the bathroom to weep quietly.

After two large helpings of her ravioli, I said, "I'm stuffed. I can't eat another bite. This was so good. Thank you for showing me. I didn't think it would take most of the day, but it did."

"Take some home to your kids," she said, then scooped the tiny dough pillows into a Tupperware container.

"Thank you."

"You're welcome."

"Well, since we've spent most of the day cooking, I forgot to give you an exam."

"Do I have to?"

"Yes. Roll up your sleeve."

"Fine, but after this, I wanna watch TV. Oh, damn it. We missed *Judge Judy*." She stomped her foot.

"How about a crossword instead? We have to exercise our brains too, ya know."

"All right, but *Judge Judy* is more fun."

I handed her the crossword puzzle, and she pulled her glasses up to her face.

"I have to get home on time tonight," I said as she examined the crossword puzzle.

"Yeah, it looks like you better. We wouldn't want him to hurt you *again*," she said, then turned her face away. "You can fool other people, but you don't fool me. I've seen the signs—bruises, broken fingernails, sunglasses to match your fat lip. Be careful, kid."

"I'm fine. I broke my glasses, remember?"

"Yeah, sure you did," she said, then stood in front of me. "Look, if you ever need anything, you let me know."

"I will. I'm fine, Ms. G. Really, I am," I said, then shut the door behind me.

I drove down her windy road, not sure whether to smile or cry.

Chapter 15

Peace Offering

IN THE BLINK OF A SWOLLEN EYE, CHRISTMAS EVE ARRIVED. I told Ms. G. I'd be coming over early because I wanted to get home to my kids. After what had happened last night, it was important for me to be home early.

I walked through her door with my Christmas dinner and my most famous sweet potato pie in hand.

"What the hell is all this?"

"This is my gift to you. You always cook for me, so it was time to cook for you. You'll like it, promise. Let's sit in the living room so we can eat and enjoy the tree."

After her normal exam and a quick walk in the garden, we sat in front of our TV trays to enjoy an early lunch. At first, she eyed the food and moved it around her plate with her fork. When she got hungry enough, she took a few bites.

"Well, how is it?"

"Not bad," she said with a half-eaten plate.

"You know, I didn't turn my nose up at your ravioli," I said firmly.

"That's because ravioli is good."

My jaw tightened. "Why are you so rude to me? Since I started here, you have been nasty and cruel at times. Is it because I'm black?"

"That's ridiculous." Her eyebrows pulled together. "Don't be so sensitive. Sheesh . . ."

"Yeah, whatever. Let me clear our plates." I grabbed the plates and walked them to the kitchen sink.

Still amped up from her blatant disregard for my effort, I marched back into the living room where she stood with a huge present in front of her.

"This is for you. Merry Christmas." She pushed a box wrapped in newspaper with a big red bow toward me.

My jaw dropped. "You didn't have to do this."

"Open it," she said as she watched with wide eyes.

I ripped the sides of the paper and pulled out an old microwave box. It smelled of mold and age. "Oh, you shouldn't have." I smirked. Inside was a huge, crocheted blue afghan made from the softest yarn I'd ever felt. On the front, she'd crocheted the state flag of South Carolina. On the bottom, she'd sewn on a square piece of red felt where she'd hand-painted a picture of a black girl holding a white girl's hand.

At the far-right corner was a red heart with the letters Vi on it, as she'd done for Gaetano all those years ago.

My insides warmed, and a smile edged its way across my face. Stroking the soft yarn of her impeccable craftsmanship, I thought about the time it must have taken her to make this.

"Thank you. It's beautiful," I croaked as the walls of my throat caved in.

She came over to explain it to me.

"See here, this is the state flag of South Carolina where you said you grew up. I had to look it up in an encyclopedia I had lying around here, but I found it. You should never forget where you came from. I never have."

"Is this us?"

"Well, yeah, I tried to get your clothes right, but the damn thing took me three tries. I was almost ready to shit-can the idea, but then by the third try, I got it." She smiled with pride over her work.

"This means so much to me."

"Try not to get the damn thing dirty. They're hard to clean—especially with the craft paint."

"I promise, I'll take good care of it. I want you to know that I care about you too." I reached over and hugged her frail body in my arms.

"Okay. You're smothering me, kid." She tried to move away from my tight grip. "I care about you too," she said, almost whispering, as if her pride wouldn't allow it.

She continued to touch the red felt and then looked up at me. "I know I can be a pain in the ass sometimes. I've become a bitter old woman, but I'm not racist. I can't stand people who treat people like that. I lived it."

"I understand. I should never have accused you of that."

"Did you know that Italians were persecuted during World War II? Homes were searched for no reason. Can you believe that crap? The government even enforced a curfew."

"I didn't know that."

"It's true. We were called the *enemy aliens* because the US was at war with Italy. And for that, we suffered. All because we were Italian. They thought we might be spies or somethin.'"

"I know how it feels to be treated differently."

"Yeah, I s'pose you would." She nodded. "You know how many times I've been called a *WOP* or a *no-good guinea*? Plenty. You know what? I don't care. Let them say what they want. Funny part is, the mob helped the God damn government during the war and still we don't get no respect," she yelled, then went to sit back in her chair. "Yeah, they used us. But what did the mob care?

It was a favor for a favor, like I told you before. So, yeah, I have felt racism too, my dear."

For a moment, Ms. G. went silent. We looked at one another. I couldn't ignore it. More alike than I'd ever thought possible, we were two women from different families, different walks of life, and even different skin tones, connecting with one another on a human level. With the words that had been spoken and the loving gestures, I had a strong belief that this day would solidify our bond.

To end the night, we played a few hands of blackjack. She told me about the things her family did on Christmas and the food they cooked as part of their traditions. We reminisced about our childhoods and things we shared in common. It was a nice afternoon, and I hated to leave her alone on Christmas Eve, but it was important that I saw my kids.

"That's game. You beat me fair and square. You're so good, Ms. G."

"You aren't leavin' already, are you? You just got here."

"Believe it or not, I've been here for six hours. Besides, my kids are expecting me. It's Christmas Eve. But don't you worry. I saved you leftovers in the fridge. Hope you eat them," I said with a wink.

Her lips pressed together in a pout—a sign she wouldn't touch another bite.

"I'll see you tomorrow at our regular time. I hate to go, but my family's waiting for me."

"Don't worry, kid. You've given me a better Christmas than you know. Now, go be with your children. That's what's most important. Never forget that."

"I won't."

I grabbed my new blanket and headed for the car. Because

I'd stashed money away, I was able to buy the kids a few extra presents for under the tree. It was the least I could do for the harm I'd put them through.

After church on Christmas morning, I checked in on Ms. G. Holiday or not, that was my job. She'd gone quiet again. The leftovers stared back at me from the garbage, untouched. I wasn't mad. I expected it, and I didn't mention a word.

I made her toast and juice and handed it to her while she watched television. Teasing her a little bit to get some kind of a reaction, I told her I'd turn on the gospel channel and sing to her. She didn't even bat an eye, and that scared me. She sat in her chair like she was somewhere else. I worried about her again. Age and loneliness were the new enemies now.

"Time for your checkup, honey."

"Okay," she said, this time with no protest.

I pressed the stethoscope to her chest.

She stared at my neck.

"You got to be kidding me. *Again*?" she said, then pulled my turtleneck back. "What the hell did he do this time?"

I thought wearing a turtleneck would cover Marcus's fingerprint bruises, but she was too smart.

"Nothing, I, uh . . ."

"Don't lie to me, young lady. I know what's going on."

"I suspect you do," I said as tears welled up in the corners of my eyes.

"You're a beautiful girl. You can get any man you want. Look at you. You're young, nice figure. Hell, things haven't even begun to fall south yet. Pretty face, beautiful eyes—when they aren't swollen." She patted my cheek. "Why you with such a loser? Can't you leave him? Get the hell out of there!"

"No, ma'am, I can't. Not yet, anyway. We live in his father's house downtown, and well, with this job, I have just enough to pay the bills, keep up with Marcus's habits, and help my daughter with her medical program."

"Medical program? She going to be a nurse like you?"

"She'll be a doctor."

"A doctor, huh? Well, I'll be. Women can be anything nowadays. Don't you have any family that can take you in?"

"My sister only has a one-bedroom apartment for her and her daughter, so we wouldn't fit there."

"Did you try the shelters?"

"He'd find me."

"Oh, he would, would he? He probably hangs out at the bars all night."

"No, the Garden Valley Casino."

"Garden what? Oh, you mean the card joint? My cousin, Michael, is a floorman there. Is Marcus a gambler?"

"Yes, he gambles our money away."

"Ha, like the *stunad*—Frank. No job?"

"He's had a hard time getting a job."

"Why?"

"He has a record."

"*Maronn*. And I thought I was the one stuck with a loser. God bless you, honey. Whatcha waiting for? Him to beat you to death? Then who's gonna take care of those babies, huh? You have to think about your kids."

"Yes, I do."

"You need a pistol? I got one around here somewhere," she said as she opened the door to the side table next to her recliner. "Cold cock him and *then* he'll leave you alone."

"No need for a gun. I'll be okay."

"Oh hey, I almost forgot. My brother Vinny called me this morning. I need to call him back before he worries. If you'll excuse me," she said, then went to her room and dialed the phone.

Before she shut the door, I heard her say, "Hey, *compadi*, it's me. I need a favor."

After her phone call, we settled in, and things got quiet again. I hated seeing her so withdrawn like she'd been in the morning, so I got her talking again.

"Ms. G., you never told me what happened after that night Frank held a knife to Tony's throat."

"Yeah, Frank was a lot like your Marcus—an asshole."

"The last time you shared, you were about to be married."

She paused for a few seconds to bring her mind up to speed and then began. "That's when I was crowned."

"What do you mean 'crowned?'"

"I transformed from a young, innocent girl to a true Mafia Queen."

"Mafia Queen. What's that?"

"By marrying Frank, I became Mafia royalty. My wedding ceremony to Frank was the closest I ever came to experiencing *La Omerta*. My ring symbolized my sacrifice. Over time, the band left an indentation, like that of the scar inflicted by a Don in a blood ceremony. The ring was my commitment to the code of silence required to survive this world. I offered my loyalty and came to the service of my husband, a soldier in this army. I had money and power. And for a time, people feared me. I learned new things and got my hands dirty. Some would say mob wives are just arm candy to make the men look good in the papers. Or we were there to continue the bloodline," she said as she wove the yarn around her fingers. "My wedding to Frank opened my eyes to many things that can't be unseen."

Part Two

Una Regina

Chapter 16

La Omerta, My Oath

East San Jose Foothills, Giordano Estate
August 1940
Violetta

I STOOD AT THE ALTAR, COVERED IN LAYERS OF WHITE FLUFF, as sweat poured down my back. Father Marco smiled and chanted words at me and Frank. Like any Italian wedding, the church was packed, and all eyes were on me. The ceremony went on forever—we'd kneel and stand and kneel some more.

I'd been coming to this church most of my life. Because my mother had made sizeable donations to our church over the years, she and Father Marco had become great friends. We were like most Mafia families, praying for our salvation in hopes of absolving us from our sins. Donations and involvement made our family look like upstanding citizens in the community. With our weekly offerings, we were able to reserve the church anytime we wanted. And they ensured the sanctity of the confessional, so what was said remained 'off the record.'

With the memory of Frank holding a knife to Tony's throat still fresh in my mind, I avoided eye contact with my soon-to-be husband. Beside me, Frank swayed. He must have been having withdrawals from the past few weeks of drinking. His face looked pale, and he perspired so badly that sweat soaked through his white dress shirt. The smell of alcohol was so strong that even Father Marco shot him a strange look.

As we chanted prayers and listened to Father Marco preach, Frank shook so badly, he almost knocked the holy candle down when we put the flame to the wick. It wobbled back and forth, dripping wax on my hand, like that of the blood in the code of silence ritual. The hot liquid stung my palm. I compared it only to holding the burning saint, the archangel Michael, in my hand. Whether I liked it or not, I was anointed.

When the priest said, 'You may kiss your bride,' I was instantly nauseous. With everyone's eye on us, Frank came in at me to put on a show for everyone. He shoved his tongue in my mouth. It tasted sour from a night's worth of vomiting. When he finally pulled away, the crowd roared in approval.

The clapping stung my ears.

Because Frank was still on the run from the feds, we couldn't put anything in the newspaper. I was glad about that because I didn't want Gaetano to read about it and see our photo. That would only hurt him more.

When we walked out of the small church, even the rice that hit my face and eyelids didn't stop me from seeing that there were a few made guys in attendance. None of the big bosses, including Frank's father, were there, as they didn't want to bring unwanted attention to his son's whereabouts. That would have turned up the heat while the Molanano family wanted things to die down.

Like most family parties, the wedding reception was in the big house out back. Mama and Carm did a good job with the decorations. Purple streamers hung down and a huge, tiered cake from San Jose's finest, Peter's Bakery, sat in the corner. As always, Mama and Pop invited all their friends and family.

Per tradition, all my aunts brought food and my uncles, true to form, played music. Everyone had a good time but me. As I was about to make my exit to the bathroom to have a private cry, Frank pulled me onto the dance floor for our first dance as husband and wife.

"Violetta, I want you to know how beautiful you look today. I'm sorry about yesterday. I got pretty drunk. I was nervous. I've never been married before. But I'm glad that it's you," he said, then pressed his cheek to mine.

"Thanks for your apology. You scared me last night. I don't want that to ever happen again."

"No, you have my word. That will never happen again. Don't look so sad, doll. I'm a nice guy. You'll see. I'm going to treat you like a real queen," he said, then came in for another kiss.

I pressed my lips together. Hoping that the music would drown out all of his bullshit, I smiled a fake smile and kept dancing. No longer allowed to be my true self, I was to be a good Mafia wife.

Pop smiled at us while we continued to dance. I tried to smile back, but it wasn't the giant toothy grin of someone who was elated on their wedding day. It was a tight-lipped stare followed by a nod to show him I'd accepted his decision.

The night wasn't complete without the father-daughter dance. Pop grabbed my hand and guided me through the crowds of guests. Music swirled around us, while Pop moved me around the dance floor. Cheers from the family echoed throughout the room. Here I was, Giuseppe's daughter—his first to get married. Pop beamed with pride, but when he looked into my eyes, we both knew we had an understanding. With apologetic smiles, we continued the dance to its finish.

"Oh, Violetta, why you so sad? I try everyting to give you a good life. Giva dis boy a chance. In time, you willa see. He willa make you happy."

I kissed him on the cheek and gave him a woeful smile. "Okay, Papa. I'll try. I love you."

"*Ti voglio bene assai bella figlia mia.* You make me so proud."

Pop hugged me tight, and I closed my eyes. And even though the words were brief, we had an accord. I'd work hard every day to bury the hatchet between us. It would be difficult, but I'd try.

After my cousins unpinned the bills from my dress from the money dance, we cut the cake and took photos by the pond. No matter how many times the photographer asked, I couldn't pull off a smile. I stood there like a statue standing next to a stranger. I understood the reality of what this day meant for my future. The minute I'd said *I do*, I surrendered myself to Frank and to being a Mafia Queen. I'd cook and clean and be ready for anything—legal or otherwise. On Sundays, I'd be in church, praying for forgiveness for my husband's misdoings. I'd seen it done by the wives so many times before. They were all such good actresses in a life that had provided as much as it had taken away. It was a bleak outlook, for sure.

Pop ushered the men down to the basement. It was customary that on special occasions—weddings, baptisms, communions and such—the men conducted business. My wedding gave them the perfect excuse to get together and plan. To make everyone feel safe, Pop paid off the mayor to keep the cops away from the party.

Frank was the last guy down. He was drunk and ran his mouth to everyone, saying how he would be the new boss out here. Pop shook his head and pulled Frank aside a few times to straighten him out. I'm sure that some of the guys who were already established here didn't want a hotshot from New York giving them orders and spying around on things. But they wouldn't cross the son of the underboss of the Molanano family. For that, Frank knew they all feared him.

After a few hours, the men came up from the basement, laughing and smoking cigars. Frank was in his glory. Everyone shook his hand and hugged him. A few of them even kissed him on the back of the hand, like a Don. He loved every moment of it—all the attention—everything. He was such a phony, and everyone knew it.

The wedding ended, and Carmela walked me to the car. Pop bought us a brand-new 1940 Buick convertible. It was another wedding gift from my parents, another monetary incentive for me to accept my new union. It was a nice car. Frank liked it because it was flashy. Not many people had convertibles, so it made us look classy. The car was packed with our bags and lots of champagne bottles.

After several attempts at stuffing the long train of my dress into the car, Pop gave me an approving nod and kissed me on the cheek. We drove away with the whole family standing in the road, waving. Everyone cheered and laughed. Some threw rice and the kids chased the tin cans that clanked against the road behind us.

I left part of myself on that road. With my stomach in knots, every mile farther down the road meant I'd said a more distant good-bye to my childhood and my innocence for a world of unknowns.

"You all right, gorgeous?" Frank put his right hand on my thigh.

"I'm fine," I mumbled.

"Don't worry about nothin' tonight. I'm gonna make tonight as easy as possible for yous," he said with a devilish smile.

I swallowed through my clogged throat and forced myself to look straight ahead.

Uncle Johnny gifted us a suite at the St. Claire Hotel. I'd only seen the building a few times when we went downtown, but when Frank pulled up, it looked like a palace. Frank parked the car in the front, and a bellhop rushed over to open my door and help me out. Other men dressed in tailed tuxedos and white gloves grabbed our bags. Frank shook their hands and tipped them lavishly.

"Oh yeah, hi. I'm a friend of Johnny Rizzuto."

The man at the concierge must have been tipped off by the name. "Oh yes, sir, we've been expecting you and your beautiful bride." He smiled at me. "Here are your keys, and we'll have someone help you with your luggage."

"Thanks. That sounds great." Frank slid the man a hefty tip.

At the top floor, Frank opened the door. As I tried to walk in, he stopped me, picked me up, and carried me over the threshold. I wasn't sure what came over him. Maybe he felt guilty and wanted to give me as much of a traditional experience as possible under the circumstances. He set me down on the bed. I was unable to smile because I didn't trust him, but I figured it was better to be kind than to object at this point.

To try and put off the obvious, I got busy unpacking our bags. As I placed my toothbrush on the counter, I heard a loud pop and rushed out to see what it was. Frank stood there with champagne in one hand and two glass flutes in the other, compliments of the hotel. A burst of bubbles spilled onto the carpet and splashed his feet.

"Hey, Vi, come here, doll," he said, attempting charm. He handed me a glass of champagne and made a toast. "Here's to my beautiful bride. May this be the first of many wonderful days together as man and wife, and may God bless us with many children so that we can continue our legacy." He tapped his glass against mine.

I smiled politely and sucked down every drop.

"Easy, sweetheart. You're gonna get a headache. But hey, you might need a little somethin' to help warm you up. And I'm all about loosening you up for tonight." A wicked grin swept across his face.

He poured me another and another. After a while, I felt numb and dizzy. I lay on the bed and closed my eyes. Then came his advances. He reached under my dress to pull off my garter belt and seamed stockings.

"Sit up so I can undo your dress."

At his command, I moved my body toward his. I got up too fast and felt like I was gonna be sick. I pushed his body to the side and ran to the bathroom, where I threw up all my aunt's fritters.

After heaving up a good plate's worth, I brushed my teeth to get the bitter taste out of my mouth and leaned against the bathroom vanity. Looking in the mirror, I noticed where my makeup had caked up around my eyes and ran down my face from sweat and tears. I removed my veil and let my hair fall onto my shoulders. Knowing what was about to happen, I took deep breaths and tried to walk myself through the process in my mind. I wouldn't fight against him because I was his wife now. But would he expect me to enjoy it? There was no way. After I splashed water on my face, I made my way out of the bathroom.

"I told ya not to drink so much, baby." He stood in his underwear; his tuxedo draped over a nearby chair. "Here, let me get you outta that dress so you can relax."

I closed my eyes as he undid the laces and the buttons in the back. It felt a bit like a scary movie when the monster approaches, yet I couldn't move—my legs were in quicksand. There was no escape, just silent submission.

When he undid the last button, the dress sprang forward and fell onto the carpet. He held my hands, and I stepped out of the garment. I stood in front of him, exposed, with only my corset and my panties. Here we were—husband and wife, staring at each other.

I never paid much attention to Frank's dramatic features before. He was, however, a decent-looking man. He had a firm jaw line that butted up against a full head of coarse, jet-black hair. His olive-toned skin complemented his intense hazel-brown eyes. They were reflective, and in the right light, I saw right through them. But it was his body hair that I was most surprised about. I'd only been with Gaetano, so I had little knowledge of men, in general. Frank was covered in hair. It was all over his chest and part of his back. A little jarring at first, but it made him look all the more like the beast from a scary movie.

Frank grabbed the back of my head and forced my face toward his. He kissed me vigorously. Kissing was the hardest part. Faking a good kiss is difficult. Motionless, I stood there while he forced his tongue in my mouth. On instinct, my body pulled away.

Once he sensed my hesitation, he squeezed me tighter. He wanted to claim *his* property. He tried to pull my corset open, but the metal latches foiled his attempts. Frustrated and filled with lust, he reached for his knife in the pocket of his tuxedo and savagely cut through the laces.

The corset dropped to my feet and my breasts sprang forward. He ravaged my chest and nipples, licking them. The sensation stimulated my insides. No matter how hard I fought against this, my physical body was turned on. Although my brain may not have wanted to engage in such activities, my body felt differently. He picked me up and laid me on the bed.

To show my willing participation, I reached for him and dug my fingernails into his back as he continued to fondle me. I felt myself rising. To help myself along, I shut my eyes and imagined it was Gaetano touching me. Then my juices really flowed.

I felt Frank pull down my panties. And then it happened. With my eyes shut, he entered me. He grabbed my legs and hinged them up around his shoulders, trying to move himself deeper inside me. And right as I began to quiver, he grabbed my face and yanked it toward him.

"Look at me," he snapped.

I opened my eyes and stared at his face. With my knees around his ears, he said,

"You like this, baby?" He grinned as he continued to thrust back and forth.

Out of fear that I might lose my concentration toward my finish, I didn't answer.

"I said, do you like this? Answer me, God damn it," he insisted. I nodded in silence while he continued.

With no response, his eyes grew cold. "Turn over," he commanded.

I turned around and got on all fours. I pushed my head deep into the pillow to obstruct my vision and hearing to make it all more bearable.

He grasped at my hips and pulled me back and forth harder and harder until I felt the echo in my pelvis. He reached around and stroked me, hard. The walls of my vagina came crumbling down, and I pulled my head to the side, away from the pillow to get air from my release.

With a few more thrusts, he claimed his victory inside me. He pulled out and fell down onto the bed next to my limp body. Both of us tried to catch our breath and lay there until he was ready to get up. There were no words. He went straight to the bathroom to clean himself up, then threw me a towel to do the same. I wiped myself, then threw the towel right back at him. He looked down at the cum-stained towel and then back at me.

"Hey, wait a fucking minute. Let me see you."

He yanked my legs apart. His cum dripped down onto the sheets beneath me. He first examined, then stuck his fingers inside. He pulled them out to look at them in the light and then he slapped me so hard it made my ears ring.

"Why didn't you bleed, you bitch? You ain't no virgin," he yelled. "Who's been in this pussy before, huh? Who do I have to fuckin kill? *Puttana!*"

I reached for the sheets and wrapped them around my naked body. "I'm no *puttana*. I haven't been with anyone," I hissed.

"Then why's there no blood?" he asked as he smeared his fingers onto my now-burning face. "See? No fuckin' blood," he accused.

"I don't know why there's no blood. I've never done this before." I raised my arms in front of my face to block the next blow.

"There's supposed to be blood. That's it," he spewed. "I'm gonna make this pussy mine, so you won't ever leave me for some other piece of shit. These are mine," he said, then bit down hard on my nipples. My breasts burned like fire. When he pulled away, I noticed he bit so hard he left bite marks.

"Stop. You're hurting me," I yelled.

"Get your little ass over here," he commanded, then pinned me down and shoved himself into me again.

Pallid light came through the hotel window. I edged my pained body to the side of the bed. From the brutal strikes to my face, I wasn't sure I'd be able to eat or speak tomorrow. Bite marks on my breasts and inner thighs felt like a swarm of bees had attacked me. They were raised and hot to the touch. I massaged my body and shut my inflamed eyes. Trapped in the blackness, I held on to my pillow tight as if it were Gaetano's arms shielding me from my reality.

I was too afraid to cry. The hairy monster got me.

Chapter 17

Wedding Gift

AFTER MY NIGHT OF TERROR, FRANK DROVE US BACK TO THE ranch. Once we stopped at the corner of Market and Santa Clara Street, Frank reached into his coat pocket and handed me some cash. "Here, doll, here's some of the money from the wedding. Go buy yourself new dresses," he said contritely.

"You paying me for my services? Look at this, Frank," I said, then pulled down my shirt to the top of my bra to show him his wreckage.

He looked over, then turned away.

"Do what you want with the money," he said, avoiding my stare. "Buy somethin' for the house then. I don't know."

"Don't talk to me." I grabbed the cash and shoved it into my purse. It was my money too, and it was only a small portion of what this whole arrangement owed me, so I took it with no more protest.

To avoid seeing anyone, I ran straight to our room and locked the door to stay as far away from Frank as possible.

"Hey, I gotta get clothes, God damn it," he yelled.

I cracked open the door. "Here," I said, then threw his suits at him.

"You can't stay in there all day. I betta have my dinna on the table when I get home." Frank snickered. "Yous keep it up, and I will break this door down, you hear?"

"Stay away from me," I fired back.

"*Vaffanculo*," he roared.

"*Basta*," Pop yelled down the hall at Frank. "Be quiet, Franco. I hava patients."

"*Mi dispiace*, Giuseppe. I'm sorry. It's just your daughter. She's in a bad mood, and, well, she won't let me into our room."

"Give her time, she canno stay in der forever," Pop said. "Das what I do wit Adelina. When she mad, I stay away. And besides, my wife carry a gun." Pop laughed a full belly laugh.

"*Maronn*, that's all I need," Frank said.

I reached in my purse and fanned out the money. Maybe that was what I needed—a gun. Then the next time he got rough, I'd shoot him right between the legs.

"I don't need this shit. I'm leaving," Frank yelled.

"Good riddance," I said through the door.

I lay in bed for the next few days and tried to put the terrible night with Frank out of my mind.

As the weeks wore on, we fell into our new titles of gangster and Mafia wife. When forced to see each other, we avoided eye contact. When he entered the bathroom, I walked out. If I came into the kitchen, he left.

Even in our bed, there was an invisible line between us that neither crossed. He didn't even try to proposition me for sex. Maybe he felt guilt for the way he had handled me. I didn't care what he did as long as he left me alone. He had a habit of getting drunk, which often accompanied outbursts. Then the next day, he'd be quiet and isolated from others. This was a pattern that I learned how to navigate.

While Frank was busy getting his hands dirty, literally, in all things mob-related, I made a home by hanging curtains and potting house plants. On occasion, I bought things to make our home feel inviting. I frequented Zavlaris's thrift shop, buying all the little things I'd always wanted to buy when I didn't have money. Secretly, I was trying to recreate the guesthouse at the Sanna winery.

After I bought decorations for the house, I picked up new dresses, as Frank had suggested. With my new 'allowance,' I wouldn't have to borrow from my sister anymore. I liked the independence that money gave me. A lot. Many things I bought made me feel happier—temporarily.

One day, when Frank was out, I went downtown to one of those fancy dress shops. I tried on everything and dropped the cash down on the counter. The woman behind the counter cocked one brow and examined me.

"Is there a problem, miss?" I asked, rather cavalier.

"Um, no, ma'am, no problem. Here's your receipt. Thank you for shopping with us." She handed me my bags apologetically.

I walked out with bags full of new dresses and shoes. I felt rich with all the bags hanging from my arms. This was one of the perks of marrying a gangster—the money. For a brief second, I felt empowered; and for that, I would ignore my conscience and revel in the moment.

At home, the weight of the bags on my arms was so heavy that I dropped the keys. When I picked up the keys and opened the front door, I tripped on a box left on our doorstep.

"*Minchia*, you stupid thing," I screamed at the box in the doorway. Angry for making me stumble, I kicked it out of the way. I stormed in, threw my bags on the ground, and retrieved the parcel.

It was heavy and addressed to me in black writing from a Napa address.

I felt like I'd swallowed a scream. I clutched at my chest to see if my heart was still beating.

I knew of only one person who lived in the Napa Valley—my love, my Gaetano.

I quickly shut the front door and checked the house to see if Frank was home. I didn't remember seeing our car in the driveway, so I went into the guest bedroom, locked the door, and drew the curtains.

My heart pounded. I had no idea what was in the box. My hands shook so badly, I struggled to open the package. Inside was a small brown box with the Sanna emblem on it. A big letter S with the sunrise in the back brought back a flood of memories. I pulled the top lid off the box to find a small note that read,

Congratulations~

-G

My heart sank.

I pulled out the bottle of red wine. It was the latest reserve of their cabernet. It even had a red satin bow tied around it. I hugged the bottle to my chest. My only connection to him. This wine was all I had left. His note made all my fears come true. He'd accepted my decision and wished me farewell.

Only a short time ago, Gaetano must have touched this bottle and thought about me and our time together. I felt connected to him. I wondered how he was and if the time between us had helped him get past the sadness. For me, no amount of time would ease the pain. For him, I hoped he'd find the happiness I'd never be able to give him.

If Frank asked, I'd say it was a wedding present from a friend of Pop's. I placed the wine bottle in the back of the glass liquor cabinet, shut the door, and threw the box in the garbage. I grabbed my shopping bags and emptied the contents onto my bed, hoping that my new gifts would fill the hole in my heart

Chapter 18
Compadi

San Jose, California
February 2002
Barbara

I AWOKE TO THE SOUND OF A DOOR SLAMMING. I LOOKED AT
the clock. It was four in the morning, and Marcus was just coming in. To ignore his ranting and rambling as he moved his way
through the house, I pulled the blankets over my head and tried to
go back to sleep.

Marcus slammed open the bedroom door and started cursing.

"Kick me out? Are you fucking kidding me? Do you know how
much money I put into that fucking place? No one kicks out Marcus
Tidwell—no one," he roared. "I'm gonna call my cousin, Leroy, and
we gonna make problems for the Garden Valley. You don't throw
me out on my ass and think you're gonna get away with it. Public
intoxication, my ass. Accusing me of counting cards? Threatening
to bar me from their establishment? No fucking way."

Marcus fell onto the bed and passed out with his clothes on.

The smell of alcohol and desperation was so bad, I got out of bed and dressed for the day. As I added a layer of makeup to my face, I wondered why they kicked Marcus out. He'd been going to that club for years.

An ominous thought came over me.

Ms. G.

She'd said her cousin was a floorman there. Would she do something like that—for me? Maybe that's who she called that day when she shut the door to her room. Was she still that powerful? As I swallowed my thoughts down hard, my gut said *yes*. And if I was right, it meant she'd protected me like I was a part of her family—even more—like I was part of the *Molanano* family. As much as I liked that Marcus was getting what he deserved, I hoped he'd never find out who really pulled the strings in this town, or my worlds might surely collide.

That thought sent a shiver down my spine.

"Well, look at you. Niner fan, huh?"

Ms. G. greeted me at the front door dressed in red and gold from head to toe.

"Best team around. See this here jersey?" She twirled around. "Number sixteen. Best quarterback of all time, and he's Italian." She smiled. "Hey, I don't want to stay in today. I want to go visit my cousin's husband, Angelo, in Goosetown. I need to pay him a visit. He has a deli there. We can get lunch." She grabbed her sunglasses and matching 49er purse.

"Okay, Ms. G., sounds good. But first I have to examine you."

"Jesus Christ, I can't go anywhere without you poking at me."

"Goosetown. Is this the same place you talked about before? The place you took *Signora* Sanna and her daughters?" I asked while opening my medical bag.

"Yes. It's like our version of a Little Italy in New York. Everyone used to go there."

"Pull up that sleeve. The longer you fight me, the longer it will take."

"Fine." She sneered and yanked up her sleeve.

Ms. G. and I got in my car. Her little eyes were wide, and a huge grin spread across her face. "So, where's Goosetown?" I asked.

"Head toward the Willow Glen area. I'll tell you where to go."

As we made our way for her old stomping grounds, she told me how things used to look, and which businesses had come and gone. She pointed out where every mobster once lived in San Jose.

"There were wise guys everywhere out here. From grocery stores to restaurants, you name it—all linked to the Molanano family. Hell, even the guy who sold my father his cars became a big boss out here. He went to the Apalachin and everything."

"What's the Apalachin?"

"Only one of the biggest mob meetings in history. Heads of the five families were there—everyone."

"What happened?"

"Some New York state trooper found out, and well . . . they raided the house. That was a dark day for the Mafia. That's when the feds found out everything," she said, then looked back out the window. "But the story that hit home was what happened at the cheese factory. Now that really screwed things up. *Maronn*, what an embarrassment. If you're gonna whack a guy, you better make sure you finish the job," she said and shook her head.

"A cheese factory? What could have possibly happened at a cheese factory?"

"Two guys were shot there and thrown in the trunk of a car. They found the car abandoned somewhere in San Francisco. One guy died, but his father lived. Lucky son of bitch survived a bullet wound to the head."

"Oh my God, really? Found in the car?"

"Yeah, apparently he was in there hitting the door of the trunk with a shovel and someone eventually heard him," she said, then laughed. "Talk about loose ends. *Minchia*. They were after all of us after that."

"I can't even believe that. Survived a bullet wound and found alive in the car—amazing," I muttered with a shaky voice.

"Yeah, they were everywhere." She pointed to various things and locations on her trip down memory lane. "Take a right here," she directed as we passed Lincoln Avenue. "See this? This is Goosetown. It feels so good to be back here," she said with a smile. "Yeah. At the next light, take a left."

As we got closer to the deli, her expression changed. "Man, what happened here? It's all beat up," she yelled, then threw her hands in the air.

We pulled up to Angelo's Delicatessen. The partially lit marquee blinked.

"This place has changed." She studied the building while I parked the car. "Let's get going."

She opened the door to the deli like she owned the place. Smells of fresh bread, spicy meats, and cheese met my nose and made me hungry. While I rubbed my growling stomach, she worked the room.

"Hey, Vi," an older, silver-haired man behind the counter shouted and came around the counter to give her a hug. "How you doing, hon? You look younger and younger every time I see you."

"Cut the shit, Ang. You better get glasses," she teased. "How you doin', *compadi*?" she asked, then tapped his cheek with her palm.

"*Mezza, mezza*," he said as he waved his hand back and forth. "We don't get the business we used to get anymore."

"Yeah, lots of changes, I see."

"And who is this with you?" The man looked at me.

"Sophia thinks I need help around the house, so they hired Barbara here to be my cleaning lady," she said, then laughed at her made-up story.

The man winked at me and held his hand out to shake mine. "Nice to meet you. I'm Angelo Sunseri."

"Likewise," I said. "Barbara Jackson. I'm her . . ." I paused when I saw her bone-chilling death stare.

"Hey, Ang, is there somewhere we can talk? I might need a favor."

Her words made me think about what happened to Marcus, and I was instantly curious.

"Yeah, sure. For you, anything," he said, then escorted Ms. G. to the back.

"Take a seat, kid. I'll be right back," she said.

I waited for Ms. G. to return when another man behind the counter stared at me intensely. He was a younger version of the man who'd shaken my hand. It might have even been Angelo's son—same face and hair—except that he had the most alluring blue eyes. The man came over to my table.

"Anything I can get you today?" the handsome-looking man said, then looked down at my left hand.

"No, thanks. I'm just waiting for Ms. Giordano."

"Oh, you're with *Zia* Vi. My godmother's a feisty one." His laugh accompanied a perfect, warm smile.

"Tell me about it," I said.

"I'm Alessandro Sunseri." He reached out his hand to shake mine. "Friends call me Alex."

"Hello, Alex, nice to meet you," I said, staring at his crystal blue eyes.

"If you need anything at all. Here's my card. Catering . . . a sandwich, maybe grab a coffee sometime—give me a call," he flirted with a dazzling smile.

Ms. G. came out with three white bags filled with food. "Alessandro," Ms. G. yelled, "get over here and give me a hug."

The man went over to her and kissed both cheeks.

"*Zia* Vi, I met your friend. You ladies should visit more often," he said, then looked me over with his brilliant blue eyes that seemed to pop against his dark hair and brows. This guy was movie-star handsome. Blushing now, I grabbed the bags from Ms. G. and smiled back at the man.

"All right, time to go," she said.

"Don't worry about nothin', *compadi.* Just call me, and it's all taken care of," the older man said.

I followed the number sixteen red jersey outside to the car.

"What's he planning to do for you, Ms. G.?"

"Oh, nothing . . . just family business," she said and got in the car.

"Family business?" I fastened my seat belt.

"I've known Angelo for years. He'd take a bullet for me," she said matter-of-factly.

"Ms. G., I have to ask you a question."

"Yeah, what is it?" she said as she struggled to click her seat belt.

"Marcus got kicked out of Garden Valley last night. You didn't have anything to do with that, did you?"

"Ha," she said in a spirited voice. "He got kicked out, huh? That's what he gets for being a *stronzo.*" She slid her sunglasses into place.

"Well, did you?"

"I'm an old lady with memory issues. Hell, until you said his name, I'd forgotten all about that piece of shit. Now, maybe he'll get a job and start providing. Let's get home. I'm starvin'," she said, avoiding my pressing stare.

I eyed her cautiously, then started the engine.

On our way home, Ms. G. looked sullen. Maybe she was sad from seeing Goosetown. According to her, San Jose had changed so much. Reality surely dated her memories and caused her pain.

I had made a right onto the Alum Rock exit when a rather wild idea crossed my mind. Without her license, she was a prisoner at the ranch. Her sad face verified it. So, without any further thought, I pulled the car over.

"Do you have your regular glasses in your purse?"

"Yeah, why?"

"'Cause you're gonna drive us home. So, put 'em on." I opened my door to walk around to the passenger's side.

"Really, kid?" Her brows rose and her eyes grew wide.

"Yes."

We exchanged seats, and she adjusted the seat to move her small body closer to the steering wheel. She shifted into gear, and we were off. She blew through one yellow light and swerved a few times as we approached the one-lane road to the ranch.

Once we hit the open road, she mashed her foot down on the gas pedal, and we flew up the hill. With white knuckles, I held on to the armrest of the door, squeezing it hard until I couldn't feel my fingers. She laughed around every turn.

"Whoo hoo," she bellowed through the car.

She flew up that road like she'd been doing it all her life. We had one close call with a truck, but she slowed and then we were back in the races again. She barreled down her driveway and slammed on the brakes, barely missing the garage door by an inch.

"That was great, kid," she gushed with wide eyes. She shifted the car into park and turned off the ignition.

"I'm glad you enjoyed it, but we can't do that every day. I might have a heart attack," I said, peeling myself off the leather seat. I grabbed the bags. She laughed all the way to the front door.

Chapter 19

Integration

AFTER MS. G.'S JOYRIDE THROUGH THE MOUNTAINS, I TOOK A few deep breaths to calm myself before loading piles of meats, bread, and cheese onto plates. I wasn't sure I could eat after our spirited little drive, but the smell of freshly baked bread took over my senses and I was hungry all over again.

Two helpings later, the elastic band on my scrubs felt tight. I'd gained ten pounds since taking care of Ms. G. I'd become a fan of Italian cuisine.

"Everything was delicious. Next time I'm in the mood for a nice hoagie, I know where to go. By the way, the younger gentleman who came to talk to me . . . that was Angelo's son, right?"

"Yeah. His oldest, Alessandro, Alex. Seems like just yesterday he was a little boy, running around that place."

My curiosity got the best of me. "Is he married?" I blurted out.

"Divorced. His old lady didn't want to be part of the *family business*," she said with a coy grin.

"Oh . . . the *family business*. Right." I swallowed down hard.

How could I be thinking about another man with the way things were? But Alex was so handsome, and he seemed interested. The only time Marcus paid attention to me was on payday. It had been a long time since someone took notice of me, and it felt good.

"He's a good-looking kid, all right. He gets it from my mother's side. Angelo married my cousin, Marie, but she died a few years back."

"Yes, Alex seems nice," I said, avoiding her stare.

"He's a good boy. He's been trying to get Ang to go legitimate for years. That kind of thing is hard—just look at my father. And poor Ang, he looks like he's struggling. Don't people appreciate good food anymore instead of this new health food crap? Who in the hell would eat wheatgrass anyway? Grass is for horses. Did I tell you my father raised horses?"

"I think I read that somewhere," I said, remembering the business cards in the desk.

"My father bred horses and had his medical practice. We were able to clean the money through both businesses."

"You mean cleaning as in money laundering?" I asked as my back tightened.

"Oh yes, bookmakin' was common in this life. See, about a month after the wedding, my father said it was time to learn the family business. I started as his medical assistant. I'd sterilize rooms, linens, equipment. Then he'd have me clean wounds and administer various painkillers. Once my father noticed I'd become more comfortable with my new role, he sat me down with this big black receipt book. And that was the first day I ever did work for the Molanano family. That's when I got my hands dirty in the business."

"Weren't you scared you'd get caught?"

"Hell no," she said, then took the last bite of her sandwich. "My father wouldn't let me take the wrap for something like that. He asked me to get involved in the finances because he trusted me with that part of the business. Since I was the first to graduate high school in my family, he thought I could handle the money side of things."

I sipped my soda while she continued.

"I remember he told me to think of it like paying taxes. Every working American had to pay taxes to the government, and in exchange, we got protection. The Mafia was no different than any government."

"Did the cops ever find out?"

"They tried a few times, but my father was smart. Deep down, whether my father wanted to admit it or not, he depended on the Mafia for lots of things—things that your basic immigrant wouldn't get on his own. He did his share of favors for them. He'd move the money when he had to. But back in my day, stuff like that would just go away. When a mob boss thought they would be linked to anything, they'd just grease the cops. If that didn't work, things got ugly and people died. It was as simple as that. So, we had to be careful, no matter what. The mob is smart. They find ways around everything, and there is always someone on the inside."

"Is it complicated to launder money?"

"No. It's pretty simple. Everything was cash. I'd write up the expenses and the charges to match how much we put in the bank. It all had to add up so that we wouldn't get in trouble. Now, you can't get away with as much as we did back then."

"That's true."

"If we were gonna get caught for anything, it would have been for taking in wise guys or for fixin' 'em up. Sometimes guys got hurt out there. Drug deals gone bad, robberies, street fights. My father saw everything from stabbings to bullet wounds—you name it."

"Bullet wounds? Seriously?" My mouth went dry.

"Sure. See, those guys didn't want to go to the hospital for fear they'd be questioned by the cops, so they came to my father, and he took care of it. As long as it all stayed under the radar, he maintained an open-door policy."

I looked around her house and tried to imagine the place as a functioning clinic. Real-life Mafia men sitting around after they may have killed someone? My heart knocked against my chest. Maybe in the room I'd put my purse and coat, there once was a gangster bleeding from a bullet wound or a robbery, or even worse. A shiver moved up my spine.

"You okay, kid? You look like you saw a ghost," she said, then put her hand on mine.

I smiled. "I'm fine. Go on." I swallowed deep when I thought about how devious she was. "You done with your lunch?"

"Yes, thanks." She handed me her plate. "I can't tell you how grateful these guys were for my father's services. They respected and admired him, and sometimes we'd even receive gifts. Once, a made guy named Johnny Spits gave my mother a brand-new mink jacket to thank my father for saving his life. Can you believe it? A mink jacket." She laughed, then went on. "My mother, being the simple woman she was, ended up having my father sell it. She used the money to upgrade the kitchen."

"Johnny Spits?" I wrapped up the leftover meats and cheeses to put in the refrigerator. "That's a strange name. Why do some of them get weird names like that?"

"They're just nicknames. Johnny used to have a lisp, and when he talked, he used to spit. I guess that's where he got the name."

I laughed with her and finished clearing the table.

"You know, even the mayor's wife came to see my father for her migraines. She'd tried everything from aspirin to morphine for her pain, and nothing worked. My father applied his touch to her temples and neck. Within a few days, the headaches went away. She was so happy with the results she told everyone about my father."

"Kind of like acupressure?"

"Well, sort of. It was more about the healing power of touch. Good news spreads fast, and because of the mayor's wife, our clinic was packed with people—including her husband. He started coming around more and more without her. Then I'd see him at Sunday night dinner and the occasional parties. And, over time, I put it together. He wanted in on the business, and since my father needed the protection, they worked out a deal. The mayor got a cut from the profits and the cops never bothered us or any of my father's friends. My father wasn't a strong arm for the mob, but he was a great negotiator, and he used whatever advantages he had."

"Ms. G., how did your father become a doctor?"

"He had a lot of friends. Some were attorneys and even a few judges. They pushed him to get his license and then they approved it. That was easy. Besides, back in those days, no one checked for licenses, unless it was threatened as a form of leverage, which happened from time to time. The cops and authorities always wanted to find a way in. The mayor was our golden ticket. By having a relationship with him, no one questioned us—ever."

"Can't really do that now. You can't just buy people off anymore. Things have changed."

"Not as much as you might think. Don't kid yourself, honey. Dirty politicians still exist," she said firmly. "The Mafia is still here, just more infiltrated now, more above board. But back then, no one ever ratted on my father because he'd earned the respect of his patients and the trust of the community for his years of service. If the mayor's wife trusts you, you're untouchable, and my father knew it."

"Tell me about the horses."

"My father bred, studded, and trained horses for racing. On paper, everything looked legal, and that's what my father and Don Molanano wanted everyone to see. He'd collect hefty fees for his services. It all looked legitimate. Sometimes he'd even gamble underground funds at the racetrack. Win or lose, it didn't matter, because the money was cleaned through the racetrack, which was connected to the Molanano family. The Molanano family was always trying to conduct and maintain business any way they could."

"So, because of your family's relationship with the mayor, you never got caught?"

"Money moved, everything moved. Things were literally falling off trucks. That's right at the time that Louie Cortese courted my sister. My father orchestrated the marriage—just like me and Frank. My sister didn't even know who Louie was until we had his family over for dinner one Sunday night. The next thing you know, he was at the house every weekend."

"So that's why your father had *you*, not Carmela, marry Frank?"

"Yes. She was promised to Louie before Frank came around," she said firmly.

I reached for her hand and looked into her eyes. "I'm sorry you weren't able to marry Gaetano." My eyes misted a bit.

"I'm okay, kid. I'm alive to talk about it, aren't I?" she said, peering over her glasses.

"Hopefully, one day, I'll be as tough as you."

"One day, you'll have to be, sweetheart."

"Did you tell anyone what happened on your wedding night?"

"Hell no. That was my business, and I didn't need a war on my hands. I focused on my patients. But living in my father's medical practice was tough for me and Frank. He and my father got into it a few times. My father made it clear to him that without the business functioning on a normal basis, he couldn't clean the money. And if he couldn't clean, trouble would follow. So Frank, being the kind of guy who knew what that meant, just sucked it up and dealt with it."

"I bet he didn't like having to cower down to your father."

"He hated it," she said with a wicked laugh. "From that point on, I didn't know where the money went. I mean, my father made money, no doubt. And there was more than money moving around, but I wasn't privy to that part of the business. I did what he asked of me, and I moved on to the more interesting parts of the job, like the patients, who later became my friends."

"Like you are to me—my friend," I said and smiled.

She smiled back with tender eyes. "Yes, but you're becoming more than just my friend. You're more like a daughter to me."

Tears I tried to hold back fell.

"Jesus, don't cry, honey. All that makeup you put on will run down your face. You get your period or somethin'?" she asked as she brushed away a loose tear.

"No, nothing like that. It's just . . . you know me like no one else. When I come here, I feel like this is my home away from home."

"I understand completely. I used to be in search of a safe place too." She placed her hand on my arm.

I wiped my tears and sniffed. "So, Ms. G., you little money launderer, you," I teased, trying to lighten the mood.

"That's how I got my feet wet in all this mess. Hell, I practically dove in. Looking back now, I can't say I was proud to do it, but I figured I'd helped my father. Working helped my mind stay busy. I needed a distraction from Gaetano. It wasn't until I moved to Brooklyn with Frank that I got a real taste of this life. That's when I met Rose and the girls, and everything changed."

"Yeah, you mentioned them before."

"I did?" She rubbed her chin. "Well, anyway, the women and wives fought for this life as savagely as their husbands did. Hell, some of them would take a bullet for their husbands. They even committed the same kind of crimes as the men, from murders to selling the poppy, from laundering to racketeering. Back in those days, mob wives were known to be tough, and their husbands wouldn't have it any other way. Most of them you could trust, but some you couldn't."

"Like a Virginia Hill type?"

"Exactly like Virginia Hill. She was one of the biggest molls in the country."

"Molls?"

"Well, that's what mob wives became known as. You know, I met Virginia once at a party."

"Really?"

"Nice but cunning. She commanded respect and, boy, did she have all the men's attention in that room—that's for sure. And she used every one of them to get what she needed. She put her female tools to work, all right."

"Female tools?"

"Women could get away with more because they had one weapon that men couldn't resist—their cock traps. Sex became a weapon. Good ole Virginia. For a while, a small part of me envied her until I found out she overdosed on drugs. I'm pretty sure I know why she did it. This life can take its toll," she said with sullen eyes.

"Wow."

"Yeah, a lot changed when I went to Brooklyn, but before I left, Frank and I went through our share of marital growing pains. We had to learn about each other—see how each other ticked in every way."

Chapter 20

Apprentice by Day,
Partner in Crime by Night

East San Jose Foothills, Giordano Estate
November 1940
Violetta

MOONLIGHT SHINED ON HIS HAIR AND BROUGHT HIS FIRM body into view. As he lay on top of me, kissing me harder, I panted with need.

"Gaetano, I love you," I said, but he didn't respond.

He moved inside me. I climbed further to my release.

Someone stood behind Gaetano.

Frozen in the dark, I focused on who was there. Frank's face came into view. He pulled back Gaetano's head and sliced his throat, ear to ear.

Blood spewed onto my stomach. Frank's eyes burned with rage. He pushed Gaetano's lifeless body off mine, then stood over me with the bloody knife still in hand, ready to pierce my heart.

I screamed into my dark bedroom.

Gasping for breath, I flicked on the bedside lamp and realized it was only a dream.

"Whew," I choked out, still disoriented. "Bad nightmare." I wiped away the sweat from the nape of my neck. When I grabbed at the covers on my bed, I felt moisture between my legs. I didn't know it was possible without being touched, but somewhere during the dream, I'd climaxed.

Heart pounding in my chest, I went to get a glass of water. On my way to the kitchen, I spotted Frank, asleep on the couch, still in his clothes. Since we'd returned from our honeymoon, he'd given me space. Frank was a bastard, but he fought against his morality and guilt. He hadn't touched me since our wedding night.

I lay back in bed and recounted the dream. Everything felt so real. I still smelled Gaetano's scent on my skin and felt the muscles on his back contract as he pushed his way inside me. My physical desires had prevailed, but the mental part of the dream, the part of Frank hurting Gaetano, was my subconscious exposing my fear. The visual reinforced my decision to leave Gaetano, but also left me feeling hollow in a loveless marriage.

Three months since the wedding, and still not a day passed that I didn't think of Guy. The only thing that helped was my new job at the clinic, alongside my father. My work routine gave me purpose and control over my life again. When I wasn't assisting Pop, I was in the office doing the books.

Over time, the muscles in my face relaxed, and a faint smile reappeared. It felt strange at first. After leaving Gaetano, I'd forgotten how it felt to smile. Thankfully, my time in the clinic helped my well-being. Above all, it provided a much-needed distraction to the huge hole that had been punched through my heart when I said goodbye to love.

"Time to get up." I dragged my body out of bed and went to the kitchen to start coffee. After my nightmare, I needed a boost to get through the day. As the pot percolated, Frank rubbed his eyes.

"You want coffffeeee?" I stuttered and stretched through a yawn. I poured myself a cup while Frank grabbed his shoes off the floor and walked toward our bedroom door.

"No, I need to sleep. We gotta get a better couch. That thing's like a rock." He rubbed his neck.

I put my coffee cup down. "Here, let me see." I placed my hands on his neck. I'd watched Pop treat neck pain many times, so I decided to give it a try. Frank eyed me cautiously while I pressed my fingers from his shoulders to the back of his skull. His neck felt like dough that needed to be rubbed out with a rolling pin. After a few minutes, I was able to get the kink out. Silent, we stared at each other, trying to gauge the other's reaction. This was the first time I'd touched him since the wedding night.

"Thanks. That felt nice." He smiled. "Maybe tonight, when I come back, I could sleep in the bed with you?"

I moved closer to his face. "Not on your life," I whispered in his ear and hummed a slight laugh.

"I ain't gonna sleep on that couch much longer, I can tell you that right now. I mean it, Violetta. I'm sorry for what happened, but a man's gotta have his limits," he said, exhausted, then grabbed his shoes and charged toward our bedroom door.

"Hope your neck feels better," I yelled sarcastically down the hall. I finished my toast and coffee and headed to the front of the house, where my patients would soon arrive.

"Hey, Pop, Paolo Caruso is in room two," I said with my hands full of medical supplies.

"Again? We just see him a few weeks ago. What for dis time?"

I looked down at his chart. "We saw him last month on the

fifth. It's hard to read your writing, but I think it says stab wound. This time he said he was attacked by a dog," I said with raised eyebrows.

"*Minchia*, dis guy," my father mumbled under his breath. "If he no careful, he gonna be dead. Okay, you follow me in to take da notes."

In the room, Paolo sat on the table, covered in gauze. He must have tried to dress the wounds himself.

"Hey, Paolo, what happen you dis time, huh, *paesano*?" Pop pulled off the gauze to examine the man's torso and forearms.

"Well . . . see . . . Giuseppe. I was, umm . . ." he started, then looked at me.

"She okay. She my daughter," Pop said.

The man smiled. "So, there is this house on Winchester. It's owned by a rich family. And well, I found out they went outta town, see, so I went over there to umm . . . I knew they had things there I needed, and when I got in, the dog was still in the house. I should have shot the mangy son of a bitch, but some neighbor started yelling that she was gonna call the cops. And well, I ran out of there." He lowered his chin.

"Dis a big dog, it look like. You gonna need stitches," Pop said, studying the wounds.

"I was gonna go to the hospital, but I knew if I came to see you, you'd fix me up with no problems."

"Violetta, get me da stitch kit," Pop said.

I opened the cabinet and handed him the box.

"Today, you gonna do it, *bella mia*. I show you."

"Really?" My mouth dropped open. It was the first time I'd ever tended to something bigger than a cut or an earache. "Okay, Pop."

"Paolo, you wan painkiller so it no hurt?"

"Sure, whatever you have," he said.

My father handed him a pill. "You no drive today. My son, Tony—he take you home."

"Okay, Giuseppe. If it's no trouble."

"Itsa no trouble," Pop said.

While my father watched, I cleaned the lacerations. Pop grabbed the threaded needle. "You ready, Violetta?"

"Yes," I said, watching intently.

Pop jabbed the needle hook into the man's flesh and pulled it through to the other side of the wound. "Tink of how you mama teach you to sew. Itsa like dis," he said and pulled the thread through again. Then he handed me the metal hook.

I did as Pop had shown me. I pulled up at the skin surrounding the bite and pierced the tip through the flesh. It made a popping sound, but I kept going until I got to the end of the wound. Then my father showed me how to tie off the knot.

"Okay, Paolo, my daughter she gonna finish up. I got a lot more patients today," he said.

The man handed my father a hundred dollars.

"Itsa on da house. *Viva la famiglia Molanano*," Pop said in Italian, then turned back to me. "I so prouda you, Violetta. You did a great job today." He beamed with pride. "Oh, and when you done, you finish da books like I show you. We got a pickup today. Paolo, tell you mama I say ello," Pop said, then left the room with his charts in hand.

I turned back to the man and continued. "Okay, *Signore*, you're all done. Remember to keep the stitches clean and dry. If the skin around them gets red, come back."

"You don't think that dog was rabid, do you?" the man asked with wide eyes.

"I wouldn't know. But if you feel strange or if you experience any symptoms like headache, weakness, or discomfort, come back and my father will know what to do next. We'd like to see you in a week so we can take the stitches out."

"*Grazie*. If there's anything, and I mean *anything*, you ever need, ask for Paolo Caruso. Giuseppe has always been good to us and my family. He's lucky to have such a beautiful daughter," the man said with a soft smile.

"Thank you." A small blush warmed my cheeks. "We're happy to help where we can. Be careful out there," I said, then grabbed my equipment to sterilize.

My father's proud eyes made me happy. I couldn't ignore why this wise guy, Paolo Caruso, was here today, but I'd done my job. I helped someone, and it felt good.

My day had been so perfect, I wanted to celebrate. Once the patients left and Pop went home, I made dinner. Then I grabbed my bottle of Sanna wine from the liquor cabinet, poured two glasses, and sat at the table. I wanted to share my accomplishment with someone, and that person would have to be Frank. Halfway through my glass, Frank came in.

"Hey, it smells good in here. Whadya you make?"

"I made pasta with meatballs." Maybe it was the two candles I lit on the table that forced him to shoot me a suspicious look. Watchful, he sat next to me to eat.

He looked down at his plate. "You wouldn't poison me, would you?"

"No, I'm saving the poison for breakfast," I said and laughed. While he ate, I took a chance on opening up to him for the first time in our married life. "Hey, guess what?"

"What?" he said as he shoveled pasta into his mouth.

"My father taught me how to stitch someone up today. I did the whole thing by myself. It was the best feeling, Frank." I poured another glass of wine.

"Oh yeah? That's nice. Maybe you gunna be a docta someday? I don't know about dat—a woman docta? That'll be the day," he scoffed.

My mood deflated. "It felt good to help someone."

"Hey, this is good wine." He picked up the bottle and studied the label. "Sanna Winery? Where did we get this?"

"Wedding present," I said smoothly as my heart pounded.

He eyed me with caution, and for good reason. Up to this point, neither one of us had paid attention to the other since our dreadful wedding night. But with my dream still fresh in my mind, I was reminded of my biological needs. I was married now. I didn't need permission from anyone but him, and I was pretty sure he wouldn't contest. The wine warmed and relaxed my muscles. Even the muscles around my private parts loosened up. Maybe it was because it had been such a long time, but I felt like being suggestive.

There was a tinge of forbidden eroticism in the moment. I remembered my friend, Julia, telling me about what the French called a *ménage à trois*. This would be the closest I'd have to that. I sipped the wine my lover made for me, and I shared it with my husband. The cabernet took on a new meaning. The bottle even resembled a certain part of Gaetano's body that I craved. Gripping the bottle in my hand, my mind went to forbidden places. I thought of things I wanted to do with that bottle when I was alone. Tiny beads of sweat trickled down my back as I poured myself another glass.

Red liquid splashed along the rim of the glass, and I imagined it was Gaetano's finish, spilling into me. I grabbed my glass and drank it down fast—every drop. His seed coated my throat. It was personification at its finest.

And although Gaetano was not there, his wine taunted and aroused me further. The idea of him being a participant in this moment gave me permission to engage in such an activity with Frank. I'd make sure that Guy would be with me in this existential way.

My intentions made my insides throb further. I imagined drinking the wine with Gaetano again. Taking him into me, inside me, where he would fill up every part of my body. It was a feeling

I hadn't felt in months, and I welcomed it desperately. Throbbing unfolded in my pelvis.

I looked at Frank's face and how the muscles on his forearms moved as he lifted his fork to his mouth.

He shot me a quick glance. When I didn't look away, his breath became uneven. He stared, waiting for me to make my next move. To protect myself, my mind transposed Gaetano's face onto Frank's. I took my last sip of wine and walked over to his chair. My cheeks were hot from the wine and my groin was damp.

With excited eyes, Frank swallowed hard.

"Whatsa matter? What are you doin'?" he asked as I advanced on him.

I straddled him on the kitchen chair and rubbed myself up and down. I arched my back for better traction. He pulled me closer to him. His lips pushed my lips apart and his tongue jetted into my mouth like a snake coming out of its hole. I kept grinding on him, letting my panties soak through onto his pressed slacks.

He reached under my dress and quickly unzipped his pants. Before he could insert himself inside me, I quickly jumped off and kneeled in front of him. I shut my eyes and let my mouth work. Tonight would be about me. I wouldn't let him finish until I was sure I could. Once he began to moan, I climbed back on top. Letting my dress fall around him, I pulled my panties to the side and forced him into me. My senses told me how far to sink and how deep to go.

It was such a role reversal between us. I was in charge this time. He let me maneuver him the way I wanted. With his hands firmly gripped on my hips, I rocked my body back and forth, searching for release.

"You like that, baby? You close? Let me see you cum," Frank said with a rough voice. Then he tangled his fingers through my hair as I continued to work.

After a few more plunges down, muscles under my belly button shook and then it happened. I exploded all over Frank. My whole body trembled against him while he held me tight to my finish. Eyes closed and trying to catch my breath, I slowed for every aftershock that surged through me.

Like a sponge that has had the water squeezed out, my arms and legs felt like limp noodles dangling around him. He held on to me for a moment and stayed absolutely still so that I enjoyed the full benefit of the experience. We both knew in that instant that we had crossed over into a new realm.

Because of my new ability to transfer Gaetano's face onto his, he didn't look so scary anymore. It was like an eclipse. My imagination was a catalyst that made it possible to continue. I needed to imagine that Frank was someone else. So, I twisted my fingers through his thick black hair and kissed him fervidly.

Impatient for his reward, he picked me up and took me to the bedroom. "Now it's my turn," he said, smiling. His eyes were powerful. He had his prize in his arms and wouldn't let go. "I promise not to hurt you this time," he said, then kissed me again. I nodded and shut my eyes.

I told myself that this was a physical need—a release. For my body, it was necessary. I could no longer hold out for fear of him. I had to take him, the bad and the good, for myself and for my sanity. I imagined it was my grape grower holding me and surrendered to the moment.

I awoke the next morning feeling revived, mind and body. Frank stood at the other side of the bed, looking at me. For the first time, his eyes appeared to search for who I was and what I meant to him.

We were two people who didn't know one another but had just shared an old-as-time experience. It wasn't lovemaking, but it wasn't rape anymore, either. It was a function. With all the pain inflicted on me recently, emotionally and physically, I wasn't afraid to test my sexual limits with Frank. I'd acted in a way I never thought possible. Our movements were harder—stronger some-how, and a part of me liked how rough we were with one another. I channeled months of self-inflicted torment and guilt onto Frank and found my escape. Our bed was a life raft for my drowning soul. And because we didn't know how to act, or what to say after our night, we searched in vain for words.

Silently, he poured a handful of jewels—five diamonds, three rubies, and two emeralds—into my palm. As I moved the shiny rocks around my palm, the facets reflected light into my eyes. My very own magic show. I'd never seen such a dazzling effect before.

He held my other hand. "These are for you. We'll visit a jew-eler friend of mine and make nice pieces out of these. See you later tonight, gorgeous. I'll make sure to bring another bottle of wine for dinna." He kissed my cheek, finished knotting his tie, and left.

It was a strange feeling. There were no 'I love yous,' no 'thank yous,' but there was a present. Maybe that was his way. I didn't feel like a whore because I was married, but I didn't feel loved, either. I was somewhere in between.

I lay there in the quiet of our room, naked under the sheets, and it all felt surreal. My heart belonged to Gaetano, but my body was Frank's. Gaetano was the love of my life—my fairy-tale ro-mance. He was innocent and represented a life to be proud of and revered. The kind of man who worked hard for what he had and someone who loved me to my core.

And now I had Frank, whom I'd finally connected with—not in an emotional way, but a physical one. We were familiar now. He represented the dangerous life, one that was chosen for me a long time ago. Frank was a feared, treacherous man, one who would kill for what he wanted. His alliance with this life required the type of wife who would lie for him and defend him at all costs.

As I balanced these thoughts in my mind, I balanced the stones in my hand. I held them up to the light and thought about what other women in my position would do. Most women in that moment would tell their husbands that they didn't want the gemstones because they were probably stolen. For all I knew, someone had died for these jewels. Truth was, I was okay with it because a piece of me had died. They were owed to me for my sacrifice.

Payment in hand, I accepted being the wife of a mobster. To my core, I knew this lifestyle was embedded in my genes. It was all I'd ever known. As much as I'd fought against it, I couldn't deny it any longer.

I'd use Frank as much as he'd use me.

Chapter 21

Ciao for Now

WRAPPED IN AN AFGHAN I'D MADE, I WALKED AROUND THE house, turning off lights and locking doors. Just as I was about to crawl into bed, I heard someone struggling with the front door lock.

Who would be here at this hour? Frank didn't usually come home until four in the morning. Chest throbbing, I reached for the silver candlestick on my nightstand. I was ready to strike when Frank stumbled in and flicked the light back on.

"Oh Jesus, Frank, you scared me. I thought someone broke in. I almost took your head off." I exhaled, then put down the heavy candlestick.

"You'd like that, wouldn't you?" he teased, then slapped my ass.

"Ouch. Quit kidding around. Why you home so early, anyway? It's ten o'clock."

I hopped into bed and pulled the covers over my cold feet.

"I talked to my father. He said the feds backed off, and it's safe to come back."

"Frank, we never discussed moving to Brooklyn. I'm not

ready to leave my family. My father needs me," I protested through clenched teeth.

"Let's get one thing straight, doll. We don't need to discuss anything. I make the rules around here, and we're going to Brooklyn. My family's there. I got things lined up. I can make a lot more money in Brooklyn than I can in this dump," he said as he undressed.

"Dump?" I sat up in bed. "This *dump* saved your ass when you had nowhere to go." I crossed my arms as my blood pressure rose.

"We're going, and that's final. Don't be mad," he said, then got into bed. "It'll be great, you'll see. You'll live like a queen ova there," Frank said, then caressed my hot cheek.

I pushed his hand off. "Don't even think about it." I rolled my eyes.

"Oh, here we go again with this shit," he said with his hands in fists.

"Why can't I stay behind for a while? That way, I can train Carmela to help out in the clinic."

"Every respected Sicilian with a wife does not live apart. I'd look like a disgrace to my father. No way. Start packin'," he said, then rolled over and was asleep in minutes.

I sat in bed, listening to him snore. My blood boiled. As far as we'd come in the last few months, my anger with him was back in full force. He didn't sit me down, try to reason with me, or even ask me how I felt. He just told me. How could I leave now? I loved working with Pop at the clinic. The books were perfect. All the deposits ran smoothly, with no red flags, and business was good. I didn't want to leave my family and the only home I'd ever known.

Frank never liked the foothills. He really had no business on a ranch, anyway. It wasn't his style. Whenever Pop asked him for help with something as simple as feeding the pigs, he always had an excuse. Pop never said much to Frank, but there were a few times I overheard him and Tony talking about how Frank was more work than he was worth.

What scared me most were the stories I'd heard about the

families in New York. They lived a different kind of life from what I was used to. I was afraid of what would happen to us in Brooklyn. From the little I'd read in the newspapers, the Sambino family was somehow implicated in the murder Frank committed. Was that why Frank's father thought it was okay to come home now, because the Sambino family took the heat? And when we got there, would Frank be targeted? If there was a war brewing between the Molanano and Sambino families, I didn't want to be in the middle of it without my family's protection. The whole idea gave me *agità*, and my stomach ached. I wasn't ready for such a move.

The next morning, I woke early and made Frank's favorite breakfast of bacon and eggs. I figured I'd try the be-nice angle. But the conversation at breakfast quickly turned into a heated argument. He screamed and I cried. No matter what I said or did, Frank didn't budge. When all else failed, I followed up with indignation, which turned into a boxing match. I threw plates at his head, and he belted me in the stomach a few times. After a few bruised ribs, and not being able to breathe well, I knew my days on the ranch were numbered.

I walked gingerly around the office as I cleaned instruments and sterilized exam rooms.

Pop stopped in front of me and studied my slow movements. "Violetta, why you walk funny? You look like you ride da mule or someting," Pop asked as I sat at my desk.

"I fell."

"Fell on what?"

"The floor."

"Whatsa going on? I hear you da udder night. You and Franco, you fighting? It sound like tings breaking."

"Yeah, like my ribs." I winced.

My father's eyes widened. "What happened, *bella mia*? He hurt you?"

I didn't have to speak. He knew.

"Pull up you shirt. I need to check."

I pulled up my shirt. He rubbed his hands softly across my ribs when I winced.

"*Che cazzo*? Das it. No more. I keep dis guy here and dis da tanks I get?" he yelled, then smacked his hands on the desk. By the time I'd pulled down my shirt, he was already out the door looking for Frank. In great pain, I tried to follow him down the hall to our bedroom.

"Franco," he yelled and banged on the door. "I needa speak wit you."

Frank came out in his underwear and scratched his head. "What's up, Giuseppe? Can't you see I'm sleepin' ova here?"

My father shoved his finger in Frank's face. "If you ever hurt my daughter again, I'll kill you. You hear me?" My father's eyes were intense and burned onto Frank.

"You're smarter than that, old man. Besides, me and your daughter are moving to Brooklyn. My father said it's time to go back. So, mind your business," Frank said with cold eyes.

Pop stood there and shook his head. "You tink you soma big shot. You disrespect me in my own house wit my daughter. Youa disgrace to dis family," he said, then marched back down the hall where I was standing.

Frank slammed the door.

Pop called me to his office. His hands trembled when he handed me the tiny, white bottle. "Here. Dis are painkillers," he said with a shaky voice. "Take dem twice a day for da next few days. You listen to me. I canno get in da middle, but if he ever hurt you like dat again you coma straight to me or Tony. You hear?"

"Okay, Pop. I will." I nodded. "I don't want to go to Brooklyn. That's why we got into a fight in the first place."

He kissed my cheek and whispered in my ear, "Remember what I tell you." Then he grabbed the charts and walked away.

After the patients left, I locked up and went to my room where I took my first pill. I felt better within minutes. Later, Frank told me that if I ever told anyone about our domestic troubles again, I'd get worse. He threatened to kill me and have Pop watch. Then he'd kill Pop because he was such a pain in the ass. Frank wasn't someone to make empty threats. He meant every word. That was the night I learned to stay quiet.

Two weeks passed. With no choice and no voice, I packed our things. Standing alone in our bedroom, I remembered everything I'd done to make this place feel like a home. I remembered the briefcase with Gaetano's letters that I'd stashed away in the filing cabinet. I didn't want anyone to find it. I went to the barn and searched for the key. When no one was looking, I buried the briefcase deep in the barn and didn't look back. Forced to start over with nothing, I was miserable and heartbroken all over again.

Frank bought two first-class seats on the airplane to New York. When the engine roared and the plane lifted off the ground, I made sure to take an extra pill. Within an hour, I was out. I woke to the stewardess telling me to move my seat forward.

After a long day, we finally made it to Brooklyn. It was dark out as we drove by some waterfront homes and a few areas that looked like parks. If I was ever to have children with Frank, I wanted them to have a place to play outside and not be caged up in some high-rise apartment complex.

After what had transpired between me and Frank, the thought of having babies with him made every muscle in my body tense up. I'd never seen him with children, but if his version of fatherhood was anything like his version of marriage, I'd be scared for my kids' lives. I wondered where all his aggression came from. Was Mr. Di Natale

Sr. hard on him or his mom? Was it from his time on the streets? I'd never seen my father hit my mother. It all felt wrong.

As much as having kids with Frank scared me, being a mother would give me purpose again. I wanted a child so that I'd have someone to love and someone who'd love me back, unconditionally. Frank told me he wanted a big family, but I didn't think it was for the same reasons. He'd want sons to help him with the family business, much like he was to his father, and how my brothers were to Pop. With a heavy heart, I pressed my head against the car window as tall buildings buzzed by.

"You ready, baby? You're gonna love it here. My parents are so excited to meet you." He kissed my cheek.

My body froze from his touch. Aside from digging my fingernails into his forearms on the plane's take-off, we hadn't touched since our big fight at the house. My gaze fell. "I miss my home. It's all I've ever known. No one beats me there," I said with moist eyes.

He gauged my reaction. "I'm sorry, Vi. It won't happen again. Sometimes you bring the worst out in me," he said, then reached for my hand. "Let's start fresh. Please, forgive me," he said with softer eyes.

"Yeah . . . sure . . ." I mumbled half-heartedly, then darted my heavy eyes away from him and back onto the road.

Even in twilight with the few streetlamps shining on it, the Di Natale estate was a massive spectacle of a house. Mr. Di Natale was not only an infamous gangster, but he had a few front companies that made him appear as a legitimate businessman. His biggest operation was funeral homes. He owned and operated several in the Northeast. He also had a few bars here and there, on top of trying to get his feet rooted in the casino business. Having his hands in different businesses afforded him a house like this. A true out-of-the-history-books mansion. A Mafia fortress. However, it wasn't the fortress

that made me nervous. It was who was in it—Frank Di Natale Sr.—
the underboss for the entire Molanano family.

Since I'd never met Frank's parents, I wondered how they'd
perceive me. For the first time in my life, I saw servants. Back on
the farm, we did all the work ourselves, so when their maid took my
jacket, I was floored. It felt uncomfortable, but I followed Frank's
lead. He showed me around the mansion. It had a library, two dens,
and eight bedrooms. I'd never seen anything like it. It smelled of old
age and money, a mix of damp wood and mothballs.

His father and mother greeted us downstairs. Frank ran right
up to his father and hugged him.

"Glad to see you, son," Mr. Di Natale said as he kissed Frank
on the cheek.

"Hey, Dad, this is Violetta."

Mr. Di Natale Sr. reached out his hand, layered with gold rings,
and kissed the top of my hand like I was a queen. A princess, maybe,
to his dynasty.

"It's a pleasure to meet you, Violetta."

"Nice to meet you too," I said back shyly.

His mother extended her hand toward me. Her three-carat di-
amond ring caught my attention.

"Nice to meet you. She's beautiful, Frank," she said with a
half-smile.

"Thank you. It's nice to meet you too." I shook her hand.

She shifted her focus back onto her son and hugged him tightly.
"So glad to see you, son, and know that you're all right. Did they
treat my baby okay over there? Huh? Look at you, all married now."
She cupped Frank's cheek in her hand and smiled through her red
lipstick.

Mr. Di Natale chimed in, "I wish I could've been at the wedding, but I had to attend to other business, as you know."

"If you'll excuse me, I have so much to do with the party and
all," his mother said.

"Party?" I asked.

"My parents are throwing us a welcome-home party and a mini-reception, since they couldn't be with us at our wedding."

"When?" I asked, then yawned.

"Don't worry, baby. Tomorrow. They knew we'd be jet-lagged," he said and laughed along with his father.

While the two men spoke in the living room, I took in my surroundings. There were a few Picasso paintings, which I was pretty sure were real. There were gold-plated lamps, fancy heirlooms, and religious symbols scattered around the room. The most interesting figure in the house was Mr. Di Natale. His reputation preceded him. He was the underboss, and he was known to be ruthless. Mr. Di Natale meant business. He seemed elusive, and that was what made him respected and feared.

Frank made fun of Pop and how we lived like animals. He said we were dirty people and called us 'basics.'

"Don't go around sayin' stupid things. Talkin' like that is what gets you in trouble, son. You keep it up, and I might not be able to help you next time. Giuseppe took you in, under my direction. Don't forget that. Let's talk later in private." He gave me a slight shrug. I smiled back. It was rather amusing to watch Frank's father reprimand him. For fear of laughing out loud, I bit down on my bottom lip. Being the cunning and sly man that he was, Mr. Di Natale changed the subject to redirect the conversation back to me.

"So, Violetta. What do you think of my little town? It must be a big difference compared to San Jose. Was the plane ride okay? You look tired," he said.

I paid attention to his words *my little town*. If I was honest, he was right. In so many ways it was his town.

"Yes, it's different than I expected. Still nice, but different. This was the first time I'd ever been on a plane. It was a little bumpy from time to time, but I slept most of the way."

"Why don't I get someone to bring your luggage up to your room so you can rest? We're hostin' a big dinner for yous two to-morra. I got a lot of people who wanna meet ya."

"Katarina," he yelled. The maid entered the room. *"Porta le valigie in camera."*

"Si, Signore," she said.

With his suggestion for me to rest, I suspected that Mr. Di Natale wanted to speak to Frank alone. I took my cue and followed the maid up the stairs to Frank's old room. At first glance, the room still had childlike elements. An old, tattered baseball and glove sat on a dresser. Wood paneling covered the walls.

Pictures on the wall told Frank's true story. Each photo displayed various stages of his life. On one wall were framed pictures of his childhood. There was one of him riding a pony and another of him playing baseball. I'd never seen this side of Frank. Seeing him as a sweet, innocent boy endeared him to me. If I didn't know he was the son of a famous mobster, I would have thought he lived the typical American life.

One photo showed Mr. Di Natale holding Frank as a baby. He wore his father's hat and Mr. Di Natale smiled at him. The image was sweet and assured me of Mr. Di Natale's love for his son.

I wondered if I would see the softer side of Frank with our future children the same way that Mr. Di Natale revealed his tenderness so many years ago. Maybe sharing a child with Frank wouldn't be so scary after all. Deep down, I knew that if I had a son with Frank, he would find his place in this life, one way or another. I didn't want to have a child, only for him or her to be killed one day or put in jail.

I wanted a child for me—*not* for the mob.

To break away from these thoughts, I continued to browse the room. That was where I witnessed the shift. Frank's transition: a picture of Frank standing next to a group of guys on the street, smoking cigarettes. Frank and another guy held guns to their chests while the rest shot brooding stares at the camera. They fit the tough-guy description.

Somehow, Frank's eyes had changed. Youthful innocence had left him. What remained was a hardened man. The toll this lifestyle had taken was evident. His duty to the cause and the need for his father's love had warped his morality.

Frank had mentioned he was in a street gang at thirteen. That was when he got into the life. I knew a few guys back home who'd done the same thing. Because Frank's father was the underboss, Frank had lots of connections. He'd told me he'd always wanted to be a gangster like his dad. Maybe now I'd understand him better and could forgive him for what he'd done to me. Frank was a product of his environment.

The photos of him burned holes in my heart and mind. I tried to settle in but tossed and turned. I wasn't sure if it was because it was a different house or the long day of travel. I felt exhausted, yet my mind was active. The photographs got me thinking about my family and my home. I wondered if my father was okay and if the patients asked about me.

By default, my mind drifted to the one place it spent most of its time—Gaetano. No matter how hard I tried, his memory always crept in and took over. For so long I'd thought of only having children with Gaetano. Just like we'd talked about, I imagined them running in the fields of the winery. Wavy-haired angels, blessed with the most beautiful black lashes, smiling back at us. And yet here I was, thinking about starting a family with a different man. My thoughts betrayed me, but I was helpless against them.

To stop my mind from torturing my heart again, I popped another pill and washed it down with water from the bathroom sink. I figured it would help me sleep and when I woke up, I'd be ready to face my *new* family.

Chapter 22

Mob Wife in Training

Brooklyn, New York
February 1941

"Hey, get up, Vi. *Minchia*. It's almost noon," Frank yelled.

At the sound of his voice, I tried to peel my heavy eyes open. My vision was foggy and unfocused.

"What the hell's wrong with you? You been sleepin' for, like, twelve hours."

"I fell asleep when I got up here, and um . . . er . . . I don't know," I croaked.

"You slept the whole night, and now it's almost lunchtime. I tried to wake you, but you slept like the dead. And I should know, I seen a couple guys like that before. I think at some point you were even snorin'," Frank said, laughing. "My mutha is gonna think you don't like her cookin' if you don't get down there soon. I told them you were sleepin' in from the time difference, but it is lunchtime now. So, time to get up." He pinched my ass.

I flinched and rolled onto my side. My arms and legs still felt relaxed from the pills, and I felt sort of wobbly. It took a few minutes, but I made my way to the shower.

With help from a little hot water and strong-smelling soap, I was awake and ready to face the day. I put on one of the new dresses that I'd bought. It was a black dress with red accents. Simple, yet classy. I finished it off with a pair of black heels. I'd be meeting new people today, so I wanted to make a good impression. I did up my hair in a bun and decorated my ears and neck with the rubies Frank gave me.

I smiled at myself in the mirror and turned to Frank for direction on what was to happen next. He stared at me for a minute, and if I thought we didn't have to be at a party soon, he would have taken me right then and there.

"You look great, baby. I got a little somethin' for you," he said as he opened the closet and pulled out a big rectangular box.

"What's this?"

"Open it. It's long overdue, and when you're here with me, in *my* town, we gotta maintain a look. Guys gotta know that we earn— keeps the younger ones motivated. So, our wives gotta look good."

I opened the box to find a beautiful mink stole. It was caramel-colored and had the loveliest gold brooch. A few of my aunts had stoles like this, and they wore them to holiday functions and sometimes to church, but I never had one of my own.

Frank pulled it out of the box and draped it over my shoulders. With suggestive eyes, he said, "The winters here are much colder than what you're used to. This will keep you warm." He grazed his fingertips from my shoulder to my chest, sending rows of goose bumps down my arms.

"Thank you," I said, charmed by his generosity. I stroked my fingers softly through the fur. Tiny hairs tickled my neck and felt silky to the touch. When I caught a glimpse of my reflection in the mirror, I was no longer a small-town girl, but a real woman. I'd matured. The stole was the perfect final touch and made a strong statement, for sure. I turned back to Frank, ready to meet everyone.

"It looks great on you," he said as he continued to touch its softness over my breasts.

"It's stunning. I've never had a fur before."

"This is just the beginning. I'm gonna shower you with gifts. For my wife, only the best." He kissed my cheek. "I'll meet you downstairs, but don't take too long. My ma wants to get to know yous betta. She has cooked up a feast for us," he said as he walked out of the room.

Before I came downstairs to meet everyone, I caught another glimpse of myself in the mirror. For a split second, I saw my mother. I remembered the mink coat she'd been given many years ago and had asked my father to sell because she wasn't that type of woman. She didn't want to parade around like she was some fancy mob wife like the others. And here I was in Mr. Di Natale's house, the mob boss of the Molanano family, with a God damn fur wrapped around my neck, ready to mingle with the biggest gangsters in the world.

The realization shook me to my core.

Who was I becoming?

Would I let myself turn into someone I didn't respect or know? The stole, mixed with my heavy, beating heart, made me sweat. The fur strangled me, somehow restricting me of breath and choking back my morality. I was at a dangerous crossroads. Not sure which direction to turn or where I was headed, I pushed back any straggling hairs behind my ear, adjusted the mink, and walked into my new life.

I strolled into the foyer when Mr. Di Natale called me over.

"Hey, kid, you sleep well?"

"I was exhausted, but I'm much better now."

"Good to hear it because Marie's been cooking all morning for you."

"Oh, thank you. She didn't have to go to any trouble."

"Oh no, no trouble. She loves to cook. She's a damn good cook too."

Mr. Di Natale put his arm around my shoulders and led me through the double French doors into the formal dining room. The room was huge and had the longest dinner table I'd ever seen. The table was set so elegantly with massive, fresh, long-stemmed rose bouquets at both ends. Gold-plated china was stacked at the end of the table, which was loaded with various trays of food. Dead center of the table was a huge glass chandelier that dangled from the cathedral ceiling, reflecting light on all the crystal glasses. The effect reminded me of Frank's words: having this *look* so that other guys would aspire to be like him.

Everything was so fancy, as if I was about to dine with a king. As I admired the room's details, Frank called for me.

"Hey, Vi, come ere."

I walked past the table into the kitchen to see the queen in her castle.

She looked up from her pot of gravy to see me in my dress and new fur. Her eyes moved over my body, followed by a half-hearted smile. Maybe she thought I wasn't good enough for her son. Little did she know, I didn't think much of him, either. She looked away, wiped her hands on her apron, and clasped Frank's face in her hands. "I sure hope you're happy, son. If you're happy, I'm happy."

That was it. Not a word to me. She turned away from us and continued to cook. I took the hint and moved closer to Frank. That's when the doorbell rang.

"Okay, lemme see who's here," Mr. Di Natale said as he went to greet his guests in the foyer.

Frank pulled me aside and whispered in my ear, "Okay, you're gonna meet some friends and family. You'll be all right, just don't talk too much. Let me do most of the talkin'. Oh, and don't go saying nothin' about our business."

"Sure," I said. I'd been silenced again.

Over the next hour, people continued to arrive. There must

have been about forty strangers in the kitchen alone. But in a fortress like this, forty people in a kitchen weren't a crowd.

Suddenly, the room quieted.

A man in a three-piece suit entered with his wife, daughter, and two sons.

"Don Molanano, we're so happy you joined us today," Mr. Di Natale Sr. said, then kissed the back of the man's hand. "Come get a plate of food. Marie's been cookin' all day," he said respectfully.

"*Grazie*," Don Molanano said, then looked around the room at the men and families assembled. He appeared to be from the old country. He had a broken accent and was soft-spoken. There was something regal about him, like he'd been born to do this. He didn't appear like a tough guy. He looked sophisticated and powerful. At his level, he had enough guys under him to do his bidding, so he wouldn't have to get his hands dirty anymore. His wife reminded me of Mama. She dressed more reserved than the others. She stood proud and elegant next to her husband.

Frank, hungry to make a name for himself, went right up to Don Molanano and made a big fuss about me and our marriage.

"This is her—my Violetta," he said, presenting me like I was a shiny new trophy.

"Dis a Giuseppe's daughter?" Don Molanano asked with wide eyes.

"Yes, this is her."

Don Molanano handed Frank a thick envelope. "Here. Dis for you, for da wedding." He lightly tapped Frank's face and turned to me. "*Congratulazioni*. I know you fater for many years."

"I remember meeting you when I was about eight or nine years old. You wanted to see one of our racehorses, Stranger."

"Oh *si, il cavallo*. I remember dat. I ma sorry I no make da wedding, but I had to tend to some biziniss," he said, then shot a bone-chilling stare to Frank's father.

Frank's father nodded, then continued talking to his guests.

"I wish you and Franco a life of love and a house full of healthy children," Don Molanano said.

"*Grazie*," I said, still shocked at who stood before me.

"My wife and I, we beena a marry almost forty years." He looked on lovingly at his wife, who sat in the corner with a plate of food on her lap.

The thought of forty years with Frank made my stomach turn inside out. "Forty years, that's quite an accomplishment. *Congratulazioni*. I hope Frank and I will be as happy as you are in forty years," I lied, trying to convince him and myself.

"Well, itsa pleasure to meeta you again, Violetta." He kissed the back of my hand. "Excuse me," he said as Frank's father called him over.

In that moment, I felt like royalty. I'd just spoken to Don Molanano, one of the biggest mafiosos in the world, and he kissed *my* hand. I knew what that meant for me. I would be regarded as someone to be feared. That felt strange in itself. I understood more clearly my father's master plan.

"The Molanano family controls both coasts. And with our move into the casino business out there, we're one of the strongest families. Right, Pop?" Frank turned to look at his father.

"Yes, son," Mr. Di Natale said.

Everyone raised their glasses. Together, they chorused, "Salute, *cent'anni . . . Viva la famiglia Molanano*."

Don Molanano stood proudly over his men and families. All the made men, *capos*, and soldiers gathered around him and glorified him like a king. Everyone went up in a line, kissed his hand, and hugged him.

After introductions concluded, the house grew loud. Cigarette smoke and the smell of alcohol filled the air. I didn't think it was possible in such a cavernous place, but I started to feel claustrophobic.

While Frank worked the room and socialized with the big guys, I nibbled on second-rate focaccia bread. It was nothing compared to my aunt's recipe, but I munched on because I hadn't eaten since the day before, and my stomach growled right through my dress.

Most of the men wore fancy suits with matching ties and pocket squares. They kissed the women on the cheeks as a sign of respect. In front of the women, they talked about things like baseball, politics, and the best places around the city to buy a suit. When the small talk was over, in typical Italian fashion, they grabbed their food and made their way outside to smoke and talk about things not suited for certain ears.

The women, however, stayed inside and were forced to mingle with each other. I'd heard about women like this before. I didn't know if I would fit in with them or if I even wanted to socialize with these types. Because I didn't know anyone yet, I wasn't in the position to go around mouthing off about people and things I didn't know about. To avoid unwanted conversation, I sat in one of the dining room chairs and minded my own business.

The women gathered and gossiped like a group of cackling hyenas. Most of them had the big hair and faces caked with dark makeup. They dressed revealing, with skintight pencil skirts and see-through blouses that put everything on display. A few in the crowd dressed elegantly.

The one thing that was true of both groups was that they had no problem flaunting their wealth. That was the allure. The silver lining beyond murders and crime—furs, jewels, huge houses, and fancy cars—were the payoff for the oath and duty we all took. I had experienced this with Frank when he presented me with jewels and the mink stole. Maybe it was out of payment or solidarity, but whatever it was, we all loved the allure. It felt good to have nice things, but at what cost? Despite the furs and jewels, they all wore gold crucifix charms around their necks to pray for their sins and the sins of their men.

As I listened further to their chatter, the room crowded with the stink of hairspray and strong perfume. I worried that one of them might catch their hair on fire every time they lit another cigarette.

One woman named Rose told a story. Not sure if it was the heavy red lipstick or the poofy hair or the way she cussed like a sailor, but she stood apart from the others. She spoke in a heavy Brooklyn accent.

"Hey, Suzanne, guess who I saw at Clamonte's last night?"

"Who?"

"Sammy Impietro. Do you remember him?"

"Um, yeah, I think so. Was he the guy you dated a few years ago? The guy with the lisp?"

"Yeah, that's him. He was there with some bimbo. I told Jimmy if she looked at me one more time, I was gonna shove an ashtray down her fuckin' throat. Jimmy marched right over there and told Sammy to have her stop giving me dirty looks. And if he didn't get her to stop, then he was gonna cut her eyes out of her God damn head and do the same to him."

The women listened and blew smoke out their mouths like dragons.

"One thing led to another, and they got into a huge fight. Jimmy ended up breaking a bottle over his head, and we got thrown out. I swear, I will neva go back to that dump. I don't care how good a food they think they got," Rose said.

"Oh, is that why he has a shina today?" Suzanne asked.

"Yeah, I didn't have the heart to tell him I used to date Sammy. If he had known that, I'm sure he woulda waited outside for him and his whore to come out and whacked 'em both."

"I can't believe they made you leave," Suzanne said.

"Yeah, they did. Threw us right out onto the street. Jimmy told the owner he would be back and that when he did, he would come packin.'"

"I can't believe it. We all spend alotta money in that joint. Besides, Pasquale knows who we are. He knows betta. He'll let us back in if he knows what's good for him. I bet we get free dinnas for a year. You watch," Suzanne said, laughing.

"I gotta admit it, though, girls. He looked so damn good that night," said Rose. "Made me think about him a little. He was really good in the sack. The only crazy part was that his *braciole* pointed in the wrong direction. It was like it made a right turn or somethin'."

They all giggled.

"Hey, girls, maybe we shouldn't talk that way in front of Miss Violetta over here," Frank's mother said. "Hey, Violetta, have you met the girls?" She motioned me over.

I walked slowly over to the pack of hyenas and sat quietly.

"So hey, Vi, or Violette, is that your name, sweetie?" Rose asked.

"Yes, it's Violetta," I said, correcting her.

"Oh, um, Violetta. So how did ya meet Frankie?" she asked.

To protect the story, as I thought Frank would want me to, I responded with a lie. "He passed through California on a trip to Nevada. We met through my brother, Tony." I was suddenly home-sick all over again.

"Oh really? Hey, Marie, what was Frank doing in Nevada?" Rose asked Mrs. Di Natale.

"He was um, investigatin'. We might get into the casino business someday," Frank's mother lied smoothly.

"Oh wow, yeah, that's good business. I keep telling Jimmy to do the same thing. We hope they will send us out there to manage things. I'd love to live in a casino. They got some of the prettiest hotel suites. You could live like a fucking queen out there. They got the best shows and nicest accommodations, and it's good money. We just gotta get the okay," Rose said as she flicked her cigarette in the glass ashtray.

The girls kept talking. Rose sat closer to me.

"So, a married girl, now, are you? You got a great catch. He's so handsome. You're a lucky girl to have bagged him. Before he left, he had so many girlfriends, but they didn't have no class. I can see why he married you, Violetta. You got the clean-cut look about you. I bet you're gonna make a good wife for Frank. You just gotta make him happy in bed. You know what I mean? You want a kept man? Then you gotta keep him there. Frank's been known to have a wandering eye from time to time. The way I see it, we gotta tame our men in the bed. They gotta know who they have before they go and put their cocks into some floozy whore, ya know? Any whore that comes around Jimmy, I'll kill her, dead. I'll do anything for my man. I will neva rat on him—neva. I'd take a fucking bullet to protect him. You know what I mean, Vi?"

"Um, yes, I think so," I said, then gulped down hard.

"Come on, let's go get a drink," she said.

After a few cocktails, I'd made a friend. I was enamored by her bravery, and I was pretty sure she'd help me find my courage. And maybe if I adopted her don't-take-any-shit attitude, Frank would fear me and leave me alone. The cackling hyenas possessed what I most desired in my new life.

Strength.

Chapter 23

Power

AFTER A FEW MONTHS OF LIVING WITH FRANK'S PARENTS, IT was time to go. We had no privacy. In bed, Frank had to put his hand over my mouth during sex because he was afraid someone might hear us. I despised that because it brought me back to our dark wedding night. It made the sex terrible. I couldn't even enjoy myself.

When Frank was out, which was most of the time, I was left alone. To avoid the loneliness and boredom, I walked through the neighborhood. Frank told me to stay home because the feds would follow me. They'd been casing Mr. Di Natale's house at least twice a day. I didn't even want to stand in front of a window in that house.

Mrs. Di Natale was extremely territorial over her kitchen. I couldn't cook what I wanted, and with the maids, I didn't even clean my own underwear. I told Frank it all felt too personal and too strange and that I wanted a place of our own to call home. A place for our kids to grow up. He agreed, and we started looking.

After three weeks of searching, I realized that most of the houses in Brooklyn were close to each other. As an occupational hazard, Frank didn't want anyone to hear what he said or did in his home, so we continued to search for the best house that accommodated both our needs. After thirty different homes and two realtors, we eventually found our dream home in Bensonhurst.

Most of Bensonhurst was loaded with Italians, so that felt good. However, some Italians viewed the mob as a kind of black mark on the Italian culture. One of the realtors mentioned that the neighbors weren't too thrilled with us moving next door. That was the day Frank fired him, and we got realtor number two. But I couldn't let that change my mind. I was happy to be out on our own.

The house was in the nicer part of town. With a white door and matching front windows, our new home had a brick exterior like most of the houses on the street. Rose bushes lined the yard, which gave it nice curb appeal. Frank made sure to buy the biggest house on the street, but it wasn't so grandiose that it screamed Mafia. It was a nice home with lots of amenities. It had a washroom for clothes, three large upstairs bedrooms for a growing family, and a basement for Frank.

While we continued to get settled, the neighbors nosed around. They'd yell things through the windows when Frank had guys over late. They called us 'guinea hoods.' Frank shut them up by firing his gun in the air and told them if they kept it up, they'd get worse. I, on the other hand, wanted to know the neighbors so that our future children would have friends.

One day I got the nerve to go and introduce myself. I put on my best dress and marched across the street with a box of cannolis.

An older woman answered the door.

"Um, hello. My name's Violetta. My husband and I just moved in across the street. I wanted to introduce myself." I handed her the box of cannolis.

Her eyes narrowed as she took the box.

I followed up with a handshake. Reluctantly, she shook my hand, then snatched hers away quickly.

"I know who you are. *Maronn*, the whole neighborhood knows who moved in. A Mafia hood, that's who," she hissed.

With raised eyebrows, I said, "I was trying to be nice. I'm sorry to have bothered you. I don't know anyone around here. I wanted to make friends, but it's clear now that I would never want you as a friend. And as for my husband, you better watch what you call us."

"Is that a threat?" She shoved the cannolis back into my hands.

"Not a threat. A promise."

She stared at me.

I curled my lip up and shot her a smug smile. "You know, it's a sad day when your own people turn against you. The same blood that runs through my veins runs through yours."

"Don't compare yourself to me. You people have given us a bad name," she snarled.

"My people? Let me tell you about my people. If I ever see you look in my direction with anything more than a smile, I'm going to tell my husband what you said to me today. He won't like that, and neither will the men who come to pay you a visit if you should dare disrespect me again."

Her eyes opened wide, and her jaw fell open.

"Have a nice day, *Signora*," I said, then turned on my heels. On the walk home, the tips of my ears burned from her harsh words, but I also felt exhilarated. My new last name had given me power. A power I'd never felt before.

I didn't tell Frank what happened. I didn't want her murder on my hands. More than likely, he wouldn't care what some old lady said. He'd wave his gun around, and they'd fear us and leave us alone. Sad part was, it didn't matter to Frank. He had his friends. I didn't. I was in a new town and alone. It'd be one thing for people to dislike me, but it would be an entirely different thing if they were mean to my children. I would need to find women who were like me and in my situation.

The mob wives—they'd be my friends.

With my new four walls, life became consistent again. During weekdays, I made our new house a home, and during weekends, we were always out on the town with Frank's guys and their wives.

Sometimes we went to the bowling alley. We formed teams and bet large. Frank would get drunk, and I'd end up having to drive us home. Other times, we took turns making dinner. Frank barbecued with the boys while I played cards with the girls. And when we were tired of doing those things, we went to a movie.

There wasn't a weekend that we weren't all together. Although I missed the days back at the ranch, I knew I had to adapt to my new friends and new environment. I was used to only trusting my family—my blood. These people were strangers to me, but after some time and many bowling alleys later, we got to know one another better.

It made sense for us all to stay together because we shared interests and lived under the same circumstances. My new friends took away the loneliness from being homesick.

I became close to two of the girls: Rose and Suzanne. Our husbands were closest in the group, so it seemed right that we formed a relationship. They taught me a lot about the life and took me to places where we were treated like queens. People knew who we were and who our husbands were. The minute we pulled up to certain establishments, we were catered to—free food, free stuff. We were Mafia royalty—Queens.

It was strange, at first. I felt guilty taking things they gave us. But Rose told me that if it wasn't our husbands providing them protection, someone else would. So, we might as well enjoy the benefits.

Deep down, I knew that was a lie we were all telling ourselves. Still, I did what she told me. I followed the rules in every way.

For obvious reasons, the girls were good at keeping secrets. I got used to talking to them about things I didn't discuss with anyone else. One afternoon, after a few cocktails, Frank and his crew drove us all out to a huge field where the girls showed me how to fire a gun.

Rose's boyfriend, Jimmy, placed empty bottles on top of tree stumps scattered around the field, and that became our practice range.

"You put the bullet in here, like this," Rose said as she pointed to the chamber of the gun.

Rose clicked the gun together. "Okay, then you extend your arm, like this, and aim and fire," Rose explained, then took her first practice shot.

Wham!

Her arms jolted back into her shoulders. Smoke from the gun slithered its way up to the sky above us. The sound was so loud it stung my ears.

"*Minchia*," I said.

"Now you try." She emptied the chamber and handed me the gun and bullet.

For a small gun, it was heavier than I expected. It got me thinking about my mother and how she'd carry her shotgun around with her everywhere. My mother was no small lady, either. I understood where she got her muscles, and it wasn't from rolling out dough.

"You ready, gorgeous?" Frank said as he pressed himself behind me to steady my arm. To adjust my position for the perfect aim, I swayed my body from left to right. His erection pressed on my ass. "*Maronn*, I never knew teaching you how to shoot would turn me on like this. Your ass is so plump," he said as he pushed himself into me further. "If no one was around, I'd do you right here. You look so hot with a gun in your hands. I'm gonna get you your own gun," he whispered in my ear.

I stood there with Frank panting in my ears and his hands under my elbows as I focused on my target.

"I'm ready." I locked my arms in position. Heart pumping through my chest, I squinted my eyes to get a good view and squeezed the trigger.

Pow!

The sound echoed through the empty field. Glass shattered

through the air from my bullet. It was such a strong and calculated move.

"Good girl," Frank whispered in my ear and licked my earlobe. I handed him the gun. "Thanks for helping me."

We smiled at each other. "I'm happy you're learnin'. Makes me feel good to know that if some son of a bitch tried to come into our house, you'd be able to take care of yourself," he said while loading the gun again.

I felt good knowing I could defend myself. With Frank's line of work, I was sure there would come a time that my practice would come in handy.

Frank fired a few more rounds and turned back to me. "Let's go home. All this shooting has got me hot for you."

"Aww, you guys leaving already?" Rose asked, stomping on her cigarette butt.

"Yeah, where yous going, anyway?" Jimmy spoke up. "We just got here."

"Nope, time to go." Frank looked at me with burning eyes. We drove back home, where the adrenaline from the day's activities bled into sex. It was another night of testing my limits—our only real connection.

In between the booze, drugs, and guns, our lives were full of parties, conversation, and, above all, confidentiality. Since we'd returned to the East Coast, Frank was back to doing jobs for the Molanano family. Some nights he told me to hide money; other nights, I hid drugs.

"Vi, get over ere," he yelled from the hallway.

"What is it? Why you yelling?" I rolled my eyes.

"Help me find a place for this." He lifted up a six-inch gold bar.

"Jesus, Frank. Where the hell did you get this? You a pirate now?" I laughed.

"This ain't no time for jokes. We need to hide this here for a while."

I thought about my backyard and how he'd made it look like we had gophers from all the damn holes Frank dug to protect us from a search and seizure situation. "What about the big planter box outside? We haven't used that yet," I suggested.

"Good idea," he said, then went to the garage for the shovel.

I woke up to the sound of a honking horn. The clock read 4:00 a.m. After grabbing my robe, I ran for the window to see who made all the noise.

It was Frank, sitting in a brand-new Chevy Coupe.

"Vi, get down here," he yelled, then honked the horn again.

Lights turned on in the neighbor's windows. I knew I'd better get outside before someone called the cops.

I put on my slippers, tied the knot of my robe, and ran out to the driveway.

"Shh. Frank, stop," I said as he pressed on the gas to fire up the engine. "Someone's gonna call the cops if you're not careful."

"Let 'em," he said, smiling. "Get in."

I climbed into the passenger seat and ran my hand over the dash.

"You like it? I got it for you."

"Really? Oh, wow, Frank. I can't believe it." I opened the glove box and tinkered with the door.

He grabbed my face in his hands. "This is for all your help, baby." He planted a hard kiss on my lips.

"It's beautiful," I said, still stunned.

"Here, let's switch seats. You drive." He got out of the driver's side. I slid in front of the big steering wheel. Once he was safely beside me, I shifted into reverse and we were off.

An hour later, with the sunrise through the back window, I pulled up to our driveway. Two cops stood, waiting.

"Don't say nothin'," Frank said. "I'll take care of everything."

I turned the engine off. Frank got out of the car to talk to the officers. He handed them something and they left. No citation, no words. They just drove away.

"What happened?"

"Nothin'. Don't yous worry about it. Let's go in. I'm beat," he said. "But before we go to sleep"—he grabbed my hips, pulling my body into his frame—"I wanna drive *this* car." With my new car in the driveway, I obliged and let him carry me inside.

After his final thrust, he fell down next to me. Within seconds, Frank was snoring. In the quiet morning hours, I thought about my house and car.

This was my life. Living with a mobster.

This was the illusion I'd warned myself about the day I stood in front of the mirror with the mink around my neck. The house, the jewels, the fur, and now the car—they were all just things. And no matter how much he gave me, I still didn't love him. I shut my eyes to try and sleep when visions of wavy brown hair and long black lashes winked at me in fields of grapevines. I reached for Gaetano's hands, but he was too far away. The wind pushed me into my lover's arms and then it all went dark.

Chapter 24
Big Brother

DAY AFTER DAY, THE FEDS DROVE PAST OUR HOUSE. THEY CAME around asking questions. Thankfully, they usually dealt with Frank. I didn't want to get caught saying something I shouldn't. On a few occasions, they followed me. If I went to the grocery store, they were there. When we went to dinner, they were there. It seemed like every time I looked over my shoulder, they were right there, watching every move.

With my wet hair in a towel, I ran down the stairs to answer the kitchen phone.

"Hello?" I said.

"Hey, Vi, I'll pick you up in an hour," Rose said.

"Okay. I'll be ready. Just honk. I don't wanna wait outside, you know," I said in code.

"Still?" she asked.

"Yep."

Rose pulled up and honked the horn. I grabbed my purse and locked the door behind me. As I approached her car, I was shocked to see Rose standing next to the police car, talking to one of the cops. Shaking my head at her, I couldn't believe my ears.

"So, how about you take us to lunch, huh, Officer? I know this great place in town they serve the best manicott in the city." Rose brushed lint from his uniform.

The officer smiled at Rose. "Is that right? Best manicott in town, huh?" He blushed as she bent down in front of him to show him her tits in her low-cut shirt.

"We better get going. It's getting late." I opened the passenger seat door and got in.

"I'll see ya around, Officer . . . Douglas is it?" She smiled and batted her eyes at him.

"Yes, ma'am," he said, then took down her plates. "Goodbye now. You be careful out there, miss," he said with a flirtatious smile.

Rose blew him a kiss and got in the driver's seat. She started the car and pulled out of the driveway slowly, making sure to wave at the cop as we turned onto the main road.

"You better be careful, Rose. One day, you might say something to the wrong person."

"It's like insurance, Vi." She lit a cigarette and turned up the radio.

Rose and I spent the morning buying new outfits and matching heels. Then we met Suzanne for lunch. After lots of talk and an endless supply of cigarettes, I looked down at my watch.

"Oh shit. It's already three o'clock, ladies. I gotta get home. You know Frank. He likes a hot dinner before he goes out."

"Oh. Let him make a sandwich for once in his life," Rose said. "You're too obedient."

I rolled my eyes at her. "That's why you aren't married, Rose." I smiled.

We paid the bill. As we walked to the car, a detective stopped us.

"Hello, ladies. Looks like you've done a good deal of shopping today. Safe to say that you paid for all this stuff from drug money or was it from the robbery?" he asked smugly. "Molanano business must be going well."

"Let's get to the car, Vi. We don't have to listen to this shit," Rose said, then flipped him the middle finger while we dashed through the parking lot.

"Do you have a mouth like your friend? You ladies think I'm stupid? I know what goes on in this town, and I'll do everything in my power to bring every last one of you down," he said, walking far too close to us now. Then he got in front of me and shoved his badge in my face.

Forced to stop, I looked down at his name. Officer Tewey. I tried to move around him to open the car door.

"You're Frank Di Natale's new wife, huh? Where's he hiding the drugs and cash, huh? We know he was in Atlantic City on March eighth. Same night a bank was robbed. We have reason to believe your husband was involved. In fact, we have eyewitnesses who swear they saw your husband at the scene of the crime before the robbery took place."

I tried to reach around him, bags in hand, for the door handle.

"Get in the car, Vi," Rose yelled from the driver's side. "Leave us alone."

"I don't know what you're talking about." I moved past him and opened the door. Once I was in, I lit a cigarette to calm my nerves.

"You know *exactly* what I'm talking about," he yelled through the half-opened window. "You know what your guinea husband does. We have proof he was in Atlantic City gambling that day and bought a car. Do I need to go to your house and verify the date of purchase from the registration? We also know that a candy-apple red Chevy was spotted in the parking lot of the bank.

We know you have no accounts at that bank—not a single one. So, you think your husband is some hotshot, huh? Let me tell you, little lady, if I find out you or your husband had anything to do with it, I'm gonna bring you all down. I can promise you that." He shook his finger at my face.

"I don't know what you're talking about," I fired back, then blew smoke right in his face.

"You don't have to answer any of his questions." Rose revved the engine.

"Mrs. Di Natale, we know your husband killed Mario Cantoni. Do you think we are that stupid?"

"Yes, we do, actually," Rose shouted past me.

The officer looked back at Rose with eyes blazing. "If you don't shut your mouth, I'll throw you in jail for jaywalking. I'm sure we could dig up some shit on you, little lady," he said, his tone sharp. Then he shifted his blazing eyes back onto me. "There was an eyewitness who gave testimony that he saw your husband shoot Cantoni two times in the chest. We know how you *WOP* pieces of shit covered it all up. And maybe we were too late to put Mr. Di Natale away for that, but he ain't gonna get away with this. Word on the street is that the Molanano family is getting sloppy. You might want to mention that to your husband because I'm pretty sure the Sambino family ain't too happy with the way it went down by trying to frame them with the little dumpster stunt. Who knows? It might start an all-out war. That would make my job easier if all you guinea hoods would just kill each other off."

I started to say something in our defense when Rose put her hand over my mouth.

"Be quiet, Vi," Rose said firmly, then gave him the finger.

As I went to roll the window to stop the interrogation, Tewey leaned his head into the passenger side, stopping it from coming all the way up. His fish breath bounced off my face as he spoke.

"Oh yeah, Mrs. Di Natale? One last thing. How's your father doing? Do you miss California? Looks like he's made a killing in the horse breeding business. Has he made any bets lately? Don't fuck with the federal government. We'll be seeing you soon," he said, then backed away from the car.

As soon as his body was clear, I finished rolling up the window. Rose slammed on the gas, and we peeled out of the parking lot. My heart pounded through my chest and sweat poured down my back. How did he know about my family?

"Don't listen to those pieces of shit," Rose said. "They don't know nothin'. They're tryin' to scare you. I'm gonna talk to Jimmy, and you talk to Frank about this. Do it in the bathroom while the shower is on so they can't hear you, and for God's sake, don't tell anyone, and don't say a fuckin' word on the telephone."

With a bone-dry throat, I felt the full weight of my involvement. The cigarette in my hand shook, flicking ash all over Rose's car and my skirt. How did they know so much? Back home, the cops were all paid off, so we never had this type of interrogation. But here in New York, things happened faster. I couldn't wait to get home and tell Frank.

Too shaken to cook a big meal, I sat in my bed with my pistol on the side table. I kept hearing noises like there were people outside. Every little crack of the house settling made me sit up in bed. Frank didn't show up until almost four in the morning. He came in drunk again, stumbling around the kitchen, looking for something to eat to sober himself up before he passed out. It must have been a bad night because he was already angry. He cursed and slammed the refrigerator door shut.

"God damn it. What the fuck do you do all day? Hang out with those whores and don't make your fucking husband dinna?

You ungrateful bitch. I'll show you," he screamed from the downstairs kitchen.

Loud, uneven footfalls pounded the stairs. Once in the bedroom, he took off his belt. I put my finger to my mouth as a sign for him to shut up.

"Shhh," I hissed, then grabbed his arm and yanked him through the bathroom door. "Be quiet. I have to tell you something," I whispered.

I turned on the shower, shut the door behind him, and started talking.

"Frank. The feds followed me and Rose to the store. They know everything. They know about Cantoni, and they know about my father. They even asked me about something on March eighth—some bank robbery. They said they saw the car, Frank. Don't tell me you were that stupid to drive the car there," I said, trying to keep my voice down.

Frank's eyes got huge, like they would fall out of his head.

He put his vice-like grip around my throat. "What did you tell 'em?"

I tried to push his hands away. "I didn't say anything," I choked out.

He relaxed his grip, then splashed water on his face.

I let the water run for at least thirty minutes while I told him everything.

"Frank, I'm afraid," I said as tears welled. "I keep hearing noises outside. Would they try to come in here?"

"Don't worry, baby. I'll take care of everything." He kissed me on the forehead. Then, out of pure exhaustion and the need to pass out, he climbed into bed and slept.

We didn't talk about what Tewey said after that. My fancy red car stayed at one of my father-in-law's warehouses, where he stored extra coffins and chairs for his funeral homes, never to be driven again.

As the days went on, I was scared from the moment I woke up to the time I went to bed. I didn't want to leave the house. To help my racing mind and pounding heart, I searched for my father's pills. Taking them at night helped me sleep. It was the only way I could function.

I needed them more and more. Frank gave me pills from jobs he'd taken. The hard part was they only helped me at night. So, Frank gave me different pills to help me function in the day. He didn't like to see me so strung out, but I didn't know how to handle the stress. A part of me was happy that Frank had a connection to the drugs because a doctor would have cut me off already.

Between the bad dreams and the need to relax my mind, I yearned to call my family to see how they were doing. Afraid they were under investigation, I didn't want to say anything over the phone. And I wasn't certain if the feds had intercepted their mail. They wanted Frank so bad that they were gonna go after anyone and anything connected to him. If they threatened my father, I prayed he wouldn't cooperate. That would put the whole family at risk.

Because of the dumpster incident, the Sambino and Molanano families were ready to go to war. It was bad enough that we had the cops on our ass every day, but now the Sambino family tailed us too. Lines would be drawn, and sides would be taken. That could expose our ranch to other things. My family was a small piece of a much larger organization. The Sambinos wouldn't think twice of wiping my father off the face of the earth. What was left of my hollow heart felt frozen from the endless possibilities of our demise.

A few weeks after I told Frank what had happened with Officer Tewey, Don Molanano wanted to have a sit-down with Frank about the whole thing. Frank confided in his father, who covered his ass by telling Don Molanano what happened with me and the officer.

Bosses didn't like when their men got sloppy. It was bad for business. If Frank didn't get things straightened out, they might come for us on both sides, and I didn't know which side would get to Frank first.

I was to stay in the house because he was afraid I might cave under pressure. Each time a car drove by the house, my heart sank straight into my gut. I was convinced they'd shoot up my house to get Frank. What if I was in the crosshairs and got shot? What felt like fun and games had become real, quick.

I was alone again. Alone in my mind. Alone in a city that wanted to kill me and my family, one way or another. I had to do something, but what could I do? Nothing.

Frank found the detective that who had approached Rose and me and did some investigating. Officer Tewey was involved in a drug ring with another boss from a different family. Tewey allowed some guys to push drugs so long as he got a cut.

When Frank found out where and when the next score would be, he had someone take pictures of Officer Tewey at the scene of the crime. Frank taped the photos to the door of Tewey's house. Frank was not above extortion. He didn't want a war with the other family, but there was no way he was gonna get pinched. So, he did what he had to do. That made Detective Tewey back off for a while. And while things relaxed for a bit from the feds, life went back to business as usual. But as far as the families were concerned, Frank had become a liability.

Afraid of my own shadow, I popped more pills.

Chapter 25

Road Trip

FOR WEEKS AFTER HEARING OFFICER TEWEY'S LATEST ACCU-
sation, Frank walked on eggshells. That made things in the house
shakier than normal. Luckily, Frank agreed to let me go to Miami
with Rose to visit her mother, who was gravely ill. With the constant
surveillance from the cops and the pressure from the other families,
I was happy to get out of town.

Since I'd never been to Florida, I didn't know what to pack.
Rose told me it was warm and humid there, so I packed a few dresses,
a swimsuit, and towel. Then I headed to the bathroom to grab my
toothbrush and toothpaste.

"Hey, Frank, can you hand me my shower cap in there?" I asked.

With soapy hands, Frank handed me the yellow plastic cap. I
shoved it in my small bag along with some perfume and other toiletries. The water stopped, and Frank threw open the curtain. Water
dripped off his naked body.

"How long you stayin' anyway?" he said, drying his hair with
a towel.

"I don't know. A few days, I suppose. I'm not driving, so it's not up to me," I said, then drew on some lipstick.

He stepped over the tub and came behind me. He wrapped his arms around my waist. Drops of water soaked my neck and shoulders.

"Stop that. You're getting me all wet," I said and tried to break from his grip.

"You look beautiful." He placed his hands on my stomach. "Anything yet?"

"No, not yet. But thanks," I said, a little surprised at his compliment.

"I'm happy yous two are goin'. With the way things are around here, it'll be good for you to get out of town for a while until things calm down."

"Yeah, things have been pretty scary lately. By the way, I'll need some more money."

"Jesus Christ. I feel like every time I turn around you want more money. I just gave you a few hundred last week. What did you do with that, huh?" He pressed my body up against the bathroom vanity, his eyes fierce for my answer. Muscles in his arms quivered.

"I don't know. Stop hurting me, Frank," I yelled back, then pushed my body weight back against him. "I bought groceries and a few things for the house. And when I went with the girls, I bought some new dresses and shoes," I said, trying to regain my footing.

Frank marched into the bedroom and looked for his wallet. "Here. And not another penny for a while. With things the way they are, business is slow." He threw some cash onto the bed.

I shoved the money into my purse and zipped up my suitcase. I made sure to grab my pills. I put them in my purse, along with my sunglasses, and sat in the front room to wait for Rose.

A few minutes later, Rose honked her horn. I opened the door as she pulled into the driveway. Circular black sunglasses covered her eyes and her red lips opened to a smile.

"Hey, you ready?" she asked, then came around to open the trunk.

"Ready as I'll ever be," I said. As we pulled away, Frank came to the door to watch me leave. Because of his anger, I hadn't said goodbye. I waved, and he waved back.

"I'm glad he's letting you out of the house again." Rose lit up a cigarette. "Me and the girls have missed you."

"Sorry. It's been crazy."

"You gotta stand up to Frank, Vi. You can't let him run you around like this."

"And what would you have me do?"

"Fight back," she said with serious eyes.

"A lot of good that'll do. You know Frank."

"Jimmy tries that shit with me, but he knows I'll put a bullet right through him if he eva disrespects me." She pressed on the gas.

With her painful words in my ears, I lit up a cigarette, hoping the smoke would fog up my vision and my reality. I turned on the radio. It was a tune I'd heard before—the song Gaetano and I danced to on our first night at the winery. No matter where I was or where I was going, he was always there in one way or another.

Gaetano Sanna haunted me.

Two hours into our road trip, Rose stopped for gas. It had been a while since my last pill, and I felt a little antsy. I swallowed another pill with vodka that Rose kept under the seat.

"Hey, give me some," she said, then ducked down to take a swig.

The gas attendant scowled at us.

"You got a problem, mister?" Rose barked.

"No. No problem," he said, then pulled out the nozzle.

"Good. Then mind your business," she said with wicked eyes.

Once he was done, he walked away. Rose started the car and turned to me. "Okay, look, I didn't tell you this before because I was afraid you might tell Frankie. We aren't visiting my mom. She died like ten years ago."

My brows tensed. "Then where the hell *are* we going?"

"Don't worry. We're still going to Florida. South Beach. I have a friend I have to meet down there."

"What kind of friend, Rose?" I asked in a serious tone.

"The kind that will make us both a little richer."

"Richer?"

"For coming with me, I will cut you in for ten percent of the job. And besides, you owe me."

"Owe you?"

"Yeah. Without me, you wouldn't be nothin' in Brooklyn."

Muscles in my jaw tightened. "What job? What the hell have you got me involved in? I have enough problems right now."

"What I'm about to tell you can neva be repeated. If I find out you ratted, it will change everything. You can neva tell Frank—eva. If you do, he'll tell Jimmy and well—" She licked her dry lips.

"I won't. What is it?"

"I have a connection down there. I've been meeting with him for a while now."

"Connection to what?"

"Drugs."

"What? What kinda of drugs?"

"Everything from pills to powders—you name it." She fixed her hair in the rearview mirror.

"Oh Jesus Christ, Rose. Are you fucking serious?" I shook my head at her. "If anything happens, I swear—"

"Nothin's gonna happen. I promise. Just do what I tell you, and we'll be fine. Stop being so serious and have a little fun." She handed me the vodka.

With sweaty palms, I grabbed the clear bottle and chugged it down.

"There you go. Now, let's go have some fun," she said, then peeled out of the gas station.

As we continued on our journey, I didn't look at her. And to think I'd actually felt bad for her mother. Her deceit made my blood boil. The closer we'd gotten to Florida, the less I knew about her.

I'd heard that she and Jimmy had problems, and there were rumors that she screwed around with other men to get money out of them. In conversation, she'd throw around other men's names. She never came out and told me she'd slept with other men, and I didn't ask. It was her business, and I didn't care if she cheated on Jimmy. He was Frank's friend, not mine.

Because of Rose's reputation, Frank was worried about me coming with her. He told me that if I screwed around with anyone else when I was with Rose, he'd kill us both. I'd seen that look in his eyes before, and I knew he was serious. But I had no desire to do anything like that. I didn't even want to have sex with Frank. I did it to shut him up. If I ever cheated on him it wouldn't be with some wise guy, it would be with the man who stole my heart that summer in the California foothills—Gaetano.

To break the silence, I went out on a limb. "Are you and Jimmy any better?"

"Oh yeah. He can't stay mad at me for long. And besides, I made sure to make up with him before we came down here. The last thing I need is for him to follow us. I can neva tell him about any of this, or he'll want in. This is my score—my money," she said firmly.

When she talked business, her tone and body expressions changed drastically. Her extreme personality was the one thing that really scared me about Rose. Some days, she was quiet. Other days, she was loud and crazy. Something wasn't right in her mind.

Because Florida was such a long drive, we took shifts. One of us slept for a few hours while the other drove. The drive was a nice distraction from the pressures of the city. The open road ushered in a freedom I hadn't felt in a long time. I stuck my hand out the window and pushed my fingers against the wind. The sensation reminded me of Gaetano. He was my wind, pushing against me, trying to stop me from marrying Frank, and, now, trying to stop me from doing something stupid with Rose. Maybe it was a sign. For some reason, I pulled my hand inside the car, and we continued on.

After a one-night stay in a cheap motel, we woke early and made our way to Miami. As we edged closer, the prettiest white-sand beaches I'd ever seen came into view. South Beach's water was a breathtaking blue. My eyes focused on the ocean, while my ears half-listened to Rose's idle conversation. And when she got quiet enough to light another cigarette, I'd think about Gaetano—how he was doing, how the wine business treated him and his family.

Was he married?

The thought twisted my guts in knots.

As jealous as the thought made me, he couldn't put his life on hold. I'd left him. He had every right to be happy. He was a good man and deserved a good life. I took another swig of vodka and shut my eyes. I remembered his face, his beautiful, dreamy eyes, and how his biceps contracted while he moved himself in and out of me when we made love. Life was so much simpler when we were together. Even though two years had passed, it felt like a lifetime ago that he'd held me in his arms. I missed the simplicity of it all. More than anything, I missed who I was when I was with him.

Rose and I drove to a beachfront hotel. It was one of those art-deco types. The guy at the front desk waited for our husbands to show up. When we paid the tab, the look on his face was priceless. Of course, Rose toyed with him. She ordered the best champagne and slid him a lavish tip to make it worth his while. He smiled, but I bet he wondered how we got the money. We laughed, pushed our big hats forward, and made our way to our room.

The bellman opened the door and placed our luggage on the bed while Rose flirted with him. I pulled back the curtains to get a better view. We were just a few feet away from the white, sandy beach. As I looked toward the horizon, the blue skies and puffy clouds were such a welcome change from the smoke-filled air I'd become so accustomed to in Brooklyn. This was the kind of place I'd have a hard time leaving.

Once the bellman left with a nice tip from Rose, I turned to her, ready to bury the hatchet. "I was afraid to come with you at first, but I'm so glad I did. It's beautiful." A smile blanketed my face.

"Yeah, Miami's a nice place. Let's get our bathin' suits on and go to the beach."

The afternoon was pleasant. We sunbathed and sipped on our drinks. They were cold and wet, with sprigs of mint. Because of the humidity, we gulped them down fast. And in between spreading our toes through the sand and getting drunk from mixing alcohol with the heat, we shared some of our histories.

She told me she'd had a rough childhood and that she'd been molested by her father. Since running away from home at thirteen, she'd been on her own. Rose divulged she'd been married twice before she'd met Jimmy and had a daughter at seventeen.

"My aunt in Idaho adopted her. I haven't seen her since she was one month old. I couldn't take care of her. I was on drugs. I had no money, and if I'm honest," she said as one tear escaped, "she would have gotten in the way."

I swallowed hard at her admission.

"It's hard to have children in this life, ya know? You always have to worry that somethin' might happen to them."

"Yes," I said. "I worry about that. The boys that get into the life, they're either put in prison or killed. This life isn't forgiving, no matter how you look at it."

"I did the right thing for my daughter. My aunt sent me a picture of her and she's beautiful. Headin' to college and everything. It was the hardest thing I've ever done, but sometimes you have to stop being selfish and accept your reality. Some women aren't mother types, you know?"

"I want a child, but I'm afraid. I don't want to wake up one morning and find out they were shot over some petty crime, or—worse yet—some war between the families."

"It will always be a personal choice," she said and took another sip of her drink.

And before she shed any more tears on the subject, she lit up another cigarette. With the flick of the match, she moved on to something else. It was as if she'd detoured off a highway flooded with memories.

"I'm made for this life. I've been on the street since I was a kid. I'm no housewife, makin' dinna, waiting on a man. Oh no. I want to be in the thick of it. I want to make my money so no man can tell me what to do. As a woman in this world, you gotta make your moves. You gotta make friends with your enemies. And if I'm being honest, you gotta use your pussy. That's the one weapon men fall for. That's the one thing they're all powerless against. I'll use what I have to get what I want. It's survival. Life is full of suckas." She blew plumes of smoke past her lips. "And I won't be one of them anymore. No. I'll never be weak again."

I stilled and took a deep breath.

"Don't look so surprised. I've paid prices too. I've even been to prison a few times. One time I was a driver on a robbery gone bad. Another time, I was busted for cleaning the money. My last stint, I was busted for prostitution. A big sting operation." She adjusted the strap on her bathing suit. "I remember the first time I ever whored myself out. When the guy gave me the money, I knew I'd found a way to eat. It wasn't glamorous, but when I bought myself furs and nice things, I felt rich. That's how I met Jimmy. He was one of my johns. Poor bastard bailed me out and tried to civilize me by giving me money and spoiling me so I wouldn't go back to the life. He wanted me off the streets."

I felt the pain in her voice when she talked about what her father had done to her. I felt sorry for her. It was the allure of *Cosa Nostra* that kept her going. She wanted a way *in* somehow; and as a woman, that was impossible. Culturally and traditionally, women couldn't be members. It wasn't part of the deal. Mob wives helped their husbands do things here and there, but they could never become a boss.

As the sun beat on our skin, she told me that Jimmy knew about her past and never judged her. I think Jimmy never wanted to lose her. She was a strikingly beautiful woman, and she was the brains between them. Jimmy was still a soldier, but Frank was now a captain. So, when Frank needed to keep his hands clean, he'd call on Jimmy to do his dirty work. Rose liked that Jimmy was the guy who took care of business. But I knew Jimmy wouldn't be the last guy in her life. Rose was ambitious—sometimes too ambitious.

"So, tell me about growing up in California. I heard it's beautiful out there. Jimmy said the family is starting to settle out that way, even getting into casinos and the movie business. What's Hollywood like? That Frank Sinatra . . . what a dream boat," she said, smiling.

"I've never been to Hollywood. I've been on our ranch most of my life. Life on the ranch is fun at times and hard work at other times. But I miss my family, the horses and . . . well, lots of things . . ."

Gaetano's face came into view. I took another sip of my drink to coat my dry throat. I didn't want to say too much for fear that something would get back to Frank.

"I think I'll take a nap. The sun feels so good," I said, trying to avoid more intimate conversations.

"Sounds nice." She tilted her big hat over her face.

With the sound of the ocean in the distance and the wind tickling my arms, I focused on the teal blue waves in front of me.

After a full day of sun and drinks, we returned to the hotel. Rose was adamant that we had to get up early because we had a big day ahead of us. We were here on business, not pleasure. We put out our cigarettes and folded our towels.

While we walked back to the hotel, I thought about what she'd said. It seemed that Rose wanted to look important to the mob, so they'd use her when they needed. She searched for purpose and importance. I empathized with her because that was something I'd searched for since I left Gaetano. He was the only man besides my father who made me feel important. I wasn't sure what I was in for tomorrow, but anything seemed better than going home.

Chapter 26

The Cuban

M Y ARMS WERE ON FIRE. SHEETS, AS SOFT AS THEY WERE, scratched my sunburnt skin. I turned my body to see Rose half naked in bed. Her hair in giant knots, she snored like a chain saw.

"Rose, get up. It's almost six a.m. Didn't you say you wanted to leave early?" I muttered, still feeling the effects of a day's worth of sun and booze.

Rose rolled over and rubbed her eyes. "Oh shit, thank God you woke me up. We gotta go."

We rushed to pack up our things and left the hotel. I was sad to leave the beach, but Rose had to meet her connection by 7:00 a.m. With roaring headaches from rum-induced hangovers, we drove west to our rendezvous place.

Rose and I headed to a private strip of homes on a sequestered island that was tangled in palms trees. The lush jungle provided the needed privacy to conduct business, far from any pain-in-the-ass cops. As we approached the gated entrance, a guard recognized Rose and was all smiles. He was an older man who spoke broken English.

His Spanish sounded a little different than the Mexicans I'd met at the winery, but I understood some of the words.

"*Hola*," Rose said, then continued several long phrases in Spanish. I'd only heard her strong Brooklyn accent up to that point, so to hear her speak fluent Spanish blew my mind. After a few more pleasantries, the guard opened the gate and allowed us inside.

We pulled up to a large white house that bordered an ocean channel. Rose parked in the car port, touched up her signature red lipstick, and blotted her lips on a piece of newspaper stashed in the glove box.

"Put on your hat and wear these." She handed me a pair of big, black sunglasses. "We don't want anyone to spot us. That's the last thing I need."

I put on the glasses and wrapped a scarf around my neck.

"Don't say anything when we're in there. Just go along with everything I tell you."

"Ere . . . okay." I adjusted my hat.

We approached the front door. A man with a dark complexion and watchful eyes greeted us. Two more bodyguards stood inside. They didn't talk much, and they didn't greet us. They eyed Rose and me with guns at their sides. With every step forward, quivers of trepidation jolted through me. Where the hell had Rose taken me? Why did I ever agree to this?

Various pelts and stuffed game animals decorated the walls. A huge tiger skin stretched above the fireplace. The animal's glass eyes followed me. It was obvious that whoever lived in this house was comfortable killing things. Death was all around me. A cold sweat flushed my body. Something was very wrong here.

I fidgeted with the button on my blouse, ready to meet *Mr. Big Drug Dealer*. My jaw tightened, and my legs shook. With only the sound of a ceiling fan above, I waited for Rose's direction as she ran her hands over the tiger's pelt.

"It won't be long now," she said.

"Thank God. I can't wait to get out of here," I whispered.

One of the bodyguards adjusted the leather straps of his gun and pulled it around his shoulders.

"*Vámonos. Síganme,*" another bodyguard commanded. He nudged us from behind to move through the house to the back.

Since Rose knew the protocol, I followed her past the lifeless walls and through a patio door. A waterway and a narrow dock stretched ahead. We walked toward a thirty-foot boat tied to a wooden piling.

The guard helped us onto the boat and stood as a lookout.

Inside, the boat was bigger than I'd expected. A small couch sat under a tiny window. To steady my legs from the boat rocking back and forth, I held on to Rose's arm. A smaller man approached. He had dark skin and thick black hair, which he had tied into a ponytail under a black cowboy hat.

He smiled at Rose and threw his arms around her.

"*Hola, mi preciosa.*" He kissed her and grabbed her ass with both hands. My stomach hardened watching them fondle each other. I felt like I'd betrayed Jimmy by just being there. She knew this man better than she'd let on.

Once the man pulled his tongue out of her mouth, he eyed me up and down.

"*Esta es mi amiga,* Violetta," Rose said.

He moved his body in front of mine and stared at me intensely. I reached out my hand to shake his. He drew my fingers up to his mouth and kissed the back of my hand.

"*Ella es muy hermosa.* Will she be joining us?" he asked.

I yanked back by hand and shot Rose a bone-chilling stare. "Joining you for what?" I snapped.

"No. Vi isn't into that kind of thing."

Rose planned to use her main weapon in her arsenal. It was between her legs—proving once again that pussy ran the world, like she'd said.

I followed his dark eyes as he looked from my breasts to my feet. He smiled back at me, then continued to make small talk in

Spanish with Rose. He made drinks behind the tiny bar in the galley. As much as I was put off by him in the short time I'd met him, it was so warm and humid that I accepted the drink. I sat on the little couch as the two of them continued to talk. Every now and then, they broke out in laughter.

The whole encounter felt invasive and awkward. I'd never been on a boat or been an accomplice to a drug deal. Trapped again, I took a sip of my drink and let Rose do what she needed to do so we could get the hell out of there.

Rose was coquettish with this man, more than she'd ever been with Jimmy. She let him grope her, then she'd laugh. Maybe this was how she intended to maintain good relations and keep the drug supply flowing. She was a natural-born salesperson. From the batting of the eyes to her endless flirtation, she lured him in sexually. She was like a snake, using its tail to attract prey by drawing them in closer for the kill.

I pointed to my watch and Rose got the hint.

"Hey, you gonna be okay here for a bit? I'll be back in a little while. I got to take care of some business and um . . . he likes to do business privately. You understand, right, Vi?"

"Yeah, just hurry up." I rolled my eyes at her.

She followed the man to the bedroom and locked the door. With nothing more than the sound of the rolling tide hitting the boat, other noises made themselves known. I'd never seen a pornographic movie, but I expected this was the closest I'd come to that.

After a few minutes, Rose came out wrapped in a bedsheet and got in my face.

"He wants you to join us," she said, straight-faced.

"What the fuck are you talking about? I'm married."

"Listen to me carefully," she whispered with a hardened expression. "If you don't, he might kill us both. I owe him money. You gotta help me out."

My entire body shuddered. "Are you serious?"

"Dead serious. Maybe I can get him to be okay with you just watching."

"Watching?" Muscles in my jaw spasmed.

"*Vámonos*," the man yelled from the bedroom.

"You better follow me in."

"Rose, I can't do this."

"We don't have a choice," she said as her lip quivered.

I stood from the tiny couch. With shaky legs, I followed behind her. The man sat naked from his session with Rose. He came over and stood in front of me. With his smoke-filled breath on my face, he grabbed the back of my head and tried to kiss me.

"Stop." I tried to pull my face away.

His black eyes held onto me intensely. "What's wrong wit you fren?" he asked Rose, then yanked my face toward him again.

"Nothin'. She's never done this before. Please leave her alone," Rose said and stood between us.

"Get back in bed or no deal." He laughed at her.

Rose shot me an apologetic stare and complied.

With one hand firmly gripped on the back of my head, he pushed me down toward his erection. The smell of his sweat and ejaculation fresh on his skin made my skin crawl. On my knees, with the boat rocking, I held on to the side of the bed. "*Chúpamela.* Suck it," he commanded.

"No," I said, almost crying.

The smells were too much. The environment was too much. This couldn't be happening. I cried. Not again.

He growled, then released the back of my head. "*Cabróna*," he yelled. "Den you watch and touch yourself. And if you don't"—he reached under the bed and pulled out a gun—"then I'll hurt both of you."

I felt like a little girl, trapped, held against my will. Not knowing what would happen, weak and powerless, I sat on the ground and prayed the Hail Mary over and over in my mind.

"*Quiero que me mires, cabróna*," he shouted. Rose started sucking him to get his attention away from me. Fearing for my life, I did as he asked and watched Rose pleasure this man in front of me. I went to that place in my mind where I thought of Gaetano. My eclipse place. Destination survival. I imagined it was Gaetano rubbing his hands over my breasts and up my skirt while this evil man watched. He cried out in pleasure, then lay back in bed and pushed Rose off him. "You and you fren can leave now." He lit a cigar. "My men will load you car like we discuss. Now get out," he said with barren eyes.

Mortified, I jumped up and ran out of the room. Rose followed behind me, fixing her dress. She handed her car keys to one of the bodyguards, who quickly headed toward the house. I wasn't sure what was next, but I wanted to scream and run out of there.

Rose pulled me aside in the empty house and said in a low voice, "It won't be long now. They have to arrange things for us. Here, try this. It'll take the edge off. I'll take half with you," Rose said as she broke the pill in half. She then turned to the guard. "*Hace mucho calor. ¿Podemos tomar un vaso de agua, por favor?*"

The guard walked away and returned with a glass of water.

"I can't believe you, Rose. I should've never come here. I'll never do this again. You make me sick," I said, seething. "What if something happened? Do you think Frank would like that? No. He'd start a fucking war, and you'd be the first to go." I swallowed the pill.

"Stop being such a baby. You better not tell anyone. I know where you live," Rose hissed, then lathered more lipstick on her naked, dry lips.

"Don't ever threaten me. You got that?" I fired back.

While we waited for the car to get loaded up, I became sleepy. The pill did its job, and the effects were welcomed. I wanted to put this out of my mind. I lay against the leather sofa in the forsaken living room. The bodyguard returned and threw the keys back at Rose.

"*Vamos, vamos, tienes que irte ahora mismo,*" he shouted at us as he pulled Rose off the couch to a standing position.

"*Cálmate, cabrón,*" Rose fired back.

The man's nostrils flared, and he nudged us outside the door.

I ran past Rose toward the car. Transaction done. Time to get the hell home.

Rose followed me out to the car, cussing. "These fucking guys got no class. They don't know how to treat a lady," she yelled as we got into the car.

"Yeah, right . . . a lady," I said under my breath.

Rose started the car to make our journey home. I threw my purse in the back seat and noticed that it looked different. I glanced at Rose and then to the back seat. Rose looked over her shoulder and then pulled over.

"I gotta check somethin'." Rose went to the trunk of the car, pulled out an old blanket, and spread it across the back seat.

"What are you doing now?" I asked, disgusted at the sight of her.

"The stuff is under the seat cushions, so just in case we get pulled over."

"The seat cushions? How?"

Rose pulled the blanket away. The back seat had been cut with a blade along the seam. She pulled the leather cushion up. The bench was stuffed with bags filled with pills and powders. I'd never seen anything like it. She pushed the seat cushion back together and put the blanket over the entire back seat as a disguise.

My heart fell into my stomach. "Oh my God. I had no idea it was this much."

"Shut up and act normal. We'll be fine. Don't worry about nothin'. Put on your sunglasses. We got a long ride ahead of us."

"Are you okay to drive, Rose?"

"I'm fine."

As she started the car, the pill crept over me like a fog. It was like a tug of war. My anxiety tried to fight its effect, but it was powerful. There were times, right before I succumbed to it, that my heart raced from fear, only to be shut down by the ringing in my ears. I fought against it as long as I could, but it finally owned my consciousness.

The sound of car horns flooded my ears.

My body jerked right to left. Oncoming car lights flashed, stinging my dazed vision.

"Fuck. Get up, get up, God damn it," Rose screamed and swerved.

"Wha-what's going on?" I mumbled, half awake.

"Oh shit," Rose yelled. "Light me a cigarette, quick. I must have fallen asleep at the wheel." Her face looked as white as a ghost.

I reached in the glove box for her smokes and lit her a cigarette. She took a deep drag and slapped her face a few times. As smoke enveloped the car, the lights and noise of a siren came from behind us.

"Fuck. We're gettin' pulled over," she yelled and grabbed for her purse. "Here. My gun's in there. Don't get it out now. Just keep it by your feet. If anything gets crazy, shoot him in the head."

"In the head? What? Are you fucking kidding me? You shouldn't have been driving. We should have stayed the night somewhere. Jesus Christ," I yelled through a dry throat.

Rose gave me a dirty look and stopped the car. My heart pounded. I looked in the side mirror to give myself a once-over. Veins in my neck popped through my skin, and my hands dripped with sweat. How would I be able to shoot the gun if it slipped out of my hand? Rose inspected herself in the rearview mirror. She pulled the ashy cigarette from her mouth and licked her red-stained lips.

The officer came up along the driver's side door and eyed Rose's car. "License and registration, please," he said. "I noticed that you had trouble staying between the lines. You okay, miss?"

"Oh, yes, Officer, yes," she said as she pulled out her paperwork from the glove compartment and handed it to him.

"And New York plates? What are you two fine ladies doing so far away from home?" he asked while looking inside the car. Thank God for the blanket that draped over the back seat.

"Officer," I said with a smile, trying to be convincing. "About a week ago, she got a letter that her brother died in the war. His plane was shot down."

To follow the act, Rose put on the fake tears and began to cry.

"And we just came back from the funeral. You can see, she's still real shaken up. Why don't you let me drive, Rose?"

"I have a few cousins stationed in the navy right now. It's some crazy times for our country. Hey, look, I understand. Why don't you take the next shift for this young lady so she can calm down? I'm sorry for your loss, ma'am." He handed back her license.

We both got out of the car and switched seats. "Thank you, Officer. I'm sorry to have done that. It's just I've been so shaken up about the whole thing, really," Rose managed to get out.

"No problem. You be careful now."

"Yes, thanks, Officer," I said, smiling back at him.

I started the car and got back onto the highway.

After a few miles of awkward silence, Rose lost it. Like a flick of a switch, she became unhinged. She punched the dashboard and stomped the floor so hard that she accidently kicked her purse.

The gun went off.

Bang!

The sound rang through me and shook my insides. I pulled off the highway and slammed on the brakes. Smoke from the tires clouded around us. She'd shot a hole right through the floor of the car.

"Look at what you did," I screamed at her. "You could've killed us. What the fuck is wrong with you?"

"I hate those fucking pigs. They think they're gonna get me? The fuck they are. You should have shot him, Vi," she said with burning eyes. "You should have shot him right in the head and let that pig bleed all over the God damn highway. Ah. I ain't neva going to prison again. Neva," she screamed at the top of her lungs.

"Shoot a cop? Are you fucking crazy? You're lucky I got us out of it. You didn't say shit! What if you've damaged the engine? Then what, huh? You think I'm gonna hitchhike home or, better yet, call Frank to come get me? He'll kill us both!"

"Pop the fuckin' hood," Rose belted out, then went to check the engine.

I sat, thinking of excuses to tell Frank when she shut the hood and came back to the passenger's side.

"The bullet didn't touch the engine or the tires. We're fine."

"How do you know?" I asked coldly.

"I used to screw a mechanic. That's how. Let's get the hell outta here before another cop comes. This time I will shoot," she said, then lit a cigarette.

To test the car, I pushed down on the accelerator, and we lurched forward. I took a deep breath, eased back on the highway, and made my way home.

We didn't talk much on the ride back. Her violent outburst made things strange between us. We both wanted to be rid of each other. To pursue any unwanted conversation seemed pointless. I'd drive and then once she was coherent enough, she'd drive. We only stopped for coffee and gas a few times. We drove cautiously to avoid unwanted attention from the cops. Any more prolonged time with these drugs in the car could mean further entanglement with the law. So, we drove with purpose.

We arrived before dawn. Luckily, Frank's car wasn't there. If he had seen us, he would've been furious. It would have cost me a beating and who-knows-what for Rose. I wanted to get out of that car and into my house. Away from Rose, away from it all. To avoid any more awkward exchanges between us, I scooped up my stuff from the front seat and slammed the car door.

"Hey, you better not tell nobody. I'll fucking come for you," she said in a clipped tone. She got out, walked to the trunk, and threw my suitcase at me.

As she got back into the driver's seat, I charged her, stood over her window, and looked her straight in the eye. "Is that a threat? I just saved your ass." Angry spit flew out of my mouth and onto her face.

She lit another cigarette and blew the smoke right back into my face.

"You just better not say nothin'. Look, I'm sorry. Yeah, yeah, I owe you one."

"I'll never do this again, Rose. Ever. There's something wrong with you. You're crazy," I belted out.

She looked back at me like she knew what I said was true but didn't have the balls to admit it to herself, much less to me. The truth of it was in the air between us now, lingering, ready to sting her to the core.

"Yeah. Yeah. I'll call you tomorra," she said unapologetically.

"No. Just leave me alone! Never call me again. I have enough problems. Keep the money. I don't want it." I searched frantically for my keys.

She screeched out of my driveway onto the street. She was on her way to deliver the stuff to whomever, wherever. I didn't care. I never wanted to see her again. To think that I might have killed a police officer. What would that have meant for my life?

It was one thing to be married to a gangster. It was an entirely different thing to live like one. The more I thought about Rose, the more I was convinced she was crazy. Her need for power would always be a motivation to stay in this life, but with the way things went for her, I didn't know how much longer she'd stay alive. After what I'd witnessed, I was done playing with fire. These were dangerous games. As I unlocked the front door, I was absolutely sure of two things: my luck had run out a long time ago, and roses always have thorns.

Chapter 27

Entrepreneur

As Rose's tires screeched down my street, I yanked my
purse off my shoulder and tossed it on the stairs. Suitcase in
hand, I threw it into the garage and slammed the door without taking out a single thing to wash, then paced the living room.

"Never again," I said as my footprints burned holes in the
carpet.

Happy that Frank wasn't home yet, I took a deep breath. I was
in no mood for an argument or to be interrogated. Nor was I about
to whip up something to eat for my master. No. I was too angry to
wait on anyone.

Frank would fly off the handle if he knew some Cuban drug
lord tried to have sex with me, that I was involved in a drug deal,
and almost shot a cop. He'd never want that kind of heat. It was one
thing to kill other members in various families and rats, but gun-
ning down a policeman in broad daylight was on a whole new level.
Not to mention the problem such an event would cause between
him and Jimmy. Jimmy was loyal to Frank, and vice versa, but not

at the expense of his future family. I was done trusting women outside my family.

Jumbled up with suppressed thoughts, my hands curled up into balls. "God damn you, Rose," I yelled, then punched the pillows on the couch.

After a few minutes of screaming and pounding furniture, I'd used up all my energy. Adrenaline left my body hollow and limp. As long as I never saw Rose again, I'd shelve the whole thing in my mind. Case closed. Time to move on.

Shaky from the drugs and the adrenaline, I needed to decompress. I marched upstairs and turned on the shower. I wanted to get the smell of the day's events off my body. I hoped the water would wash away any wrongdoing.

After the shower, I felt relaxed and more in control. I came downstairs to get a drink of water and tripped on my purse.

"God damn it," I yelled.

I bent down, snatched up my purse, and found a piece of newspaper. In my anger, I must have inadvertently shoved it in my purse when I gathered my things. I remember Rose blotting her lips with it before we went into the Cuban's house. Ready to toss it in the kitchen trash, I caught a glimpse of a man standing in a field full of vines.

Gaetano.

The room spun and my legs wobbled. I fell onto the kitchen floor and drew in big gulps of air. With shaky hands, I read the headline out loud.

"NORTHERN CALIFORNIA'S YOUNGEST WINEMAKER AND CONNOISSEUR IS POURING OUT SUCCESS IN CALIFORNIA'S NAPA VALLEY"

There he was—the man of my dreams. The only man I'd ever loved. The man who represented my innocence. My *Guy*. He looked as handsome as ever, holding a bottle of his wine and smiling my favorite crooked smile. And it was more than his physical self. He looked regal, like a true businessman. He was now an entrepreneur in one of the biggest industries in the country.

He'd cut his hair. It made him look serious and business-like. But those eyes, those same dreamy eyes, stared back at me and into my soul. It seemed as though all my questions were answered in this one picture. He looked happy, living his dream. He'd done what he said he would do. He was no longer the immigrant boy I'd taught to read and write. No. The man on the front page of the newspaper was a boss in every sense of the word.

I took another deep breath and continued to read.

Italian Immigrant Gaetano Sanna, California's youngest winemaker, is helping to make Northern California a prime vacation destination. Sanna has made his father's dream a reality. The son of Efrem Sanna has commercialized this new booming industry by creating a place where visitors can taste wine and enjoy a top-of-the-line restaurant and exclusive hotel.

Guests wake to a private tour, which includes learning how to cultivate, produce, and manufacture wine from start to finish.

The restaurant offers some of the best Italian cuisine in the Bay area, serving everything from breakfast to dinner with only the finest ingredients.

Sanna intends to build a swimming pool and a spa for his future guests to rest, relax, and enjoy themselves while sipping on some of the finest wines in the country.

"I want people to taste the wine and enjoy themselves. I want this winery to serve as a place of love and commitment to community," says Sanna.

Sanna wants to make the wine country a place, not just for wine aficionados to visit, but for lovers to come on their honeymoons and for families to enjoy. He thinks with the future amenities, like the Olympic-sized swimming pool and spa, the hotel and restaurant will attract more guests.

When asked what motivated him to become a pioneer in this market, he replied, "My father helped, of course, but

*someone special encouraged me along the way, and for that,
I am eternally grateful. Il mio sole, la mia vita. My sun, my life."
When pressed on who that someone was, Sanna would
not comment further. With summer coming, he is open for
business.*

My ears rang, and I hyperventilated. For fear of passing out, I
put my head between my knees. I was sure Gaetano meant me. I was
his sun. In my heart, this meant he still loved me. This was his way
of sending me a message. How could I tell him I still loved him? Did
that even matter anymore? What could I do? Our lives had moved
so far apart and not just geographically.

I held the newspaper close to my heart and prayed. This article was God's way of showing me there were no coincidences in
life. There was a reason why I'd accidentally grabbed that piece of
newspaper out of Rose's car and why it fell into my hands. Divine
intervention.

With my new understanding and reaffirmed faith, my mind
and body went into overload. When I looked back at what I'd been
through the past few days—from sipping drinks on a beautiful beach
to almost shooting a cop and back to this—this article reminded
me of a past I'd worked so hard to forget. A feeling of disgust came
over me so strong that I dropped the newspaper and ran to the bathroom to throw up.

After purging bad decisions and sad memories, I went to the kitchen,
picked up the article, and hid it in a place Frank wouldn't think to
look—a box of sanitary napkins.

I didn't belong here. With no real friends, Frank always gone,
and no connection to his family, I was right back where I started
almost two years earlier—trapped and alone.

With every stride I paced, I planned a way out. I always came
back to the same conclusion. I'd never be away from this life. Only

if Frank were killed or put in jail would I be free. I didn't love Frank, but he provided for me. Was financial support enough to stay committed to a loveless marriage for the rest of my life? My gaze crumbled, and I dropped to my knees.

The answer was no.

About a month later, Rose got busted for a petty crime. Turns out she had a few priors, so they gave her six months. Jimmy was heartbroken and asked if I would write to her and talk some sense into her. I told him I didn't want to get involved. Truth was, no amount of words would change Rose.

On top of that, a war brewed between the families. The Sambino family was angry at the Molananos for the Cantoni rap. With news of the bank robberies and Officer Tewey's accusations into the overall business, word on the street was that Frank had gotten careless. The cover-up, the robberies, and the impending investigation meant heat for everyone. It slowed business, and no one liked that.

The Molanano and Sambino families had worked together in the past, but this was the second time Frank was close to being pinched. To the mob, that looked sloppy—just as Officer Tewey said. The mob might warn once, but not twice. They get rid of loose ends, no matter whose son you are.

Frank's father told the Don about what had happened with the robberies and the cop. Don Molanano said he'd arrange a meeting with the Sambinos to mend fences. But Frank said there was always a chance that when he and his father went in, they might not come out.

The war put Frank on edge as the day of the meeting got closer. We fought every day. And when we weren't fighting, he took out his anxiety in other ways, which often involved rough sex mixed with booze. Almost every day, I lathered myself with makeup to cover the bruises. I was too embarrassed to look at myself in the mirror.

To escape the pain, I took pills. One in the morning and one at night seemed to help me cope with all the problems. When I wasn't calming Frank down, I worried for my family back home. I wanted to crawl into a ball and throw the covers over my head. And I did that a lot.

I was most nervous the day of the sit-down because, like the feds, the families kept an eye on us. They looked for patterns. They knew when I went to the store, and they knew when and where to attack. And since they knew where Frank and his father would be that day, they might try to do a hit on him in transport. Not knowing if they were gonna shoot up the house, I prayed I wouldn't have to pay a life-or-death consequence for one of Frank's mistakes. My hands shook as I drank my coffee.

"Calm down." Frank took my coffee cup from my hands to set it down. He offered an awkward hug, then said, "It's gonna be all right. I won't let them hurt you. Jimmy and the guys are gonna come over ere, and if that Sambino son of a bitch really wants a war, then we'll give him one." He finished tying his tie. "If things get really bad, I've made arrangements for you to get back to California."

For a split second, I thought about Frank being shot and there was no feeling. His death only represented a way out. "Well, be careful," I mumbled, then dropped my eyes from his gaze.

Jimmy and his guys showed up. With a kiss on the cheek, Frank went out the front door. The guys came prepared—all of them with guns. One guy in the back had a tommy gun, in case some son of a bitch tried to jump the fence.

During this whole ordeal, I hadn't been feeling well. I blamed the stress and weaning myself off the pills. With no energy and a constant foggy brain, I needed to be clear-minded if anything were to happen. But after a day or two of not taking the pills, I got the shakes and felt sick to my stomach.

While I detoxed, the guys took shifts eating and patrolling. Before Frank left, he asked me to feed the guys. I made trays of food while they protected me and our home.

"Hey, the lasagna's great, Vi. And the sausage and peppas . . . *maronn*," Jimmy said as he continued to stuff his face.

"Thanks, Jimmy. Is it okay if I open a window in here? The smell of the garlic is making me feel sick for some reason."

"Yeah, sure, but only the ones that look out to the backyard," Jimmy said and wiped the sauce off his face. "Hey, have you had the chance to write to Rosie yet? She's homesick, poor kid. I miss her a lot."

"Sorry, no, Jimmy, I haven't. With everything that's gone on lately, I've been too worried to write."

"Yeah, fucking Sambino pieces of shit. They want a war, we'll give 'em a war." He grabbed for his gun.

I sat at the kitchen table and stared at him. I knew he was heartbroken, but it made him look weak and pathetic, even with his gun at his side. Rose didn't love him and the second she got out of jail, she'd make her move. I just didn't have the heart to tell him.

For the next hour, he kept talking. In between all the talking, he shoved platefuls of lasagna down his throat. Fumes coming off his breath made my stomach turn. I ran up the stairs and threw up all over the bathroom floor. Jimmy ran after me and banged on the door.

"You, okay?"

"I'll be all right. Give me a minute," I said as I heaved again, this time into the toilet.

"I'll be downstairs if you need me. You don't look too good, Vi. Maybe you should see a docta?"

"No, no, I'll be fine. I haven't been feeling too good lately. Must be all the nerves," I managed to choke out, then cleaned up my mess.

After a few minutes of silence, Jimmy left. I sat on the bathroom floor and finished relieving the contents of my stomach into the toilet.

I must have fallen asleep on the floor because the next thing I knew, Frank picked me up and put me in bed.

"What happened? You sick, kid?"

"Yeah, I think so. My stomach," I muttered and rubbed my belly.

"I'll sleep downstairs tonight. Get some rest." He pulled the sheets over me.

As I was about to drift off, I put it together: Frank made it out alive.

"So, you okay? The meeting went okay? No bad blood anymore?" I croaked out. The words pushed against my raw throat.

"Yeah. Don Sambino, he gets it. He knows why I had to do what I did. Thank God my father was there to help me. It could have gone either way if he hadn't been there to vouch for me," Frank explained.

"They won't come after us now?"

"No. Everything should be fine—for a while, anyway. Go to sleep, baby," he said and kissed my forehead.

After weeks of uncertainty, I was finally able to relax. Rubbing my nauseous stomach, I hoped that tomorrow I'd wake up feeling better.

Chapter 28

New Arrival

A S MUCH AS I HATED TO ADMIT IT, DRUGS RAN MY LIFE.
What started off as harmless painkillers from my father
turned into an obsession. With sad memories looming overhead, and a husband who fed my fix, I was hooked. Everyone
I'd met in Brooklyn used something, from booze and cigarettes
to narcotics. My body suffered. Once things settled between the
families, I made the decision to wean myself off the pills.

The first few days, the withdrawals were brutal. I broke out
in cold sweat and felt nauseous. Chills followed, where I rolled
up into a ball and my entire body shook. Everything ached. The
longest I went without a pill was two days. Then I'd take the pills
and cry with guilt. I was disgustingly weak and spinning in cycles
of sickness. It was a constant battle between self-loathing and not
dying.

I lay in bed and counted the cracks in the ceiling. Frank
threw open the door to our bedroom. His eyes were red, and his
nose flared. He charged at me.

"You been in here all day," Frank shouted, then slapped my

face. "How many days you gonna lie around, huh? I got no dinna on the table and no clean shirts."

I sprang up in bed and touched the burning handprint on my face. "I'm sorry, Frank. I haven't been feeling well," I said, mindful of his fisted hands.

"Yeah, you can say that again." Frank snarled at me. "You been worthless around here. What's gotten into you? You don't cook no more, you hardly clean, you're sick all the time, and you still haven't given me a son. What good are you anyway?"

"*Vaffanculo*," I yelled, then spat in his face. "Don't ever talk to me like that again." I ran for the bathroom.

Frank grabbed me and yanked me to the floor. "You think you're some tough girl now that you can spit in my face? We'll see how tough you are. Give me a son," he screamed in my face. He lifted my nightgown and finished himself in me on the cold hardwood floor.

Once he was done panting, he hauled himself off and zipped up his pants. With narrowed eyes, he left me there. I got up off the ground, straightened my hair, and went downstairs to make *the boss* his dinner.

A few days of silence between us was always the best remedy after what happened. I made sure to have his clothes clean and his dinner made so that I wouldn't hear him complain or risk another beating. Days of the same routine made me itch for a pill. Besides the kitchen and bathroom, I hadn't left my room. So, I decided to take a walk through the neighborhood. Fresh air and some movement seemed good to me.

A few nosy neighbors gave me dirty looks. I smiled and waved. It wasn't until I'd made it past the Morrones' house that I noticed something strange. Sunlight and breezy air woke me from the pill fog and nausea. Since I'd been curled up in bed for so long, when I walked my body felt different. My insides felt like they'd shifted somehow. With each step forward, I felt better, but peculiar. The weight of my breasts was heavy against my bra. And when my legs took their natural stride, my skirt felt tighter around my belly button. How had I gained weight when I barely kept anything down?

My heart galloped in my chest and my breathing quickened. "Fourteen, fifteen, sixteen." I'd had my last period a few days before Rose and I went to Florida. My heart stopped. If my math was correct, it had been at least seven weeks since I'd been back from Florida. With all the withdrawals, I hadn't paid attention.

All the signs were there: the throwing up, the exhaustion. It wasn't the pills; I was pregnant.

"Oh fuck," I mumbled while I backtracked to the house. Why now?

In the house, I grabbed the receiver and dialed. "Um, hello, my name is Violetta Di Natale. I need to make an appointment with Dr. Jacoby. I think I might be pregnant," I said to the nurse on the other line. The word *pregnant* slipped off my tongue and made my legs shake.

"We can get you in first thing tomorrow morning."

"Yes, that'll work."

"See you at nine a.m., Mrs. Di Natale," the woman's voice said.

I hung up the phone and placed my hands on my swollen tummy. "Pregnant," I said again, then drew in more breath.

I stared at the red light in front of me. "Come on already. I wanna get home. *Minchia*," I yelled at the windshield of my new Plymouth sedan. A little make-up gift from Frank for all the stress he'd put me through with the Sambino war.

Since receiving the results of my positive test, so many

thoughts raced through my mind. How would I tell Frank? Was I ready to be a mother? How could I raise a baby in this environment? Would Frank be different with me? Gentler somehow? I glanced at the groceries sitting in the car next to me. Making Frank a special dish to tell him the news might lighten the tension between us.

Pasta *fagioli* bubbled on the stove. As amazing as it looked, I was still sensitive to smells. I opened the window and took a deep breath. "Mmmm." I sighed. Everything was in place. I'd mopped the kitchen floor and hung his fresh-pressed suits on the hook of our bedroom door, just as he liked.

The front door slammed.

"God damn, cock sucka Jimmy," Frank yelled. "He doesn't want to give me a taste. He betta, or I'll kill the son of a bitch and his whore of a girlfriend too."

He threw his suit jacket on the couch and went right to the liquor cabinet to pour himself a Scotch. He cussed in both Italian and English like I wasn't there.

I stirred the pasta and put the bread on the table.

"Everything okay?" I asked gently and served him a bowl.

He ripped the bowl from my hand, then sat to eat. Even though my stomach was still nauseous from either the morning sickness or the absence of the pills, I forced myself to eat something for the baby.

We sat across from each other in silence. The only noise in the room was the slurping of the broth at his lips and the click of the ice in his drink.

"Frank, I have to tell you something."

"Oh God, what is it now? Can't you tell I've had a bad day? What in the fuck do you need now? Don't you have enough? You spoiled bitch," he yelled in my face.

Frank bolted from the table and charged at me with his open palm raised, poised to slap me. With his hand cocked back, ready to strike, I instinctively put both hands over my stomach to protect my unborn child.

"I'm pregnant," I screamed, then pressed my eyes shut, waiting for the blow to reach my face.

Seconds dragged. No feeling of fire came across my cheek. The silence forced me to open my eyes, to look at his reaction.

Frank's eyes got huge. His hand dropped to his side and his chest panted up and down from the release of his energy.

"You're what?" He tried to steady himself against the kitchen chair.

"We're gonna have a baby, Frank."

"A baby? You sure?" he said with wide eyes.

"I was late, so I went to the doctor today to confirm it."

Frank fell to his knees in front of me. "Jesus, I'm sorry, Vi. I, uh . . . Well, that's wonderful news," he stammered.

He swallowed deep, then reached up to touch my growing belly. He looked up at me. It was the same look he had as a little boy in some of the pictures I'd seen in his bedroom. Sweet and innocent Frank perched at my feet. The one who would protect what was his, at all costs. Knowing he wasn't going to hit me anymore that night, I moved my hands to let him feel his growing child within me.

He kissed my tummy.

"I hate to say it, but I just thought you were getting fat, Vi. I didn't know you were pregnant. I'm sorry. Honest, I am," Frank said with softer eyes.

"I'm seven weeks." I let my fingers run through his course black hair.

"Is it a boy or a girl?"

"They don't know yet," I explained.

"I hope it's a boy. We need a boy in this house. Another man to run things, like his old man," he said, smiling at his new prize growing in my womb. "Here, you better eat. My son needs his food to get big and strong." He pushed my bowl closer.

I spent the rest of the meal with *little Frank*. The one who loved his child fiercely. He smiled at me and scanned my midsection as we continued to eat.

After dinner, he helped me to bed and stayed, touching and kissing my stomach.

I looked at my watch. "Aren't you going out? It's already ten."

"Not tonight. Tonight, I wanna stay right here with you and the baby," he said with gentle eyes. He held me in his arms and rocked the three of us to sleep.

Chapter 29

Every Choice Has a Consequence

MY BODY CONTINUED TO CHANGE. I HAD A HARD TIME STAY-ing awake, let alone doing my chores. But because Frank knew I was pregnant, he was easier on me. He'd rub my feet when we sat on the couch or draw me a warm bath. I didn't know how to take his softer approach. It was new for me, so I remained guarded.

Every morning I became more acquainted with my bathroom tile. My body wasn't made for pregnancy. I didn't understand how my mother did this five times, and my *Zia* Lucia seven. My new con-dition left me sleepy and swollen. My body had been invaded. After nine months, would I be left with only a shell of skin and bones? I wanted to embrace this special time, but with the constant pangs of nausea that radiated inside my gut, that seemed nearly impossible.

Since I'd moved here, I'd only talked to my family a handful of times. I avoided calling for fear of the feds listening, and for the fact that I still resented Pop for forcing me to marry Frank. I missed my family and my patients, and I missed the animals on the ranch. Most of all, I missed Gaetano. Every time I thought about home, something sparked a memory of our time together. Distance, however, helped me avoid the wistful memories.

But with my growing condition, I couldn't avoid the conversation any longer. I picked up the phone and dialed. With one hand over my now-bulging stomach and the other holding the receiver against my ear, I waited to hear someone pick up.

"Hello?"

"Hello, Carmela, is that you?" I asked.

"Yes, hey, Vi, how you doin'? How's married life treating ya?"

"It's all right, I guess."

"Really? That's good to hear. How's Brooklyn? You like it out there?"

"It's different, that's for sure," I said, thinking of Rose and my time with the Di Natale family. "It's miserably cold here in the winter and snows a lot. It's also noisy. It's taken me time to get used to it. How's Mama and Pop?" I asked.

"They're . . . okay . . ." Carmela stammered. "I was gonna call you. Mama's been sick. She can't catch her breath and yesterday she coughed up blood. Pop's been doing everything he can to help ease her with treatments and such, but nothing's working. I hoped you'd come back and help out around here for a little while."

My voice caught in my throat. "Oh no, poor Mama. Did you guys take her to see Dr. Santoro?"

"Yeah. We talked to her about that, but she only trusts Pop."

"Sounds like her. How serious is it, Carm?"

"Pop doesn't know yet. She might need some tests. I've never seen her so weak before."

"Can you put her on the phone?"

"She's sleeping right now. I have some news myself. At first, with Mama sick, I didn't really feel right about telling anyone. When I finally did, I think it made her happy. Louie finally proposed." Her voice pitched high. "Can you believe it? I was so surprised. He got down on one knee and everything. I felt like *you* were gonna be the only girl in this family to get married."

"Congratulations. That's wonderful. I'm so happy for you."

"We're hoping to get married in the fall, but with Mama the way she is, I don't know. I got a job at the cannery, and Louie's gonna manage his father's business. With the longer hours at the cannery, I haven't been able to help like I used to. And Mama can't even cook right now. Do you think Frank will let you come out here to help out for a while? We would all be so grateful."

"I'll talk to him. I'm not sure I can fly right now. Maybe I'll catch a train."

"Fly? Why not?"

"The reason I called was because, well . . . keep this a secret. I want to tell Mama and Pop myself."

"What is it? You're scaring me. What's wrong?"

"I'm pregnant."

"Oh wow, congratulations," she yelled through the phone.

"*Shhhh*, keep it down. The whole house is gonna hear you."

"Sorry. I can't believe it," she said. "Mom and Pop's first grand-child. How do you feel?"

"To tell you the truth, not so good. Morning sickness is tough."

"Sorry to hear that. Maybe when you get here Pop can whip you up some pastina?"

"I'll talk to Frank tonight and call you with my arrangements. But please remember, don't say a word."

"I know. I've been pretty good at keeping your secrets so far, sister." She laughed.

Her words locked onto me, and I fell silent.

"Hey, Vi, you there? I'm sorry. I shouldn't have brought it up. I didn't mean . . ."

"No, it's fine. I've moved on, and so has he apparently."

"Yeah, are you talking about the newspaper article? I saw it too. We were all talking about the Sannas at the dinner table the other night."

"Did Pop show any remorse for me and my situation? Any emotion at all?"

"Well, if I'm honest, he mostly talked about Gaetano's father. But after reading the article, it became clear that Gaetano is running things. Apparently, *Signor* Sanna suffered a small stroke, so Gaetano has taken over the business."

"Oh really? That's too bad," I said, remembering how last summer *Signor* Sanna couldn't wait to turn me over to my family.

"I'm glad you're okay. We were worried when you left. Pop told me what happened. But it sounds like you've started a life for yourself ova there. How's Frank feel about being a father?"

"Happy. He wants a son. Since I told him, he's been trying to be sweeter, but you know his temper. There are times he scares me, Carm," I said, then put a hand over the bump on my tummy protectively.

"Be careful. Has it been strange being so close to the big families?"

"Let's just say I've learned a lot about myself and the life." I fumbled with the phone cord, thinking about strangling it around Frank's and Rose's necks for all they'd done to me out here. "Hey, look, I got to cut it short because Frank will be home soon. I'll be in touch when I can return. Give my love to Mom and Pop. I'll see you soon. Goodbye. Love you."

"Bye. Love you too."

I hung up the receiver and another slight pang of nausea came over me. I rubbed my stomach and sat on the couch. Maybe it was all the talk about Gaetano that had me feeling sick again. As much as I tried to feel excited about my unborn child, the anxiety and uncertainty for my sick mother and the grief of a mourned relationship stifled my excitement.

Overwhelmed, I decided to go upstairs and take a nap before Frank came home so I'd have enough energy to discuss this with him. He wouldn't want me to leave in my condition, but I hoped he'd let me visit my sick mother.

Chapter 30
Homecoming

"**H**EY, VI, WHERE YOU AT?" FRANK ASKED AS HE CAME UP THE stairs to our room.

I'd stayed in bed most of the day, sick and swollen. "In here," I croaked.

"Hey, baby, how you feelin' today? Yoos tired?" Frank asked, then pulled the blankets off and kissed my stomach. "How's my little boy today, huh?"

"You know it might be a girl, Frank." Since Frank was in a good mood, I figured it was a good time to tell him about my plans. "I talked to my sister today to tell her about the baby, and she told me that my mom is real sick. She can't breathe. I'm worried about her, Frank. Carm asked if I'd come home for a while and help out."

"I don't know, Vi. You've been feelin' so bad lately. I'd be worried about you going all the way over there and somethin' happening to the baby."

"It's my mother we're talking about."

"I know, but this, this right here . . . this is our biggest blessing."

He kissed my tummy. "This child furthers our family. It furthers the Di Natale name."

"I know," I said and propped up my pillow. "If I talk to the doctor, can I go?"

He pushed my hair behind my ear. "All right, kid. If the docta says yes, then you can go. But you betta be careful," he said, then smiled at my midsection.

"I will."

He kissed my cheek. "Don't worry about cookin' nothin'. I'll get dinna out."

"Okay," I said, relieved.

After a conversation with the doctor, he said I was free to go as long as I tried to rest during the day and put my feet up. So, I packed my bags and headed for home: the east foothills of San Jose. I arrived at San Francisco Airport to find my brother Tony waiting for me.

"Hey, Vi, how you doin'?" Tony hugged me tightly.

I had to push him back a little to protect my growing stomach, and so he wouldn't notice. I wanted to try and keep the secret for as long as possible.

"You okay? You look like you don't get no sleep. Frank better not be doin' nothin' to you anymore. One day, he's gonna piss off the wrong person with that temper of his."

"I'm fine," I lied. "It was just a long flight. How's Mama?"

"She has good days and bad days," Tony said with empty eyes. "She'll be happy to see you. Pop's got me doing a lot more work around the ranch."

"Well, I'm here now. I'll do what I can to help. So, Mama decided to see Dr. Santoro, huh?"

"Yeah, me and Pop had to almost toss her in the car to get her there, but I think she knew it was time."

I took a deep breath as I approached my father's Cadillac. "It will be good to be home, anyway." Tony threw my suitcase in the back.

We made our way down the highway. On our left was the most beautiful sight I'd seen in a long time—the rolling hills that surrounded my home. It was June, and the hills had turned from green to yellow from the dusting of warmth. The closer we got, the less my stomach hurt, and my nausea seemed to disappear. Maybe the pure joy and excitement of being with my family numbed me. Whatever the feeling, I welcomed it.

I walked into my childhood home, where my brothers and sister greeted me with open arms. Pop was the last in line to hug me. I hugged him with the reluctance of past hurt feelings. He gave me a strange grin. I wasn't sure if it was to absolve himself from guilt, or if he'd missed me.

"Where's Mama?" I asked.

"She in da bedroom," he said.

Mama lay in bed in nothing more than her shift. The window was cracked open to let in fresh air. The faintest shade of gray tinted her skin. Beads of sweat dotted her forehead and upper lip. She reached out her hand to take mine. "*Ciao Bella, Violetta. Come stai? Oh, quanto mi sei mancata, figlia mia.*"

"I've missed you too, Mama. How do you feel? What did the doctor say?" I asked as I held on to her moist fingers.

She looked over my shoulder when Pop walked in behind me.

"The docta tink itsa cancer," he said as his chin trembled.

"Oh my God. I'm so sorry, Mama." I tried to blink away tears. "I'm here now. I'll take care of you." I wiped my eyes and tucked my hair around my ear. "I have some news that I think will make you feel better. I'm gonna have a baby." I placed my hand along the little bump under my belly button.

Mama looked at Pop and tears welled up in both of their eyes.

"Dat isa wunnafull news," Pop whimpered. He leaned over and embraced my shoulders, then kissed my cheek. For a moment, I forgot my anger toward him. I allowed myself to bask in the moment with them. I reached for their hands. With Mama's dying hand in mine, this was a circle-of-life moment. The kind of moment where someone I loved would eventually leave this earth and another would join. I grazed my hand over my stomach and said a prayer.

A few days after my arrival, I remembered how hard it was to live on a ranch. I'd forgotten what it took to work a large piece of land like ours. I fed the animals, cleaned the barn, made meals, and did the wash. It was backbreaking work, and my pregnancy did not respond well to any of it.

My ankles were so swollen it was hard to walk. By the end of the day, my feet looked like elephant feet. Without Carm and Mama to help out, Pop closed his practice early to relieve me for the rest of the afternoon. Tony also took some slack. Paulie helped a little too, when he'd finally grace us with his presence, but I could tell he was involved in the street life.

One morning at the kitchen table, Paulie came in from being out all night and paraded around wearing a new gold watch. I knew how he got it. How many *things* had Frank given me? In the days since I'd arrived, I heard Pop plead with Paulie to go back to school. Paulie said he'd earn more working for the mob than he ever would the honest way. I remembered Frank's words about motivating his soldiers by showing off his wealth. Paulie had fallen into that trap with both feet. What guy would rather make twenty bucks a week doing it the hard way when he could make twenty bucks a day working for the mob? Watching him transform from a sweet little boy to a hardened criminal broke my heart because I'd seen it before with Frank.

At times, I'd catch a glimpse of my father's disappointment. He'd shake his head, but what could he say? Pop had always served Don Molanano, so how could he expect any different from his sons?

I think he wished they'd become something bigger than just a gangster. Now, carrying my child, I understood his frustration.

I didn't want my unborn child to succumb to this lifestyle. That inevitable reality would be in front of me someday. I didn't want my kids to have to run from the law or hide in the shadows. I accepted my duty, but I didn't want my child to suffer the same sacrifice.

While Paulie cleaned his gun at the table, I looked at him and shook my head. I sat next to him and hugged him tightly. "Please, be careful out there. This isn't a game," I whispered in his ear.

"I'll be fine. Don't you worry, Vi. One day, I'll be a real boss. You watch."

"Are you sure that's what you want?"

"That's all I *ever* wanted," he said with hopeful eyes. He pulled away from me and left the dinner table. I placed my hand over my stomach. As much as I prayed for a healthy baby, I secretly wanted a girl, not a boy.

But a girl wouldn't be much better.

She'd end up like me.

Chapter 31

Eternal Salvation

IN THREE SHORT MONTHS, MAMA'S BODY WAS SKIN AND BONES. It hurt me to hear her wheeze in bed at night. When I'd wash her bedsheets, I'd find blood spray all over her pillowcases from her coughing so hard.

The signs were there.

It was hard to be happy about my pregnancy when she was so miserable. But when the baby moved, I placed her frail hand on my belly for her to feel her grandchild. She smiled. She'd relax and her breathing calmed when I read her the Bible.

When we knew her time was close, we asked Father Marco to administer last rites. Her cancer came in like a freight train and killed everything in its way. Mama died on a Sunday, surrounded by her family.

Carm and I made arrangements with the Loma family mortuary. Pop and Mr. Loma had been friends since the old country. Father Marco gave her a beautiful eulogy. His words were personal about their friendship.

The community joined our family to pay their respects and

pray the rosary until we were all in a trance. Repeating the words in unison to one familiar God, we hoped he'd take her into his arms and protect her forever in his kingdom.

Rosary beads in hand, I was certain Mama was right with God. She'd confessed her sins and the sins of her family to secure a place in heaven. A true mob wife. Would I be forgiven for all I'd done? At some point, I'd need to enter the confessional for my eternal salvation. Our voices filled the room. On this day, I wanted God to hear me.

After the church, we left for the mortuary. Mr. Loma had done a great job. Beautiful flower arrangements from the heads of the five families filled the room. Maybe in some small way, they owed her for all the times she took men into her home, hid them, made them meals, and provided them a safe place to heal. How many nights of sleep did she lose worrying that someone would harm her family? Mama and I were more alike than I'd previously thought. A wave of empathy rushed over me as I approached the casket to say goodbye.

I stared at her face.

"I love you, Mama," I said as a torrent of tears washed over my face. "Thank you for taking care of me that day when I was so scared that I thought I'd never see you again. And for rocking me in your arms and comforting me after some of the darkest days of my life." My voice failed as the memory of my attempted abduction came to mind. "Rest in peace."

Pop stood next to me. The love of his life—gone. Without hesitation, I wrapped my arms around his sturdy shoulders as he cried.

"I love you, Papa," I whispered.

I'd forgiven him.

We cried in each other's arms. With my unborn child moving like a handful of butterflies in my womb, I understood my father clearer now. He'd protected his family, no matter the cost. I would do the same.

After all the words and prayers came the hardest part: the cemetery. She'd be laid to rest in a mausoleum at Santa Clara Cemetery. GIORDANO had been carved into the marble of the giant family tomb.

The burial plot got me thinking about where I might go when I died. Would it be here, alongside my family? Or would it be at some strange place in Brooklyn with Frank's family? The thought shook me to my core.

Our family approached in order of age and threw our roses onto her brown wooden casket. I laid down my rose and turned toward the mourners in front of me.

A man whose face lived in my mind stood a few rows back from the others. He wore a black suit and held the hand of a woman I'd never seen before, but I knew him like no other.

Gaetano.

He was a few feet from me. His familiar eyes offered empathy while he shot me a comforting smile.

My heart dropped—like it had fallen through my rib cage onto the floor. I wondered why, in my biggest moment of grief, God would test me like this.

I froze. My mind commanded me to move, but my legs refused. My heels dug into the grass, making it impossible to retreat. He walked through the crowd, placed his rose on the casket, hugged my father, and came toward me. He reached out his arms, and I fell into his embrace. Our cheeks touched. I didn't have the strength to move my arms around him as I had hoped to do so many times before. This was not how I'd imagined our reunion.

He slowly pulled his face away, his arms still holding me. "Violetta, I'm so sorry about your mother." His gaze held, comforting me like a warm blanket.

"Thank you for coming," I croaked out, trying to gain my balance in his arms.

"Was she sick long? Your father told me she had cancer."

"Yes, lung cancer," I said, still trying to catch my breath.

"Oh, I'm sorry. This is Angelina Bustamante."

The tall, sandy-blond woman reached out to shake my hand.

"I'm sorry for your loss," she said.

Her face looked innocent enough. It was clear he'd never told her a word about us, or she might not have come off so nice. She had a pale complexion and blue eyes. With a name like Bustamante, maybe her family was from northern Italy?

"I wanted to come and pay my respects. It was the least I could do after everything that she and your father did for me and my family. If there is anything I can do, please let me know. I'd be happy to help in any way I can."

His words flowed like running water—smooth and languid. Besides this mystery woman, what was different about him? It took me a few seconds, but then I noticed. He'd lost most of his accent.

"You don't have your accent anymore." A smile crept out and warmed my face.

"Ha. Yes, well, since my father's stroke, I've taken over the business. We thought it was a good idea if I worked with a language teacher for when I meet with customers. It was Angelina's idea." He winked at his companion with my favorite dreamy eyes, the same way he used to look at me, years ago. "It's not perfect, but it's better. I wouldn't be where I am without you, Violetta. I hope you know that."

"Hmm. It was tough sometimes, but we got through it, right?" I said with a fake smile.

"How have you been?"

"Doing great. Baby on the way." I stroked my stomach, waiting for a pang of hurt to hit my gut. My words were an act to appear unfazed by his choice of guest.

He paused, as expected, and looked down at my stomach. He stared at me with a strained face. His brows pinched together, and his gaze drifted to the ground.

"Congratulations are in order then."

"Thank you," I replied, then looked at the woman who had taken my place.

"We have to get going. It's a long drive," he said.

He kissed my cheek. For the first time that I'd known him, his kiss burned like a bee sting. It would leave a mark.

"Goodbye, Violetta. Take care of yourself. I miss you," he whispered lightly in my ear. He smiled my favorite crooked smile, then walked hand in hand with his light-eyed woman to a black limousine where a driver awaited.

And just like that, he was gone.

My knees buckled as my adrenaline ebbed. I steadied myself on a nearby bench.

I realized how long I'd held onto the possibility of reuniting with him. Since I left him at the winery, I'd stashed him away in a private compartment in my mind, secretly hoping our paths would cross again. False hope, to be sure, but it was this part of me that provided an escape—a place in my mind when things got scary. His memory had saved me all these years.

How many times had I daydreamed about him when I lay in bed with Frank on top of me? I'd put his face on Frank's to make sex more bearable. When Frank slapped or punched me, I'd go to my safe place, deep inside, and think of Gaetano. He was my wind.

He'd come into my life like a storm, swirling himself against me, around me, and through me, churning up feelings of desire and love in my soul. And just like a gust of wind that exists for only a moment, he blew away for good.

My grape grower, gone.

Gone forever. And how could I blame him? I was the one who left him. I'd made my choice and continued to pay the consequences. My trick of inserting his face and memory would no longer work. How would I survive and escape my reality now? What was I to do? His total absence scared me to death.

Time had moved on. While I had played house as Frank's Mafia wife, Gaetano found love with someone else. His words in the article confused me. Maybe he didn't mean me after all. Maybe she was the center of his universe. I was instantly and insanely jealous of her. I despised her. But for what? She'd done nothing to me but extend her hand out of respect for Mama. Why did I hate her so?

Because she had what I always wanted.

The bitterness tasted sour in my mouth and the pangs of nausea crept up again. I looked down at my swollen feet and rubbed my stomach to stop it from aching. It was my heart's turn to ache. How could something that felt like it had been ripped out still ache? The only reason I still needed my heart was to keep my unborn child alive, but that was all it was now—a muscle. I didn't understand how it all worked. All that I knew was that he was no longer *my Guy.*

Chapter 32

Angel Wings

I LEFT MY HEART AT THE CEMETERY. SEEING GAETANO THREW me into a ball of emotions. To distract myself, I scrubbed floors and washed windows. Without the pills and Gaetano's memory to help me escape, I'd lost all ways to cope. It hurt too much to daydream about him now that I'd seen the truth with my own eyes. I'd been in denial.

For Pop's sake, I stayed in San Jose for a while to help. He'd relied on my mother for so long that I wanted to make sure he'd be able to take care of himself. I showed him where things were around the kitchen and how to iron his clothes. I told him that once I went back East, Carmela would help out. Sadly, a few weeks after Mama died, Carmela was nowhere to be found.

It was late after dinner. Pop sat alone on the back porch of the big house, smoking a cigar and drinking his limoncello. He was heavy in his grief for Mama, so I left him to his feelings. I had just cleared the table when Carm came in. She had magazines in her arms and laid them out onto the table.

"Look at these dresses I found in this catalog. They're so beautiful. And the bridesmaids' dresses are gorgeous. Come look," she said with wide eyes.

I flipped through a few pages. "These are nice, but where you been? I can't do everything around here in my condition. When I leave, Pop's gonna need you around here."

"I've been here," she said, annoyed.

"No, you haven't. Almost every day after you come home from work you eat dinner, then take off with Louie. You know, Carm, I don't have time for this crap," I chastised. "I'm exhausted. Every day I cook and clean, take care of the animals, and where are you, even on the weekend? With your in-laws, *schmoozing*, or out looking for a dress. It's like you think the whole world has to stop for your wedding. And to think Mama died only a few weeks ago. You parade around here, waving your magazines like nothing ever happened."

"*Maronn.* What the hell's wrong with you? Don't be pissed at me because of your situation. It's not my fault," she fired back.

"Go screw yourself, Carmela."

"I'm plannin' my wedding. I'm sorry that you didn't care to plan yours, but that isn't my problem," she said coldly.

My hands shook, and my lips quivered. "Let me tell you something. This isn't about me, and it isn't about you. Pop, Paulie, and Vinny need your help. I'll be leaving soon."

"Don't even start. Paulie's fine, or haven't you noticed?"

"I've noticed, and it scares the shit out of me. They need us right now. Not some stupid fucking dress I can't wear anytime soon," I said, then looked at my big stomach.

"Thanks a lot. You know, sometimes you can act like a—"

"A what?" I asked.

"Just because things didn't work out with Frank doesn't mean you can take it out on me. I love Louie, and he loves me. And we want a nice wedding. With everything that happened, I wanted to

have something to look forward to. Something to make me happy."
She scooped the magazines into her arms.

I took a deep breath. "You're right. I'm sorry. I've been under
stress with the baby and . . ."

"I saw him there too. I'm sorry you're hurting," she said, softer
now.

Unable to form words, I reached out for a hug. She dropped
the magazines back onto the table, and we held on to one another
for a long time. The exchange was followed by tears that lingered
from the death of our mother.

Carmela's words buzzed in my ears. I was a walking, breathing
emotion. I couldn't stop my mouth or my tears from doing what
they do. To soothe my temper, I went into the medicine cabinet
in the office and grabbed a few pills. One or two couldn't hurt. It
would help take the edge off and let me and my growing baby rest.
With a glass of water, I took one down. Then I put on my pajamas
and fell asleep in my old bed.

Like every morning on the ranch, I woke when the rooster crowed.
I rolled out of bed and stretched. Massaging my aching lower back,
minor cramps radiated into my groin. It must have been from all
the cleaning and gardening I'd done the last few days. I rubbed my
stomach and decided I wouldn't do as much today.

I got dressed and went outside to move my body. I hoped that
increased circulation would help my aching pelvis. I went straight
for the chicken coop. I bent down to grab the bag of feed and a massive pain surged through my pelvis. The pressure was so bad that
I grabbed the wooden beams of the enclosure so I wouldn't fall.

I breathed through the pain. A gush of blood streamed down
my legs and reddened the dirt of the chicken coup.

"Papa!" I screamed, trying to hold on. My legs gave way, and I
fell into the pool of bloodied dirt. "Tony! Anyone, please help me!"

With every scream, more blood gushed out of me.

Tony ran to me. His mouth dropped open. "Oh my God, what's wrong?" He tried to lift me off the ground as the chickens gathered around us.

"Get Pop, *now!*" I belted out. That was all the energy I had left. I became weak and dizzy. My eyes closed without my permission, and everything went black.

I woke in one of Pop's medical beds. My eyes didn't work right. Unfocused. My hearing was altered by a constant hum in my ears. The room smelled funny but somehow familiar—sweet and fragrant, like one of those rum drinks I had in Florida.

Licking my lips, I made the connection.

It was ether.

The room spun from all the medicine and drugs that coursed through my veins. I tried to move, but my pelvis ached something fierce. When I shifted my hips from side to side, something had been shoved inside me. It felt like a large piece of cloth or gauze. I didn't want to move until I knew what had happened to me.

With a bone-dry throat, I called out, "Papa?" I tried to scream, but it felt like I'd swallowed my voice. "What happened? How's the baby?" I barely managed to get out.

My father came to me with red puffy eyes and held my hand. He leaned over my sore body, and said, "I ma so sorry, Violetta. You *bambina*, she's *morta*. She die."

"Wait, what? What?" I screamed at him. With every wail of my voice, the pain penetrated deeper. Every time I yelled out, my abdominal muscles spasmed in a stabbing pain so strong it made me breathless until I built up enough energy for the next scream.

He hugged me gently, and I held on to him with one hand. The other searched my pelvis for any signs of life.

There were none.

No more bump.

No more little flutters under my belly button.

"No, no! This can't be true. Please God, tell me this can't be true," I cried out, followed by waves of tears. "Why would you take my child, my sweet innocent child? The only thing I lived for," I cried out and dug my nails into Pop's arm. "Why, God, would you do this to me? Haven't I suffered enough?" I cried years of grief into Pop's shoulder.

I sobbed for over an hour when Carmela came in to comfort me. I was glad she didn't hold a grudge against me for my recent outburst because I needed her. And since Mama was gone now too, I needed Carm more than ever to help me get through this. Carmela knew me inside and out. I surrendered myself to her, right there and then. I could no longer be brave.

"I'm so sorry," she said as she hugged and cried with me.

Pop backed away to let us have our private moment.

"Was it a boy or a girl?" I choked out.

"*Una bambina*," he said.

A girl. A beautiful little girl I'd never again have the chance to love or hold in my arms. I wept as my sister held me.

"What did she look like? Let me see her," I said with swollen eyes.

Carmela and Pop exchanged glances.

"If you wanna see her, I bring her to you," he said. "We can bury her beside your mama. She take care of her in heaven."

I cast my fears aside, and my motherly instincts kicked in. I needed to see her. I wanted to touch her skin and kiss her cheek. I would not spend the rest of my life wondering what she looked like—my angel.

"Bring her to me," I said through trembling lips.

Pop left the room and came back holding a white blanket in his arms. He held her out to me. I peered into the cloth and there she was—my precious daughter. She was so tiny. She didn't have any eyelashes or eyebrows, but the faintest shadow of the tiniest strands of black hair covered her head. She looked like she was sleeping. Her eyes were closed, and her tiny fingers were folded over her stomach. She looked like an angel, so quiet and gentle. My finger grazed her velvet soft cheek. And for a moment, I was blissfully unaware of the tragedy that had befallen me.

"She was two pounds," Carmela said as she watched me stare at my daughter for the first time.

"How'd this happen? I did what the doctor said. I took naps. I rested. I ate well. I did everything—now this," I cried out as tears gushed over my cheeks onto my daughter's closed lips.

"You've been under a lot of pressure with Mama's death and everything," Carmela said as her voice caught in her throat.

"Violetta. Sometime *Dio* needa da *bambini* back in heaven to do hisa work. Itsa always God's will," Pop said, trying to bring me back to my faith.

With a throbbing sensation radiating through my pelvis, I held on to my doll-like baby and retraced everything that led me here: my stressful marriage to Frank, my travels to San Jose, witnessing Mama die, seeing Gaetano again, and realizing he'd moved on with someone else. Then it hit me.

It was the pills.

Waves of guilt crashed over me. As much as I wanted the comfort of denial, I could no longer ignore the truth: I had done this. I was weak. I killed my baby. I'd poisoned her.

The room spun. My grip on my daughter loosened.

"Take her. I can't hold her any longer. Bury her with Mama. I did this," I muttered, tangled in grief.

With a blank look, Carmela took my lifeless baby from my arms and carried her out of the room.

"Violetta, sometime dis tings happen. Itsa not you fault." Pop reached for my hand.

"Get out. I don't want to see anyone," I said with acid in my voice.

Once he left, I looked around the room. Reality hit me from

every direction. Although I hadn't pulled any trigger, I was a murderer.

I mustered up the courage to call Frank. I called the house several times, day and night, and no answer. Where the hell was he? I didn't have Jimmy's number but decided to call the Di Natale home. I wouldn't tell them over the phone. This was news that Frank should hear straight from me.

"*Pronto, residenza* Di Natale."

"Yes, this is Violetta. Is Mrs. Di Natale there?"

"*Si, un attimo.*"

"Hello?"

"Hello, it's Violetta. I've been trying to get a hold of Frank, but there's no answer for two days. Do you know where he is?"

"I'm sorry, I don't. Are you okay, Violetta?"

"No, not exactly. I need to speak to Frank as soon as possible. Please have him call me at my father's house."

"Yes, I will. How you feelin'? So excited to meet our grandchild. I hope you're resting over there. Frank said you weren't feeling too good before you left."

I couldn't respond right away. My throat was so tight I struggled to breathe.

"Vi, you there?"

The phone shook at my ear. "Yes, please have him call me."

"Sure. Take good care of yourself."

I hung up the phone and cried the rest of the afternoon.

Frank called two days later.

"Whatsa matter? Ma said you called."

"Yes, I called the house several times, but you weren't home. Where have you been?"

"Out. Don't ask me about my business, Vi. You know better than that. I'm working on somethin.'"

"Frank, I have something terrible to tell you. Sit down."

"What the fuck did you do, Vi? What happened?" His voice grew frantic.

"We lost the baby. It was a girl."

There was complete silence, then wails of screams came through the line. "I told you, you should have never gone out there, but no, you neva listen. *You* did this."

I didn't admit to the drugs in that moment or Frank would've killed me. But he wasn't wrong, so I didn't protest.

"I'm sorry, Frank," I said in a small voice. "We named her Adelina after my mother, and I will bury her with my mother in two days. I wanted to tell you so that you could come here and say your goodbyes."

"I'll neva forgive you."

"I understand you're hurt and angry. I think more than ever we need each other right now. She was our daughter."

"You pill poppin' whore," he said through tears. "Probably wasn't even mine. You been around all those whores. I bet you got knocked up when you went to Florida. I provide for you. I bought you things like a God damn queen. Look what you did."

"I wanted you to know, as the father of our child, so that we could bury our daughter together," I pleaded.

"I ain't comin.'" Through the receiver, I heard things breaking and Frank screaming. Then nothing.

He'd hung up.

There was a hard side to Frank that needed to live up to his father's standards and there was still a young boy who grew up too fast and had to be tough to survive. He took to the drink when things got hard, as I had done with pills. Because I saw it in myself, I saw it in him. Sure, Frank killed strangers on the street because he didn't know them, but he didn't have the courage to bury his own daughter. As tough as Frank Di Natale appeared, there was a weak, sad little boy inside.

I buried my daughter alongside my mother. Mr. Loma made a small casket for her body that looked like nothing more than a shoebox. She lay in tiny, white satin clothes. Carmela stitched them from fabric she planned to use for her wedding dress. Adelina looked like a doll lying in that box. The only thing that got me through that process was the belief that my Mama would take care of her and that they'd be together. Once I told myself that, it was easier to watch them put her in with my mother, easier to walk away from them both and from the entire experience.

As he'd said, Frank didn't show.

My daughter's absence made me feel like I didn't have much left to live for. I had the whole thing planned. I'd get the pills and swallow the whole damn bottle. I wanted to be in Heaven, safe with my mother and daughter. I went to the medicine cabinet and grabbed the pill bottle. With a glass of water, I tilted the bottle in the air and opened my mouth.

"Violetta, no," Pop screamed and slapped the pills from my hands.

I reached for him and held him tightly.

"I'm sorry, Pop. I . . . I . . . I'm lost. I don't even want to be on the ranch anymore. With Mama gone, Gaetano, and now my daughter, death and loss are all around me. I don't want to live anymore."

My father's eyes were grave, and tears fell from his cheeks. "Violetta, I suffer da same wit you. I lost my wife and now my granddaughter. Please, dona do dis. I canno lose you too. Da one ting keeping me alive is you and your brothers and sister."

"But, Pop, I don't have any children. I have no one."

"You have us. You mussa go on. You mama, she would wan you to go on."

"Pop, it's so hard. All I want to do is take the pills."

"I willa help you get off dem. You needa get back to da church to find yourself again. Only God can helpa you do dat. My beautiful daughter, life isa bout hope and possibility. Dat isa what keep us going on," Pop said, then wiped a tear from my cheek.

I fell into my father's arms. He hugged me tightly and rocked me back and forth like my mother used to do.

"I love you, Violetta." He kissed the top of my head.

I closed my eyes and embraced the silence.

With Pop's help, I got off the pills. I attended AA meetings around town, and they helped for a while. I listened to others talk, but I knew with the kind of life I was in, I'd never be able to share my story. If anyone found out that I told someone outside the family, I'd look like a rat. So, I went to the one place most mob wives went to lessen the pain—church.

I spent many hours praying to the man on the cross. I told God I was angry at him for making me endure all that I had. I asked him why he would do this to me, and the answer that came to me was simple. He didn't; *they did*—the Mafia.

They had done it all. I was a product of their power—a puppet on their strings. Every loss I'd suffered was because of them in some way. And it wasn't just their physical power. They were always in my head, manipulating me and leaving me on edge. They controlled me—mind, body, and soul. I'd been beaten and lost almost everything I loved. I could blame Frank, I could blame the pills, I wanted to blame everyone, but it was *Cosa Nostra* that had brought me to my knees. Every sick and twisted move led me here, before God. As much as they'd given me, they'd taken.

In my mind, we were now even.

Between the Hail Mary and the Lord's prayer, I decided it was time to leave the ranch. I needed to face Frank, one way or another. I hadn't told him when I'd be returning for fear that would cause another unwanted outburst. But once I was home, I would decide if I'd stay married. I knew that the church frowned upon divorce, and divorce to a mobster was almost unheard of, but my soul was at stake. This time, God would guide my decisions, not pills, and not fantasies.

With an altered soul, I packed my things, said goodbye to my family, and left the foothills behind, ready to face my predetermined life. Again.

Chapter 33

Liberation

THE CAB PULLED UP. FRANK'S CAR WAS IN THE DRIVEWAY, ODD at this hour. Maybe he slept in from a late night out again. I didn't want to face him. I represented failure to him, as he did to me. I rubbed my stomach and felt the absence within my womb.

With every step toward the front door, I fought back my shame.

My hands shook as I inserted the key. I opened the door quietly. I walked into what looked like my house, but it didn't feel the same. It even smelled different. A blend of cigarettes mixed with perfume that I'd smelled before, but I couldn't place.

I put my bags on the sofa and took a look around. All the kitchen chairs had been knocked over. Liquor bottles littered every surface. Broken glasses and plates scattered across the floor.

Poor Frank. He wasn't handling our daughter's death well.

As much as I would've liked to avoid him, I was ready to talk. At the staircase, strange noises came from our bedroom. It sounded like the radio. I continued to climb the steps and entered the abandoned nursery. My stomach dropped and more tears welled. The hollow shell of my soul crumbled. Inside, I touched the yellow curtains that hung from her tiny window.

A familiar voice came from my room.

A woman's voice.

My mind mentally cataloged the sound, and an eerie feeling came over me.

I walked toward my bedroom door. Voices turned into groans and heavy breathing.

Heat spread through my body. A fire deep inside burned and consumed me. Blinded by red, my mind locked somewhere between consciousness and freefall. I stood in the confines of my hallway, barely holding onto my resolve of duty to family. I'd suffered every emotion but one—rage.

The anger that lay dormant in my soul was now present. Like smoke, adrenaline crept up from the ground and slithered its way around my legs, passing my heart and settling in my brain. The toxic poison desensitized all rational thought.

This felt primal.

I wanted to be hit. Hit hard. Pain was welcomed. Pain would make me feel alive again. This time, I'd hit back. Just beyond that door was my excuse—my freedom.

My heels sank into the Persian rug fibers that lined the hallway in *our* home. I would force myself through the door and face my demons. This was *my* house. The only place I had left to go. With my dead daughter's nursery behind me, the level of violation was incomprehensible.

I unclenched my fists and threw open the bedroom door.

Rose was on top of Frank, naked, while he lay like a rag doll. The sound of the door striking the wall made her whip her head around. Her eyes were doll-like, black and lifeless. She focused on me—the woman standing in her way. Her message was clear: conquer and stake her claim, like a dog marking its territory. To Rose, this wasn't betrayal—it was a business move. A divisive power play used in my absence.

"Violetta, I told you a long time ago, you gotta make your man happy in bed." She puckered her mouth with her signature red lips and kissed the air between us, while she straddled the remnants of my obligation. That was all I needed to unleash my fury.

Life would end here. Now.

Hers.

His.

Mine.

Ours.

I didn't know. I didn't care.

I leapt toward the bed and slapped Rose's ruby red lipstick right off her face.

She dropped to the floor.

I grabbed the lamp from the bedside table and hit her, again and again, with thrashing blows to her head.

Unconscious, she lay naked and bleeding, with streaks of red smeared across her face.

Frank pulled me off of her. "You fuckin' worthless bitch. This is for not giving me a healthy child!" He punched me in the gut.

"Do it, you coward. I'm begging you. Put me outta my misery, you soulless bastard!" I squeezed my eyes shut and clenched my jaw tight until I heard my teeth crack.

"And this is for the baby you killed," Frank screamed, then punched me again.

Gasping for breath and still sore from the fresh wounds of my daughter being ripped from my womb, I reached for Frank's head and scratched his face, carving a deep gash under his eye. While he tried to pin me down, I bit him, hard and violent, through his cheek. With a mouthful of his flesh between my teeth, I felt a popping sensation. I wasn't letting go. His blood trickled onto my tongue and over my chin. A metallic taste flooded my mouth. He jerked away from me and rubbed blood from the bite-sized teeth marks on his face.

"Now . . . I'm gonna kill you," he seethed.

He backhanded me with a blow so fierce it made one of my back teeth come loose. My eyes went unfocused. My jaw felt like it had unhinged from my skull. Pain surged through my head, leaving me stunned and gasping. I spat out my tooth on the hard floor of our bedroom.

I lay on the floor with the shattered lamp around me. He followed my eyes. I knew what he planned to do—strangle me with the cord. Survival mode kicked in. I kicked him in the balls so hard he lost his air, dropped to the floor, and curled up into a fetal position. He moaned and writhed in pain.

"You worthless, sad little man. You didn't even have the balls to bury your daughter. I never loved you."

Frank stood and kicked me in the stomach.

The blow knocked the wind out of me. He yanked me up by my hair and punched my face.

Immediately, my eyes watered. Blood gushed over my mouth and dripped off my chin. I'd tended to enough wise guys to know he'd broken my nose. The pain was excruciating. He finished me off with a final kick to the ribs. I heard a snap and curled into a ball, motionless.

He tried to help Rose to her feet. Blood poured from her head wound.

"Rose, get up, baby. She's barely breathing." His voice rumbled.

I ignored his words. It could have been any *goomah* I found in my bed. I knew why Rose did what she did. She was a social climber. She always wanted to be a player in the game. What better way than to fuck a guy who was high in the ranks? I didn't want her dead, but injuries happen in battle.

After a few moments, I regained my breath, but it was the worst pain I'd ever felt. Wheezing and coughing, every part of my body hurt. Frank and I stared at each other for a long moment, a neutrality moment, a white flag moment. We panted, exhausted. I waited to regain my strength to stand and leave this hell, once and for all, when the doorbell rang downstairs.

"Brooklyn Police. Open up," the voice yelled through the door.

"Fuck!" Frank dropped Rose's head onto the floor and ran over to the closet to put on some pants. Was he dumb enough to think he could escape? There was no way he'd get away from this. He grabbed and loaded his rifle, then stood over me, pointing the barrel in my face. "What did you do? Did you fuckin' rat to the cops? You stupid bitch!"

"No . . . no," I choked out.

Frank ambushed the front window and slowly pulled the corner curtains back to look outside.

"God damn it! There must be fifty cops outside! What the fuck? You stupid broads. If this is you, Rose, I'll fuckin' kill you. Who'd you run your mouth to, huh? You flip in jail? You lousy whores."

Rose lay with her eyes shut, lifeless.

The cops yelled back, "We got a warrant for your arrest, Di Natale. If you don't come out, we'll come in after you. The house is surrounded."

The next thing I heard was the sound of the front door shaking. Hinges rattled. Something big hit our door.

Frank ran down the hall and looked out the nursery window, which looked out onto the backyard.

"Fuck. They're everywhere," he screamed, as veins popped out of his neck.

Boots echoed across the hardwood floor and stairs. The noise kicked my heart back into high gear. Cops scattered throughout the house, opening doors, searching for Frank. My hands shook for what was about to happen. Frank climbed into the closet and shut the door.

I crawled under the bed and pulled Rose's lifeless body under with me. She lay naked and bloodied, after just fucking my husband. She smelled of sex, sweat, and blood mixed with the same perfume I'd smelled so many times before. Somehow, I'd shifted from primal survival mode to some form of empathy.

From my limited view, the cops' boots moved around the room

quickly. There must have been at least ten men in my bedroom. That's when I heard a familiar voice coming up the stairs. It was Officer Tewey, the same cop who'd questioned me in the parking lot. A noise emerged from the closet.

"Frank, come out with your hands up, or we'll shoot."

All hell broke loose. The closet door ripped off its hinges and landed across the room.

"DROP THE FUCKIN GUN AND PUT YOUR HANDS IN THE AIR, NOW," Tewey roared.

Frank's gun landed on the floor. Three cops threw Frank to the ground and pinned him.

"Fuck you, you fuckin' pigs. I ain't saying nothin'," Frank spat.

His face was inches from mine as they put their full weight on his bare back. He shot me a bone-chilling stare while they cuffed him. "*Puttana* . . . I'll get you for this, Vi."

The cops yanked Frank to his feet.

I tried to move my body to see what happened, but with every move, I was in agony. Afraid that if I winced in pain from my movement, the police would shoot me right through the mattress, I lay there, silent, with Rose's naked body next to mine.

"Well, well, well . . . I've been waiting a long time for this, Frankie," Tewey said. "And with the little stunt you pulled, I owed you one."

Tewey lunged at Frank. Frank's legs collapsed under him.

"Keep it up, and you'll get more," Tewey said.

Frank gasped for air.

"I don't want to rough you up too much yet. No, we have big plans for you. We want the big fish, and you're gonna help us, aren't you, Frank?" Tewey said. "Get him outta here."

The cops ushered Frank down the hall. For a split second, I was happy to see Frank receive what he'd given me all these years. A voice pulled me away from my temporary feelings of retribution.

"Search the whole house. I want everything for evidence—everything, fellas," Tewey commanded his troops.

One blink later, I saw the ceiling instead of the box spring. It must have been Frank's last threat to me that tipped off Tewey to my hiding place. The cops threw the mattress to the side of the room.

"Please, please, help us," I cried out between the popping sounds in my lungs.

Another officer bent down next to me and Rose. She was still unconscious and naked with a nasty gash on her head, and I wheezed through a blood-covered face and swollen eyes.

"Get 'em up," the officer said and helped me to my feet.

The pain of shifting my ribs was excruciating. I screamed out in agony. My screams got their attention, and they helped me to sit on my hope chest.

"Please, please. He broke my ribs. I can't breathe," I tried to gurgle out.

Thankfully, the cop called for an ambulance.

Sirens approaching brought me a sense of relief. A medical person came into my room. They placed an oxygen mask over my face. My eyes watered. Tears streamed while they took my vitals and tended to Rose. They gave her some smelling salts, and she slowly came to. They put her on a gurney, and she left in an ambulance.

The paramedic deemed that my cracked rib may have punctured a lung. They hauled me out to an ambulance. Neighbors stood outside, laughing at me. Jimmy watched from his car across the street. What was he doing here? Had he caught Rose with Frank or was it a coincidence? As questions filled my mind, we drove away from all the chaos and destruction. I'd broken through the doors of my bondage and faced my fears. From freefall to rock bottom, I was trapped no more.

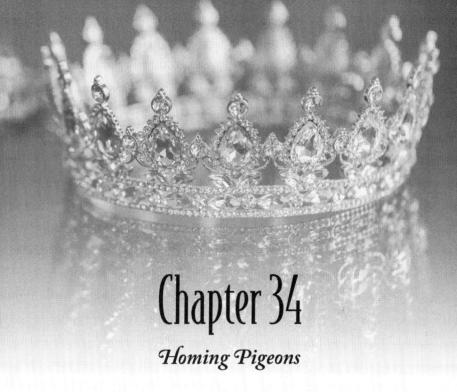

Chapter 34

Homing Pigeons

East San Jose Foothills, Giordano Estate
March 2003
Barbara

M s. G. STOOD FROM HER RECLINER, WENT TO HER ROOM, AND returned with an envelope. She reached inside and took out two newspaper clippings. The first was the write-up of Gaetano in his winery. I held it in my hands and noticed the faintest red kiss mark still stained at the bottom from Rose's red lips so many years ago.

"I figured, by now, you should know what Gaetano looked like," she said and smiled over his picture.

He was exactly as she'd described: dreamy eyes, a slightly crooked smile, and brilliantly handsome. The second article was about the bust at her Brooklyn home with a mugshot of Frank and Rose.

"See, kid, what I didn't know was that after the miscarriage,

Frank started an affair with Rose once she was released from jail. During their relationship, he learned of Rose's drug connection and wanted in. Frank wanted to impress Don Molanano with another way to score and make money, and she wanted to climb the ladder. Jimmy must have caught onto them and placed an anonymous call, or he flipped. From what little I heard, no one has spoken to him or seen him in years. Either way, he was a dead man. The things we do for love, I guess."

"So, what happened? How long did you stay in the hospital?"

"One X-ray and a week's stay in the hospital is what I got out of the whole thing. Luckily, they didn't have to set my nose. I had double black eyes, and I coughed small amounts of blood for weeks after. They said that was part of the healing process."

"Oh my God." I reached for my side, thinking of the times that Marcus had bruised my ribs. "Did you have to go to jail? How did you get out of it?"

Ms. G. sat with the envelope still in her hands. She shot me a coy smile. "I lay in that Brooklyn hospital bed and the feds came in daily. Once I was healthy enough to answer their questions, I played dumb. I said I didn't know what my husband was involved with and that he never discussed those things with me, which, for the most part, was true. They asked so many questions. Apparently, Frank was involved, not only with Rose, but with other stuff I had no idea about."

As she spoke, I peered down at the article.

"I told them I came home to find my husband in bed with someone else and that things got heated. I didn't admit to hitting Rose in the head with the lamp. I told them that during our tussle, she hit her head on the nightstand.

"I can't believe you still saved her after she betrayed you. I don't know if I would have done the same," I said.

"Many days, I wondered the same thing. As much as I didn't like Rose, she befriended me when I got to Brooklyn. Maybe it was because we'd both lost children. Hers had been given away; mine had died. Or maybe because she wasn't operating with a full deck. I don't know. Woman to woman, I couldn't let her die. It wasn't jealousy. If anything, their affair gave me a way out. But the betrayal I felt is why I have a hard time trusting women. It's why I had a hard time trusting you," she said, then cupped my cheek. "Please forgive me, Barbara, for being a pain in the ass. At least now you know why."

"I understand. But you still haven't told me how you got out of it. That one cop seemed to have it in for you."

"I told Officer Tewey that it was Frank who'd beaten me up. I didn't mention the hiding places in the house. They tried to press for those, but to my core, I'm no rat about business. It was the same business that had provided for me. It's the one rule you don't break. Apparently, Rose felt the same. Once the cops told her I'd saved her life, she didn't tell them anything about me. That was the second time I saved her life, so maybe she felt she owed me one. I don't know, but I went with it."

"Rose went along with it?"

"She did. She was wanted in two other states for drugs and money laundering. They planned to send her to prison, but she failed some kind of mental intake test and was put in an institution in upstate New York. Later, I heard she was sedated on some pretty strong drugs. Word got around that she was almost catatonic for a while. But that wasn't the strangest part of the whole thing. I still couldn't figure out why that cop didn't shoot Frank. Maybe they thought he'd be more useful if they could make Frank flip. Frank was sentenced to seven years in prison for a load of offenses."

"So, what happened to Frank? I read he went missing?"

Ms. G.'s eyes shifted back to her hands and avoided my stare. "I don't really know. He probably pissed off the wrong person or something. Who knows? A day before they released me from the hospital, Officer Tewey asked me about Frank's cheek. I told him that it was self-defense because Frank tried to kill me. He listened, and I batted my eyes a few times. A few conversations later, over drinks and well . . . let's just say I did the most mob moll thing I'd ever done. To ensure my freedom, I slept with him."

"What? Ms. G., are you serious?"

"Yes. I'm not proud of it, but I did. I needed insurance in case he ever wanted to threaten me again. If I'm honest, I needed a release. There wouldn't be feelings between us. It was just business."

"I can't believe you," I said, laughing.

"He wanted to punish me for what my husband had gotten away with all those years, and I wanted to punish him because he was a dirty cop. So, a few hours of hard sex later, I had my insurance. And I'm pretty sure that was the first night he used his handcuffs in bed." She laughed. "If he ever came after me again, I'd tell his wife everything, about his strawberry birthmark on his right ass cheek and how he made me call him daddy when he came. I was pretty sure he'd leave me alone if I threatened to tell the mother of his kids that."

"You're nothing short of ruthless."

"No, just a survivor. As you'll be one day."

Her words brought me right back to my reality. I took a deep breath.

"The girls taught me that women can be just as cunning as men. More so, because men don't expect women to behave in such a way, much less have a plan to destroy them. So, I used the one tool I had in my toolbox that they desired. Not only was it my pleasure zone, it was a weapon, and a powerful one. And in that particular time in my life, I used it to my advantage."

"When did you return to San Jose?"

"After a few weeks, I realized there was nothing left for me in Brooklyn. My mind and heart had made their natural transition. I belonged in the country, where I could roam free. I gave all the baby stuff to the church, and the rest I sold piece by piece—even the mink stole. With Frank in jail, I needed the money. I moved back to San Jose to be with my family. Frank might have been pissed that I'd left him, but what was he gonna do from prison?"

"Were you scared he would come after you when he got out?"

"A little." She swallowed deeply.

"You're so brave. I wonder when I'll be able to leave. My kids don't respect me anymore, and I don't respect myself."

"When you've had enough, you'll do the right thing. That's how it was for me. Hey, I wanna show you something. Let's go outside. It's not raining. Come on, don't deprive an old lady," she said, still holding the envelope.

"Okay. Let's go." I helped her outside to a wooden enclosure behind the barn.

"Hey, did I ever tell you the time that my father had homing pigeons?"

"No."

"Years ago, when this place ran like a ranch, my father had pigeons. Some were gray, and some were black, and some were even white. Have you ever looked at a pigeon's neck and seen the color of their feathers?"

"Maybe. I don't think I've paid that much attention."

"Pigeons have beautiful colors on their necks. In the sunlight, the gray ones have an iridescent color, almost like an opal. It's beautiful. Just another one of God's creatures at work, ya know?"

"Ya, okay."

"Anyway, my father took care of all these pigeons, made cages for them, and hand-fed them. Because they were homing pigeons. He'd tag their legs with a number."

"Those are the kind of pigeons that return home, right?"

She nodded. "When my father told me, I didn't believe him. I remember it like it was yesterday. He took me out here, placed a pigeon in my hands, and showed me the little tag on the bird's foot. It said *Giordano number twenty-six*. Pop prayed over it and told me to open my hands, so it could fly away. Then, before I could count to three, the pigeon was gone. It soared over the ranch and through the trees. Sure enough, a few weeks later, there it was. The pigeon had landed on top of its cage. Twenty-six had returned home. I didn't know where it'd been or what it'd seen, but I was so happy that the bird came back. I remember my father saying to me, 'See, Violetta, da pigeon came home. It like it here, with us.' No matter where I'd been or what I'd seen, I always came back home—just like the pigeons."

Ms. G. handed me the envelope.

"I want you to have this," she said.

"What's this?" I asked. Inside the envelope was a key. I laughed. "A key to the front door. You finally trust me, huh?"

"That's not a key to the front door. That's the key to the big house. I know things are hard at your home, and I can't stand seeing you with bruises, scratch marks, and broken nails. I want to give you a safe place to live. I've already called my cousin who's in construction. He's going to convert it for you. It won't be ready for a few months, but you and the kids can stay in my house until it's ready. You've cared for me. Let me care for you."

Tears welled up and dripped onto my cheeks. "This is the nicest thing anyone has ever done for me, but I can't impose."

"What the hell you mean you can't? How are you imposing? You're here every day, anyway. Please, let me do this for you. It'll make an old lady feel good."

"I couldn't . . . I can find a place."

"You found one, damn it. You're welcome. Now let's watch some *Judge Judy*."

"Can I have some time to think about it?"

"Don't wait until it's too late. Just today, I see the new bruises on your cheek. Your time is coming, I can tell."

I reached up and touched my face. "As much as I try not to hate Marcus for what he does, I wish he'd get a taste of his medicine, just so he'd know how it feels. I'm tired of having to lie and hide myself under makeup," I said, then stared at the ground.

Ms. G. cupped my face. "*La mia bellissima figlia.* My darling long-lost daughter, Barbara. You no longer have to hide from anyone. I had a safe place to go when I needed one, and now, so do you . . ."

Chapter 35

Freedom

I LEFT WITH THE KEY TO THE BIG HOUSE IN MY POCKET. I thought about everything Ms. G. had told me over the last few months, and I was in awe of her. She was a true survivor. Her story forced me to reflect on my own life. For the health of my family, I would make the necessary changes. Our health and safety depended on it.

When I pulled up to my house, I noticed Marcus's car wasn't in the driveway. This was my chance to explain to the kids the offer Ms. G. made us and that we needed to plan a path forward in the event things got out of hand again.

After dinner, I sat Leticia and Darnell down. I showed them the key and that we had a place to go if needed. I apologized for every act of violence they'd witnessed in their lives and took responsibility for failing in my job to protect them from the abuse. I promised to talk to their father about violence counseling. There were a few tears shed, but we all agreed to leave together if things didn't change between me and Marcus.

After a few long hugs, we all discreetly packed an overnight bag and placed them in my trunk, ready to stay with Ms. G. at a moment's notice.

Marcus came in late. As usual, he took a shower, then nosed around the house and in my purse, searching for money. The last few weeks, Marcus had become desperate. A pair of my grandmother's pearl earrings had gone missing. So, I'd made it a point to get a safe deposit box in my name at the bank.

Not only did I have to hide money, but now I had to hide possessions, just like Ms. G.

"All right, I'm off," Marcus said.

I dragged my eyes up from the *Godfather* book I was reading. "Okay, see ya later," I said, then made my way to bed.

I awoke from a nightmare about Frank kicking Ms. G. in the gut. Panting and sweating, I rolled over in bed. Fresh out of my nightmare, I tried to get my bearings when my bedroom door swung open with force. I recoiled to the other side of the bed. Marcus stood in front of me. His eyes pinched together, and his bloody lip curled at one side, exposing his missing tooth. He smelled of liquor and had a huge bump over his left eye.

"Who you been talkin' to about our problems, huh?" Marcus demanded. The words foamed at his mouth. "And don't you fuckin' lie to me. You see my face? I've lost a tooth, and look at my forehead. Some mutha fucka hit me in the face with a bat. A God damn bat."

He lunged at me, grabbed my hair, and yanked me off the bed to the floor.

I tried to loosen his grip. "Let go . . . I don't know what you're talking about."

"At first, I couldn't put it together. Now I know better. When I left here tonight, I put gas in the car, but I had to take a leak, so I asked the guy at the station for the key to the bathroom. When I got out, a white delivery van pulled up in front of me and two guys came out with masks. One of the guys had a baseball bat." He pointed to his face.

His eyes circled around in his head as his alcohol breath sprayed on my face.

"I tried to fight them off, but it was two against one. A bitch move, really. And when they were finished, they said if I ever hurt you again, they were gonna kill me. So, I'll ask you one last time. Who you talkin' to about our problems?" He cinched his hands around my throat.

I dug my nails into his forearms, trying to free myself from his hold, "No one," I choked out.

"I thought about calling the police, but I already know who done this."

"Who?" I tried to draw breath.

"I'm 'bout to confirm it with that cunt WOP you work for on the hill. I bet she knows who attacked me."

"Leave her out of this," I yelled, trying to wriggle free.

"Let me tell you somethin'. I found out the floorman who kicked me out of Garden Valley has the last name of Giordano. At first, I thought it was a coincidence and paid no mind. After tonight, it all makes sense."

"What are you talking about?" I bucked my hips from side to side to try to escape.

"When the van pulled away, I tried to get the plates, but there was a bumper sticker that read *Angelo's Deli and Catering*. And to-night, when I went in your purse, I found a card in there that said Angelo's Deli with a name on the back. Alessandro Sunseri ring a bell? You been to the deli lately?" His voice tinged on sinister.

"Only once."

He reached back and slapped me. "Point proven, bitch. You cheatin' on me? I'm gonna fuck you up good this time. And when I'm done, I'm gonna pay a visit to that bitch on the hill. I'll make you watch me beat her senseless."

"Don't Marcus. She's innocent," I screamed. Tears flooded my eyes. "We just went there for lunch. I swear. They give those stickers out at the counter. I've seen them. It could have been anyone," I said, trying to deter his actions.

"I don't believe you."

He slapped my face so hard my cheek burned.

"In fact," Marcus whispered in my ear, "tonight I'm gonna teach you a good lesson. No one fucks with Marcus Tidwell. No one."

He fled to the garage. I knew what he was getting—the one tool he used on me when his fists weren't enough—the wrench.

I jumped up and banged on the kids' doors. "Get up," I screamed. "We have to go, NOW! Leticia, take my keys and start the car."

We all ran to the car in our pajamas. We got in and locked the doors. Leticia threw the gear into reverse. Marcus ran and jumped on the hood. Leticia swerved and Marcus fell onto the street. With screeching tires, we escaped.

Something hit the back of the car.

In the side mirror, in the red glow of our taillights, the wrench clattered to the pavement.

At 11:00 p.m. I banged on Ms. G's door. She answered the door with her mother's shotgun at her side.

"Jesus Christ, Barbara, I could've killed you. What happened?" she asked with wide eyes.

"You know what happened. Can we come in?" I stood with my kids at my sides, still in tears from Marcus's violent attack.

"Yes, of course. You guys can sleep in the two spare bedrooms down the hall," she told the kids.

I locked the door and turned out the light. While the kids got settled in the rooms, I pulled Ms. G. aside.

"Ms. G., did you tell Angelo to do something to Marcus? Because if you did, he knows." Sweat formed on my forehead.

"God damn it. These guys are gettin' sloppy nowadays. Just like that *stronzo* Frank," she rebuked.

"Marcus said he's going to come here to hurt you. I think we should call the cops. I can't let him hurt anyone anymore."

"Oh yeah? If he thinks he's coming on my land, he's got another thing coming," she said, then pressed her lips together.

"When did you get this from the garage? Does it still work?"

"Today, after I offered you the key. You can never be too careful. Look, tomorrow I'll make a few calls. It'll be fine. He won't hurt you again. I'll make sure of it. No one gets away with hurting my family."

Because we were all too wired to sleep, Darnell played a few games of poker with Ms. G. I wanted the kids to get to know her. I wasn't sure I'd sleep, but it was worth a try. Tomorrow, I'd probably be at some courthouse trying to get a restraining order and close all the bank accounts.

"Okay, guys, let's try and get some rest. It's been a long night," I said.

"Yeah, I have to be in surgery at the hospital at eight in the morning."

"I'll drop you off. Then I'll go to the police station and file a restraining order. Don't go back to the house for your car just yet. We don't need to run into your father right now."

Leticia nodded in agreement.

Darnell put the cards away and followed me down the hall.

"Mom, I think Ms. G. cheats," Darnell said.

"She might. You gotta keep an eye on her, son. She's tricky."

"I heard that," Ms. G. yelled from the living room. "At least I know this damn hearing aid works."

A small chuckle bubbled up through my exhaustion.

"Wait, what about our bags?" Leticia asked.

"Oh yeah, I'll get them," I said.

"I'm heading to bed. See you in the morning, kid," Ms. G. mumbled.

Outside, I stared at the dark, windy road I'd traveled the last six months. In Ms. G.'s driveway, I drew in a cleansing breath of crisp, clean, country air. With only the sound of crickets chirping around me, I opened the trunk and grabbed the bags. I was just headed back to the front door when something hard pressed against my back.

My heart jumped into high gear.

"You didn't think I'd let you get away with this?" Marcus whispered in my ear. The thick scent of alcohol on his breath stung my nose.

"Oh my God. Marcus, leave us alone," I begged.

"You trying to take my kids too? That's not gonna happen. Now go." He pushed me through the front door with a gun at my back.

When we passed the threshold, Marcus put me in a headlock and pressed the gun to my side.

"Where is she, huh?" he asked in an ominous tone.

"I don't know," I cried, clawing at his forearm. Marcus dragged me through the dark hallway and into each of the rooms. He searched frantically for Ms. G.

Leticia screamed.

"Open the closet. Now," he roared. With the gun at my side, I opened all the doors and closets except for one.

We stood in front of Ms. G.'s door. My hands shook as I tried to turn the knob.

"It's locked," I said, trying to break away from Marcus.

"Locked, huh?" Marcus moved the gun from my side and fired at the door.

The knob blew off the door.

My legs felt like they were about to give in. With the gun pressed at my back, he dragged me around her room, searched her closet, and pulled me to the floor with him to look under the bed.

No Ms. G.

We continued to the living room, where Leticia had the phone in her hand.

"I wouldn't do that, Letty. Not tonight. Sit down and mind your business like a good girl." Marcus ripped the phone off the wall and smashed it on the ground. "You wouldn't want me to hurt your mother, would you?"

When she saw the gun at my side, Leticia cried.

Darnell flew out of nowhere and jumped on his father's back.

Marcus backhanded him with the gun.

Darnell collapsed to the floor.

"Stop it. Don't hurt him." I stood over my son. "Take it out on me, not him."

"My rebellious kids. Yep, you take after your mother all right. Where's the old bitch?"

"Get out of here," I screamed.

Marcus pointed the gun at my face. "Tell me where she is."

"Leave us alone," I said defiantly. With his hand on my throat, he pushed me against the wall next to Ms. G.'s recliner. I looked down at where'd she'd sat all these days. Where was she? She must be hiding somewhere but where? Hell, this house was known for places to hide. We'd passed her room, and she wasn't there. If she wasn't hiding, maybe she'd gone for help? Marcus swayed, waving the gun around at me.

"Stop, Marcus. You're drunk," I said, then looked outside through the glass slider to divert his attention elsewhere.

Marcus followed my eyes to the sliding glass door of the living room. As he searched for Ms. G. through the glass door, I reached down for the one weapon I could get my hands on—Ms. G.'s crochet needle.

When he turned back, I stabbed the needle in Marcus's neck as hard as I could.

He released my throat and pried the needle from his neck. I opened the slider and ran.

"Ahh, you bitch." He fired a shot.

The glass door shattered behind me.

Marcus followed me outside. "I'll get both of you. This is gonna be good. A little target practice at night." He ran through the yard, shooting at trees and walls of the big house. Bullets flew. Glass broke.

Hairs stood on my neck. *Damn it. Where is she?* What would Marcus do if he found her before I did? She must be out here, but where? Then, like a streak of lightning, it hit me all at once.

The big house. The basement. She must be there.

I followed the fence line in the dark, all while Marcus laughed and shot his gun. Afraid that a bullet might hit me, I hid behind some thick, dense bushes to stay concealed from Marcus's view. I looked up at the dark night sky. Right above me was the huge metal apparatus the Giordano family used to hang and drain the pigs after they'd been slaughtered. Two rusty hooks still hung from the bar. I reached up and pulled one down. Trying to quiet my breathing, I looked through the bushes. Marcus staggered and waved the gun around.

"I'll find you yet," he roared and swayed.

Sweat poured down my back. I sat, hidden in the bushes, hook in hand.

Suddenly, Marcus pulled me up by my hair. I swung the hook from side to side and knocked the gun from his hands. I'd sliced his wrist.

He growled, then charged at me. "Woman, you don't never learn."

I swung the hook in his direction—left, right, and left again. He dodged my attack, knocked me to the dirt, and ripped the hook out of my hands.

"Leave her alone," a low voice came from the darkness.

Darnell jumped on Marcus's back and landed several blows to his head. Marcus shifted his body weight and Darnell fell off. Marcus pulled back his hand to hit our son with the rusty hook.

"No," I screamed and threw my body in front of Darnell. My hands went to my face. Marcus came down with a glancing blow of the hook to my forehead.

With Darnell under me, blood poured from my wound. I was blinded by the darkness of night and the blood in my eyes. But my ears were still attuned.

Chak Chak.

The sound of someone cocking a rifle came from behind us.

"There's the old bitch," Marcus said.

I wiped blood from my brow and squinted. Ms. G. stood at a distance, her mother's loaded gun poised and ready to fire.

"Enough," Ms. G. yelled. "I knew you'd come, you son of a bitch. I didn't want to have to do this in front of your kids. Sorry it took me so long, Barbara, honey. I called the cops from the garage. But they asked too many God damn questions, so I had to take matters into my own hands."

That's where she went. She'd snuck out of her bedroom and come around to the garage. She wasn't hiding.

She was saving us.

Marcus searched the moonlit ground for his gun.

"I wouldn't do that if I were you. I'm a pretty good shot, and I'm not afraid to blow your fucking head off." Ms. G. lowered her face to the barrel and squinted her eyes to focus.

Marcus reached for his gun.

Ms. G. fired.

Wham!

"Ah!" Marcus let out an ear-piercing scream and held his right knee. With one leg bleeding, he reached again for the gun.

Ms. G. fired off a second shot. Clouds of smoke lifted into the night.

Marcus screamed in agony, fell back, and grabbed what was left of his legs. Ms. G. had blown out both of his knees.

Darnell got out from under me and kicked the gun away from his father.

"You old cunt," Marcus yelled through the dark night air.

"I told you not to move. You're lucky I didn't aim higher, you son of a bitch," she hissed. "Darnell, help your mother up. Cops should be here any minute, and your daddy has some explaining to do."

Darnell helped me to the house, and Leticia tended to my wounds. I'd lost so much blood I felt woozy sitting on Ms. G.'s recliner, holding a towel on my head to stop the bleeding. Sirens barreled down the road.

Shortly after, I was hoisted onto a gurney and placed inside an ambulance. I looked out the back window. Leticia and Darnell had their arms around Ms. G. as the ambulance drove me away. The paramedic placed an oxygen mask on me. Everything went blank.

I woke to the unfamiliar voice of a new nurse in my room. After two long days in the hospital, I was ready to go home.

"Hello, Ms. Jackson. My name is Lorre. I'll be your nurse today. The doctor asked me to inspect your incision. When we're done, I'll have you sign your discharge paperwork."

"Oh, I almost forgot. My Saint Christopher's medal. They must have taken it off when I arrived." I looked around the room. "Oh, there it is," I pointed to my necklace that was on top of a stack of clean clothes.

"Yes, your daughter Leticia came in and brought you some fresh clothes this morning."

"Can you get it for me, please?"

"Sure." She handed me the necklace.

I rubbed the metal between my fingers. "Can you help me put it on?"

"Yes, after I examine the wound."

I ground my teeth together as the nurse peeled away the heavy bandage from my forehead.

"It looks nice and clean," she said, gently probing it.

"That's good."

"As a fellow nurse, I'm sure you know the routine. As it heals, it may itch, but try to avoid scratching it so that germs don't get in."

"I understand."

"We've called in an antibacterial ointment to help speed up the healing process to your pharmacy along with some anti-anxiety medicine to help you sleep. You've been through a serious ordeal."

"Okay." I shifted my gaze away from hers as flashbacks flooded my mind.

"If it starts to get red or hot to the touch, make sure to call your primary physician so you can follow up with some oral antibiotics, but overall, it's healing nicely. You'll need to make an appointment with your doctor in the next few days to remove the stitches."

"Yes, of course. I'll make an appointment."

She extended her hand to the necklace. I placed it in her palm, then she clasped it behind my neck.

"I want to see my face," I said as my stomach flipped in circles.

"Okay, I can help you to the bathroom." She helped me out of bed.

A little woozy, I stepped in front of the mirror. Immediately, tears surfaced. The gash was a good two inches long. It ran above my right eyebrow and hung down toward my temple. Tiny strands of stitching material stuck out from it like hairs on a caterpillar.

I was hideous.

Marcus had taken everything from me. My money, my self-esteem, and now he'd permanently altered my appearance. I'd never look the same. The scar would be a constant reminder of my life with him. No amount of ice or makeup would hide this.

Then Ms. G.'s words rang into my head, loud and clear.

I was a survivor and my time had come.

For once, I was strong.

I'd saved my son.

I lived.

I drew the medal up to my mouth and pressed a kiss. "Thank you, Mrs. Passarelli. I know you were with me that night," I prayed.

Weeks passed. We settled into our new environment at the ranch. Men worked on the big house. Marcus was in jail, booked on violations from domestic violence to a felony possession of a stolen firearm, assault with a deadly weapon, and kidnapping. We later found out that he was also involved with trying to sell a stolen car. The depths of his problems brought him down in big ways.

With Marcus's court date a few months away, I was nervous. I felt better knowing that Justice Pasquale Caruso would preside over the case. He was the son of a Paolo Caruso, the man Ms. G. had tended to with the vicious dog bites in her father's clinic years ago. He'd always promised her a favor for a favor, so she made *the call* in our defense. Like she'd always said, she had a lot of friends.

My kids adjusted to life on the ranch. Ms. G. showed Leticia how to implement some homeopathic treatments and the power of touch techniques. And when she wasn't with Leticia, she taught Darnell new card tricks and how to cook, with my supervision, of course. I'd been in talks with a cosmetic surgeon and learned I was up against a few surgeries. I wanted to start the process soon. I tried not to feel sorry for myself and focused on the bond we'd made and how far we'd come.

Standing on this historic land, I peered over at my new home, nestled among the beautiful San Jose foothills. For the first time in a long time, I felt safe.

"Hey, Ms. G., you ready to work in the garden?"

"Yes. It's time. When the tomatoes are ready, I'll show you how to can them so we can make the gravy. And one day, God willing, I'll teach you how to make ravioli."

She'd forgotten.

"Sounds great," I said and smiled to keep my chin from quivering, reminded of her need for me and my need and love for her.

As we dug holes, working alongside each other, the sun touched my face, and the wind tickled my arm.

"Perfect kind of day, Ms. G. The sun and wind together." I smiled at her.

"Yes, it is," she confirmed, then beamed. She dropped her shovel, shuffled over, and put her arm around me. "Like my father used to say—the best part of this day is that it is filled with hope and possibilities." She winked at me.

"Endless possibilities," I said with hopeful eyes.

We shared a grin, then looked out into the distance.

We were free.

Epilogue

East San Jose Foothills, Giordano Estate
May 2003
Barbara

M s. G. lay in her bed with her foot propped up on a mound of pillows.

"I ain't eating that crap." She pushed aside the pasta I'd made for her. "It ain't even real sauce. I can tell. You expect me to eat crap from a jar?"

"Well, I'm just happy you had your Life Alert necklace on. But I don't want you in the yard by yourself. We've talked about this."

"Yeah, yeah, stop treating me like a baby," she protested.

"You have to eat to take your pain medication."

"I'm fine. Just an ankle sprain, is all."

"You're lucky you didn't break anything."

"Hey, my godson asked about you the other day when he called to check in on me. You know, he's a good kid. Comes from good stock," she said proudly, changing the subject.

"Oh, he did, did he? I can't get involved, Ms. G. After hearing about you and Frank, how could I get involved with a gangster? Besides, who'd want me now? I have two kids, I am forty-three years old with a ton of baggage, and now this." I pointed at the huge scar on my forehead.

"You could do a lot worse than Alessandro Sunseri. And from the looks of it, you already have," she said.

"Thanks a lot," I muttered, then shook my head at her.

"You're a smart, attractive young lady. You need to get back out there and give it a shot. And if he doesn't treat cha good, he'll have to answer to me. Alex has a past too. When his wife left with the kid, he had to do some soul-searching, just like you're doing now. I can tell he was taken with you that day at the deli."

"I don't know. Not sure I'm ready." I rubbed at the edges of my scar.

"I wanna show you something. Go in my hope chest. You'll have to dig for it. It's a pink box."

"Okay." I walked over to the big chest at the end of her bed.

As I dug through the chest, I shuffled artifacts of her life. She had various old records of Frank Sinatra and an old leather briefcase. Once I reached the bottom, I touched what felt like a shoebox and dragged it up.

"This?"

"That's the one," she said with big eyes and took it from my hands. She wiped off a little dust and opened it. Inside were some dried flowers and an envelope. She handed it to me. "Take a look for yourself."

The envelope was yellowed from age. Inside were some pictures and a few letters. First was a black-and-white photo of Ms. G. and Gaetano, standing in front of a big metal fence with a sign that read *Antonelli Farms*. This was her time picking prunes. Ms. G. looked so young and beautiful. With her hair in a French braid and her tattered overalls, she looked at the camera like her heart was full.

Gaetano stood a good six feet tall. He was beyond handsome, like a Hollywood movie star. His hair was just as she'd described it—soft waves that hung down over his forehead. And his eyes were like none I'd ever seen. Long dark lashes spread over his almond-shaped eyes. They were calm and peaceful. Dreamy, just like she'd said. I turned over the photo. On the back, in Ms. G.'s writing, *Antonelli Farms 1939.*

Behind that picture in the stack was another picture of the two of them standing in a vineyard. This time, the two young lovers had their arms around each other. Vines surrounded them, and sunlight shined on their faces. I turned the photo over. *Sanna Winery 1940.*

The last picture in the stack was of the two of them standing side by side in front of a large building with giant pillars. On the back of the picture, it said *Rome with my Guy 1947.*

Wait . . .

When did she go to Italy? How did I miss this?

"Wait a minute, Ms. G. You never told me that you went to Rome. This can't be right?"

"What do you mean? Of course, it's right. Let me see that," she clipped, then grabbed the picture out of my hands.

"When did you go to Italy with Gaetano? I thought Gaetano met another woman. You said she came to your mother's funeral and everything. I don't get it."

Ms. G. smiled down at her beloved in the picture.

"So, wait a minute. You came back and found Gaetano *again?*"

"It was after the war when Gaetano Sanna came back into my life. Changed my world forever. Take a seat. You need to hear the rest of the story. It's one worth telling," she mused, then smiled fondly at her grape grower.

Word-of-mouth and honest reviews are critical to an author's success. If you enjoyed this book, please consider leaving a review at your favorite online retailer.

Thanks for reading *Queen of Secrets*!

Coming soon . . .

Crown of Confessions
Book 2 in the Mafia Matriarch Series

About the Author

E.J. Tanda lives in Northern California with her husband and three sons. Growing up, she was surrounded by a large Italian family. With a rich, cultural background guiding her writing, she weaves her heritage throughout her stories. She graduated from Southern New Hampshire University with a degree in English and creative writing. When she isn't writing, she travels the globe to gain experiences for her next book.

Acknowledgments

First, I want to thank all the people who supported *Queen of Secrets* through to its completion. You have been incredibly patient and supportive along the way. I hope you enjoy this story and that it finds a place into your heart pocket.

To my 101-year-old grandmother—my Nani: I love you and hope I did our little story justice. It has been such a gift to have you in my life throughout my writing journey. Thanks for the many phone calls, for telling me the stories of the past, and for sharing your life with me. This story brought us even closer. Because of you, I am a storyteller now too!

To my husband, Eric—my rock: I love you. Thanks for being an extra pair of eyes and for dedicating your afternoon calls to me to help me get this story into shape. And thanks for wiping my tears and building me back up when I didn't think I could do it.

My boys, Michael Patrick and Justin: let this book serve as a reminder to never give up on your dreams and to stay resilient. Thanks for cheering me on throughout this process. I love you, my silly rabbits.

Dad, thanks for all the "sit-down" convos and for raising me on Godfather movies. Your love and guidance mean the world to me. Mom, thanks for all the unwavering support. You are a great little editor. Love you both very much!

To my sister, Samantha: thanks for all the positive messages and texts on days I wanted to throw my laptop out the window.

To L.A. Mitchell: best writing coach and editor in the world. Thank you for believing in me and for pushing me to make this the best story it could be. I will be forever grateful to you and value our friendship. Just thinking about these last two years and our work together puts a giant lump in my throat. *Visceral goes here* You are awesome!

A huge thank you to all my beta readers who selflessly took time out of their busy lives to read and review *Queen of Secrets*. You helped make my dreams come true. Michael and Annie Tanda, Bill Zavlaris, Barbara Riggio, Vicki Langone, Mathew Morrone, Marco Di Ianni, Karin Barbaria, Kristie Bender, Kari Schoch, Kevin Gildea, Monet Ortega Kerr, Bob and Linda Langone, Joanne Zavlaris, and last, but definitely not least, to Christine Grissom, for being a fellow team mom, one of my beta readers, and for referring me to L.A. Mitchell. Team moms rock!

Many thanks to my sensitivity readers: Nicole Langone Traoré and Jill Devinny-Peterson. Your input was invaluable. I really appreciate both of you for your support.

Thanks to the creative team at 360 Web Design. Special thanks to Charles Donaldson and Annette Frei. You guys are amazing! I absolutely love what you've done with my website and look forward to working with you in the future.

To my proofreader, Emily A. Lawrence: thanks for all your hard work in polishing and refining this story. Such an honor to work with you!

To Tatiana Vila: thank you for all your creative help in making this cover sexy and bad ass! You are a creative genius. Can't wait to see what you come up with for book two.

Thanks to Stacey Blake for formatting my novel. You did a fabulous job! I will never forget how incredibly understanding you were with my deadline when I was going through some hard times. You are a good human, and I will never forget that.

To Kelly Way: thank you for reviewing my story and for providing your expert legal counsel. And thanks for all the business convos and guidance these past few years. I appreciate you!

To Jonathon and Deanne Watts: thanks for all your help and for handling things so expeditiously. It was a pleasure to work with you both.

And to my street team for your incredible support and enduring enthusiasm. You have been by my side since day one. I'm so blessed to have you all in my life to take this journey with me.

Additional thanks:

To Caroline Leech for creating my style sheet. Thank you for reading the story with a historical lens and for doing such a thorough job. I appreciate all your hard work.

To Migi Oey, who listened to my vision and applied her artistic talents to create fictional logos and a six-scene watercolor portrait that hangs in my office. Every time I look at it, it reminds me of how these pictures in my mind finally came to life through your hands. Thank you!

To Aimee Martello: thank you for your creative expertise and for the graphic design support with the promotional and marketing content.

To anyone suffering from domestic abuse, drug addiction, or thoughts of suicide, I hope this book serves as a beacon of hope and possibility. We share a common bond. Please know that you are never alone.

Made in the USA
Las Vegas, NV
03 June 2022

49693911R00210